Love Finds You
in
HERSHEY
PENNSYLVANIA

Love Finds You
in
HERSHEY
PENNSYLVANIA

BY CERELLA D. SECHRIST

summerside
PRESS

Summerside Press™
Minneapolis 55438
www.summersidepress.com
Love Finds You in Hershey, Pennsylvania
© 2010 by Cerella D. Sechrist

ISBN 978-1-935416-64-7

Scripture references are from The Holy Bible, New International
Version®, NIV®. Copyright © 1973, 1978, 1984 by Biblica, Inc.™
Used by permission of Zondervan. All rights reserved worldwide.

The town depicted in this book is a real place, but all
characters are fictional. Any resemblances to actual
people or events are purely coincidental.

Cover and interior design by Müllerhaus Publishing Group
www.mullerhaus.net.

Back cover and interior photos of Hershey, Pennsylvania,
by Chadd Caldwell, www.caldwellphotodiary.aminus3.com.

*Summerside Press™ is an inspirational publisher offering fresh,
irresistible books to uplift the heart and engage the mind.*

Printed in USA.

Dedication

·····················

To my grandparents,
C. Orville and Irene Delbaugh,
for a lifetime of recipes, stories, and faith.

Acknowledgments

....

Because food (and a book) is always better when shared, I owe the following people gratitude and cookies:

To those who digested the manuscript, laughed at the right spots, and offered input: Carissa Sechrist, Chérie Sechrist, C. Orville and Irene Delbaugh, Elana Kopp, Janet Kahler, Donna Ferguson, and Nedra Lahr.

Enormous thanks to Chadd and Cheryl Caldwell, who helped finalize the menu by providing fun, friendship, food, and photos on one of my visits to Hershey.

To my mom and dad: Wayne and Chérie Sechrist; my brother and sister: Caleb Sechrist and Carissa Sechrist; and additional friends and family who served up encouragement, support, and prayers: you know who you are.

To Diana Flegal and Hartline Literary Agency: thanks for helping the cake to rise.

To Rachel Meisel, Jason Rovenstine, Connie Troyer, and the rest of Summerside Press: for taking a chance on an untried recipe and, of course, for the chocolate.

Finally, to my sister, Carissa: for telling me what I needed to hear, always just when I needed to hear it. It is no coincidence that our Ferguson family crest motto is *Dulcius ex Asperis*—"Sweeter after Difficulty." You helped make the struggle more sweet than sour. I owe you truffles...and then some.

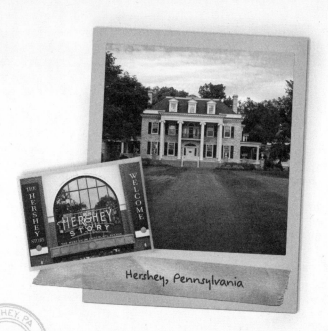

Hershey, Pennsylvania

WHEN MILTON HERSHEY ENVISIONED THE IDEAL AMERICAN community, his thoughts turned to the sweetest of ingredients: chocolate. After all, what's not to love about a town where every avenue beckons the palate with tantalizing street names such as Cocoa, Chocolate, and Reese? A simple drive down Hershey's main thoroughfare teases visitors with the mouthwatering aroma of melting cacao as it wafts through the streets, and even streetlights bear the iconic silver shape of Hershey's Kisses. It's not all about the chocolate, however. The town is also home to the Hershey Gardens, ZooAmerica, the Antique Auto Museum, Giant Center Stadium, and the Hershey Theatre, plus museums, Chocolate World, Hersheypark, Hershey factory tours, the Hershey Hotel and Chocolate Spa, and of course, the infamous yellow-and-green trolleys. Nestled among farms and woodland, the town still manages to maintain an aura of idyllic nostalgia for days gone by as well as retain its small-town feel and community values. In Hershey, you may come for the chocolate, but you'll leave feeling a sweet sense of fulfillment, richer for an experience in culture, family, and history.

Cerella D. Sechrist

Chapter One

....

He'd been coming into her restaurant for weeks now, flaunting his gorgeous black hair and icy blue eyes. She had learned that his heritage was Russian, which accounted for the roller-coaster pitch of his consonants and his sonorous name.

Dmitri Velichko.

He turned heads when he came through the front door. He melted hearts when he ordered from the menu. He was sharp, classy, and charming.

Dmitri Velichko was the enemy.

Sadie Spencer knew this well because she had learned, during her time at culinary school and her year as a cooking show host, exactly what comprised an enemy.

The sudden clatter of a pan in the kitchen arrested her attention, and she rushed from the main dining room to see what was the matter. As she flew into the kitchen, her conscience raised its hand, demanding attention.

What now? she asked it.

The hand came down, but a voice piped up. *You didn't know he was the enemy right away. You didn't know until yesterday when you overheard Mrs. Smith and Mrs. Jones talking about him.*

Sadie's eyes narrowed to slits as she put her conscience on hold and surveyed the damage to her kitchen. Jimmy, a young man who had worked his way up from dishwasher and busboy and was now being trained as one of her line cooks, was hunched over and frantically scooping the remains of a rice pilaf back into the pan from the floor, where the dish had landed. She hurried over.

"What are you planning to do with *that*?" she demanded of him.

Jimmy swallowed, his Adam's apple bobbing like her daughter Kylie's attempts to submerge her rubber ducky in the bathtub. "Er... getting ready to plate it up?"

Sadie's eyes widened with horror. "It's been on the floor!"

Jimmy stared up at her with the mournful expression of a cocker spaniel. "It's a clean floor," he lamely noted.

Sadie closed her eyes and rubbed her forehead furiously with the tips of her fingers. She forced her shoulder muscles to relax and felt a tingling relief shoot up her neck.

"Throw it away," she instructed. "Begin again. If you don't have time, ask Karl to help you."

Jimmy finished scooping the small grains back into the pan.

"You got it, boss."

"Sadie. Just call me Sadie, all right, Jimmy?"

"Sure thing, boss."

She glared at him, but he didn't notice. With a toss of her long chestnut hair, she whirled on her heel and headed to the kitchen door, stopping to stare out the clear oval frame at the restaurant's main dining room.

Where was I? Oh yes...Dmitri.

At first she had feared he was another food critic. There had been a whole slew of them the first week she'd opened. It seemed everyone wanted to critique the very first restaurant endeavor of the renowned Sadie Spencer.

Well, *minimally* renowned, maybe. After all, she'd briefly had her own cooking show, and her two cookbooks had competed moderately well on the big market. She had thought of herself as up-and-coming before…well, that had been nearly five years ago. Now she was simply Sadie Spencer once more—back at square one and working her way up the ladder to her dreams. Her restaurant venture was just over one year old and so far a great success…except for Dmitri Velichko.

Once she had realized that Dmitri was not a food critic come to criticize her efforts, she had simply assumed him to be one of her restaurant's biggest fans. The modest-sized café in her hometown of Hershey, Pennsylvania, drew all sorts of customers—locals and tourists alike, though she'd never had a regular customer who set female hearts to fluttering quite like Dmitri did. In a town where chocolate reigned supreme, Dmitri was considered an extra-sweet treat. Until yesterday, that is.

Sadie had known Mrs. Smith and Mrs. Jones from her preschool days, when they cotaught her Sunday school class at the Holy Water Evangelical Church. For as long as she could remember, the two had possessed an exasperating knack for eroding her confidence and showering pessimism on any sunny moment that came her way. She suspected it was all because of the time when, at seven years of age, she had been asked in front of the entire congregation who was older than Methuselah. In retrospect, maybe "Mrs. Smith and Mrs. Jones" hadn't been the right answer.

But twenty-two years later, one would have thought it wouldn't matter any longer. Still, whatever the reason, Smith and Jones seemed to go out of their way to rile Sadie. She supposed that at their age they didn't have many other forms of entertainment.

Being two of her most regular customers, they took every advantage of their self-appointed positions as chief tormentors of Sadie's life. Every Tuesday at precisely twelve noon, the two shuffled in and took up residence in the corner booth, beneath the display of butterfly suncatchers, and ordered their usual—the roast-turkey-and-spinach panini with garlic red lentil soup and an extra pickle with one glass of water and one cup of peach tea for Mrs. Smith and the same, minus the pickles, for Mrs. Jones. The two routinely turned up their noses at dessert, having informed Sadie long ago that her range of confectionery delights was not quite suited to their discriminating palates.

Sadie snorted at the memory and slipped out the kitchen door to keep a closer eye on her Russian adversary.

It had been at 12:49 p.m. yesterday when Smith and Jones were working their way through the dregs of their teas and Dmitri Velichko had shadowed the doorway of Sadie's restaurant. For three weeks, he had been coming and going at any hour of day or evening for a meal and a mug of coffee. That day, however, his appearance sent the old ladies tittering with delight.

Wiping down the table beside them, Sadie had rolled her eyes at their reaction. Sure, Dmitri's darkly handsome looks made quite the impression on the teenage waitresses, but Smith and Jones were pushing eighty-four and eighty-six, respectively. Sadie had shrugged at this thought.

"You're dead if you stop looking," she had once heard them say.

It was the thread their conversation began to weave, however, that caused her to linger over the table, tidying the salt and pepper shakers and carefully arranging the sugar packets.

"Russian, you know," Smith was saying.

"His parents, yes," Jones corrected. "However, *he* was born in America."

Smith's bristly gray brows rose a notch. "Are you sure, dear? His accent sounds pure European, if you ask me."

Jones had remained adamant. "I heard someone ask him the other day at the grocer's. That young girl on checkout 12 who's always flirting with any man under fifty-five." Jones clicked her tongue in disapproval.

Looking was never a crime, but apparently flirting was.

"It would seem that his parents came over from Russia before he was born. After his birth, they saved money to have his grandparents brought over, as well. Comes from the big city, as I hear it."

Smith's eyes widened. "However did he end up here?"

Jones slurped the last of her tea and daintily placed the cup back on its saucer. "Apparently smaller town life appeals to him." She leaned in conspiratorially, and Sadie took a decided interest in the tabletop she was wiping, leaning down and over to catch what was being said.

"He's opening up an eatery of some sort. The place just across the street." Jones had cackled. "Likely to send Sadie into a straitjacket when she finds out! You know how she hates competition."

Straightening up, Sadie coughed. Jones glanced over her shoulder and did not appear in the least surprised.

"Oh, Sadie dear, hello. We won't be needing anything but the check, thank you."

Sadie plastered a smile on her lips. "Are you sure I can't interest you in the dessert menu? Just this once, ladies?"

Smith shook her head. "No thank you, dear. You know your confections are simply too rich for our preference." She placed a thin, bony hand to the side of her mouth and whispered loudly, "Have to watch our figures, you know."

"And our blood sugar," Jones added.

Sadie glanced into the mirror above their heads where a flock of butterfly suncatchers reflected the afternoon light. She checked her reflection to be certain her smile remained tacked into place.

"Of course. I understand. I'll have the check brought right over."

They smiled with enough sweetness to send Sadie's own blood sugar soaring and chorused, "Thank you, dear," in perfect unison.

She had walked off in the direction of their waitress to remind her of their check and then settled herself at a booth in the back with a stack of papers in front of her, watching Dmitri Velichko as he ordered from the menu.

The full impact of Smith and Jones's conversation had slowly begun to sink in. A restaurant? Dmitri Velichko planned to open his own restaurant? Right across the street from her very own Suncatchers? The injustice! She had watched him with renewed suspicion, her eyes narrowing to slits as she contemplated how this would affect her own business.

Sure, it might create a stir at first, but then eventually things would die down, wouldn't they? And her customers would be back, ordering their same favorite dishes every day of the week, right? But as Sadie watched her female clientele drooling more over Dmitri's presence than her own mouthwatering entrees, a sinking stone of doubt had settled itself firmly in the pit of her stomach.

Dmitri Velichko could shut her down with a smile, if he so

chose—but only if she gave him the opportunity. And that, Sadie Spencer would not do.

Slipping from the booth, she approached his table with a dazzling grin of her own and sweetly asked, "Is everything to your satisfaction, sir?"

Dmitri glanced up, clearly startled. The first several times he had come into Suncatchers, Sadie had tried to be unfailingly polite, though she knew she still possessed a faint edge of steel beneath her soft exterior. Of course, she had assumed he was a captious food critic at the time and had been doing her best to smooth the way to a glowing review without allowing her distrust to show. Once she realized she was mistaken in her assumption, she had thawed a bit and genuinely insisted that if there was ever anything he should need to please let her know.

But never had she greeted him with the syrupy grin she presented now. She noted he recovered instantly, however, and smiled that engaging smile that sent half her staff to swooning.

"My order hasn't arrived yet, but I am sure it will be to my liking as always. Thank you."

Sadie swallowed and fought the heat flaming up her cheeks. Maybe he would think she'd just come from the kitchen. The heat in there always left her flushed.

He turned his attention back to the article he had been reading. Sadie swallowed a second time and ventured, "W–what is that you're reading, if I may ask?"

Dmitri glanced up again, his expression puzzled. He held up a newspaper. It was the business section. Her resolve stiffened.

"I see."

His eyebrows dipped together in confusion. "I'm sure you do." Clearly, *he* didn't see whatever it was *she* was seeing.

His pale blue eyes were clear, but Sadie fancied a challenge in them. Well, if he thought Sadie Spencer was going to give up without a fight, he was dead wrong. She straightened to her full, magnificent height of five feet eight inches.

"Please enjoy your lunch," she offered in a tone that indicated he should choke on it. She turned on her heel and marched away.

That had been yesterday, and now Sadie stood well away from Dmitri's table, covertly watching him take bites of his creamy shrimp tart and mentally casting about for a plan of attack.

She had checked at the county courthouse yesterday and managed to ascertain that the worst was true. One Dmitri Velichko had indeed recently purchased the property across the street from Suncatchers.

What to do, what to do? Sadie sighed.

"Isn't it about the time you head for home, boss?"

Sadie looked up as Jimmy spoke to her from behind the counter. Sparing a glance at the wall clock, she nodded. Six o'clock. Time to head home and relieve Jasper of babysitting duty. She smiled at the thought and lightened considerably.

Gathering her paperwork, she purposely kept her back to Dmitri's table as she left final instructions with her evening shift manager, Glynda, before slipping out the back door, successfully sidestepping her Russian competition.

She reveled in the late spring air, savoring the dewy warmth brushing her skin. The last remnants of winter had been swept out with the spring rains, and now there was only heat and sunshine to look forward to for the next several months.

Slinging her bag over her shoulder, Sadie set out toward her house, only a few blocks away from Suncatchers. Although she still possessed a driver's license, she hadn't bothered to purchase a car upon her return to Pennsylvania some three years ago. In fact, she hadn't driven much at all since her husband's death from a car accident several years before. The lack of a vehicle didn't bother her much, however. "Practically born walking" had always been her mother's motto for her. Sadie smiled at the memory. Amelia Cameron used to assert that Sadie had taken her first faltering steps at a mere nine months of age. Since Sadie's father hadn't been a very constant figure in her life, there had never been anyone to dispute Amelia's claim.

Thoughts of Mac Cameron brought a momentary shadow to Sadie's features, but she forcefully locked away the memory of her father and concentrated on more recent remembrances.

There was Kylie, her daughter, who would be turning five years old on Saturday. And Jasper, her best friend since those early days when she truly had taken her first steps. Sweet, constant Jasper who had been with her through the worst of it all. For with the sweet also came the sour—a lesson, she had learned, that applied to cooking as well as to real life.

Kylie's birth had ushered in an entirely new world of joys and fears, and Sadie's time of bliss as a wife, mother, and cooking show host had been purchased with several subsequent years of failure, death, and change: Ned's death in that tragic accident…the swift ratings plunge for the cooking show…her mother's diagnosis of cancer and Sadie's move back to Hershey…reconnecting with Jasper and learning to laugh and cry in side-by-side moments…and Amelia's last breath, drawn as Sadie held her hand and promised to never forget the lessons her mother had taught her.

The ache in Sadie's chest prickled sharply as she drew in a lungful of fresh evening air. Expelling the breath, the ache eased and happier memories began to buoy her. The down payment on her restaurant… Jasper helping her choose the name *Suncatchers* and decorating the mirrored walls with dozens of colorful glass art pieces…Kylie's first day of kindergarten…Suncatchers' grand opening…

Life could be bitter. But it could be sweet too. And no one knew better than Sadie how well sour balanced sweet.

She smiled beneath the glow of the street lamps and picked up her pace a little. She had paid her dues for this sweet time in her life. Nothing and no one—not even Dmitri Velichko—was going to take that from her now.

* * * * *

Sadie slid her key into the lock and turned it with a satisfying click. She entered the warm comfort of the home she had grown up in— now hers, since her mother's death—and dropped her bag to the floor. It fell with a reassuring *thud* as she tossed her keys onto the hall table and slipped out of her jacket.

While she hung her jacket on a peg, her mind hummed over how to best conquer the problem of Dmitri Velichko's interference in her life. She usually listened for the sounds of Kylie and Jasper's chatter as they played or finished homework or started dinner, but, preoccupied as she was, Sadie didn't pay much attention to the fact that the house remained strangely silent in the wake of her arrival.

"Jas? Kylie?" she called absentmindedly as she stepped from the hall and into the kitchen.

No dinner preparations. No boiling water or preheated oven. No salad fixings out to slice. She often brought dinner home from the restaurant for them to eat, but she thought she'd told Jasper that wouldn't be the case tonight. She frowned as she reached for the mail and began flipping through the layers of thin white envelopes.

"Jas?" she mumbled distractedly.

He appeared in the doorway, his disheveled blond hair brushing against his eyebrows, as she tossed the remains of the mail onto the counter. She smiled at his boyish features. Jasper's appearance never failed to tickle her in an odd way. He had never quite managed to refine a specific look and so forever had the appearance of a surfer dude gone country.

His skin bronzed lightly in any weather, and his wheat-colored hair never stayed neatly combed. His features were masculine with a strong jaw and an angular chin, but his lips pouted in an adorably childlike fashion. He was muscled and lean and, at the moment, dressed in his typical after-work attire of a T-shirt, faded jeans, and bare feet.

"Hey," she greeted him with a grin.

He smiled back, but there was something uneasy in the gesture. She cocked her head for a moment and waited, but he said nothing.

"*He* came in today," she volunteered, to begin conversation.

"He?"

Sadie stepped to the fridge and opened it, reaching inside for a bottle of apple juice. She affected a Russian accent as she replied, "*Da. Dmitri Velichko.*" She pulled out the juice and opened the cupboard for a tumbler.

She reverted to her regular speech as she continued. "He was in twice today, if you can believe it. For breakfast—strawberry pancakes with fresh cream and a side of sausage. And coffee, of course," she added as she poured the juice into the glass. "And again for dinner—creamy shrimp tart with a side salad. Russian dressing." She raised her juice in salute before sipping. "What else? He's a patriot, that's for sure."

Sadie drained the juice in seconds and rinsed the tumbler in the sink. "Who does he think he is, anyway, breezing into town like this and assuming he can just start taking over? I was born and raised here—*born and raised*," she repeated emphatically, "and even I knew better than to assume I could make a go of it just like *that*." She snapped her fingers.

"Maybe he doesn't know he can make a go of it," Jasper suggested. "Maybe he's just holding onto a dream. Kinda like you." He winked at her.

She refused to be charmed. "Oh, don't even, Jasper." She screwed the lid tightly onto the apple juice bottle and jerked the refrigerator door open to deposit the container inside. "Don't even bother comparing Dmitri Velichko to me."

"Why not?" Jasper prodded in that annoyingly ingratiating way of his. "Moving from the big city and attempting to make a go of a restaurant on his own? Sounds a *little* familiar, doesn't it?"

Sadie slammed the refrigerator door shut. "For your information, wise guy, I was raised *here*—Dmitri Velichko was *born* in the big city. Or so Mrs. Jones claims."

Jasper raised an eyebrow. "You're basing this entire vendetta on information from Mrs. Jones?" He clicked his tongue in an uncanny resemblance to the very woman in question. "You and your sources."

"I would hardly call it a *vendetta*. And Jones and Smith are unimpeachable sources."

"Oh, just like when they claimed that *your* restaurant was going to be a huge flop since no one around here would want to eat 'fancy, TV-style cooking'?"

Sadie couldn't help but smile maliciously at that comment. "Hmm. Yeah. Crazy old biddies." She shook herself. "But in this instance, I believe they are *dead-on* to something."

"Oh, they're on something, that's for sure. I'm just not sure if it's the Valium or the Prozac that's doing it."

Sadie turned her back to Jasper so he couldn't see her grin. No use in letting him know she found his commentary amusing. His head was big enough as it was.

"Like it or not, my friend," she said as she began rummaging through the cupboards for dinner ideas, "Dmitri Velichko isn't going to get the best of me. I've worked too long and too hard to be ousted by some reformed KGB wannabe chef."

Jasper frowned. "Come on, Sadie. That's harsh."

Sadie pulled a couple of chicken breasts from the freezer and stuck them in the microwave to thaw before opening the refrigerator once more. "If there's one thing I've learned in my time in this business, it's that all may be fair in love and war but nothing's fair in the food industry."

Jasper snorted.

"You're staying for dinner, right?" she questioned with her face to the lettuce crisper.

Jasper and Sadie had worked out an arrangement following the opening of Suncatchers. Jasper worked as a teacher at Kylie's school,

Agape Christian Academy, and each day when classes let out, he picked up Kylie from her kindergarten class and drove the three miles to Sadie's house. They spent the next few hours playing, working on homework, or doing chores until Sadie was able to get away from the restaurant and come home to join them. In exchange for this, Sadie usually cooked Jasper dinner (if he hadn't already cooked it for her), and he often spent the evening at Sadie's playing board games or watching *Beauty and the Beast* with Kylie (their favorite) or simply chatting about old times with Sadie. All this was done out of the goodness of his heart. Sadie had offered to pay him a couple of times for his help, but he always refused.

Now there was sudden silence in the kitchen following her offer of dinner. She pulled her head from the crisper, her arms loaded with salad ingredients, and glanced over her shoulder.

Jasper's face had paled beneath his sun-bronzed skin, and his arms remained crossed over his chest. Sadie frowned and noticed, for the first time, that her daughter hadn't come to greet her yet.

She dumped the salad items onto the counter.

"Where's Kylie?"

"Upstairs in her room."

Sadie immediately found that odd. Kylie didn't usually linger in her bedroom, especially not when Jasper was around. Where Jasper went, Kylie followed. She practically attached herself to his hip.

"Oh?"

He shifted from one foot to the other. "Need some help?" He gestured to the carrots.

Sadie looked carefully at him. "What's Kylie doing in her room?"

Jasper attempted an expression of nonchalance, something he usually achieved with considerable ease. But now he simply looked as though he were in pain.

"She got the Barbie dolls out. You know I hate that. Ever since Malibu Ken lost his leg and Kylie accidentally flushed it down the toilet and said it got taken by the volcano…it's just not the same."

Despite his obvious attempts at distracting her, Sadie had to laugh at this.

"Taken by the volcano?" she repeated skeptically.

He nodded in all seriousness. "Yeah. Mount Thousand Flushes."

She choked and then coughed.

"Not to be confused with the Scrubbing Bubbles Lagoon," he added. Then he leaned in and quietly whispered, "That's the bathtub." He made a face indicating that this admission could cost him his very life and then mouthed, "Shh! Don't tell!"

Sadie covered her mouth to keep from laughing out loud. When she was able to control herself, she removed her hand and whispered, "Your secret is safe with me. I wouldn't want the locals to know you were telling island secrets."

"You'd better not," Jasper soberly agreed. "Or it could be my leg that's taken by Mount Thousand Flushes next."

She smiled. "You *do* look a little like Malibu Ken, though."

"That's what Kylie said. But I told her the resemblance stops at the hair."

Sadie grinned, shook her head, and pulled the defrosted chicken from the microwave.

"Um, Sadie…there is something you should know."

Finally he comes out with it, she thought.

But following this statement, Jasper once more fell silent. She glanced at him.

"What's wrong?"

A slow-working dread began to steal along her nerve endings, causing her skin to tingle. Jasper took several steps toward her.

"It's about your dad," he softly said, his breath brushing her eyelashes.

Sadie's stomach dropped several inches.

"What's happened?"

"Nothing's happened." Jasper quickly tried to calm her. He reached out to smooth the layers of her long brown hair behind her ears. "It's just that…" He took a breath, and she wanted to slug him.

Out with it! her mind screamed.

"He's here."

"*What?*"

Before Jasper could repeat himself, Sadie sensed movement. Jasper's hands lay gently on her shoulders, but she shifted out of their reassuring embrace to see past her best friend.

There, in the doorway of her kitchen, stood an older man with thinning brown hair and watery eyes. Her father.

"Hello, Sadie," he greeted her.

She sighed. "Great."

Chapter Two

....

"Just *what* are you doing here?"

Not exactly the greeting Mac Cameron was looking for, Sadie was sure. But she couldn't help herself. On her fifteenth birthday, it had finally dawned on her that Mac really wasn't planning on being a regular figure in her life. Ever since that day, Sadie had assembled walls around the memories of her father. Nothing got out, and Mac never got in, no matter when he showed up or for how long.

Noting the tense set of her shoulders, Jasper took a side step. "I'll give you two some privacy."

Sadie whirled. "Oh no. Stay. You're as much family as he is." She gestured with contempt at the man before her. "More, in point of fact."

Jasper glanced at Mac. Mac nodded.

"It's all right, Jasper. You can stay."

Sadie's eyes narrowed. "Excuse you? Jasper is *my* best friend. I'll be the one to tell him if he can stay or not." Her gaze remained trained on her father. "Maybe you'd better give us a minute, Jas."

Jasper shook his head but didn't say a word as he turned and strode down the hall.

"Still taking him for granted, are you?"

Sadie's lips pursed together. "What do you want?"

Mac swallowed and lowered his head for a moment. "I heard about your mother."

"What about her? That she had cancer and was dying? Or the part where she *did* die and I had to bury her? Without you."

When Mac's head lifted once more, there were tears in his eyes. "Both, actually."

Years of practice prevented Sadie from weakening at this sign of remorse. "And when did you find out, exactly? It's been two years since her funeral."

"I've known for a few months," he admitted. "She sent me a letter…."

Sadie couldn't believe what she was hearing. "A letter?"

Mac swallowed, his soft brown eyes—the same eyes both Sadie and Kylie had inherited—staring a hole into the linoleum.

"I guess she sent it before she died—mailed it to the last known address…." He swallowed again. "But I wasn't living there anymore."

Sadie felt her face flush, thanks in part to a surge of anger. "Surprise, surprise." The sharpness to her tone stung even her.

Mac raised his eyes. "I did a lot of thinking after I got that letter."

Sadie turned her back on him and sliced open the plastic bag of carrots with unnecessary force.

"Oh?"

"I did a lot of soul-searching," he said.

"Uh-huh." She rinsed the carrots thoroughly before subjecting them to her full fury. A dull *whack, whack, whack* drowned out whatever Mac might have continued to say, and bits of orange confetti flew through the air.

After a moment, Sadie realized what she was doing and laid the knife aside. She turned and faced her father once more.

"My daughter turns five years old in two days. Did you know that? Do you even realize how much time has passed? It's been over four years since the last time you saw her, after all. *Four years*. I mean, when *was* the last time you decided to drop by?" Sadie made an exaggerated gesture of pressing her forefinger to her lips and then snapping her fingers. "Oh, that's *right*! It was after my husband's funeral! Good to know you could make it for that—missed the wedding, but you got to the funeral, so I guess that's what counts, right?"

She whirled, and carrot pieces filled the air around her once more.

"Sadie."

She stopped her mad dicing and cocked her head. She'd heard Mac say her name before, of course, but never like that. Something lingered in those two simple syllables. Something like…regret.

Sadie turned to look at him again.

"What?"

Mac's eyes were filled with emotion. "I am sorry."

Sadie felt it. A bit of the wall chipped. She quickly sent gallons of mortar to cover the spot.

"Too little, too late, Mac." But curiosity got the better of her. "What prompted this gallant reparation anyway?"

Mac stepped a little closer to her, and she noticed new wrinkles around his eyes. At least, she didn't remember those little lines in particular. But then again, four years was plenty of time to forget such things.

She nearly shook her head. No. They were new. She knew Mac's face as well as she knew her own daughter's. She had never forgotten his face. Couldn't, in fact. She'd tried—God knew how she'd tried, but it stayed.

Mac's eyes, Mac's smile, Mac's nose…they were a persistently indelible image that had affixed themselves years ago to her memory. Each time he made a brief stop into her life, she absorbed any changes that had taken place and so the image revised itself after every encounter. But it never went away.

"I got God, Sadie."

Her response came automatically, without forethought. "I thought you always had God. That's what you used to say."

He'd come back one summer when she was eleven. She'd just spent a week at Bible school and was filled with the love and compassion of Jesus. Mac had ridden into the driveway on a red Harley and scooped her up in his strong arms. The smell of gasoline and wind was thick on him, and she'd happily buried her nose in his leather jacket.

She'd told him about Jesus and how she'd accepted Him as her Savior while at Bible school. Mac had smiled and tugged her braids and replied, "That's good, Sadie girl."

But when she suggested he do the same, his reply had been flippant. "I already got God, sweetheart."

It had taken her years to understand that. She even feared, for a time, that it was Mac's jealousy of her love for God that kept him away. So she had rebelled for a while, avoiding church and the Bible and stretching her hope so thin that it had nearly snapped.

Thanks to Jasper, she eventually came to her senses.

Mac faced her now with open honesty. "I lied."

She scoffed. "Good of you to admit it."

Mac didn't say anything for a while, just watching her as she finished chopping the salad ingredients and tossing them into a bowl.

When the salad was prepared and the chicken frying in a pan, he asked her a question.

"You know what that letter of your mother's said?"

Sadie pumped a palmful of soap into her hand and lathered furiously. She didn't answer him, despite her overwhelming curiosity on the subject.

"It said she loved me. And not only that she loved me, but that she forgave me."

The hot water stung Sadie's fingers, and her eyes watered.

"But it didn't really matter what it said," Mac elaborated, "because she'd been saying it for years—that she loved me and forgave me and understood why I…" He stopped.

Sadie slapped down the faucet handle, and the stream of water abruptly ceased—just like Mac's words.

"Yeah, well…she was like that," Sadie replied.

"That's what got me to thinking," Mac said. "*Why* was she like that? What made her different? I knew how she was from the moment I met her…but how did she get like that? Was she born that way, or did something happen to her?"

"She tried to tell you," Sadie cut in, avoiding his gaze by carefully drying her hands on a pale blue dish towel. "She tried to tell you a thousand times. I heard her, late at night, when the two of you sat up— you drinking coffee and her drinking tea—after you thought I'd gone to sleep." Sadie neatly folded the dish towel and draped it over the lower cupboard door. She looked at him. "She *told* you," her voice accused.

"I didn't listen, Sadie girl."

"Stop it!" She smacked a palm against the counter. "Don't *call* me that! I told you a long time ago not to call me that anymore." Fearful that Kylie might overhear, she dropped her tone several decibels. "I'm not your little girl anymore."

His eyes were nearly apologetic as he said, "But you are. You'll always be my Sadie girl."

"Well, you may be my father, but you'll never be my dad," she shot back.

He nodded in seeming acceptance, and Sadie felt the sharp bite of disappointment.

"I'm not going away this time, Sadie."

Against her best intentions, she felt a small wave of elation.

"I can't turn back time, but I'm hoping I can salvage what's left of it."

"Tell that to my mother."

To her surprise, his lips turned up in a small, secretive smile. "I already have. I think she gave me her blessing to try."

Sadie suppressed a snort of derision. "Good luck with that."

"It's just my poor fortune that you inherited my own hard-headedness."

"Mmm." Sadie didn't dare comment on that one.

"But I figure I'm more experienced at it than you are."

"You'd be surprised how much practice I've had."

He locked eyes with her, and suddenly Sadie realized he was serious. He meant to elbow his way back into her life and carve out a niche there.

Clearly, this was her month to meet arrogant men head-on. Well, she dared them to try to break down her defenses. They'd see soon enough how well she stood her ground.

She stared straight into Mac's eyes, daring him to look away first. He blinked, and his eyes shifted. She grinned smugly.

First round, me!

"Sadie?"

"Yes?"

"Your chicken's on fire."

She whirled around to see bright coral flames licking the side of the pan. By the time she dumped the entire contents of an Arm & Hammer baking soda carton onto the fowl flames, Mac had gone. She tossed the empty carton into the wastebasket.

"Figures. At the first sign of trouble, he bails."

She surveyed the frying pan with its powdery white hills of baking soda nestled against coal dark regions of ruined meat.

Jasper entered with Kylie in tow.

"We're having blackened chicken?" he queried with raised eyebrows.

Kylie wrinkled her nose. "Kylie's *not* eating that," she announced.

Sadie lifted the pan from the stove. "Don't worry, Kylie girl. We're going to offer it to the volcano instead."

* * * * *

Sadie hated fast food. And junk food. And pretty much processed food of any kind. It wasn't real food, after all. Jasper occasionally tried to convince her of its merit, more to see her bristle than because he really championed the cause, but she refused to budge.

Fast food was from the devil, and Sadie considered all forms to be poison to the system.

But at nearly five years old, Kylie didn't see reason with her mother's patiently illustrated discussions on what chemically laced corn chips and preservative-packed pastries did to one's internal organs. Most of the time, Kylie could be placated with homemade cookies (containing wholesome, natural ingredients) or Sadie's own dehydrated potato chips. After all, it wasn't that Sadie was against sugared or fattening foods (in moderation, of course)—only the kind that was chockful of additives and preservatives.

But children, Sadie had learned, operate on a need-to-have basis. And one moment after the chicken catastrophe, Kylie made it known that she needed to have food. Right then. Right away.

Salad had no appeal by this time, and Sadie's own nerves were too frazzled to concoct anything more than peanut butter sandwiches, which, of course, Kylie had already had for lunch. When Jasper suggested going out for pizza, Kylie had hugged his knees with such force that he nearly lost a leg, just like his counterpart Malibu Ken.

Sadie could have ripped it off herself for his suggesting such a thing.

"It won't kill her," he pointed out as Kylie rushed back to her bedroom to put on shoes. "She's young; whatever they put into it will work through her system in no time at all."

"That's comforting," she replied with sarcasm.

"I promise that if she goes into a meltdown, I'll take full responsibility."

"I promise that if she goes into a meltdown, I'll take your head."

Jasper grinned. "Noted."

So within the hour, despite her better judgment, Sadie found herself sandwiched next to Jasper in a small red booth at the Pizza Playhouse. Across from her, Kylie slurped her orange soda noisily, and

Sadie tried very hard not to wring her hands with motherly concern over the amount of sugared beverage her daughter was consuming.

Jasper eyed her with profound amusement, that ridiculous grin fixed permanently onto his expression, as Sadie repeatedly asked Kylie if she wouldn't prefer some water.

"Can Kylie go play in the ball pit?" the little girl eventually asked.

Sadie gulped. The ball pit? With its myriad of unseen bacterial microorganisms? Sadie had long been convinced that fast-food ball pits were nothing more than breeding ground oases for germs and other communicable diseases.

"Can *I* go play in the ball pit?" Sadie attempted to correct her. For the past three months, Kylie had found it most enjoyable to speak of herself in the third person. She only reverted to the first whenever she felt extremely tired or ill.

"Well, yes, Mommy, if you want to," Kylie answered her.

Jasper snorted, and Sadie kicked him under the table.

"Kylie—" she began again, but she was quickly interrupted.

"*Puh-lease*, Mommy?"

Sadie hesitated. Kylie looked at Jasper with large brown eyes.

"*Puh-lease*, Jasper?"

He didn't hesitate. "Just don't put any of the balls into your mouth," he cautioned.

Kylie didn't hesitate either, as she bounded off to the adjoining room with the glass windows to cavort among the plastic rainbow mounds.

Sadie watched her go with a shudder.

"It'll be all right," Jasper soothed.

"For years, I had no idea what my mother meant when she said, 'Worry and motherhood were born hand in hand.'"

Jasper stretched an arm around the back of the booth and rubbed her shoulders gently. "Hold her too close and she suffocates, you know."

Sadie sighed. "I know. But don't hold her close enough and I lose her entirely."

There came a companionable pause, the kind Sadie liked best. She could lean into Jasper's side and relax for several moments, feeling secure and protected in the warmth of her best friend's strength.

After several minutes—during which Sadie's eyes continually darted to the glass window to spot Kylie's tiny figure—Jasper spoke.

"Did you want to talk about what happened with Mac today?"

Sadie toyed with her straw, capping the upper end with her fingertip and suspending the liquid inside the plastic tube.

"Not really." She shrugged.

"All right." Jasper pulled his arm from the back of the booth and took a swig of his iced tea.

"He says he's found God, and I think he thinks he's come back to set things right," she blurted.

"What do you mean, you 'think he thinks'?"

"That's what I think he wants to do, but it's tougher than he thinks."

Jasper sighed. "That's what I thought."

Sadie dropped her straw back into the glass. It buoyed for a moment before slowly sinking down and tapping the bottom.

"I mean, who does he think he is to come back again after four years—after everything I've been through—and just fire up a relationship like he'd fire up a weed whacker?"

Jasper quirked his lips at Sadie's examples. "First of all, you're not a weed whacker. And secondly, you think too much."

"So? What if I do?" she sullenly asked.

"Why don't you just go with it?" he asked.

She arched an eyebrow. "Go with what, exactly?"

"Why don't you just go along with your dad and see where it leads?"

"He's not my dad."

"Fine. Mac, then. Why don't you just go along with Mac and see what happens? See how you feel about it."

"Clearly, you don't know Mac."

"Ah, but I do," Jasper corrected. "I've known him just as long as you have."

"And with similar results," she pointed out. "You don't understand him any better than I do. It's not the same thing, Jasper, and you know it."

He backed off. "I know it's not. But maybe it's worth a try."

She grew suspicious. "Why are you taking his side?"

Jasper shrugged. "I didn't know I was. But I did notice when he showed up today that he was…different."

"Different how?"

"Mellowed. Content. Not the same old Mac."

Sadie paused. She hadn't considered that, but there was an echo of truth to what Jasper said. There *had* been something different today.

"You remember what it used to be like when he'd come back? Like he wanted to be here, but you could just feel it…something… pulling him away?"

Sadie frowned sadly. "Yeah. I remember."

"But it wasn't there today. There was no pull. There was just Mac."

Sadie blew out her breath, fluttering the strands of hair framing her face. "Just give it some time."

Jasper smiled triumphantly. "Exactly. Just give him some time, Sadie. Time and another chance."

She stared stonily at Jasper. "Mac used up all his chances a long time ago."

Jasper's eyes softened in response to hers. "Maybe," he said softly. "But I guess only time will tell."

Sadie groaned and stretched her neck muscles to relieve some of the tension she felt. "You can be *so* irritating sometimes."

"Only sometimes? I have to try harder, then."

"Great," she muttered sarcastically.

Just then their pizza arrived. Like a hound on the scent, Kylie came bounding over. Sadie grimaced as she doled out a slice of pepperoni to her daughter. She had attempted to convince Kylie that green peppers gave *color* to pizza, but it hadn't worked. Noting her expression, Jasper grinned all the broader as he slid a piece of pepperoni pizza her way.

Swallowing hard, she took a bite and chewed it down.

"Huh," she mumbled. "Not bad."

* * * * *

With Kylie's birthday party taking place in just two days, Sadie was in desperate need of essential party items. Because Jasper owned the only car between them (willed to him by Sadie's mother, Amelia, upon Amelia's death), he offered to drive her to the supermarket following their time at the Pizza Playhouse. He had even been chivalrous enough to pay for their meal, and by the end of dinner, Sadie felt quite bad for her poor attitude.

She accepted his offer for the trip to the grocer's and laughed loudly as he and Kylie serenaded her the entire way with the song "Be Our Guest" from Kylie's favorite Disney movie. Upon arriving at the supermarket, Kylie begged to be "lifted up" as Sadie pushed the cart through the aisles. Jasper, as usual, succumbed to her pleas and carried her in his arms for their first half-hour through the store.

At last, Kylie grew bored with this and demanded to be put down. He did so with firm instructions that she was not to go wandering off. She skipped a few feet ahead of the cart, humming snatches of "Be Our Guest" as she went.

The waiter at the Pizza Playhouse had presented Kylie with a cherry lollipop for dessert, which the little girl had accepted with glee. Having thoroughly smeared her own mouth with sticky sweetness, she had pushed the diminished bright red orb into Jasper's mouth. He held its remains firmly in the pouch of his cheek as he and Sadie strolled through the supermarket.

Sadie's eyes narrowed to slits as they passed a display of ethnic foods with Russian caviar at its center.

She muttered something about global conspiracies, and Jasper raised an eyebrow. Removing the lollipop from his mouth, he commented, "What makes you so sure this Russian dude has got your number?"

Sadie pursed her lips before answering. "It's obvious, isn't it? He's been coming into my restaurant for the past three weeks in order to stake out the competition. That gives him a three-week advantage over me, the dirty rat."

"Dirty rat?" Jasper coughed and reinserted the lollipop. "I'm just saying…maybe you're jumping to conclusions."

"There you go again, defending the other team!" She dropped a box of whole-grain crackers into the cart.

Kylie came running back to them from farther up the aisle, waving a box of fruit roll-ups in the air. "Kylie wants *this*!"

Sadie gave her one of the "I'm-the-mother-and-that-means-no-is-no" expressions, and Kylie turned around with a frown and marched back to return the fruit roll-ups on the shelf.

"I'm not defending the other team," Jasper inserted. "I'm just making sure *our* team doesn't make any premature moves."

"As team captain, my decision supersedes yours," she teased.

"But as team strategist, *my* rulings are final."

"Then I quit," she responded.

"You're under contract," he shot back.

She frowned. "True. You've got me there."

He grinned smugly. Kylie dashed in between them.

"This one, this one!" She held up some sort of sugary gelatin in plastic tubing. The color of the liquefied candy was neon green.

Jasper took it from her. "Kylie, even *I* wouldn't eat this stuff."

She ran off again. Jasper removed the lollipop, which was considerably smaller by now, and waved it in the air. Before he could comment, Sadie cut him off.

"Listen, Jas, I've worked long and hard to get that restaurant running. It's been a dream of mine for years—even before Ned died. I'm not about to take any chances on it. Let's just say the Russian's motives are innocent—and I'm not saying that they are, mind you…but it's very hard to make a go at that kind of business. What are the odds that two restaurants like ours could exist side by side, even in a tourist-traffic town like this?"

"But if there's even a *slim* chance," Jasper argued, "don't you think he deserves the right to try?"

Sadie paused to read the ingredients label on a spice container. "In a perfect world, yes. In my world, unfortunately not."

Jasper crunched the final knob off his lollipop stick and ground the ruby shards between his teeth.

"So what are you planning to do, then?"

Sadie wheeled the cart around a corner and into the next aisle. "I don't know. But I'll figure something out, don't you worry."

"Me? Worry?" He stuck the white lollipop stick between his lips. "That's your department, sweetheart, not mine."

She rolled her eyes at him as Kylie came running up once more.

"Can Kylie have this, Mom, *puh-lease*?"

The soon-to-be five-year-old held what appeared to be a can of edible silly string. Jasper and Sadie exchanged a worried glance.

"Uh…" Jasper took it from her outstretched fingers. "Why don't we see what's in the organic foods section, huh, Kylie?"

Kylie pouted. "But Kylie wants *this*!"

Jasper crossed his arms and stood toe-to-toe with her. Sadie thought they looked adorable like that.

"Kylie." He used the "grown-up" tone. "We got pizza, didn't we?"

Her head dropped a little. "Yes," she mumbled.

"You got a lollipop, didn't you?"

Her head went lower.

"Yes."

"So how about if we go look at the birthday cakes, and you can pick the design you want your mom to put on *your* cake this Saturday?"

Her head lifted a little.

"And then maybe we can stop by the ice cream case and pick a tasty, sweet, *natural-ingredient*"—he glanced at Sadie here—"dessert."

"That would make Mommy very, *very* happy," Sadie declared.

Kylie's head bobbed back up like the bobble-headed dog on her teacher's desk at school. Jasper winked at her.

"And if Mommy's happy…," he began.

"Then Kylie and Jasper is happy!" she finished with glee.

"Kylie and Jasper *are* happy," Jasper corrected.

She frowned at him. "That's what Kylie said, silly."

Jasper looked at Sadie as Kylie dragged him toward the bakery. "You know, she took *two* for the team with that one."

Sadie shrugged helplessly as Jasper and Kylie exited the aisle. Glancing back at her list, she frowned as she noticed she had forgotten to pick up a jar of nutmeg in the previous aisle. With a sigh, she swung the cart in an arc and propelled it around the corner. She felt the crash even before she heard it, a rattling connection with a shopper just beyond her line of vision.

She gasped as a groan hit her ears, and she flew around the side of the cart and out of the aisle to see what mayhem she had caused now.

Please don't let it be Smith or Jones…please don't let it be Smith or Jones!

Her heart sank when she saw whom she had leveled with her cart. He leaned against an end display of cookies, holding on for dear life to a cardboard cutout of one of the Keebler elves and rapidly rubbing his shin.

Dmitri Velichko. The Russian.

Great.

Chapter Three

....

"It's you." Sadie realized her tone lacked something in the way of apology, not to mention the simple fact that she *hadn't* apologized.

Dmitri rubbed his shin a few more times before releasing the cardboard Keebler elf, albeit with some obvious reluctance.

"Are you always this reckless?" he asked with a hint of irritation.

Sadie failed to smother a grin. "Yeah. It's just part of my natural charm, I'm afraid."

Apparently he found her brazen lack of remorse rather engaging, because he smiled. Straight, dazzling white teeth too, she noted.

"I suspected as much," he admitted.

"So…you come here often?"

She mentally slapped her palm to her forehead as soon as the words left her mouth.

Way to go, Sadie. Score one for the other team.

He arched an eyebrow. "Whenever I need groceries. And yourself?" His accent was endearing, and she knew her blush was alarming.

"I–It's just that, well…you know…my daughter's birthday is on Saturday, and uh…we could've gone to Wal-Mart instead of coming here, but…and um…some people, they uh, well…prefer to go there."

What am I doing—a Forrest Gump impersonation?

She made a second attempt at coherence. "So…you know."

Oh yes, much better, Sadie.

He looked concerned. "Are you all right?" he questioned.

Why did he look so concerned? "Sure. Why?"

"You're turning *very* red."

"Oh, it's—it's allergies."

"Allergies?"

"Mmm…yeah."

No, it's stupidity syndrome.

"I just get in grocery stores, and I—I—" *I—what?* "I tend to break out."

Sadie could have sworn his eyes were literally going to pop out of his head.

"You what?"

"I just… Okay, you know what? Never mind." She covered her face with her hand. She couldn't believe how poorly this was going. Where was Jasper when she needed him?

She turned on her heel and prayed that her face would start cooling any second. She grasped the handle of her cart and grimaced as Dmitri took a step back.

"I'm only lethal when I drive," she tried to reassure him. "And I don't have a car, so I hardly ever drive."

"That's…comforting."

She thought he was probably lying but was beyond caring at that point.

At long last, Kylie came bouncing over and tugged on her shirt hem. Thank goodness for five-year-olds and their constant interruptions.

"Mommy! Kylie found the cake she wants! It's gots yellow icinining"—Kylie had yet to learn the correct pronunciation of "icing" —"with blue curly edges and guess who's in the middle of it! Guess, Mommy, guess!"

"I can't possibly, sweetheart."

"BELLE!"

Sadie frowned in confusion. "There's a bell on the cake? You want a yellow cake with a bell?"

She looked at Jasper as he approached, begging for some sort of assistance. He made a face at her as though she were a bit simple.

Well, of course she was. She had Forrest Gump–syndrome and a tendency to break out in grocery stores after running over "innocent" Russian immigrants.

"*No*, Mommy." Clearly, Kylie had inherited the brains in this gene pool. "Belle from *Beauty and the Beast*."

"*O–Oh! Belle!*" She glared at Jasper. Like it would have killed him to throw her a bone on that one. "Well…that sounds wonderful."

She made a mental note to return to aisle 12 and procure two more packs of yellow food dye. She didn't even want to begin to consider the effects of that much artificial product on a five-year-old's internal system.

Jasper read her mind and said, "It'll wash right out with the fruit punch, so don't worry about it."

As Sadie considered this, the group fell silent. After a moment, she took notice of the quiet. Glancing up from her grocery list, she saw that Jasper and Kylie were staring at Dmitri and vice versa.

"Oh! Sorry! Uh, guys, this is Dmitri Velichko." She turned her back on Dmitri and made a face at Jasper, gesturing stiffly with her hand and mouthing, *"He's the one!"*

She turned back around. "And Dmitri, this is Kylie and Jasper."

Jasper and Dmitri shook hands, and the Russian smiled warmly at Kylie. "Pleased to make your acquaintance, Kylie."

"You talk funny," she bluntly announced.

"Kylie!" *Why me, Lord?*

Dmitri was not in the least offended. "That's because my family is from Russia," he explained.

"Oh." Kylie chewed her lip for a moment. "Is that where Sesame Street is?"

Dmitri faltered. "Excuse me?"

"You know. Where Elmo lives?"

"No, Kylie," Jasper jumped in, "Sesame Street is in New York."

"Then where's Russia?"

"It's across the ocean," said Dmitri.

Kylie's eyes lit up. "Like Belle?"

"Mmm, sort of. Belle lives in France, yes? And Russia is several countries over. Closer than America, though," Dmitri explained.

Sadie was impressed that Dmitri was familiar with the Disney story. Kylie, on the other hand, was eyeing Dmitri Velichko with a whole new form of awe.

"Can you take Kylie there?" she asked.

Her use of third person confused him. "Take who?"

"Kylie."

"You?"

"Yes."

"Oh, well, it's a very long way away."

"That's all right," Kylie assured him. "Kylie doesn't mind."

"Yes, but Mommy does," Sadie at last intervened.

Kylie looked at Sadie with her "not-now; stay-out-of-this" expression. "Kylie wants to go."

Jasper sniffed and affected a look of pure distress. "But if you leave, Kylie...who will play with me?"

Kylie grew alarmed. She hadn't thought of that. "*Oh*," was the only response she could utter.

"Poor Malibu Ken," sighed Jasper. "First his leg and now this."

It was too much. Kylie grabbed Jasper's hand. "It's all right, Jasper. Kylie will stay."

He looked down at her. "Are you sure? I wouldn't want you to regret it later."

Kylie released his hand to wrap her arms around his legs. He grabbed onto the Keebler elf cutout for balance.

"Can't leave Jasper! Won't!"

Jasper glanced up and mouthed, "She's going to break my legs!"

Sadie inserted her hands in between Kylie's arms and Jasper's legs. "Let go now, baby."

Kylie released Jasper and promptly held her hands upward. "Lift Kylie! Lift!"

Jasper hoisted her up, where she promptly tightened her arms around his neck. He choked and Kylie loosened her hold.

"Kylie wants to pick ice cream now. Jasper promised."

"Yes, Jasper did…I mean, I did." He turned to Dmitri. "It was nice meeting you."

Dmitri said the same. As Jasper was toting Kylie away, he gave Sadie a warning expression and mouthed, "Be nice!"

Deciding to give Jasper's advice a spin, Sadie gestured to Dmitri's leg and smiled apologetically. "Sorry about whaling you with my cart."

Dmitri smiled. "It's all right."

An awkward silence fell, and Sadie shifted from foot to foot. She noted the Keebler elf grinning smugly and felt the urge to topple him.

She cleared her throat. "Well…if you'll excuse me…I need to get some yellow food dye."

"For the cake," he clarified.

"Yes, the cake."

She licked her lips and mentally cast about for some sort of graceful good-bye.

"It was, uh…nice seeing you."

Brilliant.

If only he didn't look so self-satisfied. Him *and* the Keebler elf.

"Likewise."

"So, I'll…see ya around."

He nodded.

Just walk away, Sadie. Just…walk…away.

She swung the cart away from him with an exaggerated amount of force. It knocked into a pyramid of cereal boxes and sent the entire display crashing to the floor. A box of Fruit Loops landed at her feet, and Toucan Sam stared up in shame, his feathered finger outstretched and pointing at her. Sadie hung her head and sighed.

She was too embarrassed to even look at Dmitri.

A voice blared over the loudspeaker: "Clean-up on aisle 14."

Sadie finally glanced at him. "It's all right. They know me here."

He looked as though he were going to burst out with laughter at any moment. She wheeled her cart down the aisle and attempted to hold her head high, ignoring the *squeak, squeak, squeak* that had suddenly developed in the cart's wheels.

"Ms. Spencer?" his accented voice called her name.

She swallowed and turned. "Yes?"

"I believe the allergy medication is in aisle 7."

Sadie blinked.

"Thanks."

* * * * *

Sadie nearly sank through the floor the next morning when Dmitri Velichko entered Suncatchers and sat in his regular booth. The waitress on duty (a tall, waifish specimen appropriately named Willow) instantly inserted a menu in his hands and smiled with enough radiance to illuminate several city blocks.

Willow had poured him a mug of coffee and taken his order before Sadie mustered enough courage to approach his table.

"Morning," she offered with what she felt was the appropriate amount of contrition.

He smiled a greeting, which she took as a promising sign. She slipped into the seat across from him.

"How's your leg this morning?"

He laid aside his newspaper, which Sadie noted was once more open to the business section. A competitive wave of jealousy bit into her, and she had the unexpected urge to swing her foot under the table and into the same shin she had rammed with her cart the evening before.

"It's a little stiff, but I'll live."

"Oooh. That's a shame."

Dmitri raised an eyebrow at her tone. She sounded anything but sorry.

"So…the business section, huh?" She gestured to the paper.

He was eyeing her warily again. She seemed to have that effect on him. Sadie thought he probably wondered how many personalities she possessed.

"I was a business major in college," he tentatively offered.

"Really?" She affected an air of detached interest while mentally filing away this new information. A business major. He probably knew all about running a restaurant. And then she brightened as another thought occurred to her.

Sure, he knew about business. But did he know about *food*?

"Listen, Dmitri…may I call you Dmitri?"

He nodded.

"Okay then, Dmitri. About last night. I just wanted to apologize again for—for—well, for everything."

He seemed to relax once more. Sadie decided it must be her friendly personality in control today.

"I would feel so much better if you'd accept your breakfast on the house this morning as my way of making it up to you."

He held up a hand. "That's really not necessary—"

"Please." She smiled as sweetly as she could manage.

That's right, Sadie. Honey, not vinegar, remember? Kill him with your kindness and then take him out at the knees. Well, actually, she'd almost succeeded in doing that just yesterday.

"I'm not usually so…accident-prone," she explained. "At least not *that* accident-prone. I just…yesterday was just a bad day."

His blue eyes softened with compassion. "I'm sorry to hear that." His warm voice was so genuine that she felt her heart give a momentary flutter.

"Yeah, but it's…" She suddenly felt the need to elaborate. "It's my father. He sort of abandoned my mom and me when I was a kid, and ever since then, he's been this kind of off-again/on-again type of figure in my life. And he showed up yesterday, talking about making amends and regrets and God and…" She waved her hands helplessly. "What're you gonna do, you know?"

She sighed, but Dmitri actually appeared to be quite interested in her story. She found herself babbling on. "And then the chicken burned, and Kylie wanted pizza, but there were germs in the ball pit, and Kylie's birthday party is this Saturday, and I needed stuff for the party. So Jasper drove us to the grocery store, and I nearly took off your leg, but Kylie picked the cake design she wants me to duplicate, which requires an *insane* amount of yellow dye, which will probably stain her intestinal tract *permanently*, but it's okay because she only turns five years old once, you know? And I want her to be happy so she can grow up and get into a decent college and have a good life."

These words came out in a rush of thought, but Dmitri seemed to be following her just fine, so she went on. "I mean, why is being a mother so hard? Why doesn't anyone tell you how many things there are to worry about? How did my mom do it? And the thing is that she did it without my father, which is why I was so upset when he showed up yesterday. Who does he think he is to just sail back into town and expect everything to be like old times? And anyway, who said our old times were really all that great?"

Dmitri blinked several times. "I can see why yesterday must have been difficult."

"You have *no* idea."

He frowned. "I hope you don't mind my asking, but are you always this…" He seemed to be looking for a word that wasn't offensive.

"Psychotic?" she inserted for him. "I used to think it was just temporary, but Jasper has assured me that after twenty-nine years, it's probably permanent."

Dmitri took a sip of his coffee and proceeded to ask a question that caused Sadie's jaw to drop.

"Jasper's your husband?"

"*What?* No!"

Now it was Dmitri's turn to look surprised. He set his coffee cup back down. "Oh. But I thought…well, last night…with your daughter, Kylie. I just assumed…"

"Oh, no! Jasper is my very best friend in the entire world, but we've never been like *that.*" She abstractly wondered why she made "*that*" sound like such a bad thing. "Jasper is like…well, like…"

"A brother?" Dmitri attempted to help out.

She frowned. "Well, no. Not exactly."

She'd never thought of Jasper as a brother, strangely enough. He was her best friend. Did it really require further description?

Dmitri, however, appeared to be very confused.

"Jas and I were nearly born on the same day. His mom and mine shared a room at the hospital. They were good friends, so we spent a lot of time together growing up. After his mom passed on, my mom practically adopted him. So yeah…I guess he grew up like my brother, but…not."

Well, so much for clarification.

"We went separate ways when we got out of high school. He left for college to get his teaching degree, and I went to culinary school. I got married, signed a contract for two cookbooks and a television show, had Kylie, finished the cookbooks, lost the television show, and came back to Pennsylvania when my mother was diagnosed with cancer three years ago. Jasper and I reconnected when I came back home. He's been such a huge help to me the past couple of years—especially with taking care of Kylie."

"And your husband?" Dmitri questioned. "You're divorced?"

"No." She swallowed painfully. "Widowed."

"Oh. I'm so sorry."

She licked her lips and looked away. "It's been almost five years. It was a car accident—a drunk driver. Kylie was only a few months old when it happened."

She stared out the front windows of her restaurant and watched the suncatchers there make cherry rivers on the glass. Like a bleeding heart. She shook her head.

"So that's *my* life in a nutshell. And as for Jasper—a girl couldn't ask for a better friend. He even plays with Barbies when Kylie asks him. How many guys do you know who would do that?"

Dmitri cocked his head and studied her with a strange expression. "Sounds like he'd make a great father."

Sadie thought that was an odd remark, so she decided to ignore it.

"And yourself?" she asked.

Now he looked startled.

"You wonder if I'd make a good father?"

She coughed. "No...I meant, what's your story?"

His expression of relief struck her as extremely comical. She bit back her laughter.

"Oh... My parents are Russian immigrants. I grew up in a Russian neighborhood in the city and decided to give small-town life a try."

Hmm. Not very detailed, is he?

"And your parents?"

"They still live in the city."

"Friends? Girlfriends?" she pushed for more information.

He smiled somewhat bashfully, and Sadie found it cute.

"No," he whispered shyly, "nothing like that."

"Not even friends?"

He glanced up. "A few."

"You're not much of one for sharing personal details, are you, Dmitri Velichko?"

To her surprise, he blushed. "It doesn't come naturally to me."

"Meaning I've probably shared enough for both of us?" It was cruel to tease him, perhaps, but she found a perverse glee in it nonetheless.

"No, no! That's not what I meant!"

"Oh, calm down. I'm not offended, if that's what you're worried about."

An expression of relief washed over him once more. If she persisted in these encounters with him, she was very likely to give him ulcers. Which he'd probably blame on the food she served, thereby provoking a lawsuit and putting her out of business. She narrowed her eyes.

"Start simple, then. What are your hobbies?"

"Hobbies?"

"Yes, hobbies. You know. Things one does for fun? Such as running people over in grocery stores and babbling incoherently to restaurant patrons?"

"I believe those are quirks, rather than hobbies," he corrected her.

"Touché. Score one for the Russian."

"We're keeping score now?"

Oh, we've been keeping score for a while, Velichko. Get your game on.

"So. Hobbies." She was going to find something she could use, one way or another.

He thought about it for a moment. "I like to read."

"That's good. What else?"

She forced herself to relax, her hands folded in front of her on the table.

Tell me the truth! Say it. Say it! "I enjoy putting independent restaurant owners out of business." Tell me how you're planning to take me down. Go on, I dare you!

He mumbled something she couldn't quite catch. Unfolding her hands, she laid them palm-down on the table and leaned closer.

"What was that?"

Here it comes… The confession…

"I like old movies," he repeated again, his voice still soft.

Her eyes widened in surprise as she straightened up.

"Really? You do?"

He nodded, and suddenly an interested fire lit his pale blue eyes. "When my parents brought my grandparents over from Russia, they couldn't speak any English. It was my job to try to teach them. My grandfather had a very difficult time of it until one particular day when I turned on the television set and this black-and-white Cary Grant picture came on—*Arsenic and Old Lace*. My grandfather sat through the entire thing, demanding me to translate. He was simply enthralled."

Sadie felt drawn to the way Dmitri held out his hands as he spoke and the gentle rush of his words. It was like watching ice cream melt—tempting and sweet without even taking a bite.

"From that moment on, I taught him English through old movies. And until the day he died, Cary Grant was always his favorite."

"Like in *Charade*?"

If possible, Dmitri's eyes sparkled even more. "You know Cary Grant?"

She smiled in bemusement. "Not personally, but my mother once had a thing for him."

"What thing?"

"A thing, like—like she thought he was cute."

"Ah."

"My grandfather also loved Greta Garbo."

"Oh yeah! Like in *Ninotchka*?"

"You've seen it?" Dmitri's expression rivaled Kylie's when Jasper had suggested they go out for pizza last night.

"Sure, I've seen it!"

Sadie flung back her hair and attempted her most serious Garbo impersonation. "'And there is an old Russian saying—the cat with cream on his whiskers had better find good excuses.'"

Dmitri was positively exuberant. "Yes! Yes! You do a wonderful impersonation of her."

Sadie couldn't help glowing even as she blushed slightly. "Thank you."

Willow reappeared then with a steaming plate of eggs tostada and a jealous expression. Sadie waited as Willow laid out the food and sweetly asked if there was anything else she could get for him. He replied there was not and thanked her.

She backed away from the table with a girlish grin. Sadie watched her go for a moment and then turned back to Dmitri.

"You know, the Hershey Theatre here in town shows classic films once a month on the big screen. They're running one this Friday."

Dmitri's eyes lit with interest.

"I haven't been over there in ages, but it used to be pretty cool. If you're ever interested in going, let me know."

It took a second, after the words left her mouth, for Sadie to realize what she had just done.

Oh…my…word. Did I just ask Dmitri Velichko out?!?

His delightfully endearing grin returned. "Ms. Spencer, are you asking me out on a date?"

Sadie made a face. "What? No! Besides, I'm not even in the market, if you know what I mean. Well, not that I'm *not* in the market, exactly…it's just that it's been awhile since I've seen anyone—or seen them in that context, I mean, and although I'm sure you'd be a lovely date, I just don't think—"

He grinned at her. "Well, in that case…sure."

"W–what did you say?"

"I'd be delighted to go to the theater with you—you said this Friday? Tomorrow night then?"

Sadie wasn't entirely certain what had just happened or even whether it was a good thing, but she had the distinct feeling she could use this to her advantage. Of course, there was no point in looking desperate.

"Tomorrow? I'll have to check my schedule."

Clearly Dmitri wasn't fooled. "I'll pick you up at six? Will that be enough time?"

Her voice cracked when she attempted to answer. Clearing her throat, she tried again. "Plenty."

She slipped out of the booth with what she hoped demonstrated more elegance than Grace Kelly. "Enjoy your breakfast," she casually tossed over her shoulder.

She was grateful she couldn't see his face when he bemusedly answered, "I intend to, Ms. Spencer."

Chapter Four

....

"You *what*?"

Sadie had never seen Jasper so shocked. While he was thus distracted, she stole a french fry (made from organic potatoes with no unnecessary preservatives) and popped it into her mouth.

Suncatchers was now knee-deep into the lunch rush hour, and Jasper had stopped by, as he often did, to grab a bite before heading back to his class at Agape Christian Academy. If she had known that her announcement would provoke such a reaction from him, she'd have saved the news until later that night.

"It's not like I *tried* it," she defended. "It just sort of happened."

"Sadie." He gave her the "don't-feed-me-that" kind of look. "With you, nothing 'just happens.'"

"But it did!" she insisted. "One minute I was telling him about the downtown theater, and the next minute, we had plans to go out tomorrow night!"

Jasper frowned. "Tomorrow night? What about Kylie's party?"

"What about it?"

"It's on Saturday."

She looked at him as if he were simple. "Yeah, I know. Like I said, we're going out *Friday* night. I'm going downtown, not to Kansas. I'll be back by midnight, I swear. It's not a problem for you to watch her, is it?"

Jasper toyed with his napkin, shredding the edges. Sadie couldn't help thinking he looked a little ragged at the edges himself, following her announcement.

"Jasper? Do you mind?"

He looked up, and she touched his shoulder with concern.

He sighed. "No, it's not a problem. I just thought you'd be busy with last-minute party preparations and stuff."

"Well, I've got Karl delivering the cake on Saturday morning, and then I'll decorate it with Belle and all that cursed yellow icing. I'm finishing up the other stuff tonight. No worries."

He looked at her sharply. "With you? No worries?"

"Have a little faith in me, Jas."

"I do, Sadie, I do…but don't you think—" He dropped the rest of his sentence when she looked away, distracted by movement near the front of the restaurant. From the corner of her eye, she saw Jasper's head swivel as well.

Oh no.

It was Mac. He'd entered the restaurant and was self-consciously scanning the room, most likely looking for Sadie. To her annoyance, Jasper suddenly raised his hand and waved him over.

Mac spotted them with obvious relief and smiled, threading his way around the customers and toward the back of the room. Jasper jumped as Sadie smacked his hand down.

"*Ow!* What was that for?"

"What are you doing?" she hissed.

"He looked lost out there," he reasoned.

Sadie scowled.

"Chances, Sadie," he reminded her. "It's all about second chances."

"Easy for you to say. It's not *your* chances he's been using up."

The remark cut, and Jasper's expression told her so. But there was no time to discuss it further before Mac was upon them.

"Hello, Sadie girl," he greeted her.

Sadie clenched her jaw. "Hi."

"You really oughta lay off those lemons," Jasper murmured to her.

Okay, maybe she deserved that, but still…

"Can I get you anything?" Sadie attempted to treat her father with some small measure of civility.

Mac didn't answer her right away. Instead, he let his gaze wander over the restaurant, seeming, in particular, to focus on the myriad of suncatchers gracing the mirrored walls.

"It's really pretty in here," Mac finally commented. "Like walking underneath a rainbow."

Despite her best intentions, Sadie warmed at the compliment.

"It was Mom's idea," she softly remarked.

Mac turned, his eyes alight in a way Sadie had never noticed before. "You don't say. Did she make all of these?" His hand swept the room.

Amelia Cameron used to make suncatchers and display them, even selling them for a time. She'd give them as gifts or donate them to church fundraisers. People from several counties over would come just to purchase one of her detailed suncatchers. Sadie swallowed at the memory.

"Most of them," she quietly offered. "I made some myself, but I was never as good at it as she was. Kylie made a couple." Sadie gestured to an octagonal mirror behind her. The set of suncatchers displayed there was a smear of blended colors, clearly a child's work of art.

"That's another reason it's named Suncatchers," Jasper joined in. "'Cause Amelia always said that Kylie's smile was just like a suncatcher—it'd light up a room with color."

Mac grinned at this, and Sadie felt a strange little feeling in the pit of her stomach, almost as if a dozen caterpillars were suddenly crawling around and tickling her insides with their furry spines.

Sadie cleared her throat, and Mac focused on her. She cocked her head expectantly, silently communicating her growing impatience with this unexpected visit.

"That's what I came to talk to you about." He finally came to the point.

"Suncatchers?"

"No. Kylie."

Sadie felt every muscle within her tense unmercifully.

"What about her?"

Mac swallowed and shifted his weight. Sadie felt Jasper's eyes on her, silently pleading for her to at least make the effort to get along. She ignored him.

"I wondered if I might take her out sometime. For ice cream or something. You know—whatever she likes."

Sadie frowned unhappily. This was *not* something she felt prepared to allow.

"Or maybe I could come see her?" Mac hastily amended. "You know, at the house."

She pursed her lips in silent answer to this question. "I didn't know you'd be in town long enough to do that," she acidly stated.

Mac looked her straight in the eye. "I'm here for as long as it takes."

It was Sadie who dropped her gaze. "Well, promises are cheap, Mac. You know that better than most." Her voice grew soft and filled with remorse. "I spent half my life looking forward to when you'd show up again and the other half dreading when you'd decide it was time to move on."

She lifted her eyes and met her father's squarely. "I'm sorry. I really am. But I can't put Kylie through that."

Mac seemed to respect her honesty. He nodded, and Sadie realized her heart ached. It ached for the understanding in his eyes. He might have been a scoundrel and a poor excuse of a father, but at least he knew it. The worst part was that he seemed to accept how *she* felt about it. Something inside her cried out, *Wait! Don't give up on me yet—try again!*

But Mac had already turned to go.

"I'll be seeing you, Sadie."

"All right."

When he was gone, she blinked her eyes several times and rearranged the remains of the Cajun burger on Jasper's plate.

"Do you think I'm a terrible person, Jasper?" she suddenly asked.

Jasper stilled her fingers by wrapping them in his own.

"No, Sadie. I've never thought that."

She looked up and stared at the door where Mac had just exited.

"Yeah? Well, sometimes I do."

* * * * *

Dmitri Velichko shook hands with the contractor before bidding him farewell. Left on his own, he turned and stared up at the face of the building he had recently purchased. The late afternoon sun shone on the structure's exterior, and he felt a swell of optimism at the dappled display of light. He wished his grandfather could be here with him now, to witness this. He liked to think the man would be proud, seeing his grandson take this step of faith on his own terms.

"Whatcha lookin' at?"

Dmitri jerked in surprise, just now realizing that someone had come to stand next to him. He turned and looked into the expectant face of a young man who appeared vaguely familiar. Dmitri cleared his throat.

"I'm, er…just…looking," he lamely answered, feeling foolish for having been caught daydreaming.

But the younger man nodded as if this made perfect sense. Dmitri watched his face as he continued to stare at the edifice before them with an inexplicable absorption. Hesitantly, the Russian's gaze returned to the front of the building.

"Was there something *you* were looking at?" Dmitri couldn't help asking, not quite understanding why his building should hold such fascination for this stranger.

The other man shrugged and turned toward him. "Nah. Just looking."

"Ah." Dmitri wasn't sure what to do next, but he decided to be friendly. Extending his hand, he said, "I'm Dmitri Velichko."

The boy accepted the gesture. "Jimmy Craley. I work at Suncatchers." He tossed his head in the direction of the café across the street.

"Yes! That explains why you look so familiar."

"I'm a line cook there," Jimmy proudly announced, his thin face exuding a glow of satisfaction.

Dmitri smiled. "It's a wonderful establishment. I particularly enjoy the breakfast menu."

"Dude, totally. Sadie gives us a discount, you know, for working there. 'Course Karl—he's the head chef—says I should spend less time eating and more time working." Jimmy shrugged again.

Dmitri scratched the back of his head, trying not to let his amusement show. "I'm sure he's only teasing. Sadie must have faith in you to have given you the job."

Jimmy's head bobbed with enthusiasm. "Sadie's the best. She never yells, like other bosses. She just, like, sighs and then tells me to try again. Or if she's really upset, she pinches her nose, like this—"

Jimmy proceeded to demonstrate by gripping the bridge of his nose in between his fingers and sighing in imitation of Sadie on a bad day.

"But she's always really cool about it, you know? She rocks."

Dmitri coughed into his hand to hide his smile. "She's a good employer, then. And she seems very successful. I've noticed that her customers are extremely loyal—many of them come in several times a week."

"Oh, yeah," Jimmy agreed. "She grew up here, you know? So she knows a lot of people in town. I guess her mom was really well-liked or something—always helping people out and stuff. So maybe everyone feels like they're returning the favor, even though Amelia's been dead for a couple of years now."

"Mmm," Dmitri vaguely offered. He hesitated only a moment before saying, "Sadie...she seems, how would you say..." He searched his vocabulary for a suitable English description and finally touched on one a college professor had once employed. "Mercurial."

Jimmy blinked, clearly out of his range. Dmitri gave it another attempt, again searching for the proper English application. "Erratic?"

"You mean like unhinged?"

Dmitri looked at him, puzzled at this description. "She is without a hinge?"

"Like, a little nuts? Well, sure, but, dude, can you blame her? I mean, have you met those two old biddies that come in every week—Smith and Jones? Total harpies, man. They'll complain about anything, but they're so sneaky about it."

Jimmy glanced stealthily around before leaning in to confide, "They're always stiffing Willow on her tips—cheapskates. Still, Willow's super-nice to them, for Sadie's sake. But Sadie, she feels so bad about it that she always gives Willow extra tips on Tuesdays—out of her own pocket."

Dmitri softened at this. "That is very kind of her," he observed.

"Yeah. Like I said—Sadie's a cool boss." Now Jimmy turned the tables as he nudged Dmitri. "So what about you? You've been coming into Suncatchers a lot lately, right? All the girls talk about it." He rolled his eyes. "When they're on break and stuff, they're always like, 'Isn't his accent hot?' and 'You're so lucky, Willow, that he sits in your section!'"

Jimmy scoffed, and Dmitri felt a warm blush work its way up his neck. He looked away, resting his gaze on the building before him as he reluctantly responded, "Oh, well...as I said, I enjoy the food at Suncatchers."

"Dude, I know. Man's gotta eat, right?" He waited for Dmitri to speak once more, and when he didn't, Jimmy probed further. "You just moved here?"

Dmitri nodded at this question. "Yes, I have purchased a house." He gestured vaguely in the other direction. "As well as this establishment…" He glanced up at the structure before them. It showed only mild signs of damage, and the contractor had given him promising news on the remodeling.

"Cool," Jimmy said and then waited for Dmitri to elaborate.

The Russian man cleared his throat, feeling awkward. "Have you… lived here long?" Dmitri finally asked, trying to shift the conversation away from himself once more.

Jimmy answered, "I'm from Etters originally. Then Harrisburg. My girlfriend got a job at Chocolate World and moved here a few years back. She loves seeing the little kids getting all worked up over the candy and stuff." He blew out a breath. "I had to move too if I wanted to stay with her. She laid the law down on me."

This admission drew a grin from Dmitri. He relaxed again, resting easier now that the attention had moved to Jimmy. "A person will do many things for love," he commented.

"You have no idea," Jimmy told him. "I rode the Kissing Tower three times in a row because Annie asked me to…and dude? I'm totally phobic of heights." He shuddered at the memory. "I puked for like twenty-four hours straight. I haven't been back to Hersheypark since."

Dmitri burst out with laughter at this. He liked Jimmy, odd though the younger man was. "You must love her very much."

Jimmy grinned. "Dude, totally." He cast a glance behind him at Suncatchers. "Gotta go. My break's probably up by now. It was nice talking to you, Mr. Vel–itch–k…ko." Jimmy stumbled over the foreign name.

"Dmitri," the other man offered.

"Cool. Dmitri." He pronounced it "Dim–a–tree." "What is that, by the way, like, French?"

"Russian."

"Sweet. See ya later, man." Jimmy gave him a salute, and Dmitri waved.

"Good-bye!"

Standing alone once more in front of the building he now owned, Dmitri released a little sigh. He met his own gaze in the reflection of the dusty windows, startled to see the smile that still lingered on his face. After the last few conversations with Sadie Spencer and this latest encounter with her employee, he found himself feeling slightly less lonely than he had been when he first arrived in Hershey weeks before.

* * * * *

Although she found it very difficult to believe, Sadie was actually having a good time that Friday evening. Dmitri proved to be an extremely entertaining date on their night out.

Of course, things had started off rather shakily. Following her arrival home from the restaurant that night, Jasper had said he had a couple of items at his house that needed to be taken care of. He promised to return soon to keep an eye on Kylie while Sadie went out. An hour and fifteen minutes later, he called to say he would be a little late but that it shouldn't interfere with her plans with Dmitri.

Immediately after hanging up the phone from Jasper's call, an unnatural calm filled the house. Sadie cocked her head, listening with the sixth sense she had honed in recent years. "Kylie?" she called out.

Silence.

Sadie's heartbeat tripled as she rocketed up the stairs toward Kylie's bedroom. She poked her head inside the bedroom and scanned the perimeter of the room. Sadie's gaze landed on Kylie's bed with its spread of butter cream yellow and *Beauty and the Beast* pillowcases. Jasper had gotten her the set for her birthday last year. Sadie had never seen a happier Kylie than the day she unwrapped those pillowcases. She'd never slept a night without them since.

But there was no sign of the little girl now, not in the bed nor on the floor.

"Kylie?"

Sadie's heart hammered frantically against her rib cage as she wheeled out of the room and started back down the hall.

"*Kylie Amelia Spencer,* answer me right this minute!"

And then she heard it. A distinct "Uh-oh" that came from the crack in the ajar bathroom door. Sadie pushed open the door and found Kylie seated calmly by the toilet, with its lid propped up against the tank.

Kylie stared deep into the toilet bowl, and Sadie swallowed nervously.

"Kylie?"

The little girl jerked around in surprise at her mother's entry. She bit her lip as she looked up.

"Problems," she announced matter-of-factly.

Sadie felt a growing hysteria. "What kind of problems, Kylie?"

"Grandma's ring."

Sadie's eyes widened. "Her wedding ring?"

"The volcano took it—just like Malibu Ken's leg!" Kylie stated this with an indignation that indicated that all of this was the volcano's doing and that five-year-old girls were merely innocent bystanders to this type of injustice.

"KYLIE!"

She looked up with enough innocence to charm the saints. "What, Mommy?"

Sadie got down on her hands and knees and held her hair off her neck as she stared, along with Kylie, into the toilet bowl.

"What were you doing with Grandma's ring?"

Kylie frowned at her as if grown-ups shouldn't be asking those types of questions. "Kylie tried to put it up her nose."

Sadie's gaze snapped from the toilet to her daughter.

"You *what*?"

Kylie sighed. The tediousness of adults. "Jasper said that canninabals"—Sadie quickly translated this to *cannibals*—"wear rings in their noses. Kylie wanted to be a canninabal."

"Kylie, you're *not* a cannibal!"

"But Kylie wants to be! Jasper said that maybe the canninabals took Malibu Ken's leg!"

"When Jasper gets here, you can give *him* to the cannibals. Tell him Mommy gave you permission!"

Sadie rolled up the sleeve of her beaded mesh top as far as it would go and plunged her hand into the commode, glowering as she felt along the toilet's basin and attempting not to think of all the things that had been in this dark hole before.

Kylie watched her with fascination.

"Mommy, you look pretty."

"Thank you, sweetheart."

"Can Kylie do that next?"

"Do what, baby?"

"Stick her arm in the volcano?"

"*No.*"

"Do you wanna hear a joke, Mommy?" Kylie grinned mischievously. "What did one volcano say to the other?"

Sadie bit her lip and strained her fingers, desperately hoping to feel the smooth circle of her mother's wedding band. "What?"

"I *lava* you," Kylie sang out.

Sadie smiled faintly at this. Just then, the doorbell rang.

"Oh, thank heavens! Kylie, that's Jasper. Go and bring him up here."

Kylie scrambled to her feet and thundered from the bathroom as Sadie continued to explore the inner realms of the toilet's interior. She couldn't feel a thing but cold porcelain. This did *not* rank up there with life's most pleasant experiences.

"Kylie! Bring Jasper up here! Tell him Mommy needs help!"

She began mumbling to herself, a personal tirade that involved a lengthy description of what she thought about Malibu Ken and Jasper, as well as a few choice details on nose-piercing cannibals and the island paradise that was otherwise recognized as Sadie's bathroom.

"It's not Jasper, Mommy."

Sadie shifted, with her arm still submerged in the toilet, to see Kylie standing in the bathroom doorway and Dmitri Velichko towering behind her.

Sadie gulped and pulled her hand from the bowl. It dripped water across her skirt and onto the tile.

"Uh…hi there."

Can life get any worse at this present moment?

Dmitri smiled with pure amusement. "Hello," he responded. "Kylie mentioned something about volcanoes eating Mommy's hand."

"And Grandma's canninabal ring," Kylie added.

Sadie reached for a towel but found she didn't have the strength to stand. Her knees were weak with mortification.

"My mother's ring," Sadie attempted to explain. "Kylie attempted to stick it up her nose because Jasper"—here she made a face of extreme annoyance—"mentioned something about cannibals, rings in their noses, and Malibu Ken's leg. So apparently the ring fell into the volcano, er, I mean the toilet, and it's really quite priceless to me, you see, so cannibals or no, I *have* to get it back!"

She sighed with a quavering breath that indicated tears. Kylie's lower lip trembled also.

"It's all right, Mommy. Jasper will fix it."

This childlike confidence sent an unnatural surge of relief through Sadie, and she expelled a half-sob, half-laugh as she realized that Kylie was correct. Jasper could fix it. He always did.

"Jasper can fix what?"

All eyes in the bathroom turned as Jasper spoke from behind Dmitri. Kylie rounded on him in exasperation.

"Mommy said Kylie can't be a canninabal!"

"Of course you can't," Jasper declared. "What gave you that idea?"

"You said canninabals took Malibu Ken's leg!"

Jasper swallowed. "I did?"

Kylie scowled at him. "Kylie tried to put Grandma's ring in her nose, and the volcano got it! 'Cause you said canninabals wear rings in their noses!"

"Oh. So I did." He looked helplessly at Sadie. "I forget she's only four, you know?"

"*Five*," Kylie stated. "Kylie will be five tomorrow!"

"Kylie…" Dmitri attempted to help out. "Why don't we go downstairs and you can tell me all about your birthday party tomorrow? And we'll let Mommy and Jasper see if they can…um…retrieve the ring from the, uh, volcano."

"It's a toilet," Kylie corrected him.

He smiled. "Right."

Dmitri politely offered Kylie his hand, which she accepted, and the two made their way back into the hall and down to the first floor. Jasper entered the bathroom and sat on the floor beside Sadie.

"I am *so* sorry!" He was already rolling up his sleeves. "I forget that she takes things so literally."

"Jasper, she's five years old."

"I know, I know. But she's just so easy to talk to…" He stuck his hand into the bowl. "Whew. That's cold."

Sadie was finally able to stand to her feet. "Believe me, I know."

She turned on the water at the sink as hot as she could stand it and lathered her arm with soap. She washed in silence and then repeated the action two more times. When she finished, Jasper's arm was still in the bowl, with it practically up to his shoulder.

"Do you think we'll be able to get it back?"

Jasper frowned with concentration and absently remarked, "It took Ken's leg—it's not getting your ring too."

She laughed at him then, the complete seriousness of his expression amusing her.

"My knight in shining armor," she stated with a thread of breathlessness.

Just then he grinned.

"I think I got it!"

She fell to the floor beside him and leaned close as he attempted to extract his arm. He drew it out, dripping wet, a band of gold gleaming in his fingertips.

"Oh, Jasper—I could *kiss* you!"

He looked at her with a wry expression. "What's stopping you?"

Something in his eyes made her hesitate. What *was* that? If she didn't know better, she'd think it was...but no, it couldn't be.

Sadie looked away and at her watch.

"Oh! Dmitri and I better get going. The movie starts at seven!"

"Right."

Sadie ignored the strange disappointment in his voice as she checked her reflection in the mirror one last time.

"I won't be late. Kylie's dinner is in the microwave—just heat it up. There's some for you too. Have a good night!"

She rushed for the door and then paused, turning. "And Jasper?"

He looked up, and the little boy sadness in his eyes tugged at her heart.

"Thanks."

He smiled. "No problem."

Two and a half hours later, Sadie and Dmitri finished viewing *To Have and Have Not*, a film Dmitri had not experienced before tonight. He had been enraptured from the moment they walked in the door, his jaw dropping at the opulence of the Hershey Theatre lobby's Italian lava rock floors, marble walls, and arches and bas-relief ceilings.

Sadie had felt a strange swell of pride—the theater was impressive, rivaling the best of European architecture. It left a little glow of triumph warming her insides, knowing that her little town could possess such a gem of a building.

"Parts of it are modeled after St. Mark's Cathedral in Venice," she couldn't resist informing him as they'd made their way through the inner foyer. She'd tried to keep the smugness from her tone, but it was impossible.

Take that, Mr. European Entrepreneur, she couldn't help but think.

The main auditorium, with its Byzantine design and firmament-inspired ceilings, had left Dmitri equally speechless. And when the pre-show music started—an impressive round of music on the Theatre's Aeolian-Skinner organ—Dmitri merely shook his head with awe.

Sadie had smirked, feeling both childish and triumphant at the same time.

"Not bad for a small town, huh?"

One corner of Dmitri's mouth twitched in response. "As they say…not bad at all."

They'd settled in for the film, though Sadie couldn't resist nudging him playfully in the side once in a while when his eyes would wander from the screen to the ceiling, where a display of man-made starlight twinkled.

Sadie had tried not to dwell on that last look in Jasper's eyes before she'd left the house that evening, though her stomach fluttered in agitation every time she thought of it. His eyes had been faintly murky with a sadness she was unaccustomed to seeing in him. It was an expression that had taunted her all night, but she once again forced the image from her mind as she and Dmitri left the theater and walked the short distance to Café Zooka, the local coffee shop attached to the Hershey Story Museum.

Dmitri held the door for Sadie and placed their order at the counter. After receiving their beverages, they settled themselves at a booth and resumed their conversation.

"Absolutely wonderful." Dmitri summed up the experience with boy-like glee.

Sadie smiled. "If I had known it was going to get you this excited, I'd have waited a month and taken you to their double feature night."

Dmitri's face glowed. "They have one of those?"

"Yep. I can see we're going to mark it on our calendars."

Dmitri couldn't have looked more pleased. They paused to enjoy their drinks—a café Americano, black, for Dmitri and a chai latte for Sadie. After a moment, Dmitri swiveled the subject to matters closer to home.

"Kylie is a most…interesting child, isn't she?"

Sadie felt a surge of motherly pride coupled with endless frustration, her lips twisting in wry amusement at this observation. "You can't even begin to imagine."

She leaned in. "When she turned two, she painted the walls with my lipstick. All twelve tubes of it." She cupped one hand beside her mouth and whispered confidentially, "I used to have an obsession with lipstick." Leaning back, she ran two fingers across her chin in order to showcase her lips. "And now? Clear lip gloss or chapstick only."

He laughed.

"I had thought, of course, that the lipstick episode indicated she would become a child prodigy. My darling girl would be a Picasso by age six." Sadie sighed. "Alas, she had no desire to paint on canvas or paper…or even with water paint or crayons, for that matter. Walls and lipstick all the way."

She folded her hands in front of her. "I know they say not to stifle your child, but honestly—how many coats of paint can one wall take? I began to be afraid of what would happen if she discovered my secret stash of nail polish."

"I suppose parenting is at times a case of erring on the side of caution."

Sadie nodded in firm agreement. "That's something they will *never* tell you in the books."

Sadie blew on her latte and then sipped it carefully before continuing.

"Then came her interest in fashion. My mother had saved all sorts of clothes over the years, and Kylie loved to drag them out and try them on. Which is fine, you know? Kids do that."

Sadie paused to sip her drink once more.

"Except Kylie…?" Dmitri prompted.

"Except Kylie loved to place my great-grandmother's brassieres on her head and the girdles around her waist and then march outside into the yard and announce to the neighbors that she was Thor, God of Thunder."

Dmitri choked on his coffee, and Sadie smiled. "Yeah, that was my reaction too when they told me. But of course, nothing compares to six months ago when she decided she was finally old enough to drive. She waited until Jasper was occupied with something else, stole the keys to his car, started it up, and clapped her hands with glee as it rolled out of the driveway and down the street."

Dmitri's eyes widened with shock. "What happened?"

"Jasper realized what was going on in time to chase the car down the block and hop inside before any real damage occurred. And he keeps his keys pinned to him at all times now, by the way."

"She's not even five yet!" Dmitri remarked.

"I know. I figure she's already discovered makeup, though—after the lipstick thing—and the driving issue's already been dealt with, so at least that's out of the way. All that's left now is boys, piercings, and drugs."

"You're very optimistic," he commented.

She grinned. "You know…cliché as it sounds, it's Kylie herself that gives me whatever optimism I have. After she was born, I was on this huge upstroke. I had book contracts and a cooking show and a husband who loved me. My life couldn't have been better. And then there came this huge wave of change—the cooking show failed, the contracts ran out, Ned died, and Mom was diagnosed with cancer. And there would be days where I'd just lie in bed and cry and cry until Kylie came in and pressed her nose to mine."

Sadie shook her head. "You can't…" She drew a breath and looked off into the distance for a moment. She took another deep breath and continued. "You can't look into eyes identical to yours—eyes that place such complete faith and trust in you—and not make a choice to go on living. I don't know how to do that. I don't know how to look at her and *not* be optimistic."

She focused on Dmitri once more. "She's all that makes life worth fighting for."

He raised his mug. "Here's to Kylie, then, and all that's right in this world."

Sadie raised her cup. "Hear, hear."

They drank to it. "So, what about you?" she prompted. "Any fatherly inclinations?"

He raised an eyebrow, and she rolled her eyes. "I'm just *asking*, for heaven's sake. I didn't ask if you wanted to be *Kylie's* father, did I?"

He ducked his head in embarrassment. "Sorry. It's just that I get a lot of…interest that way."

Sadie smirked. "I bet you do, good-looking Russian man such as yourself. But you mean to tell me there's never been anyone who actually caught your eye?"

Dmitri shrugged.

Sadie leaned her back against the booth. "Ahh, man of mystery, huh? I think you've watched one too many of those old movies, Mr. Velichko."

He didn't respond. Sadie's curiosity sparked. She did love a challenge. Time, though. That was what was needed. Time and patience. She'd crack Dmitri Velichko yet, just wait and see.

"So why is it that you're *really* in Hershey, hmm?"

He drained his coffee. "I'm looking into new opportunities."

Sadie's jaw clenched. Was he going to reveal *nothing* to her? She toyed with her latte and grew silent as the drink grew cold.

It was several moments before Dmitri spoke.

"I was looking for a change. A chance to start over. Everyone's entitled to that, aren't they? A second chance?"

His words struck so swift and so deep that she nearly gasped. What was it Jasper had said?

Chances, Sadie. It's all about second chances.

She figured God was probably trying to get her attention with that one, but she decided to block it out.

"Some people use up their chances," she quietly remarked, thinking far more about her father than Dmitri at that moment.

Dmitri frowned. "Do you really think so?"

She looked up, realizing what she'd said. She thought about it for a minute. "I don't know, Dmitri. I guess it depends on the circumstances."

He leveled his gaze on her and asked an unexpected question. "Are you a Christian, Sadie?"

She swallowed. "Yeah, actually, I am."

"Then do you believe what they say—that God is a God of second chances?"

She hesitated. Where was he going with this? She answered softly, "I'd like to think so."

He didn't say anything more.

She frowned. "What, that's it?"

He looked at her. "What's it?"

"That's all you're gonna say?"

"That's all I wanted to know."

"Oh." She hadn't expected that.

* * * * *

When they returned to Sadie's, Dmitri walked her to the door like a true gentlemen. They lingered on the front porch for a moment, him thanking her for mentioning the movie and her thanking him for buying her a latte.

She reminded him about marking the double feature on his calendar, and then he turned to go. On impulse, she grabbed his hand, and he turned.

She stared up at him, fighting a mix of confused emotions. On the one hand, she found him deceptive and conniving—not telling her his true reasons for being in town. But then, on the other hand, he really was quite handsome and awfully charming.

It had been a long time since Sadie had been kissed by a man. Not since Ned had died. For a moment she stared into the cool, pale wells of his eyes and wondered what it would be like to be kissed by someone as good-looking as Dmitri Velichko.

She practically dared him to do it, and whatever he saw in her eyes must have sparked him to take the initiative, because the next thing she knew, he leaned in and their lips met. It took her a moment to adjust to the sensation. Other than Kylie's, no other lips had touched hers in several years.

Once she got used to it, a certain familiarity returned. As the kiss lingered, she waited…for what, she wasn't certain. Whistles? Bells? Fireworks? The horn section of a band?

But as Dmitri finally pulled away and their eyes met, she felt a sinking disappointment.

Nothing. Not a thing. She could have been kissing her brother, for all the chemistry she felt there. Sadie touched her lips with her fingertips.

They were still there. Still in working order, as far as she knew. Maybe she needed practice.

She smiled at him as though everything had been as it should be. "I'll see you at Kylie's party tomorrow?"

He returned the smile, though it was a trifle awkward. "Tomorrow," he echoed.

He turned and headed down the steps and back to his car as Sadie slipped inside the house. She moved quietly, shrugging off her coat and hanging it in the closet, laying her house keys on the foyer table.

Tiptoeing inside, she searched the lower level for any signs of life. All was still and empty. Walking up the stairs, she headed for Kylie's bedroom and eased the door open enough to stick her head in.

There they lay, side by side, on top of the *Beauty and the Beast* bedspread and pillowcases. Kylie's hair spread in a fan across Jasper's chest, her thumb tucked firmly in her mouth. Jasper's arm stretched protectively across her back, his eyelashes feathering his cheeks as he dozed. Something pulled in Sadie's heart—pulled hard—and she had the overwhelming urge to wake them both and hold them tightly in her arms, never letting go.

As she deliberated the wisdom of such an action, Jasper stirred. Seeing her standing there, he blinked the sleep from his eyes.

"Hey," he whispered softly.

"Hey," she whispered back.

Easing his arm from beneath Kylie's body, he moved off the bed and joined Sadie in the doorway.

"She went right to sleep?" Sadie questioned softly.

Jasper shook his head. "Three glasses of water, four stories, two bedtime prayers, and a partridge in a pear tree."

"Three glasses of water? She'll be up every half hour!"

Jasper shrugged. "She was thirsty."

Sadie eyed him suspiciously. "What did you give her?"

"What did *I* give her?"

"You know what I mean."

He looked away guiltily. "Maybe some Cheetos."

"The baked kind?"

He swallowed loudly. "Not exactly."

"Jasper!"

Kylie stirred, and Jasper tugged Sadie out of the room. "Just kidding," he teased.

She sighed and then shook her head with a smile. "Not funny."

"Yes, funny," he replied.

They headed downstairs together and spoke in a more normal tone of voice since they were away from Kylie.

"So, how did the date go?"

Sadie shrugged. "It was all right. They showed *To Have and Have Not.*"

"Really? Good one. Wish I could have seen it."

"Maybe we can go another time," Sadie suggested. "You, me, and Kylie."

"That would be nice," Jasper said as he paused at the hall closet to retrieve his jacket. He followed Sadie into the kitchen where she was leaning against the counter, staring off into the distance. He pulled on his coat and then touched her lightly on the arm. "Hey, is everything okay?"

She swiveled her head and looked him in the eye. "Jasper, am I… attractive?"

Something sparked in his eyes, a fire that made her unexplainably wary. "Sure, Sadie. Of course you are. Why?"

She purposefully dropped her gaze, wondering if maybe she should have kept her thoughts to herself. "No reason."

Jasper cocked his head. "Did Dmitri say something to you? Something he shouldn't have?"

Her eyes jumped back up to his. "What? No! I just wondered. That's all." She looked away again.

Jasper touched her cheek and slid his fingers down to her chin, drawing her face toward his. "Sadie, you're the most beautiful woman I've ever met. Why do you think I never married? I'm still holding out for you." He winked.

Her heart fluttered with a will of its own. She forced her voice to lighten as she said, "You don't fool me, Jasper Reeves. I know you got dumped by your fiancée back in college."

He clicked his tongue at her. "Ah, but maybe you don't know the story as well as you think you do, Sadie Spencer. See, *I* broke it off with *her*."

Sadie frowned, suddenly serious. "Are you kidding me? You never told me that."

He shrugged and brushed back the hair from her eyes. "Doesn't matter," he answered.

"Yes, it does," she persisted. "Why didn't you ever tell me that?"

"Would it have made a difference?"

"What do you mean…made a difference?"

He shook his head. "Never mind."

"Jasper—"

His expression silenced her. Suddenly she realized that he was standing extremely close. Not that it was unnatural for Jasper to stand close to her. But this was different. She felt soft and vulnerable at the moment, and Jasper's hands still lingered on her face. She could feel his breath steaming the side of her cheek.

The words seemed to come from some dark well Sadie didn't know existed. "Why haven't you ever kissed me?" she asked him.

His lips turned upward a little bit into a slightly cocky, absolutely breathtaking grin. "I have kissed you, remember? Second grade, on the swings. You knocked me out cold. The school nurse thought you'd broken my nose."

She laughed in such a low, gentle way that the air between them barely moved.

"So, what, you're telling me you're afraid of me?"

He wasn't smiling anymore. "I've always been afraid of you, darling Sadie."

He did it then, though she hadn't quite been expecting it. His lips brushed hers as lightly as butterfly wings with a sweetness no sugar could replicate. She had never known this sensation before, not this. Nothing like this. Not this electrifying, flashing light of perception, as if the entire world had flamed like the touch of a match to newspaper. And like a match, the moment extinguished far too quickly.

Whatever he'd been anticipating, Sadie didn't know if Jasper had realized his expectations or not. He pulled away and turned his face before she could read the emotion there. He left her with something about being back tomorrow in time for Kylie's party.

Sadie listened as he stepped into the foyer and locked the door behind him. And suddenly, without him standing beside her, it was she who felt afraid.

* * * * *

There was only a half hour left until closing on Friday night when Mac Cameron entered Suncatchers and made his way to the counter. He slid onto a stool and waited patiently for the waitress to approach, a carafe of coffee in her hand.

She gestured toward a mug with a friendly smile, and he nodded, watching as she filled it to the brim.

"Welcome to Suncatchers. I'm Willow. What can I get you?" she questioned, not bothering to remove the pad from her apron.

Willow was pleasant and cheerful despite how near it was to closing time.

"I thought I'd have a go at the dessert menu," he said.

This statement caused her to hesitate for a moment. "Um…sure." She reached beneath the counter and had to search for several long moments before she could slide a menu in front of him.

"We don't get many requests for the dessert menu," Willow explained.

Mac studied the list, scanning the offerings thoughtfully.

"The chocolate cake is good," Willow offered. She nibbled at her lower lip. "Really. It seriously is. Karl adds a little chili powder to the batter. I know it sounds a little 'out there,' but it really adds something."

Mac's eyebrows raised at this. "Chili powder?" He cleared his throat. "I thought Sadie created all the recipes here."

"Oh." Willow looked abashed. "She does. Pretty much. Only Karl… he knew it needed something else, so…he toyed with her recipe a little." She eyed him with a vague sort of distrust shining through her eyes. "Um…do you know Sadie or something?"

Mac couldn't stop the proud smile that broke through his normally somber expression. "I'm her father."

Willow's eyes widened in astonishment. "Seriously? Mac Cameron? I thought you were AWOL or whatever."

He felt his smile melt and vanish as he dropped his head to look at the menu once more. "Yeah," he murmured. "I was. For a while." Gathering his determination, he lifted his head once more. "But I'm back now…for good."

Willow studied him for a long moment and then grinned. "Good for you. Sadie's gotta be thrilled."

Mac didn't respond to this, and Willow chattered on, "That granddaughter of yours is such a pistol! She keeps everyone on their toes. And you must be so proud of Sadie. She's practically my role model after everything she's been through—and then making a go of this place, to boot." She gestured to the dining room at large.

Mac's head looked down once more, and he struggled to keep his breathing even. These mentions of Sadie left him feeling winded and a little gloomy. He had missed out on so much. So, so much.

Trying to shake his melancholy, he said, "Chili powder, huh? Well. Not sure I'm up for that just yet. But I really wanted to try some of my daughter's recipes. What else would you recommend?"

Willow leaned forward, her tone lowering. "Truthfully, if you want to try one of Sadie's dishes, I'd recommend an entrée. Or an appetizer. Or even one of the sides. Just steer clear of the desserts, okay?"

He ran his eyes over the menu once more. "They can't be so bad."

"Oh, they're not," Willow hastened to reassure him. "It's just, well, desserts aren't really Sadie's thing. That's why Karl does *all* the baking and stuff around here." Mac must have looked dismayed because she rushed ahead, "But all the other items on the menu are *brilliant*. Trust me."

Reaching beneath the counter once more, she immediately drew out Suncatchers' dinner menu and placed it before him. "You look like a meat-and-potatoes kind of guy. How about the beef-stuffed potatoes? Or the burger stroganoff? It's got a reduced sherry base, and it's absolutely to die for."

"Sounds good," Mac admitted, his mouth watering. "But you're getting ready to close up soon…"

Willow waved a hand. "Are you kidding? You're Sadie's *dad*. I'm sure we can throw some stuff together before closing." She looked around the dining room. "Besides, things have slowed up in the last twenty minutes. It'll keep Jimmy on his toes."

Still, Mac hesitated. "I wouldn't want to inconvenience any of you. I just thought a cup of coffee and dessert would suit me—"

Willow clicked her tongue. "Trust me. Jimmy needs the practice." She winked at him. "And I could use the tips."

Mac relaxed. "All right, then. Bring me…" His eyes scanned the assorted offerings. "Um…"

Before he could make a decision, Willow whisked the menu out of his hands. "Don't worry, Mr. Cameron. I've got it covered."

He had no time to protest as she sashayed toward the kitchen, calling, "Hey, Jimmy, I hope you kept the grill hot!"

Mac Cameron ducked his head with a smile, a comfortable warmth settling in his stomach. For the first time perhaps ever, he felt like he was home.

Chapter Five

. . . .

Jasper had heard, from a buddy of his at the gas station, that Mac was renting a room at a motel on the outskirts of town and had taken a job at a local mechanic's. Since his gas station friend was known as the touchstone for all sorts of local information, Jasper figured it must be true.

On Saturday morning he gave up on sleep as the sun peeked over the hillside, finally rising from bed and prowling his house for the better part of an hour as he thought about what to do.

He'd kissed Sadie last night. *Kissed* her.

But even that wasn't nearly so spectacular as what had happened next.

Sadie had kissed him back.

Now Jasper was forced to consider a conclusion he'd been skirting for the better part of twenty years.

He was in love with his best friend.

Maybe it had happened over time or maybe it had really started when she'd first returned to Hershey three years ago or maybe it hadn't been until she'd announced her date with Dmitri Velichko just this week, but the point was it had happened.

The lingering question was what he planned to do about it.

Sadie wasn't exactly the type of woman to swoon over flowers and chocolates. They lived in Hershey, Pennsylvania, for crying out loud—chocolate was everywhere. But she *was* a woman, with certain triggers and emotions like any other. He could use that. He could do something about it.

He could convince her they were perfect together. Sure, they worked on each other's nerves sometimes, but what couple didn't? And their laughter always outweighed their tears. Always.

Jasper ran over this synopsis a thousand times as he showered and dressed. How to win Sadie's love? How to reason with a truth he was sure, deep down, she already recognized? Eventually, his thoughts shifted to Kylie. She was like a daughter to him already; it wouldn't be such a stretch for him to actually become her dad in time, would it? Sadie would see that, wouldn't she?

He stood in front of his refrigerator with the door hanging open for four full minutes before the cold air jolted him back to reality. Breakfast. He had planned to eat breakfast. He figured Sadie would be more than happy to scrounge up something for him when he got to her place, but he didn't want to put that on her this morning. Kylie's party was this afternoon, and he was sure she was going crazy with last-minute preparations and cake decorating.

He slammed the fridge door shut. He was never in his house long enough to keep a stocked fridge, and moldy cheese and mayonnaise did not present a very appetizing meal anyway. Besides, he couldn't eat a thing if he wanted to. Nerves.

It was too early, he knew. Too early to go over to Sadie's and tell her how he felt. The timing was off anyhow—today was not an easy day to delve into such a pool of emotions.

That's when he decided to seek out Mac.

It took him less than a minute to grab his coat and keys, lock the house, step outside, and head to the car. Pleased to feel that summer was on the threshold and melted the need for even his lightest jacket, he tossed the coat onto the seat beside him and revved the 1972 blue Chevy Nova to life.

Before he had even learned to stick a key in an ignition, Jasper had loved Amelia's old car. Memories of hot summer days riding with Sadie in the backseat, the windows rolled down, as the two of them and their mothers drove to the local pool, were part of the very reason he treasured this vehicle. It was filled with happy recollections of his life. Knowing how fond he was of it (and what a mess Sadie could be when driving), Amelia had left it to him in her will.

It was just a car, some could argue. But no, it was a link to Amelia and days gone by. A purely temporal thing, perhaps, but it was a link nonetheless. Amelia had been kind to this car, and it had been kind to him in turn. Regardless of its age, it was in excellent condition.

Now he took his time, despite his wish to lay pedal to metal and fly, and cruised the car along Chocolate Avenue while breathing deeply of the constant, heady smell of cocoa on his way to the local mechanic's shop.

He pulled in at ten minutes till 8, according to his Relic watch. He parked the car and pocketed the keys (since there was no need to pin them without Kylie around) and headed to the front office. He greeted the local boys and asked about Mac.

He was out back.

Making his way around the side of the building, Jasper approached the rear lot, where a configuration of cars and trucks sat in haphazard precision. Jasper noted Mac instantly, bent at the waist with his head immersed in the engine of a 1986 Buick.

Jasper approached the car and leaned on its side, waiting for Mac to take notice of him. When the older man finally sensed a presence, he pulled his head out from under the hood, a smear of grease dotting his forehead, and looked at Jasper.

He nodded. "Jasper."

"Hey, Mac."

Jasper suddenly felt a little lost. Sure, he'd known Mac all his life (at least the parts Mac had hung around for), and Sadie didn't put much stock in her relationship with her father anyway. But still, Mac was her dad, whether she admitted it or not…and Sadie was Mac's little girl. Jasper swallowed.

"Mac, I've got something to tell you."

There was a disturbing gleam in Mac's brown eyes, and Jasper didn't know whether to be encouraged or wary. Mac reached for a rag resting on the bumper and began to wipe his fingers with it.

"Go ahead, Jasper."

Jasper swallowed again and decided that forthrightness would probably serve him best.

"Mac, I'm in love with your daughter."

Jasper had expected at least a *little* bit of surprise, maybe even shock. A widening of the eyes, an *O* shaping his mouth, a raising of the eyebrows, *something*. What he got was far less.

"You think I don't know that?"

Jasper frowned. "How could *you* know? I didn't know myself, at least not for sure, until sometime this week."

Mac's expression was entirely amused. "Jasper…I loved Sadie's mother. I really did—more than I've ever loved anyone else on this earth, except maybe Sadie and Kylie. But I couldn't stay, even when she begged me to." He took inordinate care with wiping the grease from his knuckles. The dark stains remained. He looked up and locked eyes with Jasper.

"You, on the other hand, have never claimed to love Sadie—at least not in the way that a man loves a woman—and yet you've stayed by her side, day after day, for years. Didn't that tell you something long before now?"

Jasper considered. "That she was a good cook?"

Mac made a noise of disbelief. "And Sadie calls me the thick-headed one."

"Cut me some slack, Mac. You're older, wiser, more experienced…"

"Older, I'll admit to; more experienced, probably. *Wiser* is hardly a good description of me. But it doesn't take any of those things to recognize love. You've had it all over you for quite some time."

Jasper grew silent in the face of this small speech. He scuffed the dirt with his boots, like a little kid scolded for doing wrong. "How long have you known?" he finally willed up the nerve to ask.

When Mac smiled, it was always with a sad, hound dog–like expression. He wore that face now as he looked at Jasper.

"For about as long as it takes a father to notice these things."

"Which is pretty much since grade school, then?"

"From the time she knocked you out at the swings, yeah."

"Why didn't you say something sooner?"

Mac tossed the rag down. "What was there to say? I was never in Sadie's life long enough to offer much commentary on it."

Jasper didn't have a response to that. They stood in silence for a minute, both of them musing on their lives with Sadie. At last Mac cleared his throat.

"Why exactly did you come to tell me this, Jasper? Not that I don't appreciate the visit," he quickly added.

Jasper considered his question for several moments. "Well, Mac," he finally said, "I figure I've come to get your blessing."

Mac chuckled at this. "I don't think Sadie gives a hoot one way or another what I think."

"Yeah?" Jasper looked at him. "Well, I do."

Mac paused. "You mean that?"

Jasper nodded sincerely. "I do."

The older man turned slightly and fiddled with the rag in his hands, but Jasper saw him wiping briefly at his eyes. His voice was gravelly with emotion when he spoke. "It ain't easy, you know. This work of redemption."

Jasper didn't know how to respond. He wanted to encourage Mac—to tell him it would all work out in the end, that Sadie would forgive him and he could build a relationship with his granddaughter. But those would be empty promises. Jasper didn't know anything of the sort. Forsaking hollow words, he simply laid a reassuring hand on the other man's shoulder.

Mac drew a deep breath and sniffed, turning back toward Jasper. "I couldn't think of a better man for Sadie. I always regretted never meeting her husband, Ned, before he died. I guess maybe it was hard for me to imagine my little girl with anyone, especially someone other than you." Mac shrugged. "For what good it does you, son, you have my blessing. You've always had it."

Mac smiled that sad smile again. "I never felt right, walking away from Sadie all those years. But I never worried she'd be alone. Not as long as you were around."

Jasper's voice was quiet but without malice. "But it wasn't always me she wanted—or needed."

Mac sighed. "I know it. God help me, I know that now. I only hope He gives me the chance to make it right."

"Oh, He'll give it to you," Jasper assured him. "But He'll probably give you more than you bargained for in the process. He's like that, you know."

"Yeah. So I'm finding out."

Jasper pushed off the Buick and stretched his neck to work out a few kinks. "Well, I'd better get going. Kylie turns five today, and I guarantee you *that's* more than any man bargained for."

Mac straightened with him. "That reminds me. Can you hang on a minute?"

"Sure."

Jasper waited as Mac walked several yards to the beat-up Ford he'd driven into town. He disappeared inside the cab for a moment and re-emerged with an awkwardly wrapped, rectangular package in tow. Jasper's heart ached for him as Mac returned and clumsily held it toward him.

"I got this for Kylie's birthday. I wondered if you could give it to her for me."

Jasper made a decision then, one he found every bit as important as his newly recognized love for Sadie. He pushed the present back into Mac's hands.

"Why don't you give it to her yourself? Come to the birthday party this afternoon."

Mac smiled with pleasure at the invitation, but he shook his head. "Couldn't do that. Sadie'd have a fit."

Jasper shrugged. "She has one fit or another at least twice a week. She's due for one today anyway."

Mac hesitated but then shook his head again. "No, it wouldn't be right. I don't want to spoil the party."

Jasper laid a hand on his shoulder. "Mac, Kylie asks me sometimes about you. She knows her grandma's in heaven, but she wants to know about *you*. I think she'd be thrilled if you came."

Mac raised his head, and Jasper sensed a thread of hopefulness in his tone as he said, "Really? You think so?"

"I know it. Save your gift. The party starts at two."

Mac nodded. "I'm off at two thirty. I'd be late…."

Jasper smiled. "No problem. It'll give Sadie time to get in the flow of things."

Mac looked nervous.

"Mac? Don't worry so much. Just come. Please…come."

Mac drew a deep breath. "All right. I will."

Jasper grinned. "Great." With a farewell wave of his hand, he began to walk away.

"You know, Jasper…"

Jasper turned around.

"If you're looking to woo my daughter, this is hardly the way to do it."

Jasper looked up at the sky. It was a perfect stretch of unmarred blue. "The way I see it, Mac…I want her to be a fool over me. Not you."

Mac hooked his thumbs in his belt loops. "If anyone has a fighting chance at that, son, it would be you."

* * * * *

Sadie didn't have a fighting chance. She was in a kindergarten nightmare. Twelve screaming four- and five-year-olds blowing party horns; boys chasing the girls with shrieks of delight; wrapping paper crunching like gravel underfoot; Kylie pulling on her sleeve every five seconds and demanding the cake; and Jasper and Dmitri, calm as only men can be in the midst of utter chaos, sipping from Styrofoam cups and discussing the finer points of an Italian coffee roast.

She had never been so stressed in her life. A five-year-old's birthday party made running a restaurant seem like a piece of cake, no pun intended.

"*Mommy!*"

Sadie felt the familiar tug on her sleeve.

"Kylie wants cake...*now!*"

Sadie gathered up several empty punch cups and felt relieved that the weather had permitted her to move the party *outdoors* to the backyard. Otherwise, she'd have had to permanently dye her carpet fruit-punch red.

"Not yet, Kylie. Why don't you go open another present?"

"No presents left!" Kylie explained in exasperation.

"Well, why don't you go play with one of your new toys?"

"No good toys to play with!" she argued.

"Then how about one of your friends?"

There was a constant stream of children, but Kylie had long ago lost interest in the boys chasing after the girls.

Sadie dropped to her knees, grabbed Kylie by the shoulders, and looked lovingly into her eyes. "Kylie? Mommy is about to have a nervous breakdown. Do you know what that means?"

Kylie considered this. "You're going to stick your arm in the volcano again?"

Sadie couldn't help it. She smiled. "No, but maybe I'll put my head in this time."

Kylie frowned. "That's gross, Mommy."

Sadie agreed. "Give Mommy a few more minutes, and then she'll bring out the cake, all right?"

Kylie eyed her carefully. "Promise?"

"Promise."

Kylie grinned. "Okay." And off she skipped, nary a care in her world. Sadie sighed and tossed the punch cups into the trash can.

She passed Jasper and Dmitri on her way into the house and failed to stifle a fresh wave of irritation. The two men, both of whom had kissed her last night, were bonding over coffee without so much as a hint of jealousy for each other.

Granted, was there any reason for jealousy between them? Perhaps neither kiss had meant anything. Certainly neither of them had bothered to bring it up when they arrived at her house that day. Jasper had used his key to let himself in this morning and sailed into her kitchen with a smile to rival the glow of the sun. She had expected something from him—an apology or an explanation. Maybe, on some level, she had even expected another kiss. But all she'd gotten was a cup of tea he'd picked up from Suncatchers for her and a question as to whether Kylie was up yet.

He'd gone to help Kylie prepare for the day and to give her the birthday present he'd purchased—a *Beauty and the Beast* tiara just like Belle wore, with slippers to match. These had thrilled Kylie far more than the Cook and Serve Playset Sadie had presented her.

How did Jasper do it? He was a far better parent than she was, it seemed, and Kylie wasn't even his daughter. Although she could have been, for all intents and purposes. Even now, bored with her playmates, she had approached Jasper and was raising her arms, crying, "Lift Kylie! Lift!"

He hoisted her up without a break in his conversation with Dmitri and stood patiently as Kylie wrapped her Belle tiara in his hair.

Sadie turned from the scene with a sigh and went inside to check on the cake. It sat in sugary perfection on the counter, layers of thick yellow icing shining in mouthwatering decadence. Sadie looked into Belle's face on the cake's surface and critically assessed whether she had gotten the pretty young princess's features just right.

"You're the lucky one, you know," she told Belle. "He may have started out a beast, but you managed to turn him into a prince with love and a rose. How many girls can claim that?"

Belle smiled up at her with sweet grace such as Sadie couldn't comprehend. She began to position the candles and was just preparing to light the five of them when the doorbell rang. She tossed a glance over her shoulder toward the front hall.

Everyone had arrived ages ago, all munchkins present and accounted for. Who could possibly be standing at her door right now?

Leaving Belle unattended, Sadie headed for the foyer. She didn't really have any expectations as she swung the front door open, but the person who stood before her certainly would not have been at the top of her list of anticipated arrivals.

"Mac." Her voice came out flat and unyielding, and the doubt that washed through his eyes told her what she sounded like.

"Now's not a good time," she said.

He swallowed hard, and she watched as his neck muscles tensed to force it down.

"I…" He stopped.

"What?"

He was holding something in his hands, she noticed. A package. A present. It was rectangular and wrapped with bright yellow paper. Kylie's favorite color. There was a white bow on top, the cheap kind that you buy already pre-sticky from a grocery store. Something about the sight of that roughly wrapped package pierced straight to Sadie's soul.

Mac had never brought her a present like that. Not once.

She stared at it and found no will to move or speak, not to offer Mac inside nor to shoo him away. They stood for several moments like that, the clock on the foyer table chirping mechanically.

Tick, tick, tick.

"Hey."

Sadie jerked in surprise at the sound of Jasper's voice behind her.

"Glad you could come, Mac."

Jasper somehow managed to move her stiff form from the doorway in order to allow Mac entry. Sadie was still too stunned to react and found herself shifting where Jasper directed her. Mac took a couple steps inside, his shoulders sagging with relief.

"The party's out in the yard." Jasper gestured with his thumb pointing to the back of the house. "We're just getting ready to bring out the cake."

Mac nodded and followed Jasper's directions. Sadie's motor functions seemed to stall for a moment and then kick in at high gear.

"Wait—Kylie!" she called, but Mac had already moved beyond earshot.

Jasper grabbed her outstretched hand and held it against his chest. "Let him go, Sadie. It'll be all right."

She snatched her hand away. "What were you thinking? Kylie doesn't remember him. If a strange man shows up…"

"She'll know who he is."

Sadie's eyes grew stormy. "What do you mean—she'll know who he is?"

"Hasn't she ever asked you about him? Because she asks me all the time."

Sadie's jaw dropped a little. "She does?"

"Yeah. She does."

"Oh."

"It can't hurt anything, right? It's already been a red-letter day for her."

Sadie gulped. "Maybe…" She stared in the direction Mac had gone.

"So how 'bout that cake?" Jasper prompted her.

"Right. The cake."

She turned toward the kitchen.

Moments later Sadie and Jasper emerged from the house, a glowing rectangle of silky golden confection balanced between them. Every minute of effort became worth it when Sadie saw Kylie's face light as bright as the candles that burned. She had been standing by Mac—and Sadie didn't fail to notice that Kylie's hand had been holding his—when they entered with the cake.

Now she left him to race over, her eyes wide with childish delight.

"Cake, Mommy! It's Kylie's cake!"

"Hang on, baby—wait till Mommy and Jasper set it down."

Kylie scampered impatiently at the fringes as Jasper and Sadie placed the cake in the middle of the table. Kylie's friends gathered round, mouths salivating, and stared at the delectable object before them.

Sadie swelled with pride. It *was* rather impressive. Homemade vanilla batter baked to a fluffy gold and covered with a layer of thick, sweet (and very yellow, as per Kylie's request) icing. The detail on it was stunning, with several ruffles of royal blue lacing the sides and an elaborate swirl of thin blue curls coursing across the background. And then there was Belle, in all her regal glory, her golden dress glittering and her mouth temptingly red with a halo of "HAPPY BIRTHDAY, KYLIE" circling her head.

"Mommy," Kylie breathed, "it's so pretty."

Sadie nearly burst with satisfaction. "Make a wish and blow out the candles, sweetheart."

Kylie scrunched her eyes very tight for a long moment, and when she opened them, she did a funny thing. Rather than blow out the candles right away, she looked at Jasper. Sadie's gaze flicked to him, but he was staring back at Kylie without any indication that he understood what the little girl's intensity meant.

After a second, Kylie turned back to her cake and puffed with enough breath to extinguish fifty candles instead of five. Sadie clapped with the children and decided that Kylie's odd stare meant nothing— she'd probably imagined it anyway.

After allowing Kylie a moment more to gaze longingly at Belle, Jasper began to cut the cake, with Kylie's instruction. No one could have a piece with even a centimeter of Belle on it. Belle was all for her. Fortunately, the others were perfectly content with the blue netting and ruffles, and everyone was served with remarkable ease.

Leave it to Jasper—the only man Sadie knew who could serve cake to kindergartners without any fuss.

At last the children were served and sat in a sugared haze, gorging their tiny bodies on sweet delight. Sadie tried not to think about that dye permanently staining their young little systems. They were so achingly innocent, and Kylie sat in their center, stuffing a layer of Belle's dress into her mouth and smearing yellow icing across her chin.

Sadie felt an intense wish to hold her there forever and keep the other birthdays at bay. To hold time still, at least for a little while— that's what Sadie would have wished, had she been blowing out her own candles that day.

Leaving the scene with a dull ache in her chest, she joined Jasper, Dmitri, and Mac where they sat inhaling their own large pieces of cake.

"Looks like I did *something* right, didn't I?"

"It's fabulous!" Dmitri gushed. "How did you do it?"

This was where things became difficult. The truth was, she hadn't made the cake. She'd only *decorated* it. But she couldn't admit the truth to Dmitri—she couldn't even really admit it to herself. The truth was…Sadie Spencer, restaurateur and professionally trained chef, could not create desserts. Not to save her life. It had been a skill she'd always coveted and never possessed.

Desserts were Sadie's Achilles' heel. Not that she could tell that to Dmitri. Not her arch-nemesis—the man who was even now secretly plotting to steal into the empty building across the street and renovate it as his own. She'd rather bring back Kylie's lipstick phase than reveal that critical bit of information to her competition.

So instead of admitting the truth—that she'd asked Karl, her head chef at Suncatchers, to do the baking, she simply smiled with forced cheerfulness and answered Dmitri's question by saying, "I could tell you, but then I'd have to kill you."

Ha. Take that, Mr. Russian Entrepreneur. I can compete with you any day.

Jasper, oblivious to her intentions, stabbed a large chunk of fluffy white cake and announced, "She's just kidding. Sadie can't bake a dessert to save her life. She had one of her staff from Suncatchers whip this up—like she does all the desserts at the restaurant."

If ever Sadie had wanted to throttle her best friend within an inch of his life, this was that moment. She attempted to maintain a pleasant exterior while her eyes shot sparks at him. When Jasper finally turned to catch her eye, he blanched under her fiery gaze and gulped the rest of his cake down quickly.

"I *did* do all the decorating," she defended through clenched teeth.

Jasper held up a hand. "Now, no one's disputing your decorating talent, Sadie. You can make a dessert *look* better than Martha Stewart does."

Jasper wasn't smoothing things over very well. Apparently Mac could see that, for he tried jumping in to rescue him.

"I was in your restaurant the other night. Tried a bunch of dishes on the menu. Every single one was delicious."

Although she was still offended by Jasper's remarks, her heart involuntarily warmed by knowing Mac had gone to her restaurant and tried several of the items. But she was still feeling defensive.

"Not only did I do all the decorating, but *I* was the one who suggested to Karl that for the batter, he use half cake flour and half peanut flour, to give it that special something." She felt a rush of triumph at this pronouncement...until Dmitri uttered a choking, strangled sound.

All eyes shifted to where he sat, halfway through his cake with another bite stretched toward his mouth. In the span of seconds, he had turned as pale as the inside of an eggshell.

"Dmitri?" The sight of him sent a stab of fear through her heart. "What is it?"

"D–did you say...the cake has...*peanuts*...in it?"

Sadie felt bands of perspiration circling her forehead. "Uh...yeah. It's a trick I learned in culinary school—"

Dmitri gasped as the cake he'd been holding dropped from his fingers.

"Dmitri! What is it?!" He was really starting to scare her now.

He gagged out the words as his fingers went to his throat. "I have a serious allergy to peanuts."

Sadie's heart stopped beating for what seemed like a full ten seconds. Her hand flew to her lips as she and Dmitri locked eyes. It was Jasper—calm, stable Jasper—who took charge of the situation and asked the vital questions.

"Do you have an epinephrine shot?"

Dmitri nodded, wheezing with visible effort. "Car. Glove compartment." He dug into his Dockers for the keys and passed them off to Jasper, who hurried around the side of the house. By the time he raced back to the group with an EpiPen in hand, a cluster of children had gathered around Dmitri, watching with wide-eyed fascination as he struggled for every breath. Mac had his hand on Dmitri's shoulder, speaking to him in soothing tones. Sadie held the kids at bay, trying to give Dmitri room and air.

Jasper pulled the cap of the shot and helped Dmitri stick it into his outer thigh. The boys gasped with awe, whispering, "Cool...," while the girls wrinkled their noses in disgust.

Dmitri's breathing slowly regulated, and by agonizing centimeters, Sadie felt herself reach a state of semi-calm. Once the initial danger was past, Jasper announced that they should probably take Dmitri to Hershey Medical Center in case a second attack should occur.

"We can take my car," he said. "Mac, can you help Sadie call the parents so they can come and get their kids and take them home?"

Mac nodded as Jasper reached into his jeans pocket to retrieve his car keys. Sadie stared at Jasper while her best friend went as white as Dmitri had been moments before. His hands moved from one pocket to the other and then up and down as he patted his torso.

"They're not here," he whispered. "My keys are gone."

Sadie and Jasper's gazes met, and they immediately turned to look for Kylie. The last thing they needed was for her to decide that her fifth birthday had liberated her enough to attempt driving once more.

But she sat with the rest of her friends, eyeing Dmitri's wan exterior with wonder.

Sadie lifted her up from the group and looked into her eyes.

"Where are Jasper's keys, Kylie? Did you take them?"

Kylie suddenly clammed up, her gaze shifting back and forth but not meeting Sadie's eyes. Jasper took over.

"I won't be mad, Kylie, honest—but I need to have my keys. Where did you put them?"

She gulped, not buying it.

"*Kylie.*" Sadie and Jasper spoke in unison.

Kylie bit her lip. "The volcano ate them."

Sadie groaned.

"Here." Mac waved his key ring. "Take my truck, Jasper."

Jasper grabbed the keys and helped Dmitri out of the backyard. As he shuffled the Russian around the side of the house, he glanced back over his shoulder and waved at Sadie.

He mouthed, "Don't worry."

Sadie wanted to burst into tears.

Great.

Chapter Six

Sadie didn't hear anything from Jasper or Dmitri for the rest of the afternoon. As Jasper had suggested, Mac helped Sadie call around the neighborhood, telling the parents that the party had ended early and asking them to come and pick up their children.

Kylie didn't mind this abrupt conclusion, as it gave her the opportunity to work at charming her grandfather, asking him question after question on topics she thought grandpas would be familiar with.

"And does Tommy Fitzkee's grandmother *really* have a wooden leg?"

Mac explained that he didn't know Tommy Fitzkee's grandmother but that it was possible she had a *prosthetic* leg, although probably not one made out of wood, exactly. Kylie was most satisfied with this answer and brought up another item requiring her concern.

"Then we can get Malibu Ken a *post-fat-tick* leg too, can't we, Grampa?"

Sadie wasn't entirely comfortable with Kylie's quick familiarity with her grandfather, but there didn't seem to be anything she could do about it. "Hardheaded" wasn't a trait that applied only to Mac and Sadie, after all. When Kylie decided on something, she clung to it like mildew to tile.

And Kylie had decided she liked Mac Cameron.

Mac hung around for the rest of the afternoon and most of the night, keeping Kylie distracted and out of Sadie's way as she cleaned up the party items with a mad fury born of frustration.

What could she have been *thinking*?

One line in particular kept playing over and over in her mind: *I could tell you, but then I'd have to kill you.*

Every time she thought about it, she felt a sharp pain stab her gut. What an insensitive remark. How *stupid*. And now she probably *had* killed Dmitri Velichko. She wanted him out of the restaurant business, not out of life altogether. Truth be told, she kind of liked the guy. He was charming and mysterious, and his enthusiasm for certain topics reminded her of Kylie's own childlike glee.

The mother in her wanted to wrap Dmitri Velichko in a warm blanket and tell him that everything was going to be all right.

It was unfortunate that the businesswoman in her simply wanted to strangle him.

Strangulation. She let out a weak sigh. He'd probably suffocated to death by now, his airway passages closing in on themselves. A *peanut* allergy, of all things. How could she possibly have known?

After the remains of the party had been cleaned away and the rest of the cake tossed into the garbage—she couldn't bear to save it after what had happened—there was nothing left to do but wait. Sadie put the time to good use by continuing to mentally flagellate her own self-centeredness and stupidity.

She barely noticed as Mac prepared Kylie some dinner, helped her brush her teeth and say her prayers, and tucked her into bed. He came and sat beside Sadie then, making one weak attempt at consolation by saying, "I'm sure Jasper's got everything under control."

Sadie didn't respond, but she relaxed ever so slightly at these words. Jasper would make sure it was all right. She hoped.

Not another word passed between Mac and Sadie until Jasper pulled into the driveway at 11:13 p.m.

* * * * *

Jasper greeted Sadie with a weary smile as she flung the door open and ushered him into the house. Stepping inside, Jasper tossed Mac his truck keys.

"She drives like a dream, considering what she's been through," he commented.

Mac smiled. "You gotta know how to stroke her. You must have the touch." He cleared his throat as Sadie glared.

"How can you be discussing vehicles at a time like this?" she questioned in exasperation. Mac and Jasper exchanged glances. Clearing his throat, Mac bid them a good night before slipping out of the house.

After closing the front door behind him, Sadie followed Jasper as he shuffled down the hall and into the living room with a groan, where he sank in exhaustion onto the couch.

"If you think I look bad," he said, "you should see the other guy."

Sadie let out a sob and sank onto the couch next to him. He looked at her in surprise.

"I'm a horrible person!" she wailed. "Just horrible! I don't deserve to live!"

Jasper sat up and laid a comforting hand on her knee. "Aw, Sadie...don't think that way."

She turned toward him at his reassuring words and launched herself at him, burying her face into his neck.

"It's true! I'm an awful, awful, mean, mean person!"

It came out muffled as "ma-fell, ma-fell, bean, bean parson!" but Jasper understood the context of it. He rubbed her back gently.

"It's not your fault, sweetheart. You couldn't have realized…"

"I said I'd have to kill him!" she argued. "But I didn't mean it— I didn't!"

Jasper made soothing noises of reassurance. "He knows that, Sadie; he does."

She sniffled and pulled back a little. Her eyes were red, but it only made the brown in them stand out all the more brilliantly. Her little crying fit had pinked her cheeks and cast a rosy glow to the end of her nose.

Jasper thought she looked lovely.

"Do you really think so?"

Her little-girl vulnerability nearly made him sweep her into his arms right then.

"Think what?" he asked her, momentarily confused by the sight of her lips so temptingly near to his own.

"Think that Dmitri knows I didn't mean it?" she prompted. "Do you think he can forgive me?"

"Why wouldn't he?" he softly asked, his eyes lingering on those lips. "I always do."

"But you're different," she argued, completely oblivious to the direction his thoughts had turned. "You're Jasper. You're my best friend. You're *required* to forgive me!"

It took a moment for her words to get through, but when they did, it was a bucket of cold water on the thoughts he'd been having. He shifted back a little to give himself some air that *didn't* include the scent of Sadie in it.

"I wouldn't take such things for granted if I were you."

Her eyebrows lowered together severely. "What's that supposed to mean?"

"What it sounds like. Don't always assume I'm going to just up and forgive you because I'm your so-called best friend."

"What do you mean by—so-called? You *are* my best friend."

Jasper scoffed. Sadie scowled.

He looked at her and forgot his irritation.

"Look, I don't wanna fight."

Just the opposite, in fact, he thought.

She nestled into his side exactly like Kylie did when they watched *Beauty and the Beast*.

"I'm sorry," she whispered. "Some days it feels like that's all I get done saying. Why do I keep messing up?"

He stroked her hair, gently pulling the strands back from her face and smoothing it to a rich, chestnut gloss.

" 'Cause you're human, Sadie."

"Then what are you?" she asked him. "You don't have to apologize for something three times a week."

He teased her. "That's 'cause I'm special." He added more seriously, "And I don't fanaticize over things as much as you do."

She looked up into his eyes, her lip quivering slightly. "Do you really think I'm a fanatic?"

"Fantastic?" He pretended to hear her wrong. "Absolutely! I think you're phenomenal!"

She poked him with her finger, and he squirmed.

"Be serious."

His eyes grew warmer now. "I am serious. Believe me, I've never been more serious."

She swallowed with some difficulty, and to his delight, Jasper noticed that her eyes focused on *his* lips now.

"Jasper...about last night..."

His arm tightened ever so slightly around her.

"What about it?" he murmured.

His breath tickled her nose, and she twitched.

"I don't think..." She began inching upward by mere hair lengths, getting closer and closer to his face. "I don't think...," she repeated and then released her breath in a sigh. "I can't think."

The next thing he knew, they were kissing again.

* * * * *

Sadie had told herself, late last night, that the first kiss between her and Jasper was, as the Brits said, a "one-off." The charged current between the two of them had been a fluke—an anomaly. There was no need to assume that the same static charge could happen twice. It was an unexplained phenomenon with a low recurrence rate. Like comets and shooting stars. These things flashed and then burned up...or something like that. It would be the same if she and Jasper should ever happen to touch in that way again.

That was what she told herself. These were the examples she outlined.

She had been wrong.

Somehow this kiss was even more electric than the first one. Jasper's lips on hers felt the same way she'd once heard someone describe fireworks—a sudden explosion of light and flame entering the world with a shaken bang.

She didn't want it to stop. And it didn't. Not right away, anyway.

Jasper kissed her passionately and then tenderly and then, just when she thought she might drown without air (and had passed the point of caring), he let her go.

She stared up into his eyes. They were blue, but not like Dmitri's. Dmitri's eyes were pale and pure, but Jasper's were a rich, cobalt blue and warm as tropical waters. She licked her lips now as she gazed into those molten pools of blue lava....and remembered the volcano. Er, the toilet.

"Your keys," she stated.

"What?" His voice was gravelly with an emotion Sadie didn't dare dip into at the moment.

"Mac got your keys from the volcano. I mean, the toilet."

"My keys?" Jasper blinked several times, and Sadie wondered if he could see her all right.

"The volcano took your keys," she prompted. "Mac had to rip out the entire toilet to get them back."

Things must have been becoming clearer to Jasper. He straightened, and Sadie, who had been leaning heavily against him, shifted down into the folds of the sofa.

"You're worried about my keys? At a time like this?"

She cleared her throat. "Why? What are you worried about?"

"I..." He opened his mouth and then closed it, repeating this action several times. He reminded Sadie of Kylie's guppy impersonation.

"You look like a fish," she randomly commented.

His nostrils flared. "A fish?"

She shrugged.

"Sadie…do you want me to leave? Is that what you're hinting at? Because you can just say so, you know."

She sat up, and the heat between them dissipated as swiftly as a match in the Arctic.

"I didn't say that."

"Then what's all this talk about my keys?"

"Kylie said the volcano took them. I just thought you'd be worried."

Jasper just stared at her. "I'm worried about Malibu Ken's leg too, but you don't see me bringing it up right after we *kissed*, do you?"

She made a face. "That's different."

He looked away with a weary sigh, and Sadie felt a twinge of guilt at his beaten expression. He stood to his feet. "Fine. You're right. It's late, and I'm going to the nursing home tomorrow."

Every other Sunday, Jasper visited the nursing home in York County to take his great-aunt Matilda to church and then out for lunch. She was a senile old woman with a wealth of eccentricities, but she and Jasper got along famously. Sometimes Sadie went with him. She didn't think tomorrow would be one of those times.

The tone of his voice left Sadie feeling sad.

"Where are the keys?"

She gestured to the coffee table. She thought about reassuring him that she had washed them thoroughly after their adventure through the commode's hidden orifices but decided that now was not the time.

He lifted them into his hand and turned to go.

"Tell Kylie I said happy birthday," he said. "And since I'm sure you're wondering—Dmitri's going to be fine. He even managed to drive his SUV back home."

A wave of remorse washed over her. She had been so possessed with her own guilt in the matter, she hadn't even asked if Dmitri was okay. Funny how that worked.

Jasper turned toward the doorway, but she noticed he paused for a long time. He was waiting, she knew. But she didn't know what to say.

Finally he left her.

He didn't say good-bye.

* * * * *

Sunday morning dawned clear and warm—another glorious promise of the summer to come. When it came time to wake Kylie, Sadie slipped into her daughter's bedroom and crawled under the covers. The little girl stirred and rolled toward her mother, tucking into a ball right at Sadie's stomach. Sadie smiled in remembrance of the months Kylie had nestled right there, a tiny round ball riding in blissful oblivion inside the safety of Sadie's body. It was fantastically difficult to believe that miniature life had grown into the five-year-old before her—still a smaller version of Sadie herself but clearly an individual all her own.

Five years. She felt like time was slipping through her fingers.

"Kylie," she whispered. "Kylie girl…time to wake up."

Kylie mumbled something, and Sadie gently pulled the covers away from her face. Her features slumbered in angelic repose. Sadie had never seen anything more beautiful.

"Kylie…time to get ready for church."

Kylie's eyelids fluttered.

"Church day?" she asked.

Sadie brushed the hair off her forehead. "That's right. Today is church day."

The eyes widened, and the pupils focused.

"Can Kylie have her bath in the Scrubbing Bubbles Lagoon?"

"What? *Oh*." The bathtub. "Of course."

Kylie rolled out of bed with an energy only the very young possess directly after waking. Sadie listened as her bare feet slapped the tile in the bathroom. There was a tiny grunt as she forced the water on, and then the splash of liquid as it filled the tub.

Sadie sighed. It hadn't been that long ago that she had given Kylie all her baths, had it? When had her little girl become so independent?

"Mommy?" Kylie stood in the doorway. "Kylie can't get the plugger thing to work. The lagoon won't fill up."

Sadie smiled and climbed off the bed. "Mommy's coming."

Kylie loved "church days," so she presented minimal fuss to Sadie's brushing and braiding her hair, putting a suitable dress over her head, and buckling her black OshKosh shoes.

Usually on the Sundays Jasper went to York County to visit with Aunt Matilda, Sadie and Kylie hitched a ride to church with the neighboring family. Today, however, Sadie had a mission in mind. With the warm weather to encourage her, she took Kylie's hand and marched her out of the house and up the street.

Kylie protested. "Kylie waits for Jasper!"

"Jasper's going to see Aunt Matilda today," Sadie explained.

"Then Kylie go to church with Mrs. Smelly!"

The neighboring family's last name was Snelling, which Kylie persisted in translating to *Smelly*, much to Sadie's constant mortification.

"Not today, sweetie. Mommy has a stop to make, and then we'll walk to the church. It's not too far on a day like today."

Kylie sulked and pulled on Sadie's hand. "Mommy! Kylie doesn't wanna walk!"

"Mommy will let Kylie order *any* dessert she wants at the restaurant this afternoon, how about that?"

Kylie frowned. "Kylie doesn't like Mommy's desserts."

Sadie stopped mid-step and stared down at her daughter in surprise. "What? You don't like my desserts? Are you serious?"

Kylie must have realized what she'd done, because her eyes were round with shame. "Kylie didn't mean it! Kylie loved her birthday cake!"

Sadie squatted down so she could see Kylie at eye level. "It's all right to tell me the truth, Kylie. Don't you like the desserts Mommy makes?"

Kylie bit her lip and began to sway from side to side. "Sometimes. Sometimes not. Kylie likes ice cream, mostly."

It shouldn't have mattered so much, but it did. First Jasper going all moony on her and now Kylie. Was everyone out to get her?

Kylie laid a hand on her shoulder. "Mommy worries too much."

She looked at her daughter, in whose eyes lay such innocent trust in the world that Sadie couldn't help recalling what she had told Dmitri about Kylie being a constant source of optimism to her.

"Well, if Mommy's desserts aren't good enough, they'll just have to get better, won't they?"

Kylie nodded emphatically.

"And if Kylie likes mostly ice cream, then Kylie should have ice cream today after lunch, don't you think?"

Again, the nod was emphatic with an extra bounce in it for good measure. Sadie straightened.

"But that means Kylie will have to walk a little bit with Mommy."

Kylie shrugged. "All right."

Sadie shook her head, wondering why some days it was so easy and other days anything but. They continued down the street, hand in hand, glorying in the fresh morning air.

Twenty minutes later, Sadie led them down a tree-lined drive. She stopped at the house near the end of the way and studied it with hesitation.

"Is this it, Mommy?"

"This is it."

Sadie continued to stare at the house.

"Is Mommy afraid?" Kylie asked.

Sadie's gaze dropped, but she didn't answer her daughter. They started up the walk together, and Sadie drew a deep breath before knocking on the door.

Seconds seemed like days as Kylie released her hand and began toying with her shoes. It was then Sadie noticed that Kylie had replaced her OshKosh footgear with the Belle slippers Jasper had gotten her.

"What are—" She didn't even finish the question. Kylie must have made the switch when Sadie went to apply her makeup.

Before she could reprimand her daughter for the sneaky move, the front door swung open and Dmitri Velichko stood before her.

He looked wary, but he hadn't slammed the door in her face.

Yet.

"Hello, 'mitri!" Kylie greeted him with a huge smile. "Kylie is a princess! See!" She held out one dainty foot.

The little yellow bows positively shined.

Dmitri grinned. "And what a lovely princess you are, Kylie. Would you like to come in?"

"Thank you, please," Kylie said and brushed past the two of them as if she truly were royalty.

Dmitri stepped aside to allow Sadie entrance. Kylie had already found several objects worth her fascination, not the least of which was the large cage in the corner containing a snow-white ferret.

She stood before it with wide eyes.

"Is it a rat?" she asked in a hushed tone.

It was a rat that tried to kill the baby in *Lady and the Tramp*. Sadie knew her daughter possessed somewhat of a personal vendetta against vermin ever since viewing that particular film.

"No," Dmitri assured her, "it's a ferret. His name is Mikhail. Would you like to hold him?"

Kylie considered this. "Does he bite?"

"Only when he's playing," Dmitri answered honestly.

Kylie nodded in understanding. "All right. Kylie will hold him."

Dmitri removed Mikhail from the cage. Kylie made fast friends with the creature. And then with one eye on the ferret and one eye on Kylie, Dmitri went to stand with Sadie.

"Are you feeling okay?" she asked him.

He was still terribly pale, and she couldn't help comparing him to Count Dracula with his dark hair and romantic accent. But she felt desperately responsible for what had happened.

"I'm all right," he assured her. "It wasn't your fault, Sadie."

She must have looked as sick with guilt as she felt.

"If I had known, I never would have—I never—I didn't mean—"

He held up a hand. "Enough. We'll put it behind us. Friends?" He held out a hand, and she felt guiltier than ever.

She had never intended to be Dmitri's friend. Just the opposite, in fact. But she placed her fingers in his and attempted a weak smile.

"I brought you something." She held up a brown paper bag, carried the whole way from the house.

"Not peanuts, I trust?" he teased her.

She blushed. "No," she softly said. She held it out to him.

Inside was a bagful of top-quality French roast coffee beans.

"They're gourmet," she told him. "It's the same kind I serve at the restaurant." She always kept a bag on hand at the house for Jasper —she didn't drink coffee herself. "I hope you'll accept it as a peace offering of sorts."

He nodded with pleasure, a bit of color lightening his countenance. "It's perfect. I love the coffee at Suncatchers," he told her.

She beamed.

"Well, I don't want to impose. Kylie and I were just on our way to church. Weren't we, Kylie?"

Kylie didn't answer—she was too absorbed with the ferret, Mikhail.

"Oh?" Dmitri replied to her statement with interest. "I haven't attended church since I arrived in town."

"Really?" She had been wondering about Dmitri's spiritual side. The conversation on their date indicated he had Christian leanings, but she hadn't been entirely sure. She took a chance now. "Would you like to come with us this morning? Jasper's out of town this weekend, visiting his aunt, so we wouldn't mind the company."

Kylie's ears perked up at this.

"Kylie thinks Dmitri should come! And Mikhail too!"

Dmitri grinned at her. "I don't think Mikhail is quite ready for church attendance yet, but I would love to come."

Kylie smiled. "All right. But can Kylie use your volcano first?"

Chapter Seven

. . . .

Dmitri and Jasper had an arrangement. They had worked it out in the hospital the day before while they waited for the results of Dmitri's bloodwork.

Dmitri had been lying there in a cold sweat, his arm flung over his eyes to block out the light, when he became aware of Jasper's intense gaze. He moved his arm and opened one eye.

"How ya feelin'?" Jasper asked.

Dmitri sensed true concern in him, and though he hadn't known Jasper long, he felt like they could be friends.

"Like a geyser erupted in my stomach," he answered. "Yourself?"

Jasper smiled. "Just fine, thanks. No nut allergies that I know of."

Dmitri's skin was pasty, and he grimaced at the mention of nuts. Jasper frowned.

"Are you sure you're okay?"

"I will be," Dmitri assured. "Once my heart rate normalizes."

Jasper pulled up a seat next to the hospital bed. "I figure you and I should have a talk, Dmitri."

Something about the way he said it made Dmitri's stomach flip. It wasn't a good feeling. Dmitri didn't say anything, so Jasper went on.

"I need to know exactly what your intentions are concerning Sadie."

"Sadie? I plan to stay as far away from her as possible."

Jasper got a good laugh out of that.

"No, no," he said as he rubbed tears from his eyes, "seriously."

Dmitri raised up on one elbow. "What makes you think I'm not serious?"

Jasper took note of his expression and sobered. "Oh. That bad, huh?"

Dmitri laid back. "You tell me."

Jasper ran a hand through his hair in thoughtful concentration. He seemed to be wrestling with a dilemma, and Dmitri didn't have the strength to help him out.

Finally, he decided to be honest. "Here's the thing, Dmitri. I'm trying to decide right now if I should defend Sadie to you and explain how she's really not all that bad and she just has these crazy strings of bad luck now and then…or whether I should let you go on thinking she's jinxed so you can get the heck out of Dodge."

Dmitri looked at him.

"You're in love with her, aren't you?"

Jasper jumped up out of his chair. "Does *everybody* know this?" He paced fretfully, and Dmitri couldn't help smiling.

"What can you do? Love *shows*."

Jasper sighed and sank back into his seat.

"Then Sadie's blind, because she hasn't noticed *anything*."

Dmitri considered this. "Perhaps she hasn't *wanted* to notice anything."

Jasper lightened. "Ya think?"

"It's possible. She doesn't seem like the type of woman to really… embrace such things, if you know what I mean."

"Are you kidding? I think love probably scares her to death." He paused. "She keeps losing the people she loves," he softly noted.

The two men sat in silence for a time. Dmitri rubbed his stomach, mentally crooning to soothe himself and occasionally sneaking glances toward Jasper, who was chewing his lip in silent contemplation. A nurse came in to check on them and lingered for quite some time over Dmitri, fluffing his pillows, refilling his water, checking his temperature, asking if he needed anything…. He treated her politely without being flirtatious.

After the nurse left, Jasper addressed him again. "You're sure you don't have a thing for Sadie?"

"A thing? Oh, you mean do I think she's cute?"

"Yeah," Jasper confirmed.

Dmitri shrugged. "Sadie is a very pretty woman, but I fear she is too…what did she call it? Accident-prone, for me."

Japer grinned delightedly and with a dreamy sigh said, "Yeah. Yeah, she is."

Dmitri couldn't help thinking that if Sadie was crazy then Jasper must be too. They were perfect for each other.

Jasper snapped out of it. "In that case, Dmitri Velichko, I think I'm going to need your help."

* * * * *

The sermon that Sunday morning was on forgiveness. About how God granted second chances and people should too.

Sadie found herself sinking lower and lower into her seat as Dmitri listened with attentive interest. What made matters worse was the man who sat in the very back of the church—the last row on the left-hand side. Sadie had noted him when she entered but pretended she hadn't seen as she took her seat halfway up the aisle. Dmitri took the end beside her, amid many a jealous glare shot at Sadie from numerous single, eligible young ladies.

Sadie didn't notice any of them. She was too concerned with whether the guy in the back had seen her.

The guy was Mac.

And the sermon was for her. She was sure of it.

"What kind of life would that be like?" Pastor Samuel asked. "What kind of *love* is that like? To forgive the worst of transgressions—to love despite the most horrific of misdeeds? Jesus was mocked, spit on, and despised for what crime? Because He *loved*. Not only loved of His own accord, but He demanded that very thing from those who followed Him. What kind of God demands you to love not only your *own* enemies...but your neighbor's enemies? Your best friend's enemies? Even the enemies of your child? What kind of God does He think He is?" the pastor demanded, before answering his own question.

"A God who weeps with you. Who cries your tears and then wipes them away. A God who sees your worst and loves you in spite of it while all the time cheering for the very best He knows you can be. What kind of God demands that we forgive our enemies? A God who forgives His. A God who forgives *us*."

Sadie felt a lump form in her throat. She couldn't resist the urge anymore. She glanced over her shoulder, back at Mac. He didn't see her gaze, though. His eyes were closed, and there were tears on his cheeks.

Sadie wasn't even sure he'd heard the pastor's words. But it looked like he'd *felt* them. Maybe that was the better way to receive them anyhow. She turned back around.

When the service ended, Dmitri thanked her profusely for inviting him. He'd been looking for a church for some time and thought that maybe this could be it. He wanted to go speak with the pastor, but he had to ask her something first.

She waited politely, all the while wondering if Mac was still sitting in the back row. She dare not look.

"Would you have dinner with me tomorrow night?" he asked.

Her eyes, which had wandered surreptitiously to the side, suddenly flew back to his face. His expression was open, innocent of deceit. His cool blue eyes reflected honest invitation, and his perfect white teeth were aligned in a smile.

What? Really? Had yesterday's experience affected his short-term memory? Didn't he realize she was jinxed? From the expectant way he was grinning at her, he was apparently serious.

Oh...why not. "All right," she conceded. "If Jasper is willing to babysit, that is," she amended. Something about suggesting that Jasper babysit while she went out on another date with Dmitri twisted her tongue and made her feel as though she'd swallowed a mouthful of Tabasco.

It hurt.

But Dmitri grinned broadly. "I doubt Jasper will have a problem with it."

Oh? And how do you know so much?

She only smiled weakly.

"I'll call you," he told her.

"All right," she agreed.

"Do you need a ride home—you and Kylie?"

She shook her head. "We'll be fine. Thanks."

He rushed off to speak with the pastor. Sadie turned. Just as she'd thought, Mac still sat in the back row...watching her.

She made her way down the aisle, stopping to greet acquaintances as they called her name. One mother thanked her for the party—Billy hadn't stopped talking about it since he'd returned, telling a fascinating story about poisoning one of the guests. She hadn't known it was one of those murder-mystery parties. Sadie didn't tell her otherwise. Smith and Jones cackled behind their hands as she went by, but she smiled brightly at them, taking a stab at the forgiveness thing by genuinely wishing them a wonderful afternoon.

They stopped laughing.

By the time she reached Mac, he was waiting for her. She didn't know what he expected, nor what she was there to offer. The sermon had spoken to her but not enough to warrant forgiveness for nearly thirty years of bitterness and disappointment. She gripped the back of a chair and attempted to offer a stepping-stone, if nothing else.

"Would you like to have lunch with Kylie and me?"

Mac's smile found its way straight to her soul and warmed her with the assertion that she had made the right move.

"There's nothing I'd like better, Sadie girl."

* * * * *

Mac knew, from Jasper, that Sadie and Kylie had a tradition of eating Sunday luncheon at Suncatchers each week. Kylie didn't get to come into the restaurant much otherwise, but Sundays were special. She and Sadie sat at the same table—beneath Kylie's display of suncatchers—and talked, Mac supposed, about anything and everything mothers and daughters share. At times, Jasper said he would join them, when he wasn't visiting his aunt. But sometimes he knew it was best to give them their girl time.

Now, sitting in the atmosphere his daughter had worked so hard to create, amid her mother's collection of suncatchers, with Kylie chattering at her side, Mac felt another piercing stab of regret for the years lost, the moments squandered, the time spent.

How could he have wasted so much?

Sadie and Mac didn't do much talking over lunch. What was there to say, after all? Kylie easily filled the void, however, with her chatter about the birthday party, the cake, Jasper running off to the hospital, and "Grampa" tearing apart the volcano to get Jasper's keys.

Kylie dunked her french fries into her ketchup (three dunks per fry, precisely) and then chewed them around a mouthful of words about yesterday's adventures. Mac answered questions when asked but mostly sat basking in the glow of the girls' companionship.

His girls.

He tried not to think of them in quite that light, considering that Sadie hadn't said a word about actually forgiving him and letting him start over. But it was difficult not to see them that way. They were both such a delightful blend of him and Amelia.

They had long chestnut hair—long like Amelia's, brown like his own—and matching chocolate eyes. Their skin was smooth, and their noses slightly indented at the tip. Amelia's had been the same. Sadie's lips were like hers, but Kylie's were a little wider than Sadie's. *Must be Ned's mark on her,* Mac thought.

And then there were their mannerisms. Kylie dunked her fries just like Sadie had as a child. Most times when Mac sailed back into town, he'd take Sadie out for a burger and fries. And she'd dip each fry three times in the ketchup before popping it into her mouth. Just like Kylie was doing.

Mac looked at Sadie now. She chewed a bite of her salad and nodded at Kylie's latest comment. *She doesn't even know,* he thought sadly. She didn't remember. But of course not—why should she? He hadn't given her much worth remembering.

"You used to do that, you know."

This sudden declaration, after so long in silence, caused both Kylie and Sadie to instantly fall quiet and turn their heads. Embarrassment shot through him.

"Do what?" Kylie asked.

Mac dropped his fork, wishing he hadn't spoken aloud. Sadie's soft voice eased him, however.

"Do what, Mac?" she echoed Kylie's question.

He cleared his throat and gestured at Kylie's fingers, still clutching the ketchup-coated spine of a fry.

"Dip your french fries in ketchup three times before eating them." Despite his self-consciousness, he smiled his typical sad smile at the memory. "Three times. No more, no less. I'd take you for cheeseburgers and fries at—"

"The Bridge Diner," Sadie filled in.

He nodded. "Yeah. You always got—"

"A cheeseburger, plain, except for relish and mustard. And french fries, the crimped kind, and the edges were always a little burnt."

"But you liked them that way," he whispered, stunned that she remembered such details. She'd only been a little girl. They'd stopped going to The Bridge by the time she turned twelve.

"And you had the Big Burger with all the toppings except onions—never onions—and your fries were always crimped too," she said. "If I ate all mine, you'd give me some of yours. And we had milkshakes. Strawberry for me, vanilla for you. You'd give me a quarter for the jukebox and tell me to choose any song I liked."

Mac felt his insides tearing in two. "And you always chose Elvis Presley."

"'It's Now or Never.'"

"It was your favorite," he said.

"No." She frowned. "It was yours. That's why I picked it."

Their table fell silent once more, the tension stretching in a palpable plane between them. Mac's appetite disappeared, but it was Sadie who pushed her plate away. Kylie glanced at her mother's unfinished food and then laid her tiny fingers over top of Sadie's.

"You dipped your fries like Kylie?" she asked in her breathless child's tone.

Mac was blinking rapidly. "She did, Kylie. She did."

"Why don't you do that anymore, Mommy?" she asked.

Sadie didn't say anything.

"Mommy?"

"We'll talk about it later, baby." Her voice cracked on the last syllable.

The quiet that followed was extremely awkward. Kylie couldn't stand it for more than a few moments.

"Grampa, Kylie wants to thank you for her birthday gift," she said.

He smiled at her, his heart twisting with happiness. "You're welcome, Kylie girl."

Sadie emitted a choked sound from deep in her throat, and Mac looked her way in concern. Clearing her throat, she changed the topic. "Jasper said you got a job."

Mac turned his attention away from Kylie and picked up his fork once more. He was having the herb-crusted chicken, at Sadie's recommendation. He hadn't eaten much of it, but it wasn't because he didn't like it.

"At the mechanic's shop."

Sadie nodded and reached for her plate again, pushing a section of her lobster salad around the rim of the dish. "Do you like it there?"

"Only been there a couple days. Hard to tell yet."

She nodded again. "Do you have a place to stay?"

"That old motel on the outskirts of town. I've stayed there before, a time or two."

Mac hadn't always stayed at the house when he'd come back to town over the years.

Sadie stiffened her spine before saying, "Mom left a couple of things for you. We've been keeping them at the house. A few old letters, I think. Some books. I don't know if you're interested in them—"

"Of course I'm interested." He met her eyes squarely this time, and his tone indicated his hurt that she would assume he didn't care.

She looked down at her plate. "Well, whenever you want them, you can come and get them. It's not like they're going anywhere."

Mac knew better than to remind her that he didn't plan on going anywhere either.

* * * * *

Lunch sort of went downhill after that. Kylie insisted on her ice cream and regaled Mac with tales of Tommy Fitzkee's grandmother, even suggesting that Mac should date the old woman so they could find out whether Tommy had lied about the wooden leg.

Mac told her he didn't think that would be a good idea. "It's not polite to date a person just because you want to find things out about them," he explained to Kylie.

Sadie bit her tongue when he said that and reached for her water glass.

"You should date a person because you find them interesting and because you're starting to care about them," he continued.

Kylie listened with rapt attention, and Sadie bitterly wondered whether she would have had the good sense to leave Dmitri Velichko alone if Mac had stuck around for more than five minutes while she was growing up.

After their meal was finished, Mac offered to drive them back home. Normally Sadie would have insisted on walking, but Kylie's eyelids were sinking like rocks. Sadie knew that if Mac didn't give them a lift, she'd be carrying Kylie the whole way.

By the time he pulled into the driveway, Kylie had already sagged against Sadie, her mouth turned upward in sweet, blissful sleep. Ah, the sleep of the young.

"Do you need help getting her inside?" Mac politely offered.

Sadie shook her head and expertly hoisted Kylie into her arms. "No thanks. I'm used to it."

She sat in the truck a moment longer than necessary, staring at the front door of her house. Pastor Samuel's words kept drumming inside her head.

What kind of God demands that we forgive our enemies? A God who forgives His. A God who forgives us.

Sadie blinked several times. What would her mother have done if Mac were here? An even better question occurred to her: why couldn't Amelia have lived long enough to hear about Mac's remorse?

Then again, maybe if she'd lived, Mac would never have felt regret.

What kind of love is that like?

"I didn't mean it. About the Elvis song." Sadie looked at him. "It was always one of my favorites too."

Then she opened the door and stumbled out of the vehicle with Kylie before Mac could say anything in reply.

* * * * *

Sadie laid Kylie down for a nap, waited as long as she could bear it (which was about three and a half minutes), and then went to the phone and dialed Jasper's number.

Brrriiing!

"Please pick up…"

Brrriiing!

"Please pick up…"

Brrriing!

"Oh, please—"

"Please what?"

She sank to the ground with relief.

"Pick up," she answered, surprised at the thrill she felt at the sound of his voice.

"I did pick up," he replied.

"I know—I meant, please pick up."

He didn't say anything.

"That's why I was saying please, because I wanted you to pick up. I—oh, never mind."

"No, wait, wait!" He sounded frantic. She wondered if he thought she planned to hang up on him.

"Are you still there?" he asked.

"Yeah, I'm here." *Of course I'm here.*

"Good."

She sat on the floor with her legs tucked up tight to her chest. "How did your visit with Aunt Matilda go?"

"Enlightening as always," he remarked. "She ordered a pack of Depends from the waitress at the restaurant."

Sadie clapped her hand to her mouth and stifled a giggle. "She didn't!"

"Oh yes, she did. And she insisted on leaving a tip that included two Rolaids coupons and a six-year-old prescription for hemorrhoid medication."

Sadie burst out laughing.

"Sure, you can laugh," Jasper reminded her, "because you weren't there. But I think one day you're going to be as senile as she is."

"Mmm. And will you be so sweet as to take me out every other weekend like you do her?" she teased him.

"I'd take you out every other weekend right now, if you'd let me."

The suggestion sobered her, but it left her curious too. "Sure. You would now, while I'm still young and attractive and have all my teeth."

She could tell he was smiling when he answered, "Sadie, I'd take you out even if you were bald, toothless, and only had one leg."

"Malibu Ken and I would be a matched set, then. Maybe you should try Tommy Fitzkee's grandmother. Kylie has her number if you're interested."

"What?" He sounded thoroughly confused. Kylie must never have mentioned Mrs. Fitzkee to him.

"Never mind."

There was a brief lull.

"So, how was your day?" he asked her.

"Not bad, I guess. I went to Dmitri's this morning to apologize. He came to church with us." She paused. "Mac came along to lunch."

"To Suncatchers?" Jasper sounded surprised. Little wonder, after the way she'd railed on Mac's presence all week.

"How'd that go?" he asked.

"I don't know," she softly replied. "Like old times but reversed. Like I was the one taking him out now, and I held all the power on who got to leave and who had to stay."

A pause.

"How did that make you feel?" Jasper wondered.

Sadie thought about it for a long moment, her eyes tracing the patterns in the wallpaper: blue-and-white lines running parallel from floor to ceiling. Like her and Mac. Running parallel and never intersecting. Same direction, no common ground. "Sad," she finally answered. "It made me feel really sad. Like I wanted him to have the control back, but I was scared about what he'd do with it if I gave it to him."

"Maybe you'll have to learn to trust him again."

"He still hasn't given me a lot of reason to do that."

"Coming to Kylie's birthday party was a start," Jasper pointed out.

"That's just the problem, though. What if he keeps coming around and gets her attached to him, and then he leaves her? Can you imagine that? Think about how attached she is to you. If you ever left us— if you ever left her—" There was a rising edge of hysteria to Sadie's voice, and Jasper caught it.

"Sadie," he stopped her, "I'm not leaving. I'm not going anywhere. Ever."

"You don't know that," she whispered. "You don't know. People leave. They leave all the time—whether they mean to or whether they don't. They still go."

Jasper didn't say anything at first.

"Don't be scared, Sadie. Remember the time you got stuck in the tree house?"

"Jasper, we were *nine*."

"Remember?" he pushed. "You couldn't see the steps to find your way back down. You were scared, and you started to panic. And remember what happened?"

Sadie felt the edges of anxiety begin to soften into something far more comfortable. "You talked me down. And you stood on the ground. In case I fell."

"That's right." He sounded pleased that she'd remembered and outlined it so clearly. "I'll always talk you down. I'll always be there to catch you if you fall."

"But what if…" She hated to suggest it, but it lingered in her mind nonetheless. "I used to hear Mac talking to my mom. Every time he'd come back, he'd say it was for good. That he wasn't leaving. I believed him, the first six times I overheard him say it. And then I realized it was just something he said. That it was like this

143

thing he couldn't help. No matter what he said, he always ended up leaving."

"I'm not Mac, Sadie."

She knew that. But she couldn't make herself believe it.

"Why did you kiss me?" she asked him.

"Why do *you* think I kissed you?"

"I don't know; that's why I'm asking."

He answered more quickly than she thought he would. "I kissed you because I couldn't imagine *not* kissing you anymore." He paused. "Why did you kiss me back?"

"*What?* I didn't kiss you back."

"You most certainly did."

"I did not!"

"You did."

"You're crazy."

"Of course I am—I'm crazy for you."

Sadie nearly dropped the phone. "Jasper Reeves, after all this time, are you saying that you're—you're....well...are you?"

"Am I what?"

"Jasper!"

"Am I what?" he repeated.

"Are you...you know."

"I am."

"You're not."

"Oh, but I am."

"But you can't... Wait. You're—what did you mean when you said 'I am'?"

"Sadie, how many times are you going to do that?"

"Until you answer me."

"I think you can answer yourself. I've gotta go now—things to do. I'll see you tomorrow night."

"Wait! Jasper! Tomorrow…" She felt like scum. "Dmitri asked me out to dinner tomorrow." She winced. "I said yes. Can you—"

"No problem."

She frowned. "Jasper, are you really—"

There was a click. Sadie stared at the phone. Had he hung up on her? Was he angry? And exactly what did he mean when he said he was…? He couldn't be… But he said he was! But he never said what exactly.

Sadie felt a massive headache coming on.

Great.

Chapter Eight

....

Jasper thought it was time to have a talk with Kylie. They had each done their homework (him grading papers and her coloring a sheet of the alphabet) and eaten their after-school snack before retiring to Kylie's bedroom to lay out the Barbie dolls. Jasper gently suggested taking a go at the Cook and Serve Playset Sadie had gotten for Kylie's birthday, but the little girl only wrinkled her nose at the suggestion.

"That's Mommy's toy, not Kylie's toy," she informed him.

She seated herself on the floor, an assortment of Barbie's wardrobe spread out around her. Jasper lifted a hot-pink cocktail dress and studied it for a moment before laying it back beside a leopard-print jumper.

Barbie had style, that was for sure.

He cleared his throat, and Kylie looked up at him.

"Kylie, there's something I want to talk to you about."

Kylie laid aside the brush she had been running through Barbie's soft flaxen hair and stared up at him with sweet, innocent eyes. Jasper felt his insides tremble. She was five years old, and she could reduce him to putty with one heartfelt look from those wide brown eyes.

"You know how your mommy and Jasper have been friends for a long time?"

Kylie nodded, the somberness in his tone causing her to reflect an equally solemn demeanor.

"Years and years," she affirmed, "even a'fore Kylie was born!"

Clearly, by her expression, this was an infinite length of time. Jasper smiled, though he still quaked slightly with nervousness. He considered putting this off for another day, but Sadie would be home in an hour or less to prepare for her date with Dmitri. He had to speak with Kylie before then.

He had practiced a speech of sorts, though it hardly seemed fitting for a five-year-old's ears: *In the past week, I've come to the realization that I'm in love with your mother, and I'd like your permission to begin courting her.*

No, no, no. All wrong.

Kylie blinked up at him, waiting with such uncharacteristically childlike patience that his heart melted.

"What would you think," he finally asked softly, "if one day I would become your dad?"

Kylie looked puzzled. "Jasper *is* Kylie's daddy."

He blinked. "What?"

"Teacher said Daddy is the man who stays at the house and loves Kylie and Mommy and takes care of them." She stared at him as if this were common knowledge. "Jasper *is* Kylie's daddy."

Jasper swallowed. "Oh. Well." How in the world did he refute that kind of logic? "That's true," Jasper admitted. "Sort of. But…see… Mommy doesn't *know* that. She thinks Jasper is just…a friend," he finished lamely.

Kylie made a face. "Mommy's silly. Jasper loves Mommy and Kylie!"

He smiled. "Yes, he does—I mean, I do. But now I need to make your mommy know just how much I love her."

"That's easy. Just tell her."

If only Sadie still reasoned like her daughter did.

"I have, but Mommy is scared."

This brought a whole new level of soberness to Kylie's expression. "Mommy's scared?"

Jasper nodded and tried to think of a better way to explain it. "Mommy is afraid that I might hurt her feelings one day."

Kylie shook her head. "Kylie hurts Mommy's feelings sometimes, but she doesn't mean to. Kylie always says she's sorry."

Jasper was beginning to think that Kylie had a better chance of convincing Sadie than he did.

"I know, but Mommy's afraid I might go away one day and leave you and her alone."

Kylie was positively incensed. "Jasper wouldn't do that!"

At least someone had faith in him.

"That's right, but…" He drew a deep breath. "When Mommy was a little girl, her daddy left *her* mommy, and now Mommy's scared Jasper might do the same thing to her."

Kylie frowned. "You mean Grampa?"

Jasper winced inwardly. "Yeah, sweetheart. Grandpa."

"Oh." A pause. "Why did Grampa do that to Gramma?"

"Grandpa had some problems that he couldn't fix. Sometimes…" Jasper hesitated. "Sometimes people think that their problems will get better if they go away. They don't know that when they leave, they just make more problems—for themselves and for the people who love them."

Kylie picked at a fraying thread on her T-shirt. Jasper sensed that he had made her sad. He didn't say anything more and waited for her to come to her own conclusions. After a time, she looked up at him, her brown eyes trusting. He didn't lie to Kylie. He never had. He might try to soften the truth as best he could, but he never told her anything other than what he knew to be true.

"Is Grampa fixed now?" she asked him. "Is he going to leave again?"

Jasper brushed the hair back from her round little face. "I don't know, sweetheart. I think he's better. I think he's going to stay now. But I can't promise you that." He swallowed. "And one day—hopefully not for a long time—Grandpa will go to see Grandma again."

"In heaven?"

"Yeah. In heaven."

She bit her lip. "Not for a long time?"

"I hope not. I like having Grandpa around too."

Kylie licked her lips. "Mommy doesn't always like it."

"She does. But Mommy's still afraid Grandpa's going to leave again."

Kylie fell silent once more and began putting the pieces together. Jasper sat and watched while her face went through several different emotions as she attempted to reconcile everything he had told her. At last, she expelled a breath.

"If Jasper makes Mommy not afraid…then will he be like a *real* daddy?"

Ah, so Kylie *did* know there was a difference in the role he played to her and Sadie.

"Yeah. Then Jasper will be like a real daddy."

She clapped her hands with glee. "Then Jasper should make Mommy not afraid!"

He grinned. "I'm gonna try, Kylie…but I need your help."

"What can Kylie do?"

"First—you can't tell Mommy we talked about this. It needs to be a secret."

"Kylie keeps secrets! Kylie never told Mommy she made the volcano take Malibu Ken's leg on purpose!"

Jasper's eyes narrowed to slits. "Kylie never told Jasper that either."

She gulped. "Oops."

"What did Malibu Ken do to deserve that?"

"Nothing. The volcano was hungry."

Jasper suppressed a smile. "Second, Kylie, I'm going to need your help tonight. When Mommy comes home, she's going to get ready for a date with Dmitri. But Mommy doesn't know that Dmitri is really going to take her somewhere so she can have a date with *me*."

"Ooooh!" Kylie thought this positively mischievous. "Can Kylie come?"

"Not this time. Dates are just for mommies and daddies."

"Like Mommy and Jasper!"

"Right! So Grandpa is going to come after Mommy leaves, and then I have to go get ready for my date with Mommy. And you can't tell Mommy *anything*."

"A secret," she confirmed.

"A secret."

"Just like Kylie and the volcano."

"Just like that."

"Okay!"

He beamed at her. He was so proud.

"Jasper?"

"Yes?"

"Can we play now?"

He reached for a Barbie. "Should she wear the hot pink dress or the blue one?"

Kylie shrugged. "Kylie doesn't care. Jasper can pick."

Jasper chose the pink.

* * * * *

Sadie didn't understand. If Jasper had indicated yesterday on the phone what she *thought* he had indicated, then why was he seemingly so at ease about this date with Dmitri? She didn't have the nerve to ask him. Maybe she had imagined it all. The kissing, the phone conversation…maybe she was losing her mind.

She had thought that before. Maybe it was really happening this time. Usually when that fear crept up out of nowhere, she'd go to Jasper to set her straight. No doing that this time, however, since Jasper was the reason she was in this fix.

Sadie brushed a pale swath of blush on her cheeks. Jasper had retreated to the kitchen to fix himself and Kylie some dinner. She swallowed nervously. She didn't want to go out with Dmitri tonight. In fact, at the moment, she wanted nothing more than to curl up on the sofa against Jasper's chest with Kylie in her arms and watch *Beauty and the Beast*. She considered calling Dmitri to cancel. She glanced at her watch. He would be here in ten minutes. No time. She sighed.

Suddenly feeling eyes on her, she looked into the dresser mirror to see Kylie inching around the doorway of her bedroom. She turned.

"Hey, baby."

Kylie used this invitation to vault herself into the room and toward the dresser where Sadie sat applying her makeup.

"Hi, Mommy."

Sadie looked at her. "Hi." Where in the world had that impish smile come from? She waited for an explanation, but Kylie only stared up at her, swaying back and forth in some sort of personal delight.

"You okay there, Kylie?"

She grinned broadly, a clean row of baby teeth shining through. "Fine, Mommy."

Her eyes narrowed. "Is there something you want to tell Mommy?"

Kylie considered. "Mommy looks pretty."

This observation sufficiently distracted Sadie. She looked back into the mirror and critically surveyed the pale blue top and cocoa brown skirt she wore.

"You think so?"

Strangely enough, she knew it wasn't Dmitri she was taking such care for. It was for the three minutes she'd be in Jasper's presence *before* Dmitri arrived that had her going to such fuss. Ridiculous. Absurd even. Jasper had seen her in all states of dishevelment. Did it really matter what he thought of her now?

"Mommy is prettier than Barbie," Kylie stated with sincerity.

Sadie grinned and pulled Kylie onto her lap, kissing her soundly on the crown of her head. "Thanks."

Kylie took this opportunity to stare deeply into her mother's eyes.

"What is it, Kylie?"

Kylie continued to search—though for what, Sadie hadn't a clue.

"Mommy shouldn't be afraid," Kylie declared. "Jasper would never hurt Kylie or Mommy."

Sadie pulled back in surprise. "W–what? Kylie, I—"

Just then the doorbell rang. Sadie bit her lip to keep from pronouncing something she shouldn't. Dmitri was early.... Kylie squirmed and dropped to the floor.

"Kylie, wait—"

But the little girl was already hustling out of the room.

"Sadie!"

Jasper's voice echoed up the stairs.

"Dmitri's here!"

Sadie bit her lip again to keep from muttering. Jasper didn't sound in the least bit distressed. If he had said what she thought he had said, then shouldn't he be sullen with jealousy along about now? Or maybe what he had said had nothing to do with what she thought, in which case...she might be in even more trouble than if he had said what she thought he had said. She sighed.

"Sadie!"

"*I'm coming!*" she snapped sharply.

It seemed as though a blanket of silence fell on the floor below her. Grumbling, she finished applying the last few strokes of her makeup. With a final glance at her reflection (and a prick of irritation for realizing that Jasper would barely see her before she went with Dmitri), she left her bedroom and descended the stairs.

They lined up in a row before her, staring as she made her way down the steps. Dmitri, Jasper, and Kylie each looked up at her with an odd light in their eyes. Her own gaze fastened on Jasper and, curiously enough, his was the expression that seemed the most neutral. What was going on behind those warm cobalt eyes?

"Are you ready to go?" Dmitri held out her jacket for her.

She stepped onto the floor and met Jasper's eyes as she reached for her purse on a nearby table.

Jasper's look told her nothing.

Are you angry? Jealous? Happy?

But her silent questions went unanswered.

She turned to go, but Kylie suddenly grabbed her hand.

"Remember, Mommy! Remember what Kylie said!"

It was only then that Jasper's disinterested expression faltered as his eyes jerked to Kylie.

"Remember!" Kylie emphasized.

Sadie touched her lightly on the cheek. "I will, Kylie."

Satisfied, Kylie whirled and went to Jasper's side, grabbing tightly onto his hand. Dmitri held the door and ushered Sadie out into the mild evening air. She had time for only one last look at Jasper's impassive face before he was blocked from her view.

* * * * *

The instant the door closed behind Sadie and Dmitri, Kylie tugged Jasper toward the stairs.

"Hurry, Jasper! Not much time!"

He bolted upstairs. "Like I need you to remind me!"

Kylie waited impatiently as he changed in the bathroom.

"Hurry, Jasper!" she kept urging through the door, to which he continually replied, "I *am!*"

Kylie passed the time by performing a ballerina dance in the hallway, occasionally pausing to press her ear against the door to listen for Jasper's progress. When at last she was allowed to enter, she scurried over to the counter, climbed up, and sat beside the sink. Jasper ran his fingers through his hair.

"What do you think?" He looked at her for approval.

Kylie held out her palms and, with her tongue, gave each one a long, juicy lick. She reached out a hand to each side of Jasper's head and smoothed down any flyaway strands of hair.

"There," she declared. "Jasper looks pretty."

He grinned at her as the doorbell rang. Mac.

"Thanks."

Jasper hoisted her off the counter, and the two vaulted downstairs to answer the door.

* * * * *

Sadie didn't really understand what Dmitri was doing. He had been driving nearly in circles for the last fifteen minutes. She hated to criticize—he was new to the area, after all—but what little patience she had brought with her on this date was quickly dissolving to dregs.

After three more minutes of aimless driving, she cleared her throat.

"Are you sure you know where you're going?"

Dmitri didn't seem worried.

"Mmm-hmm."

She pursed her lips tightly and then relaxed them. "And…where is it we're going again?"

"A surprise," he chastised in that lilting Russian accent. "It's a surprise."

"Oh, yeah. A surprise."

He slid her a glance, and she knew she sounded less then pleased. "Sadie...is something wrong?"

Her gaze jerked to his. "Uh, no. No. Why would anything be wrong? I'm fine. Nothing wrong here."

Oh, good grief, I'm babbling!

"You don't seem happy to be here."

"Uh...no, I...it's just..." *I sound like one of the Teletubbies.* "It's nothing. Just a long day at the restaurant. That's all."

Dmitri seemed to accept this explanation. He nodded in understanding. "You know, I meant to tell you from the moment I met you—I really admire how well you run your restaurant."

This admission momentarily caught her off guard. "Really?"

"Really. You're very good at what you do—designing the menus, creating recipes, managing the staff, making sure everything runs smoothly. It's all quite impressive."

She allowed a small smile of pride. "Thanks."

"I wish I were more like you."

This statement caused her satisfaction to deflate a bit. Did this have something to do with his own restaurant?

"Oh? What do you mean?"

He seemed to think he had said too much, because he fell silent for a moment.

"Nothing," he awkwardly answered her. "Just that I wish I had your...natural business sense. Your intelligence."

They lapsed into silence and drove for another few minutes. She watched the familiar local icons sliding by—the streetlights resembling wrapped and unwrapped Hershey's Kisses, the green-and-yellow-trimmed trolleys shuttling tourists around town, the words "Hershey

Cocoa" spelled out in brown-tinted shrubbery in front of the Hershey Foods Plant. She breathed deeply the rich, unmistakable aroma of cocoa permeating the streets of her hometown. Chocolate. It was soothing.

Let aromatherapists tout their lavender essential oil any day; a fragrant drive through Hershey soothed her faster than any scented diffuser.

Just as Sadie was getting ready to ask if she could take the wheel to get them to their destination, Dmitri turned onto a street they hadn't encountered yet. His driving suddenly acquired a more definite purpose.

Sadie frowned. If she didn't know better, she'd think Dmitri was driving to Agape Christian Academy—Kylie's school, where Jasper was employed as an elementary teacher.

"Dmitri…do you know where you're headed?"

He nodded.

"But…"

Thoughts of chocolate decadence fled as they approached the street leading to the school.

"Are we going to the school?" She twisted in her seat to view the road behind them. "Dmitri, is that where you're taking me?"

What could he possibly have planned? He didn't answer her, so she simply sat back and waited. Within several minutes' time, they pulled up to the back entrance of the academy's auditorium. Dmitri put his SUV in park, slid the keys from the ignition, and exited the vehicle.

Not bothering to wait for him, Sadie pushed open her own door and swung her feet to the ground. Dmitri came alongside and extended his hand, but she ignored him. He waited until she was out and then closed her door.

"This way," he gestured, toward the entrance.

She raised an eyebrow before forging ahead of him. A brief scan of the parking lot revealed no other vehicles on site.

Approaching the auditorium door, she saw lights seeping warmly through the cracks. Dmitri jumped ahead to open the door for her, and as it widened, she could see that all the lights were glowing—on the stage and on the auditorium floor.

Stepping inside, she stared at the stage. It was set for a production, although Sadie was certain there was no drama currently in the works. And classes were nearly finished for the year.... A summer production maybe? Neither Kylie nor Jasper had mentioned anything, however.

But something surely must have been planned, for the stage had become a romantic world of arched doorways and twinkling white lights with vines of roses stretching up a latticework to touch the edges of a painted marble balcony.

The scene, for whatever story, was simply breathtaking. A few of the props were familiar to her from the hours she had spent here in helping Jasper with school plays and watching Kylie perform in the preschool productions.

Kylie had played a carrot in the last presentation. At first, she had demanded her hair be dyed green, but following the entire exhibition, she had refused to touch carrots for a week. Yet this was no vegetable pageant. Whatever the school was staging, it had to be a glorious story. At least if the stage was any indication.

Coming back to herself, Sadie turned to ask Dmitri what this was all about, but to her bewilderment, he had gone. The door was closed, and only now did she note the soft rumble of his SUV as it pulled out of the parking lot.

"What is going on?"

Too enthralled with the soft lights and magnificent stage to even care, Sadie turned back to the auditorium and took several tentative steps toward the front. It was like a wonderland.

There was a river of golden carpeting across the stage floor that pooled beneath pillars of slim white stone. Wreaths of ivy and pale blue silk draped a colonnade that accommodated a circular stone fountain. And to her right slanted a tall, oval balcony, fenced in by a row of what appeared to be iron scrollwork. Rose petals littered the ground like crimson tears fallen from heaven. Ascending to the platform, she bent to touch them.

They were real.

"Do you like it?"

She whirled. She knew the voice but found her heart wedged so tightly in her throat that she couldn't acknowledge it.

Jasper came from backstage, his steps falling lightly on the golden carpet. He looked different than when she had left him at the house. He was dressed in black slacks and a white dress shirt. Simple. But the classy outfit certainly made him stand out in these surroundings.

Unable to look at him without her heart pounding erratically, her eyes faltered from his as she scanned the set once more.

"It's gorgeous," she murmured softly. "It must have taken ages to assemble."

"Oh, not so long as you think," he answered. "Remember Ray, who works for the Hershey Theatre? He let me borrow some props and helped set it all up."

"What's it for?" she asked, her eyes still avoiding his.

"For you," he gently declared.

She couldn't help but look at him then. "For me?"

He nodded, taking two steps closer to her. "Remember in tenth grade, when the school put on *Romeo and Juliet*…and you wanted to play the lead?"

"They gave it to Allison Seitz," Sadie remarked in distaste. "And she forgot her lines only halfway into her first scene."

"But they still wouldn't let you be Juliet," he said.

"No," she remarked with a touch of bitterness. "They wouldn't."

"Even though you'd have made the most *perfect* Juliet."

She glanced at him. "What are you getting at, Jasper?"

He held his arms out at his sides to encompass the whole of the stage. "Now's your chance. This is for you." He lowered his arms. "You get to be Juliet."

She turned and moved several steps in the opposite direction of him. "Oh, that was forever ago, Jasper. I don't want to play Juliet anymore."

He took several steps forward to compensate for the distance she had placed between them. "Every woman wants to be Juliet," he softly replied. "To be wooed and won. To have someone love her so much he'd rather die than live life without her."

Sadie swallowed. "Life didn't turn out so well for Juliet," she pointed out.

Jasper conceded, "No, it didn't. But she was happy. For a while."

"Not long. Never long enough."

"How long is long enough? Would it have been better to never have known love than to live a lifetime without it?"

She trembled. He stood only a couple steps away now. "I've had my love, Jasper. There's nothing left for me now."

"How do you know unless you give it a chance?"

"With great passion comes great risk," she noted.

"But without great risk comes no passion at all," he retorted.

It was a compelling argument.

"Here." He reached out a hand, which held a worn, yellow copy of *Romeo and Juliet*. "Give it a try. It might surprise you."

She hesitated a moment, but he winked and she felt herself relax. "It's only a play…right?"

She moved, touching the playbook. Her fingers tingled as her knuckles brushed against Jasper's hand.

"There was no time for costumes," he apologized. "But we'll just call this a rehearsal." He motioned toward the gilded steps leading to the balcony.

"Go ahead."

She licked her lips.

"Go on," he urged.

She glanced at him.

"I'm right here to catch you if you fall," he murmured.

She took several tentative steps, and before she knew it, she stood on the balcony, looking down at Jasper.

He opened his own copy of the play and cleared his throat.

"Act two, scene two?" he suggested.

She swallowed. *Of course. What else?*

Jasper began the scene. "'He jests at scars that never felt a wound… But soft! What light through yonder window breaks?'"

He ran through Romeo's lovesick lines with a passionate tenderness that could have melted the hardest of hearts. Sadie's own pulse quickened at the rough compassion in his voice.

When it came time for her to speak, she faltered the one line she had. "'Aye me!'" Her voice cracked. It actually sounded like Juliet was in distress, as she should be.

Jasper said in a stage whisper, "Good!"

She gulped. He continued his lines. When it came time for her to speak once more, she sounded firmer, though no less nervous. Jasper continued as if this was truly a performance, though they were the only two in the auditorium. His enthusiasm was catching, and Sadie soon found herself playing along.

"'How camest thou hither?'" she asked, "'Tell me, and wherefore? The orchard walls are high and hard to climb, and the place death, considering who thou art, if any of my kinsmen find thee here.'"

Jasper only glanced at the script. "'With love's light wings did I o'er-perch these walls, for stony limits cannot hold love out: And what love can do, that dares love attempt; therefore thy kinsmen are no let to me.'"

They went on. Sadie found herself staring down at him as he spoke, the stage lights bouncing golden off his light-colored hair. When he looked up at her, his eyes were filled with warmth and a longing she had never known. She had no reason to fear him, she realized. Not Jasper, who had dried her tears and long held her steady through life's hardest blows. Dear, loving Jasper, who had known her through her best and her worst and loved her in spite of it.

He stared up at her now and fell silent. Her heart swelled with... could it really be...love?

"Sadie?"

"Mmm?"

"Your line," he whispered.

"Oh." She looked down at the script, but the words were a blur of sweet nothings. "What's my cue again?"

Jasper repeated his last line. "'O, wilt thou leave me so unsatisfied?'"

She found her place. "'What satisfaction canst thou have tonight?'"

He answered, again without looking at his script, but staring up at her with his heart in his eyes. "'The exchange of thy love's faithful vow for mine.'"

Something in the way he said it... It was a line from the play, Sadie knew. But the words were meant for more than that. Could she give him her heart? Could she love him as he... Had he even claimed to love her?

"Sadie?" he prompted.

She leaned down. He was so handsome in the white shirt with his blond hair dropping into his eyes.

"'The exchange of thy love's faithful vow for mine,'" he repeated his line.

Sadie stretched toward the balcony's edge, suddenly wishing she could touch him, if only for a moment.

"'I gave thee mine before thou didst request it,'" she softly told him—and then, before she realized what was happening, she toppled over the balcony's edge toward the stage.

It wasn't a high balcony, for the auditorium wasn't large. But it was enough of a drop that Sadie gasped and squeezed her eyes shut as she fell. At any second, she expected to feel the hard slam of the wooden floor, cushioned slightly by the gold carpeting, against her body. But in an instant it was over, and she fell neatly into Jasper's outstretched arms.

His broad grin told her he was thrilled with the way things had played out.

"See? I told you I'd catch you if you fell."

And she kissed him then to let him know she believed he would.

Chapter Nine

. . . .

It seemed too perfect to last. That was the thought continually whispering through the hallways of Sadie's mind. Maybe Jasper really did love her, and maybe she really did love him. But she had long ago quit believing in songs and poems that declared love could move mountains, plumb the ocean's depths, and overcome any obstacles set before it. Sadie didn't really believe love had ever halted a catastrophe, and she was too focused on that thought to realize that love had done its fair share of aiding in the recovery of several tragedies.

Love was a season, and in Sadie's case, the seasons had always ended up being rather short ones. So the dark winds in her mind murmured through the night.

But when Jasper was with her, the voices silenced, and she was able to believe, for fleeting stretches of time, that he really could outlast the inevitable. He could love her long enough to make her believe it was worth trying.

Jasper's hand on her face, his fingers in her hair, and his eyes on hers…these were the things that banished the black thoughts and left her hopeful. As long as Jasper was near her…

But not even Jasper could forever hold off the inevitable.

* * * * *

There had been two weeks of bliss between Jasper and Sadie. For two weeks she had been able to push the threat of Dmitri's new restaurant to the corners of her mind, strike up tentative conversations with Mac, and bask in the glow of Jasper's hand holding hers. Even Kylie reacted positively to the change, and as the school year ended and summer break began, there were fewer incidences involving one-legged dolls and man-eating volcanoes. Of course, that's not to say the bathroom gods slept—just that fewer mishaps occurred during that time. Life was lulling Sadie into complacency, she was certain of it.

And then Jasper suggested a visit to Aunt Matilda.

They left Sunday morning in Jasper's car, Sadie and Jasper in the front and Kylie settled in the back with a supply of Barbies and storybooks at her availability. It was only an hour-long drive to York County, but Kylie wasn't known for her patience with drives of any sort.

Aunt Matilda didn't remember Sadie. Even worse, she immediately took her to be a kleptomaniac.

"Where did you put them, you hussy?"

Sadie blinked at this greeting. "Hello to you too, Aunt Matilda."

"Where are they?"

Kylie's eyes were round with surprise. She looked at Jasper and then at Sadie and then back at Matilda. She had never encountered anyone who was both accusatory and insulting right from the outset.

"Aunt Matilda, this is Sadie, remember?" Jasper prodded, seemingly not in the least embarrassed.

For her own part, Sadie was too surprised to be embarrassed. She'd never been called a hussy before.

"I don't care who she is!" Aunt Matilda cried. "She stole my dentures, and I want them back!"

Sadie bit her lip. Matilda's dentures were clearly already affixed in her mouth.

"Um…" She looked to Jasper for help.

Jasper patted Matilda's hand. "You have them in already, Aunt Matilda."

Matilda leaned forward. "What did you say?"

Jasper spoke loudly and with precise enunciation. "Your dentures are already in your mouth!"

Matilda touched a wrinkled old hand to her gums. "Oh." She calmed somewhat, and her pink face paled to a more manageable color. "So they are."

She rounded a worn blue eye on Sadie. "But mind you they stay there, young lady. I know your sort. Don't be getting any ideas!"

Jasper straightened and winked at Sadie. "I always knew you were a troublemaker."

She rolled her eyes at him.

By the end of the day, Sadie would look back and realize this not-so-auspicious beginning should have warned her as to how the rest of the visit would go. Unfortunately, she hadn't taken any warning from Matilda's first outburst.

It happened again in the church. They had loaded Matilda into the car for an uneventful ride to the Good Shepherd Chapel. Jasper greeted a few of the congregants as they settled Matilda in what Jasper claimed was her typical seat—center aisle, eighth pew back from the front. Jasper assured Sadie that if Matilda did *not* sit in this seat, an apocalyptic judgment such as defined in the book of Revelation was likely to rain havoc upon the world.

Sadie made sure Kylie was well supplied with coloring books and

Bible stories to last her throughout the service. Jasper had suggested the children's Sunday school class, but Kylie would have none of it. She'd made it clear there was no way she was leaving Sadie alone with someone of such suspicious character as Matilda Reeves.

And so the service began.

Everything went smoothly through the welcoming prayer and hymns. There was a brief period set aside for time at the altar, as well as an update on a missionary family in Liberia. Jasper reached over and grabbed Sadie's hand halfway through the altar time, and Sadie warmed at his touch.

With Matilda seated on the end, and Jasper to her right with Sadie and Kylie beside him, everything seemed normal. A family at church on a glorious Sunday morning. And Sadie suddenly felt the need to smother a smile at this terrific fortune.

That's when Matilda stood up.

The preacher was only ten minutes into his sermon and about to highlight the second point in his message when Matilda cried out.

"This woman!" Her bony, gnarled finger pointed past Jasper and directly at Sadie. "This woman has taken my dentures, and I demand that something be done about it!"

Jasper nervously tugged on Matilda's arm and pleaded in a loud whisper that she sit down. She only glared at him with one filmy eye and shouted, "Eh? What's that, boy? Speak up!"

Jasper placed his face in his hand while Matilda glared at Sadie. Kylie hissed beside her, "Mommy, Kylie thought we couldn't talk in church!"

The congregation in front of them had twisted in their seats and were staring at the display. The preacher had frozen at the pulpit, one finger pointed heavenward in a freeze-framed moment.

"Well?" Matilda demanded of Sadie. "Where are they, you hussy?"

"That's twice in one morning," Sadie stated incredulously. She looked at Jasper. "I just got insulted by Aunt Matilda *twice* in one morning."

Clearly, the name-calling affected Sadie more than the public humiliation.

When Sadie made no move to restore Aunt Matilda's property, the old woman attempted to shuffle out into the aisle. Without Jasper's arm and the assistance of her cane, however, this took quite a bit of maneuvering, which included her grasping the hair of the woman in the row in front of them.

By the time Matilda at last made it out of the pew, the victimized lady before them was clutching her hairdo and preparing to make a run for the rear exit. Matilda hobbled toward the front.

Sadie thought perhaps now was the time for Jasper to make a move, but he seemed rooted to the spot in absolute denial that such a thing was really taking place.

"A tooth for a tooth!" Matilda declared. "If the Good Book says so, then I demand that my teeth be restored!"

Sadie gaped. "I suppose I should be grateful that she doesn't think I took her glasses."

Jasper still didn't have the strength to comment. Nor, apparently, did the rest of the congregation. They sat in slack-jawed stupefaction, watching the drama unfold before them. Several of the younger congregation members were giggling sharply, but the majority simply stared in shock.

Jasper found his voice and leaned toward Sadie. "How do you always manage to bring out the best in people?"

She shrugged. "It's a gift."

He looked at her with a mixture of embarrassment and humor in his eyes. "Does it come with a return policy?"

She suddenly found herself wanting to laugh and cry at the same time.

Kylie, seeing that neither Jasper nor Sadie was making a move to end this madness, apparently decided to take matters into her own hands. Dropping to her hands and knees, she crawled under several seats until she found her way out into the clearing.

Sadie noticed her daughter's appearance in the aisle and felt her heart skip a beat.

"Kylie!" she whispered as quietly as she could.

Kylie either didn't hear her mother or chose not to answer as she approached Aunt Matilda near the front. Tugging firmly on the old woman's sleeve, Kylie at last gained Matilda's attention. The older woman turned her sharp eyes on the little girl.

"Maybe the volcano took your teeth," Kylie suggested.

Matilda frowned. "The *what*?"

"The volcano!" Kylie shouted.

Matilda waved her hand at this nonsense. "What volcano?" she demanded.

Kylie sighed and announced in the loudest voice her five-year-old lungs could muster, "THE TOILET!"

A collective gasp rose from the congregation, effectively drowning out whatever Matilda might have said next.

"Okay, *that* was my cue," Jasper decided. And with that, he darted out into the aisle to gather the two girls he was forced to claim as his own. Sadie made quick work of scooping up Kylie's coloring books and Bible stories as well as grabbing Aunt Matilda's six-pound purse before jumping out of the pew.

Jasper managed to herd the two offending parties down the aisle and toward the door, offering sincere apologies as he went.

"So sorry... Won't happen again... Sincere apologies..."

Sadie stood waiting when Jasper at last got Kylie and Matilda out to the car. She felt the heat of embarrassment upon her face but couldn't help smiling broadly.

He sighed as Kylie helped Aunt Matilda into the car. "What do you look so amused about?" he asked her, his smile belying any real irritation.

Sadie held out Matilda's heavily weighted purse. "Take a look."

Jasper peered inside and groaned.

There were several sets of dentures grinning morbidly up at him.

* * * * *

Following their getaway from the Good Shepherd congregation, Jasper decided to risk a lunch at a local restaurant. His reasoning was that if they placed their order early enough and ate quickly, they could be out of there before any of the churchgoers arrived at the place.

Sadie thought it was a good plan.

Following the denture adventure, Aunt Matilda settled down a bit. She was fascinated with Kylie's volcano stories and demanded that the little girl give more details on what had happened to Malibu Ken's leg.

Kylie told the story flawlessly time after time, neatly leaving out the part where she purposefully flushed Ken's leg down the toilet. Sadie didn't notice anything amiss in the story.

Kylie's good, thought Jasper. *Too good for her own good.*

Heaven help the boys when she reached dating age. Jasper thrilled a little at the thought. Much as he hoped the day would take a long time in coming, he still felt a satisfaction at the anticipation of running any would-be suitors through the gauntlet as Kylie's dad.

Kylie's dad.

Jasper had to bite his tongue to keep from grinning. He found Sadie's hand beneath the table and squeezed it gently. She looked at him, her eyes a bottomless swirl. It tempted him to kiss her right then and there, in front of Aunt Matilda and everyone.

The reminder of Aunt Matilda was what held him back.

"I think you should plow this volcano to the ground!" Aunt Matilda insisted to Kylie.

"Oh, please, don't give her ideas!" Sadie begged with honest fear.

Jasper and Sadie exchanged glances. He could just imagine her coming home to shards of porcelain littering the bathroom floor and Kylie triumphantly holding Ken's leg in homage to island justice.

Matilda looked at Sadie with sharp, all-knowing eyes. "It's not wise to have that type of thing in your home, dear. Who knows what it will begin eating next? One night while this child is in her bed—why...think of it!"

Clearly, Kylie *was* thinking of it. Her eyes were round with fear.

"Mommy?" she asked in trepidation.

Jasper shook his head at her. "It's not that kind of volcano, Kylie. Don't worry."

"But then there are those cannibals to consider," Matilda pointed out. "Rings in their noses! *Shah!* Who knows what godless heathens like that will do? Why do you let them stay in your bathroom, dear?" she asked Sadie with a critical air.

Sadie took a sip from her iced tea. "I dunno. They just moved in one day, and it seemed too much of a hassle to have them evicted. At least they don't eat much," she lightly suggested.

Matilda narrowed her eyes. "No, the volcano seems to be doing that."

Jasper snorted and shook a sugar packet. "She's got you there, Sadie."

"So, Aunt Matilda…how do you like your corn chowder?" Sadie must have decided it was time for a subject change.

Matilda took a spoonful of her soup and dribbled it onto the floor in reply. Kylie slapped a hand to her mouth, unsuccessfully covering a delighted giggle.

"It tastes like they scooped it off the floor," she declared.

Jasper rather agreed with the old woman but still thought the action a bit unnecessary.

"And how's your salad, dear?" Matilda asked.

Sadie blinked at the gentle kindness that suffused the older lady's tone.

"It's all right," Sadie warily answered.

Matilda huffed. Leaning forward, she reached her finger into the bed of lettuce greens and fished around. Grabbing hold of an olive, she pinched it between her wrinkled fingers, plucked it from the plate, and threw that on the ground as well.

"There," she pronounced. "I never did like those things."

Sadie pushed her plate aside.

"Thanks, Aunt Matilda."

The old woman beamed.

"Is schizophrenia generally a problem in old age?" she asked in a whispered aside to Jasper.

He grinned but didn't reply as he kindly edged his plate toward Sadie, offering her some of his fries. She smiled gratefully at him and reached for a few.

"Aunt Matilda," Jasper began in an effort to get things back on track, "have I mentioned that Sadie and I are dating now?"

"What?" Matilda leaned forward. "What was that?"

"We're *dating*," Jasper repeated with succinct pronunciation.

"You're mating!" Matilda leaned back in shock.

Sadie immediately stood to her feet and extended her hand to Kylie. "Come on, baby, time to go to the bathroom."

Kylie looked up at her in confusion. "But Kylie doesn't have to go, Mommy—"

"Now, Kylie—*now*."

With a weary sigh, Kylie crawled under the table and out of the booth, slipping her hand into Sadie's with a grumble. As Jasper attempted to calm Matilda, they headed off toward the back of the restaurant with Kylie asking in a much-louder voice than necessary, "Mommy, what's *mating*?"

* * * * *

When it came time to return Matilda to the nursing home, Sadie and Kylie helped the old woman to her room as Jasper lingered at the nurses' station to speak to someone in charge about Matilda's denture collection.

While Jasper was occupied, Sadie pulled forth a decorative tin filled with cookies, which she had carried in with her from the car.

"Aunt Matilda, I brought you a little special something."

Matilda tugged an orange-and-brown afghan around her shriveled thighs and eyed Sadie warily. Clearly, her assessment of Sadie's character had not been entirely reformed just yet.

"Mommy, Kylie doesn't think that's a good idea," the five-year-old girl piped up, eyeing the tin with a similar expression of wariness.

Sadie glanced at her daughter. "Why not?"

Kylie just sighed in a way that made Sadie narrow her eyes at this seemingly long-suffering forbearance.

Ignoring this reaction, she turned her attention back to Matilda. "I made them myself," she assured the elderly lady. Removing the tin lid, she waved the container back and forth beneath Matilda's nose.

"They're chocolate chip–walnut."

"Ohhh." Kylie's little hands covered her face.

Sadie felt a prick of irritation at that. "Come on. Try one." This was a new recipe, and Sadie felt absolutely confident that, this time, her dessert-making efforts had been a success.

She'd been practicing.

Removing a walnut-encrusted disk from the tin, she waved it under Matilda's nose.

Matilda sneezed. "Smells like cat litter," she declared.

A few stray crumbs floated onto the afghan. Matilda stared at them. "*Looks* like cat litter."

Kylie giggled, and Sadie threw her a look. The expression on Sadie's face instantly silenced her.

Sadie's teeth clenched tighter than a vise, and she forced through them the suggestion, "Why—don't—you—just—try—one?"

Matilda may have been old. And she may have been senile. But she was certainly not stupid. "Do I look like your guinea pig, young lady?"

Sadie pursed her lips. "Eat it."

"No."

"You'll like it."

Matilda crossed her arms. "Why don't *you* eat it?"

Sadie's hand, hanging in midair, drooped slightly. "You want *me* to eat it?"

Matilda nodded.

Sadie swallowed.

"Well, I—I suppose I could...." She lifted the crumbly cookie toward her face.

Kylie's eyes grew round. Sadie licked her lips, and Matilda's eyes narrowed to thin slits.

With a little breath, Sadie stuffed a bite of the cookie into her mouth and chewed vigorously.

"Mmmm! *Dell-esh-us!*" she muttered around the dry mounds. Cardboard cutouts tasted more appetizing. But it had to be just her. She could whip up bisques to soufflés, appetizers to entrees...surely her desserts were not so bad.

She grinned confidently and extended the remains of the cookie. Kylie's eyes darted rapidly back and forth between the two women.

Matilda's head cocked.

She's buying it....

The old woman leaned forward and opened her mouth, the clean line of her dentures standing at arms. Taking no chances, Sadie immediately stuffed the rest of the cookie into Matilda's mouth and waited breathlessly.

The wrinkled jaws chewed seemingly involuntarily. Chew, chew, chew…a few attempts to swallow…no swallowing…

Matilda opened her mouth and attempted to gasp but managed only a raspy, sucking sound. Her bleached blue eyes widened and filled with liquid, but no sound escaped her lips except that constant rasp.

Sadie grew alarmed as Matilda's bony fingers reached for her throat. Kylie scurried over.

"Mommy! She's choking!"

Matilda's vein-thickened hands clutched at her neck.

"Matilda?"

Only the sucking sound in reply.

"Mommy! She's *blue*!"

Matilda's skin *had* taken on a color similar to that of her now-wide eyes. Sadie jumped to her feet and reached for the pitcher of water. She poured it with shaking hands, sloshing liquid over the sides and onto the floor.

Rushing to Matilda's side, Sadie thrust the straw between her crumb-speckled lips and urged the old lady to drink.

This complicated matters as Matilda attempted to inhale the liquid and only served to pull more crumbs even farther back into her throat. She sputtered like an old engine and grabbed Sadie's hair, tugging in desperation.

"Ow, ow, ow, ow, *ow*!" Sadie cried, as she attempted to pull her head free.

"Purple!" Kylie cried as Matilda's color heightened to an entirely new shade.

Sadie pulled at Matilda's skeletal arm, attempting to free herself, but the woman had a death grip on her hair.

"Kylie! Get Jasper!"

Kylie whirled and pattered out into the hall, looking both directions in an attempt to remember which way they'd come in.

"Kylie!" Sadie called.

The little girl turned.

"That way," Sadie pointed.

Kylie raced off in the direction her mother indicated, calling Jasper's name at the top of her lungs.

Matilda continued to struggle futilely, pulling in small tufts of cookie-crumb air into her failing lungs. Sadie still fought for control of her head, praying for a miracle and inwardly listing cookie ingredients.

One cup brown sugar—check.

Two teaspoons vanilla—check.

One-half teaspoon salt—check.

I didn't forget the eggs, did I? No, I couldn't have. Two eggs—check.

She had gone through the recipe one whole turn and was starting it a second time when Jasper finally arrived in the doorway with a squadron of nurses on his tail. Kylie worked her way through a forest of legs and pointed out the obvious.

"Aunt Matilda is choking!"

The nurses swarmed the room with SWAT-like efficiency. It took two of them to disengage Matilda's fingers from Sadie's hair. The others went to work gently pounding Matilda's back, rubbing her throat, and finally administering a version of the Heimlich maneuver that made leg-eating cannibals look tame.

A congealed glob of cookie matter, peppered with walnut-and-chocolate-chip remains, flew across the room, hit the wall, and dropped to the floor right beneath Matilda's framed print of *Whistler's Mother*.

Oh, the shame.

Sadie dared not look at Jasper, but after a moment, she felt his reassuring hand against the small of her back. She relaxed, though she still didn't look at him. But a moment later, she stiffened as Matilda drew in a clean lungful of air and screeched in indignation.

"The hussy tried to kill me! Murder! Murder!"

The crew of nurses each turned to stare at her. Sadie felt her eyes fill with tears.

"It was a cookie," she tried to explain. "I just wanted her to try my cookies!"

With a clicking of tongues, the nurses turned and attempted to comfort Matilda. They fluffed her pillows and rearranged her afghan and crooned and cooed at her until she settled down.

Sadie felt it was all a colossal conspiracy. Honestly. The old woman's system had probably dried up on its own. Her cookies hadn't really had anything to do with it...had they?

A dark-haired nurse with full cheeks and sharp eyes stalked over to them. "I believe that's enough for one visit."

"Yes, I quite think so," Jasper agreed. His voice held just the faintest shadow of amusement, although Sadie also thought she detected a note of relief in there too.

For once, Kylie didn't have to be told to gather her things. She did so quite efficiently all on her own.

Another nurse, smaller in stature and with kind gray eyes, brought over the tin container of cookies. She held them out to Sadie.

"Don't worry, honey," she whispered. "I'm not much of a cook myself."

Sadie took the cookies and left the room without a word.

* * * * *

The ice cream was supposed to make up for the trauma of Sadie's day, but somehow not even the idea of mocha chocolate chip with hot fudge quite salved the wound to Sadie's spirit. The quaint little ice cream parlor along 322 on the way back from York was one of their favorite stops. Jasper held her hand as they stood in line, his thumb gently stroking hers while Kylie ran in circles around them and vibrated her lips in imitation of a plane's buzz.

"They were only cookies," Sadie repeated for the fourteenth time.

"You can't win them all, Sadie."

She sighed. "You don't understand."

Jasper raised an eyebrow in challenge. "Oh, really? I understand you can be obsessed—that you're a bit of a control freak." He nudged her to ease the sting of this remark but then grew serious. "You can't always be the best, Sadie. You can be good—really good. Maybe you can win a few...but you can't win them all. Be content with what you're good at and let the rest go. It's only food."

"It's not just food! It's a type of *art*!"

He faced her directly, and Kylie wove her way in between them with a *putt, putt, putt* sound. The plane's engine was failing.

"Sadie. It's a cookie."

"It's *not* just a cookie."

"Aha! See! That's my point. Where it should just be a cookie, you turn it into a competition."

Sadie rolled her eyes and took a step forward as the line moved. "But I only wanted Matilda to *try* one. I just wanted to prove that… that…" What *was* she trying to prove? She bit her lip. "Who do you think I'm competing with, anyway?"

Jasper draped an arm around her shoulder. "Yourself, sweetheart. Only with yourself. Besides…" He gave her a lecherous grin. "I'll try your cookies any day." He wiggled his eyebrows in a ridiculous gesture she couldn't help but smile at.

Her smile quickly turned to a frown as the customer in front of them ordered.

"Two of the chocolate chip cookie dough, medium size."

Sadie sighed.

"It's just that…" She turned then and faced Jasper, her desperate brown eyes staring into his soft blue ones. "I can *do* this. I know I can."

Jasper brushed a strand of hair from her cheek, his touch feather-light and tender. "But what if you can't?" he asked her.

Sadie's lips parted with an answer even she was not sure of when a voice came between them.

"Can I take your order?"

Jasper turned his attention to the counter staff, and Sadie distractedly admired the way his jaw flexed strongly as he ordered ice cream for the three of them. Kylie had stopped her airplane imitation and now clung tightly to his legs. He laid a hand atop her soft brown head as he accepted the change from the bill.

It's so easy for him, Sadie thought. So simple to just accept who he was—his talents and limitations—without fear of rejection, self-loathing, or ineptitude. Jasper made life seem effortless. She didn't know how to do that. She had never known how to do that.

"Wanna go outside?"

He was looking at her again, his hand extending her own dish of mocha chocolate chip with hot fudge toward her. Kylie had released his legs and now stretched her tongue to new limits as she licked the sides of her chocolate cone.

"Sure." Sadie took the plastic dish and allowed Jasper to lead the way out into the warm summer sunshine.

They settled at a tarnished table in a sea of newly sprouted grass. Kylie crawled onto one of the aluminum benches, her little legs swinging beneath her as she continued to take methodical licks of her cone. Jasper ran the tiny white spoon around the edges of his vanilla mint, creating a pool of chaos in a cup before stabbing out a chunk to eat. Sadie glanced down at her own dish. She ate ice cream carefully, always smoothing out the sides as she went, to maintain an outward facade of perfection while inside…everything was melting.

After several minutes of sugar-induced silence, Kylie held out the bottom half of her cone.

"Kylie's done."

Jasper held out his dish, and Kylie deposited the chocolate remains right on top of his pristine vanilla pool. Sadie looked at the two of them, blending disorder like that. How did they do it?

"Kylie wants to play." She pointed to a rusty swing-set creaking softly in the breeze. Visions of corroded metal rupturing and falling atop Kylie filled Sadie's head.

"Hands first," Jasper commanded.

Kylie held out her palms. Jasper took her little fingers and popped them in his mouth, licking away the stickiness. He wiped down each digit with his napkin and then set it to work on her lips, carefully cleaning the gooey smudges that clung to her mouth.

She squirmed. "Kylie done?"

"Kylie's done," he confirmed with a smile.

She scampered off without another word, content under Jasper's watchful supervision. Sadie hadn't said anything, but she marveled—marveled at how he made even parenting seem easy.

"Jasper, why *didn't* you ever get married, have kids?" Her ice cream was melting hopelessly, the malleable chocolate walls falling in on themselves.

Jasper stuck his spoon in the center of her collapsed fortress and stole a bite. He shrugged. "Guess I always figured, deep down, that you were the girl for me…but seeing as how you were already taken…" He trailed off.

She swallowed. "What about your fiancée from college…what was her name? Veronica?"

"Victoria."

"Right. Victoria."

He bit off the end of Kylie's ice cream cone and chewed it down. "What about her?"

Sadie swung her foot back and forth beneath the table in nervous agitation. "Did you love her? I mean, you were engaged to her."

Jasper balled his napkin between his palms and dropped it to the table. "I think what I always liked best about her were the things that reminded me of you."

Sadie felt a little tug at her heart. "Such as?"

"Oh, she was high-strung…stubborn…*totally* high-mainte-nance." He nudged her teasingly, and she slapped him lightly on the arm. He grabbed her fingers in his and held them tightly as he grew serious.

"I couldn't imagine making a home…having children…with anyone else. It was strange. Every time I tried to conjure the image, I kept seeing myself in the front yard, looking down the street, 'cause I always knew that's where you'd be. Just like when we were growing up. And I couldn't be happy where I was even when you were only several doors away."

"You knew that…all along?" she asked.

He shrugged again. "I don't think I knew it consciously. But deep down…" He paused. "Yeah. I think I did."

They were silent for a while, fingers intertwined and their eyes fixed on Kylie as she swung back and forth on the swing-set. Clouds moved sluggishly overhead, and the scent of car fuel and freshly churned ice cream floated by them.

"What about Ned?" Jasper finally asked, his voice soft. "What was it like being married to him?"

Sadie smiled a little wistfully. It didn't escape Jasper's attention. "Like a train wreck and a jet flight all at the same time. I was the train wreck—he was the jet flight."

She laughed lightly at this analogy. "No, it was…exhilarating, at first. And then it was steady. Easy. Comfortable. And when Kylie arrived, there was a rhythm all its own." She swallowed. "The hard-est part was that I felt like I wasted that last year we had. If I had known I'd only have him one more year, I would have dropped the cooking show and pushed back the deadlines for the cookbooks.

Ned took care of things, and then he watched Kylie while I dashed around from here to there, signing contracts, doing interviews and promotion spots, filming...."

Jasper's eyes were intent on her face, but Sadie kept looking at Kylie.

"If I had known how quickly some things end, I think I'd have learned to live in the moment a little more."

She looked at him, and something in his eyes shadowed the doorway of her heart.

"What's wrong?"

"Do you think you could learn...to live in the moment?" he asked her.

Sadie bit her lip. She wasn't really that type of person. No one knew that better than Jasper. She just couldn't be still, be happy. She didn't know what it was to hold an infinitesimal moment in an encapsulated bubble of time to cherish and examine over and over again. She knew what Jasper was asking her.

Could she learn to let go and simply love him without letting every little thing come in between them? Could she avoid making the same mistakes she had made before Ned died?

"I don't know," she finally answered. Because she didn't. It was against her nature, and she didn't know if that could change.

His next question surprised her, however.

"Do you think you want to learn?"

Sadie cocked her head. There was a tug deep inside her, but for what or whom, she didn't know. She didn't answer him this time.

They both settled on watching Kylie and avoiding the rest of the implications this conversation suggested. Sadie's mind continued to churn and foam as they sat there, basking in the fresh, warm breeze and the sound of Kylie's laughter.

After some time, Sadie turned to Jasper once more. "Do you really think I can't make desserts?"

He smiled at her. "Does it really matter to you?"

"Well, *duh*."

"*Should* it matter to you?"

She made a face. "Jasper, this is my *career*. What do you think?"

He looked away. "I think you're already phenomenally good at what you do, and you should stay focused on that instead of trying to be perfect at things you'll probably never be perfect at."

Her eyes narrowed. "So you're saying I'm an awful dessert chef."

"Sadie." His tone was both warning and exasperated.

"I'm just asking!"

"No, what you're doing is beating a dead horse."

"So you're saying my desserts taste like *dead horse*?"

His eyes widened in disbelief. "Sadie, I never—"

There was a slight twinkle in her eyes.

"Are you kidding me, or what?" He wasn't quite sure.

She shrugged. Jasper smiled in contentment and drew her close to press a kiss to her forehead. She leaned against him and didn't push the subject further.

But no matter what she told Jasper, Sadie knew one thing for certain.

Dead horse or not, this was no laughing matter.

Chapter Ten

....

First thing the next morning, Sadie dropped a note of apology in the mailbox to Aunt Matilda before heading into Suncatchers to start the day. The surprise that greeted her as she walked through the back kitchen door caused her heart to stop and then flutter with delight.

Flowers—everywhere. Dahlias, lilies, sunflowers, asters, zinnias, chrysanthemums… And a card lying in the center, in a scented pool of red rose petals. It read only, *"Love, Jasper."* Her heart did several backflips before righting itself with a soul-shuddering quiver.

Jasper Reeves.

She had never known he could be such a romantic, although she supposed the signs had existed all along. Her best friend. And now…more.

So much more.

Sadie's fingers trailed through the river of petals. She scooped one up with her fingertips and brought it to her lips, breathing deeply of the heavy, intoxicating scent.

He loves me.

It was both a realization and a warning. Jasper loved her. Not just as a friend but as a woman. He really did love her.

Sadie nearly gasped with the full force of such a thought. When it settled in the pit of her stomach once more, she felt it clearly—a weight on her system. For reasons she dared not define, it felt nearly like an ache. She swallowed.

"What in the… Did we buy out Hershey Gardens or what?"

Jimmy had just entered through the back door and noted the greenhouse that had seemingly sprung up overnight. Karl pushed past the younger man and came to stand beside her. He glanced down at the note, and his bushy eyebrows raised.

"A regular Don Juan, isn't he?"

Despite the pain in her stomach, Sadie couldn't suppress a smile. "You have no idea."

Jimmy came closer, his eyes round as the plates they served dinner entrees on. "How did these get here, boss?"

Sadie shrugged. "Jasper must have pilfered my keys."

"Dude." Jimmy shook his head. "Wish I'd have thought of something like this."

Karl turned to him. "What—you're planning to woo our employer here?"

If possible, Jimmy's eyes widened further. His gaze darted between the two of them. "What? No, I—it's not like that, boss, I swear! I was thinking of my own girlfriend, Annie." He ducked his head. "We got in a fight a few nights back, and now she's not speaking to me…." His shoulders slumped with despair.

Sadie took several steps over to the grill top and lifted the lavish display of zinnias and roses that rested there. She presented them to Jimmy.

"Here. Give her these. It'll do wonders, I'm sure."

Jimmy positively beamed. "Sweet! Thanks, boss! I owe you one!"

Sadie began gathering the rose petals into a bowl. "You can repay me by helping me get these flowers out onto the tables and then starting the coffee brewing." She smiled happily. "I'm hoping for a large breakfast crowd."

It took Sadie and Jimmy twenty minutes to distribute the wealth of flower arrangements onto the dining room tables. When they finished, the effect was magnificent—a soothing atmosphere of the suncatchers' brilliant, jeweled colors and the flowers' soft, transparent light. Sadie sighed with contentment.

This was what a dining experience should be: ambience, texture, flavor, and comfort.

She touched a hand to the back of a chair and felt a wave of nostalgia wash through her.

"You should see this place now, Mom," she whispered. "You'd love it."

Sadie adored this restaurant. It represented fulfilled dreams and sweet memories, and she couldn't imagine anything better. Life seemed achingly perfect right now, and she suddenly distrusted the reality of it all.

"Hey, boss!" Jimmy hollered from the kitchen. "We're out of coffee."

Sadie sighed. She knew it was too good to last.

Several hours later in the day, the worst of the morning crises had been efficiently avoided. Willow's quick trip to the grocer's had restocked the empty coffee supplies while Sadie made a note to order more of the gourmet variety, and Karl's swift competency had salvaged several of Jimmy's failed dishes.

By afternoon things were back on track, and Sadie's euphoria once more began to rise…until Smith and Jones darkened the doorway of Suncatchers.

Sadie gulped and ran to check the calendar.

Monday. Definitely Monday. Not Tuesday, when they usually came in. And one o'clock instead of their regular hour of twelve noon. What was going on?

They settled themselves at their typical booth, however, and this eased Sadie a small amount, though not by much. And when Willow took their order and they chose the grilled chicken green salad with five-spice potato wedges over their usual turkey-and-spinach panini, Sadie's stomach cramped with nervous anxiety once more.

She couldn't stand it much longer. She approached their table after Willow had delivered their drinks—orange juice for Smith and apple for Jones instead of their customary cups of tea.

"Mrs. Smith, Mrs. Jones…how are you?"

Their beady old eyes targeted her with ill-concealed disdain. What *had* she ever done to earn their malice? She wondered if they were in cahoots with Jasper's aunt Matilda.

"Fine, dear," Smith replied to her inquiry. "And yourself?"

"Oh, I'm just dandy." She stood there expectantly, though they only gave her the once-over—several times.

"We hear you've been seeing that friend of yours," Jones finally remarked.

"Yes, the Reeves boy," Smith added.

Sadie affixed a smile and wondered if maybe she should invest in a set of dentures to keep it in place for when the two old crones came around. Of course, Aunt Matilda would probably take her to court if she found out. "He's hardly a boy anymore," Sadie pointed out, in response to their observations.

"Mmm." A collective acknowledgment that hardly granted their approval.

"He's a nice lad, though," Jones said, more to Smith than to Sadie.

Sadie took that to mean he was too nice for the likes of her.

"So what brings you into Suncatchers this fine day?" She steered their attention back her way.

They looked at her once more as if she were a fly they had failed to successfully squash.

"Lunch, dear," Smith said. "We may be nothing more than skin and bones these days, but I do assure you that we must eat, the same as the next person."

Yeah, probably small children, names of Hansel and Gretel.

Sadie's smile never faltered through this thought. She even managed to force a delighted-sounding laugh. "Oh, you." She wagged a finger in mock amusement.

She was tempted to ask if the pickin's were too slim in the forest since Hansel and Gretel had found their way back home but choked off the rude comment at the last minute.

"Well, please let me know if there's anything I can do for you, ladies."

She turned to go.

"Yes, there is one thing," Jones called to her.

Sadie took a moment to slap the smile back on her face before turning. "Yes?"

Jones held out her untouched glass of juice. "This glass appears to have a smudge. Could you replace it for me?"

Sadie accepted the juice with a smile the size of Montana. "Why, certainly. Anything else?"

Smith shivered and tugged her crocheted shawl closer around her bony shoulders. "It's a tad chilly in here, dear. Do you think you could raise the temperature a bit?"

Sadie ground her back molars together. "I'll look into it."

She whirled without another word, not trusting herself to speak.

Apparently it was the day for unexpected arrivals. Just as Sadie finished delivering a second glass of juice to Jones, Lucinda Lowell, the office secretary from Holy Water Evangelical Church, came staggering through the door.

Now, Sadie was aware of the ill luck seeming to continually hover just on the outskirts of her peripheral vision, but even her own misfortune seemed a trivial thing compared to the downright unlucky streak that plagued Lucinda Lowell.

A woman of perpetual mishaps, Lucinda could not only be described as clumsy but awkward and bungling, as well. She made Jimmy seem like the height of efficiency.

Lucinda was the only woman Sadie had ever pitied.

She entered the room now with a stumble—the heel of her shoe caught in the fine fibers of the doormat. She swayed back and forth several times, clutching the umbrella rack for support, until she managed to disengage herself from the mat.

Or rather, she removed her foot from her shoe and then got down on her knees to pry the cheap suede pump loose.

Sadie winced. Poor woman.

When an insistent tug finally freed the shoe, it was released with such force that the shoe came back and socked Lucinda squarely in the face. She gasped and rubbed furiously as her nose glowed a Rudolph-worthy crimson.

Sadie didn't know whether to laugh or to cry for her. She decided simply to offer her assistance instead and hurried over to support Lucinda as she struggled to her feet. The rest of the restaurant slowly returned to their meals as Lucinda smiled breathlessly at Sadie.

"Thanks."

"No problem." She guided Lucinda toward the counter. "Here, take a seat."

Lucinda sank into it with an offending squeak that Sadie was positive had come from the chair but sounded suspiciously as though it had come from Lucinda herself.

"Don't worry about it," Sadie soothed her, as Lucinda's cheeks flamed to match her nose.

"It wasn't—"

"I know."

Lucinda sighed. Her frizzy dark hair stood straight up on her head and persistently reminded Sadie of the bride of Frankenstein. She shoved her thick, black-framed glasses higher on her still-pink nose.

"Would you like something to drink?" Sadie offered.

"Yes, please. A water would be fine."

"One water, coming right up." Sadie stepped behind the counter and filled a glass. She remained behind the counter as she deposited it in front of Lucinda.

"Is there something I can help you with, Lucinda?" Sadie asked, curious. Although Lucinda visited Suncatchers on a fairly steady basis, she rarely showed up for the lunch hour.

The other woman took a long drink of water. "Thanks." She pushed her glasses upward again.

Lucinda swigged her water again, accidentally dribbling several drops against her blouse. Sadie wordlessly handed her a napkin. As Lucinda dabbed at the water spots, she answered, "I'm having a luncheon meeting with Mrs. Smith and Mrs. Jones."

Sadie's eyebrows rose by several notches. What could Lucinda Lowell possibly have to do with Smith and Jones?

As if she had spoken the question aloud, Lucinda offered, "They're on the committee for the community fair this year. They're helping me plan the Cocoa Cook-Off competition."

"Cocoa Cook-Off?"

Lucinda nodded. "It's new this year, but the committee wants to make it an annual thing. A chocolate-themed competition—with first, second, and third prizes."

Lucinda balled up the napkin and dropped it on the counter. Inspiration suddenly seemed to strike her, and she jumped to her feet. "Hey! You're a chef! You should enter!"

Sadie hesitated. Clearly, Lucinda was unfamiliar with her dessert repertoire. She shrugged and picked up the napkin, depositing it in the wastebasket at her feet.

"Oh, I don't know…. Things have been so busy lately…."

The nonchalance in her words didn't match the way her heart hammered inside her. A dessert competition… The very thought of it made her teeth clench. But this was her chance! Her chance to prove herself worthy in the final stage of the cooking arena! To show all of her peers—and especially herself—that there was no task too great for her to overcome.

And just as she opened her mouth to say, "I'll do it!" Jasper's words from the day before pulsed through her.

"I think you're already phenomenally good at what you do, and you should stay focused on that instead of trying to be perfect at things you'll probably never be perfect at."

Sadie swallowed. *What are You saying, God? That I shouldn't do this?*

But why in the world not? She could conquer this thing—this one fatal flaw in her ability. She could make it right.... She knew she could.

And yet something told her not to.

"You can't always be the best, Sadie. You can be good—really good. Maybe you can win a few...but you can't win them all. Be content with what you're good at and let the rest go. It's only food."

Jasper again.

Oh, what does he know? a tiny voice snapped.

"Me," Sadie whispered. "He knows me."

"What?"

Sadie jerked to attention. "Oh. Sorry." She drew a deep breath. "I'm really sorry, Lucinda, but I can't."

Lucinda's eyes registered surprise. "But—but—why not?"

Sadie forced the words out. "I'm afraid desserts just aren't something I'm very good at. *Any* kind of desserts—cookies, pies, cakes, puddings, tarts, you name it. It's just not my gift."

Lucinda looked crushed.

"I'm sure you'll still have *loads* of people sign up," Sadie encouraged. "Really. But as for me...well, I just...can't."

Inwardly, she sighed.

Lucinda nodded, though she was clearly disappointed. "I understand."

Sadie awkwardly patted her arm. "It'll still be terrific. You'll see."

Lucinda managed a dejected smile. "Sure. I'm sure it will."

She stood to go, knocking over her water glass as she rose. Liquid washed across the countertop and over the hem of Sadie's blouse.

"Oh! Oh, I'm sorry! I didn't mean—I—Oh!"

Sadie held up a hand. "It's all right." She grabbed a dish towel and mopped at her shirt. Raising her head, she smiled at Lucinda. "Really. It is."

Despite her own disappointment, Sadie felt really good about herself. She'd done it! She had stared her shortcomings in the face and decided not to be ruled by them. She couldn't wait to tell Jasper.

She finished wiping down the counter and raised her head to check on Lucinda. Her eyes widened at what she saw.

Jones had slipped out of the booth to meet Lucinda and was practically dragging her by force back to the table. But it was the other occupants of the booth that arrested Sadie's attention.

For there, under the display of butterfly suncatchers, sat Dmitri Velichko, leaning in politely to catch what Smith was saying to him.

Sadie's jaw dropped. *What in the—*

She should have known those two would pull him into this. Well, it simply was not something to be borne. How could she, Sadie Spencer, in all good conscience, allow her archrival, Dmitri Velichko, to get the better of her at her own town's dessert competition? She'd never be able to live it down.

Clenching her jaw, she flung the towel onto the counter. No *way* was she missing this. She made a beeline for that booth.

"…hear you're a *delightful* chef, Mr. Velichko," Smith gushed.

And with those few words, Sadie made up her mind. She towered above the foursome at the table, her flaming brown eyes silencing whatever conversation might have arisen next.

"Lucinda? I changed my mind." She glared at Dmitri. "I'll do it."

* * * * *

Jasper and Kylie were cooking…with Sadie's help.

"Now combine the cheese, eggs, and milk."

Kylie dumped the three items into the mixing bowl under Jasper's watchful eye. "Okay, Mommy. Now what?"

The little girl looked up. Jasper held the bowl steady on the counter.

"She can't hear you, Kylie."

Sadie's face smiled brightly from the glow of the television screen. "I have to take one more commercial break, but when I come back, we'll get this quiche in the oven!"

Kylie shrugged her shoulders at Jasper. "Kylie knows."

It seemed to be no problem for Kylie—communicating with her mother through the filter of the TV set. A minor blip flipped through the screen—evidence of bypassed commercials—and then the theme song chimed once more.

Kylie hummed along, running a spoon through the egg mixture.

"Welcome back to Comfort Cuisine. If you're just joining us, what we're cooking up today is a simple but delicious cheddar quiche. The thing that's great about this dish is that it's so fast and easy. If the in-laws unexpectedly drop in, it's the simplest thing in the world to just throw together a few ingredients and come up with this scrumptious meal. It's practically foolproof."

Jasper felt his heart flutter as the on-screen Sadie winked for the camera. He wasn't entirely sure why Sadie's cooking show had failed. He'd found the food practical but tasty (at least the few recipes he'd tried were), and who could resist Sadie's adorable smile week after week? Frankly, Jasper thought she deserved an Emmy.… Did they give Emmys for cooking shows? He shrugged.

"Now we're going to add a bit of seasoning to really accentuate that cheesy quiche flavor…."

Kylie stood with her tiny hands at the ready.

"First, take a pinch of salt."

Kylie shook the salt shaker over the counter and then pinched a minuscule amount between her fingers. She mimicked Sadie's movements as she sprinkled salt into the dish.

"Now for some of that parsley I mentioned earlier…"

As Kylie reached for the dish of parsley Jasper had chopped—there was the "no-knives" rule for Kylie, of course—the sound of the front door opening and closing could be heard. Kylie looked up briefly but then hurried to catch up with the cooking show as Sadie moved from parsley to paprika.

The real-life Sadie swept into the kitchen seconds later.

"Hey, you're home early," Jasper remarked, with one eye on Kylie's ingredient-tossing.

Sadie didn't seem to hear him. She threw her bag to the floor with a *thud* and jerked open the refrigerator door. Jasper raised his eyebrows. Kylie continued to follow along to cooking-show Sadie.

"I need the kitchen," Sadie announced, her upper torso hidden by the refrigerator.

Jasper frowned. "Sure, as soon as Kylie and I finish making dinner, then you can—"

"Now." Sadie emerged. "I need it *now*."

Even Kylie paid attention, upon hearing the strain in her mother's voice.

"What's going on?" Jasper asked. "Did the kitchen burn down at the restaurant or what?"

Her eyes flared hotter than a bottle of Tabasco. "Not funny, Jasper. Simply…not…funny."

"What's the emergency? Can't you see you're teaching your daughter to cook?" He gestured to the television set he had hooked up in the corner of the kitchen.

Kylie pointed. "That's you, Mommy!"

Sadie stiffened as she noticed the television, and Jasper knew he'd made some sort of mistake. He just wasn't sure what it was.

"I see that, baby. Now, can you do me a favor and go upstairs by my bed and bring me the cookbook on top of the nightstand?"

Kylie scrambled off her stool. "The one with the yummy brownies on the front?"

"That's the one."

"Kylie will get it!"

She thundered from the kitchen, and then Sadie turned on Jasper with lightning in her eyes.

"What are you *doing*?" she snapped.

Jasper suppressed the urge to roll his eyes at her dramatics. "Cooking. Or do you have exclusive rights to that pastime?"

Sadie waved her hand toward the television screen where her other self smiled dazzlingly, hardly breaking a sweat. "I barely remember that woman—five years younger and fearless in the face of pressure." She glared at her TV persona. "I *don't* need you parading my failure before my daughter's eyes. That's hardly the life lesson I want her to learn."

Despite his attempts to hold it up, Jasper's jaw dropped. "What? You call that failure? Sadie, you hosted your own cooking show on national television! I'd hardly call that a reason to be ashamed."

Sadie made a weak attempt to straighten her spine and hold

her chin up high. "I'm *not* ashamed. But I don't want Kylie knowing about—about—you know."

"What?"

Sadie clenched her jaw and then released it. "About how hard it is to hold onto your dreams in this world. About how just when you think you've achieved something, something happens or someone comes to take it away from you!"

"Ahh." Jasper crossed his arms over his chest. "So that's what this is about."

Her eyes spit sparks at him. "About what?"

"Dmitri Velichko."

Apparently he had hit the mark, because Sadie's face flamed the exact shade of red that comes from pickling beets. However, she did not seem to be willing to admit that.

"What does *he* have to do with it?" she demanded loudly.

Kylie scampered back into the kitchen at that moment, a large cookbook balanced on her head.

"Kylie brought the cookbook," she sang.

Sadie seethed as Kylie deposited the book onto a chair.

"Kylie, go upstairs and color your number pages," Jasper commanded, his eyes never leaving Sadie's. Jasper did his best to keep Kylie in practice over summer vacation by presenting her with daily learning pages.

Kylie pouted. "But you said Kylie could finish them *after* dinner."

"*Now*, Kylie."

Jasper rarely used that disciplining tone with Kylie. She immediately left the room, and, seconds later, they heard her soft footfalls up the stairs.

"What happened?" Jasper demanded.

Sadie wouldn't look at him. She reached for the cookbook and began flipping through it with such fury that several of the sheets ripped from the force of each turn of the page.

"Nothing."

"*Sadie.*"

She glanced up. "There's a dessert competition at the community fair this year. Some annual thing they're starting called the Cocoa Cook-Off."

He licked his lips. "I know."

"And you didn't tell me!" Her cheeks flared all over again.

"I didn't want you to flip out. I can see I made the right move."

She waved a hand. "I'm not flipping out. I just need to start practicing."

Jasper cocked his head but remained silent. Sadie didn't say anything more at first. He could see her struggling, her fingers trembling as she flipped through the cookbook. He was fairly certain she hadn't really looked at a single recipe yet.

"They've convinced Dmitri Velichko to enter," she finally admitted with a quivering note to her syllables.

Jasper gentled his tone. "First of all, who is 'they'?"

"Lucinda Lowell."

"Lucinda?"

Sadie nodded.

"Why would Lucinda ask Dmitri? I don't think she's ever even met him."

"Well, she did today." Sadie's tone rang bitter.

"How? When?"

"At Suncatchers. Smith and Jones made the introductions. I think they planned the whole thing."

"Sadie. They're two harmless old ladies."

Sadie's head snapped up. "They *are not*. You don't understand! They *want* to see me fail!"

Jasper fell silent, chewing on his lip as he studied the woman before him. Was she paranoid? Or did her anxieties have an echo of justification to them?

"So what did you do?" he asked.

"I told Lucinda I planned to enter the competition."

Jasper swallowed. "You what?"

She couldn't meet his eyes. "I tried, Jasper, I really did. I turned her down at first. And then when Smith and Jones started interfering, well, I just couldn't let this opportunity slip away."

Another long pause dragged between them as Jasper contemplated this. At last he tentatively said, "You do know this is a *dessert* competition, don't you?"

Her reply was meekness itself. She ducked her head and softly answered, "I know."

"And you do remember what happened with Aunt Matilda, don't you?"

Her glare answered that one. "They were just *cookies*, Jasper. That's different."

He sighed. "I want you to be happy, Sadie. Do you really think this will be enough?"

She looked away from him and came face-to-face with the perky, on-screen version of herself. Jasper had lowered the volume when Kylie went to get the cookbook, so there was only a soft hum to indicate Sadie's instructional dialogue.

"You don't understand. This is my shot, Jas. I can do this. It's now or never."

He didn't want to argue with her. He never wanted to argue with her. He just wanted her to understand that if she couldn't be happy without a certain thing then perhaps she couldn't be happy *with* it, either. Perhaps her happiness hinged less on her own personal skill and more on the gifts God had given to her.

He shook his head. "What do you need me to do?"

Sadie leaped to her feet with a grin and threw her arms around him. "Fix Kylie some dinner and then keep her occupied while I do some practicing."

She pulled back and placed her palms on his cheeks. "Then maybe some taste testing?"

His stomach recoiled at the thought, but he nodded bravely.

"And I may need you to do a grocery run for ingredients."

"Whatever you need," he said.

Before she could rush off, he placed his palms on her neck, his thumbs brushing against her jawline.

"Sadie…I love you. You know that, don't you? That no matter how wonderful or how bad your food is…I love you just the same?"

A flickering fire in her eyes worried him.

"Sure, Jasper. I know that. I love you too."

Her reply had been too flippant.

"Did you…" He felt foolish bringing it up. "Did you get the flowers?"

An honest joy crossed her face. "I did. They were beautiful. Thank you." She planted a kiss against his cheek and offered nothing more. He knew she was eager to get started.

He released her, and she immediately began clearing away the remains of his and Kylie's cooking lesson. He took the mixing bowl from her, his fingers brushing hers.

"You can't make yourself any better to me than you already are, Sadie."

She forced a bright smile that didn't quite light her eyes. "I know that."

Jasper didn't really think she did.

Chapter Eleven

. . . .

It was impossible to say how many hours Sadie devoted to perfecting her recipe for the community fair competition. If it couldn't be measured in hours, though, Jasper thought later that it could certainly be measured by degrees of catastrophe—both inside the kitchen and out. Sadie's sole attention and purpose became focused on chocolate. While in many situations this might have led to heady smells and mouthwatering taste tests, in Sadie's case, it translated to bitter samples, sour expressions, and smoke alarms ringing all hours of the day and into the night as dessert after dessert sacrificed itself to the altar of Sadie's obsession.

Two weeks after Sadie's sign-up for the competition, both Jasper and Kylie were at wit's end with her and found themselves avoiding the kitchen at all costs. Unfortunately for Jasper, Kylie was able to manage this much easier than he could. When the phone rang at the Spencer household, Jasper was inevitably forced to answer, and when the caller asked for Sadie, he was then obliged to penetrate the off-limits sanctity of the kitchen to tell Sadie she had a call.

Countless times it seemed he stuck his head around the corner, one eye nearly closed with wariness, to announce the latest intrusion. On one such occasion, Sadie actually threw a spatula at his head following the pronouncement. He ducked and retreated, returning to the phone to inform the caller that they must have the wrong number.

But even worse than the spatula incident was when he had to start telling Belva—Ned's mother and Sadie's mother-in-law—that Sadie would not come to the phone. At first, Belva contented herself with speaking to Kylie. Living in Alabama, Ned's childhood home, Belva didn't get to see Sadie nor her granddaughter nearly as much as she wished, but throughout Sadie and Ned's marriage and even following her son's death, she had made it a point to keep in regular contact with Sadie and the family. And although Sadie had never been especially close with her mother-in-law, she did love Belva and was never too busy to talk with her about the everyday happenings she was missing out on.

Until now, that is. And Jasper hated the position Sadie had put him in, having to explain to Belva nearly every day that he was sorry but Sadie couldn't drop what she was doing to come to the phone just now.

After several days of this pat answer, Belva finally asked him in a suspicious Southern drawl, "Is it just me, sugar, or is something going on up there? Either Sadie dear is avoiding me or you've murdered her and disposed of the body."

"No, no, it's nothing like that," Jasper hastened to explain. "It's just this dessert competition she's preparing for, and all the practicing doesn't leave her much free time."

Belva clucked her tongue. "Competition? I thought she had her hands full running the restaurant."

Jasper swallowed. Truthfully, Belva had hit on one of his own major concerns at the moment. Sadie had shoved virtually every aspect of managing the restaurant into her night manager's hands, forcing Glynda to work double shifts nearly every day of the week. And while

Glynda seemed more than up to the task, Jasper didn't suppose she could go on that way forever.

But then, he didn't see how Sadie could go on like this much longer, either.

"Mrs. Spencer—"

"Call me Belva, sugar."

Despite how harried he felt, Jasper smiled. He had only met Belva on a handful of occasions—Sadie's wedding and Ned's funeral being two of the major ones—but he had always liked her warm Southern drawl and constantly amused tone.

"Belva…you know how Sadie can sometimes be…well…what's the word…?"

"Neurotically fixated?" Belva offered.

Jasper paused and nodded his head and then realized that Belva couldn't see it. "I was going to go with 'obsessed,' but that works too."

Jasper imagined Belva waving a hand with genteel Southern dismissal as she said, "Oh, sugar, don't you worry none about all that—Sadie's always been obsessive, for as long as I've known her. But she's a sweetheart—she'll be back to her old self soon enough."

Jasper swallowed and hesitated, his voice dropping several degrees. "I know, Belva. I've known Sadie my whole life, but this—this is different. It's getting worse, not better. It's…"

The smoke alarm whizzed into action with a series of ear-piercing shrieks. Jasper clenched his jaw and stifled a groan. He might as well just remove the batteries and put them away until the Cocoa Cook-Off was over. It was the only way they'd get more than thirty minutes of peace at a time.

"I've gotta go, Belva," Jasper shouted over the din of the smoke alarm. He faintly heard Sadie in the kitchen, talking in angry tones to the oven as faint wisps of smoke stole down the hallway. "I'll have Kylie call you tomorrow!"

Jasper didn't catch Belva's good-bye save for her placating "Bye now, sugar" as he pulled the phone away from his ear. He dropped the receiver into the cradle and ran for the kitchen, determined to take his frustration out on the wild screeches of the smoke alarm.

* * * * *

Despite Belva's optimistic predictions, Sadie's obsession did not burn out over the next week. As Jasper had stated, things only grew worse… until he began to fear he'd never see Sadie—nor her kitchen—returned to a state of semi-normalcy ever again.

The days became a blur of runs to the grocery store, depositing Sadie's requested ingredients onto the counter, and then being shooed out of the room to amuse himself and Kylie until well after midnight, when Sadie would at last emerge, kiss him good night, and stumble up the stairs to her bedroom for a brief rest. He would return to his own house to fall into an exhausted slumber for a few hours before rising, showering, and driving back to Sadie's to begin the entire routine all over again.

The phone calls piled up, countless failed recipes overflowed from the trash, and Kylie asked Jasper several times when they were going to start seeing Mommy again. But each time he hoped Sadie might relent, something would set her off once more and she'd start baking from scratch in an effort to conquer what seemed to be the impossible. The nearer they drew to the day of the competition, the worse her moods became until Jasper finally just stopped answering the phone and popping into the kitchen to check on her. He felt as if they were on the Great Bear roller coaster at Hersheypark, just holding on with all their might and praying that the ride might be over soon.

When Mac braved a visit one night, he unknowingly provided Jasper and Kylie with a much-needed taste-testing respite. Sadie spooned three different chocolate puddings onto his palate and then forced a cocoa cream puff down his throat. He winced when her back was turned but wisely mumbled, "I think you might have something there," when asked how her recipes measured up.

Upon emerging from the scene of destruction, he calmly asked Jasper for a bottle of Mylanta and spent the remainder of the evening watching TV with Kylie and dividing his time between the Mylanta and a roll of Mentos to attempt to clear the taste from his mouth.

With Kylie engaged by her grandfather, Jasper was left free and without excuse not to answer the phone, although he cringed with every ring that sounded. For the most part, he screened the calls as best he could; unless it was someone from the restaurant, he made his apologies and declined to disturb Sadie in the kitchen. But when Lucinda Lowell called concerning the details for Sadie's entry in the competition that weekend, Jasper knew he had to steel himself for a visit to the kitchen. He politely asked Lucinda to hold, drew a deep breath and, as the theme song to *The Swan Princess* built to a crescendo in the other room, entered Sadie's domain.

She stood at the counter with her hands in a mixing bowl, up to her elbows in chocolate glaze. A coating of confectioner's sugar lay so thickly on her head she looked as though she'd gone prematurely gray. The kitchen counters were splattered with a variety of cocoa-brown splotches in varying states of congealed puddles. The mixer, a host of ingredients, and nearly every piece of cookware Sadie owned lay strewn about, and in a mound of crumpled paper around the waste bin were the remains of failed recipes from the week's experimentation.

Sadie didn't look up as he entered the room but continued to whip the glaze in the mixing bowl. Jasper cleared his throat, to no avail. Sadie's lips were moving in silent calculation, but the only sound was the rattle of the bowl as it rolled against the counter from the force of her movements.

"Sadie?"

She was oblivious to his interruption. He coughed, bit his lip, debated whether to return to take a message from Lucinda, and then figured he'd try again.

"Umm…Sadie? There's a telephone call for you."

Her head shot up in sudden attention, like a lion smelling prey nearby. Jasper, having never been a very big fan of the Discovery Channel, wished he had left well enough alone. He didn't like the feral gleam in Sadie's eye.

"*What*…did you say?"

He knew then that breaking her concentration was the worst mistake he could have made. He shuffled his feet, ran a worried hand through his perpetually disheveled hair, and then dug his fists deep into the pockets of his jeans.

"Uh…telephone's for you?" He offered it as though it were the answer to a quiz question, and he had a fleeting appreciation for what his fifth-grade class felt when he called one of them to answer a tough question on the spot.

Fortunately for his students, he never reacted with the response Sadie fired at him now. She exploded like one of her desserts from the oven.

"How many times do I have to say it? *Absolutely, positively,* no *unnecessary interruptions!*" She threw the entire bowl of glaze she'd been working on—spatula, whisk, and all—into the sink.

Jasper realized then how poorly timed his intrusion really was. Lucinda had called right in the midst of another dessert disaster.

"This is my life's work at stake!" she continued to rant. "And the entire world has suddenly chosen *this week* to lob itself at my door-step!"

She raised a sugar-coated finger and pointed at him with all the chilling haughtiness of Martha Stewart on a bad day. He felt very much as though he deserved to be flushed down the volcano along with Malibu Ken's leg. "And *you!* Jasper, of all people, *you* should know better! I would have thought *you* could understand how im-portant this is to me!"

He sighed but didn't interrupt. At least he knew that much.

"I simply cannot accept any interruptions at this crucial stage—the competition is this weekend...*this weekend*, Jasper! Now get back in there"—her finger shifted to the door—"and *take...a...message*."

Jasper ducked out without even offering an apology. It was like *Chefs Gone Wild*. If he had taped the entire thing, he could have at least sold the past three weeks as a viable reality series. He was sure of it.

Returning to the hall, he noticed that the television had fallen silent. He hoped to high heaven Mac had removed Kylie from the room so she hadn't been forced to listen to Attila the Pastry Chef in there. It was as if they'd been treated to a real-life reenactment of *Saving Private Ryan*. He prayed it hadn't carried through the telephone receiver.

Jasper picked it up and cleared his throat.

"Uh, Lucinda? Yeah, Sadie can't come to the phone right now. Perhaps you could give me the details of where she needs to take her entry, and I…uh…can get back to you on…um…what type of dessert she's going to be making."

As Jasper scribbled down Lucinda's instructions, he repeated what she said. He knew that if he valued his life then he needed to copy down the words verbatim. Over the course of his conversation, he became vaguely aware that things had grown deathly silent in the kitchen. Studying his handwritten notes, he tried to ignore his feeling of dread as he read back to Lucinda, "Take her entry to the church's fellowship hall kitchen."

"JASPER!"

Sadie's indignant yelp startled him so much he dropped the phone. It clattered to the hardwood floor with a rattle, and Sadie yelped again in dismay.

"Why didn't you tell me it was about the competition?"

Her words were a stage whisper, but the fury in them was clear. He was beginning to feel like one of those sad desserts he'd been catching glimpses of all week—deflated, bitter, and scorched. The desserts couldn't do anything right, and neither could he.

Sadie rescued the phone, miraculously intact, and as Lucinda's concerned, "Hello? Jasper, are you there?" came through the receiver, Sadie gave Jasper a glare so sharp that it felt like Furi knives slicing him to paper-fine strips.

But when Sadie spoke into the phone, her voice was the stuff of angel food cake: soft, sweet, and light.

"Lucinda? It's Sadie. So sorry about that—Jasper failed to tell me it was you."

Another knife-slashing glance.

"...phone dropped, yes. So, anyway, you were saying?"

As Sadie took down the details herself this time, Jasper stood to the side, arms folded and eyes narrowed. Sadie scribbled Lucinda's instructions down furiously, completely oblivious to Jasper's expression.

When the phone was laid to rest in the cradle once more, she stared at the notes she had written for such an inestimable length of time that Jasper's frustration slowly ebbed to a soft pricking and not the piercing gash it had been several moments before.

He watched as Sadie raised a palm to shield her eyes, as though by blocking out Lucinda's message she could erase the strain the past few weeks had cost her. Jasper's frustration melted completely at the sight, and he quickly stepped forward to lay his hands on her shoulders. She jerked in surprise and glanced at him. She hadn't even known he'd been standing there all this time.

"Oh," she softly muttered. He worked his fingers into her shoulder blades, his pity swelling even more as he felt the mounds of knots pinching her nerves.

She sighed happily and dropped her chin to her chest to signal that he could continue for as long as he desired. He worked out a few kinks, mentally made a note to buy Sadie a gift certificate to the Hershey Hotel's Chocolate Spa for her next birthday, and then wrapped his arms around her waist from behind, tucking her firmly against him.

She kept her head lowered as he nuzzled her neck.

"So tired…," she mumbled sleepily and then dispelled a massive yawn.

"You've been working hard," he murmured, before planting a row of kisses behind her ear. She shivered a little.

"I just can't get it right," she spoke more to herself than to him.

"You will," he recklessly stated, at the moment far more interested in the curve of her jawline than the sampling of desserts that had passed through the kitchen.

"You don't know that," she declared somewhat snappishly.

"Sure," he whispered distractedly, "you'll get it right. And if not, what's it matter? It's only dessert…."

Had he been in a more cognizant state of mind, Jasper would have been fully aware of what he was saying. But tempted by Sadie's warmth and the tangy taste of the perspiration along her forehead mingling with the sweet layer of confectioner's sugar, he wasn't paying complete attention.

"It's only dessert?"

"Mmm-hmm," he mumbled as he continued to press his lips along her hairline.

"*Only dessert?*"

"Not that important at all," he foolishly replied, as he marveled at the softness of her skin. He was in the midst of contemplating what sort of flavor of truffle Sadie might be, were she in fact a candy and not a flesh-and-blood woman, when the next thing he knew, the phone's message pad was slammed against his ear with resounding force.

"It is *not* just a competition! Don't you get it?"

Jasper took a step back, rubbed his ear, and desperately tried to cast his mind backward over the last three minutes to figure out what he'd said to put the savage glitter back in Sadie's eyes.

"No, I do, Sadie—I do get it! I know how important this is to you…." He stretched out his arm in reconciliation. She slapped it away.

"You just said it wasn't important at all!"

"I did?" He bit the inside of his cheek. It did sound familiar— something about importance when he was really thinking just how important it was that Sadie had such sweet-tasting ears. He winced as her words sank in. "I didn't mean it wasn't important…not exactly, anyway…but Sadie…"

Whoa, boy. It was probably just sugar, but it looked as though steam were puffing out her ears.

"There *is* the matter of priorities," he gently protested in his defense.

Wow. He didn't know her nostrils could flare like that.

A long, deafening silence stretched between them. To his horror, Jasper watched as tears filled Sadie's eyes.

"You don't think I can do it, do you?" she sniffled.

"Sadie," Jasper softly pleaded, "you know that's not what I meant."

She hiccupped and ran a palm against her cheek, catching the droplets that flowed from her eyes and creating a sticky paste of sugar and water against her skin.

"Why doesn't anyone believe in me?" she questioned, more to herself than to him.

"Aw, Sadie…" He stepped forward, his own frustration forgotten in the face of her vulnerability. "Come here."

She didn't hesitate stepping into the warmth of his embrace, burying her face in his chest, and leaving several sugary imprints against his T-shirt.

"Shh," he soothed, as he ran his hands over her smooth hair. "It'll be all right," he consoled.

She dug her face in deeper, and he briefly wondered how she could breathe.

"You've just been totally stressed out the last few weeks," he excused her.

"Butter half tu-tu dis," she protested to his chest.

He wrapped his hands gently around her shoulders and drew her back a little so that her mouth was free to speak.

"Run that by me again."

Her brown eyes swam with desperation. "But I have to do this," she repeated, this time in distinct tones. She leaned forward once more, this time resting her cheek against his chest.

He didn't understand why the dessert thing was so important to her, but he accepted it. At the same time, he didn't know how to help her past her desperate attempts to be something she was not meant to be. If loving her unconditionally wasn't enough, then what was?

She melted against him in slow degrees. The television had started humming once more in the other room, and Jasper recognized the theme song to one of Kylie's favorite cartoons. Sadie sighed, and he sensed she might finally be relaxing. He stroked his fingers up and down her back to calm her and hoped it was having the proper effect.

After a while he thought maybe now was the time to broach a subject that had lain heavily on him for the past couple of weeks. He had received a phone call weeks ago, something that could change everything for him and for Sadie, but up until now, he had found no opportune time to share his news with her. He could hardly compete with the smoke alarm or homemade chocolate icing, not in Sadie's world anyway.

But with Sadie tucked tightly against him and the competition momentarily forgotten, perhaps he could hope for some measure of rationality when he announced his news to her.

"Listen, Sadie…there's something I've been meaning to tell you."

She snuggled closer, wrapping her arms around his waist and sighing contentedly. He felt a small trickle of relief at this.

"Now, before you jump to conclusions, I just want you to know that nothing has been decided yet. There's still plenty of time for us to weigh the options and make a decision."

Sadie swayed a little on her feet, and he hoped she wasn't so exhausted she'd fall asleep on him.

"The truth is, I'm not really sure how I feel about it, but…well… I might as well just go ahead and tell you."

He felt a wave of apprehension and hoped Sadie wouldn't blow things out of proportion. She was humming ever so slightly beneath her breath as she continued to slowly sway in his arms.

"I received a phone call the other day, and it gave me mixed emotions."

He hadn't expected the introduction to his announcement to grip her by such surprise, but apparently it did. She stopped swaying and pulled back, her eyes wide.

"What did you say?"

His eyebrows drew together in confusion. "I didn't say anything yet…well, not really. Not what I meant to say, that is."

"No, before that," she pressed.

"Before what?" He was completely baffled.

"Something about emotions," she prompted.

He frowned. "Mixed emotions? The call gave me mixed emotions?"

"That's it!" She snapped her fingers, her eyes lighting with that wild gleam again. "Mixed! Of course! Why haven't I tried that already? A *mixed-berry compote*! In a chocolate trifle!" she added as his face still registered confusion.

A prick of annoyance dug into him. "Sadie, can we please forget the desserts for a minute?"

"Raspberry and peaches! Or strawberry and cherry! Huckleberry and blueberry!" She spun around at the very idea, and then her eyes widened again as a new thought struck. "*What if* we placed *different* flavors in every layer? Like those candles you see in the craft shops? A peach base with a raspberry middle and blueberry on top! Or wait!" She held out a hand to silence him although he hadn't even been trying to continue. "Maybe bananas followed by strawberries and then the blueberry? Like a red, white, and blue theme!"

"Sadie," Jasper pleaded, his tone much quieter than it had been, "I really have to tell you this. *Now*." He didn't think he could wait another week to share his news. And at the rate Sadie was going, Sara Lee herself couldn't schedule an appointment. The competition was still several days away, and as long as it lingered on the horizon, it seemed he'd never get a chance to have a heart-to-heart with her. "Please?"

But Sadie's eyes were all scrunched up, and he recognized the signs of her visualizing the steps for the recipe and composing the trifle layers in her head.

She did another twirl and whirled herself right into Jasper's arms, pecking him on the cheek. "I've finally got it, Jas! This one *can't* go wrong!"

Still humming under her breath, she danced back into the kitchen, leaving a forlorn and disappointed Jasper staring after her. With Sadie determined to compete, he didn't see how he ever could.

He sank down onto the hall steps and sighed. Mac entered the room with two cans of cola in his hands. He must have snuck them into the house in his coat pocket, since Sadie didn't generally allow soda around. If it could corrode a penny, she didn't want to begin to consider what it did to a five-year-old's gastrointestinal tract.

"Still no luck?" Mac asked with sympathy as he handed over one of the cans.

Jasper popped the tab with a weary sigh and shook his head.

"I don't know how much longer this can go on, Mac."

Mac settled himself beside Jasper on the steps. Kylie's cartoon continued to play in the other room, keeping her contentedly occupied for the time being.

"Are you talking about Sadie…or yourself?"

Jasper dropped his head. "I don't really know."

Mac paused for a moment. "Have you prayed about it?" he asked at last.

Jasper scoffed, though it wasn't really out of scorn. It was still an adjustment—hearing Mac mention spiritual things. But it was a habit he was growing to enjoy. Tonight, though, he just didn't have much spiritual energy in him.

"Yeah, absolutely," Jasper responded in an effort to be more conciliatory. "It just seems like God's holding the ball on this one rather than sharing it with the team."

Mac nodded with an expression of such complete understanding that Jasper felt a great relief. The feeling caused him to open up a little more.

"I'm just so…" He paused to gather his thoughts. "I'm so afraid of losing her, Mac. But if she's always going to be like this, I don't see how I can ever keep her. She likes to think of herself as totally independent, not needing anyone. No offense, but I think that's partly because of your not being around when she was younger."

Mac dropped his head in acknowledgment but did not appear offended.

"But it's not like it's just your fault. I mean, there's Ned's accident and Amelia's death, and in some ways, I don't blame her for not wanting to rely on anybody else."

"But she does, son," Mac cut in. "She relies on you more than either of you realize. She always has."

Jasper fell silent at these words, analyzing the truth of them. He didn't voice his thoughts aloud, however, when he continued. "I have to tell her about that phone call," he determined, "but what'll I do if she… What if she thinks…" He couldn't go on with scenarios too dreadful to think about.

"She'll know you love her," Mac assured. "That'll count for something."

"Yeah," Jasper admitted, "but I'm really not sure if it'll be enough."

To add to his apprehension, Mac didn't disagree with him.

Chapter Twelve

....

Jasper made several attempts throughout the remainder of the week to tell Sadie his news, but each time, his announcement was foiled by her preoccupation with the Cocoa Cook-Off competition. His nerves began to stretch nearly as taut as hers over the dessert distractions, the added responsibility of full-time care of Kylie, and the occasional conversation with Glynda regarding the restaurant. No wonder Sadie lived in a nearly perpetual state of agitation. He'd thought several times over the last few days that he'd lose his mind completely if he had to constantly put up with such pressure.

But the strain bearing on him the heaviest was the knowledge that Sadie must be told, one way or another, what was going on, and he didn't have the faintest clue how to break the news to her. In a rational world, it needn't be such a dramatic moment, but Sadie's outlook was anything but rational. And he knew, as surely as he knew how disastrously the Cocoa Cook-Off was fated to turn out, that Sadie would see his news as the inevitability she had known would eventually come.

Uneasiness left him feeling slightly queasy as the Saturday morning of the community fair and dessert competition dawned flawlessly sunny and bright over Hershey. He picked up a cup of coffee at the gas station before driving over to Sadie's to help load Kylie and Sadie's dessert into the Nova.

Sadie's constant agitation of the past few weeks had mellowed into a rather sickening silence as Jasper carefully laid her dessert entry on the backseat. She bit her lip and wiped several beads of perspiration from her temple before breathlessly suggesting that perhaps she should sit in the back and Kylie could have the front this time around.

Kylie had no problems with this. She had informed him the day before that she'd be happy when Mommy was herself again, which indicated how thin her five-year-old patience had grown. Jasper couldn't blame her. At this point, he too would have liked nothing better than to have Sadie back in place of the harried madwoman who only *looked* like his best friend.

The drive to the church was tense and quiet as Sadie guarded the backseat with all the possessiveness of a lioness while Jasper and Kylie exchanged "Oh boy" looks in the front. They knew better than to indulge in sing-alongs or banal chatter at such a crucial stage of the game.

The parking lot was already one-third full when they pulled up beside the church, a fact that caused Sadie to mutter ominously but unintelligibly from the backseat. As Jasper turned the car toward the front of the building, he spotted Mac's pickup sitting nearby. Sadie's father was leaning against the door with his face upturned to the warm sunshine. He must have felt the same apprehension for Sadie that Jasper and Kylie did; his presence hours before the activities began proved it.

Kylie clapped her hands together in delight at the sight of her grandpa, and Jasper slowed the car to a stop by the pickup so she could jump out and join him. Mac's grin and Kylie's exuberance in their greeting warmed Jasper's heart, thawing some of the worry he felt. He tried to meet Sadie's eye in the backseat, but she was distractedly checking off cars in an attempt to discover who had beaten her to the setup table.

So instead of sharing a glance with Sadie, he ended up sharing one with Mac—a mutual frown of distress. Jasper waved Kylie into Mac's care and then drove on to a parking space before slowly turning off the ignition and gathering his strength.

It took him by surprise when Sadie didn't immediately vault from the car as soon as it ceased motion. Everything thus far indicated that she was tearing to get inside and start things rolling. He shifted in his seat to get a good look at her, the vinyl creaking in response to his movement.

She sat there staring straight ahead, with flickers of fear dancing in the depths of her eyes. Her fingers clutched the edges of her dessert containers with such a pale steel grip that he feared she might actually bend the plastic and ruin her entry before she even got it through the door.

She swallowed loudly and then expelled a little breath. Jasper didn't think it would take more than one loud "Boo!" to send her running in retreat. His heart ached for what she chose to put herself through, so he tried one last time to talk sense.

"You don't have to go through with this, Sadie. Whatever you think you have to prove, I think you proved it a long time ago. You've got Suncatchers; you've got Kylie. You've got Mac, and"—he grinned in an awkward attempt to coax a smile onto her pinched face—"you've got me. I think all that speaks pretty well to what you've been able to accomplish in your life."

The silence stretched out thinly as Sadie made no response. He wondered if she had even heard him.

"Sadie?"

She kept staring at the church door, keeping a white-knuckled grip on her dessert. He reached out and laid a hand on her knee. This action finally drew her to attention, and her eyes darted to his face… but everything in her gaze felt hollow.

"You don't have to do this," he repeated.

She hesitated, and for one brief, hopeful moment, he thought she might relent. But then there came the sound of two high-pitched voices, hallooing another arrival as they made their way to the door.

Jasper inwardly groaned as he watched Sadie's eyes flicker toward the sound. Smith and Jones ambled across the parking lot, a small cooler held tightly between them, as they accosted Dmitri Velichko before he could enter the building. He paused politely to greet them, flashing a charming European smile and holding the door as they cooed and fussed.

He held a white cardboard box in his hands. A dessert. His dessert. His entry.

Sadie's eyes flashed fire.

The sight of Dmitri sparked the initiative she needed, and she reached for the door handle with sudden decisiveness, tugging it toward her with a vicious jerk and then stepping outside. Jasper lowered his head and allowed himself a brief sigh before rushing to catch up with her.

* * * * *

Registering for the competition took all of ten minutes, and after Sadie set up her display inside the church, there was little to do but mingle and wait until things got under way.

After weeks of experimenting, taste-testing, and analyzing, Sadie had at last decided on a dish. A creamy mousse base, flavored with almond extract, rested atop a graham cracker crust. The cocoa confection was topped with a rich berry compote comprised of blackberry, raspberry, and blueberry and would be garnished with a thick dollop of cream along with a strawberry fan. Jasper had to admit that it looked and sounded tantalizing. Each contestant was required to make two of the same dessert for their entry. The first one was plated up for the display so that every angle of the entry could be viewed and analyzed, and the second was set aside or refrigerated for the judges' taste-testing.

Sadie's dessert sat in deceptive decadence, the berries swimming in a thick syrup of sticky delight atop the creamy chocolate mousse. Sugary brown crumbs peeped out from the bottom, looking temptingly tasty. It *appeared* to be a perfect offering.

But looks could be deceiving. And Jasper knew better than anyone how well this old adage applied to all of Sadie's desserts. The amazing talent God had given her for recipes, cooking, and even restaurant management did not make up for what she had not been blessed with—the ability to create a tasty, truly delicious dessert.

As Jasper stood staring at the display, he marveled at mankind's constant attempt to strive beyond the abundance they already possessed.

When was it enough? When could they learn to be happy with what they had and stop worrying about what they didn't? He sighed and turned away, his eyes seeking out Sadie's form as she bent in consultation with Lucinda Lowell. She had pasted a satisfied smile on her features, but it didn't serve to conceal the tension he recognized in her tightly squared shoulders and rigid posture.

He chewed his lower lip with worry, wondering how they were going to get through the day. As he stood there working at his lip and digging his hands into his jeans, Dmitri suddenly appeared beside him.

Jasper shifted a little to look at Dmitri's face and saw that his gaze had also focused on Sadie. The same concern Jasper felt now radiated from Dmitri's interested blue eyes.

"Is she going to be all right?" he asked, his tone filled with distress.

Jasper was moved by the other man's worry. "I don't know," Jasper admitted after a moment. "I guess it'll depend on how the day goes."

Dmitri considered something for a moment. "She tries too hard, doesn't she?"

The observation startled Jasper for some reason. He studied Sadie's smooth but tense movements on the other side of the room. "Yeah," he softly acknowledged. "Something like that."

With a shake, Jasper drew himself back to the man in front of him. "So, you've got your entry all registered and ready?" he asked, longing for a change of topic.

Dmitri nodded, easily shifting the conversation. "It is a chocolate ganache and ginger tart topped with poached pears."

Jasper raised his eyebrows at how easily those words spun off Dmitri's tongue. Dmitri had apparently done this before. Suddenly Sadie's paranoia over the Russian as possible competition didn't seem so far-fetched.

"It begins with a cocoa-and-crumb base for the tart shell, followed by the ginger-and-ganache filling," Dmitri explained. "Pears poached in cinnamon and wine are served on top."

Jasper's mouth watered at the mere thought of it. This was clearly something he had to see. Besides, his convenience-store cup of coffee had long since failed to satisfy his empty stomach. Not that Dmitri would give him a taste, but just seeing such deliciousness might be enough.

"Mind if I take a look?" he asked as casually as if he were popping the hood of a Chevy.

Dmitri didn't need to be asked twice. He steered Jasper toward his table, where the two stared in childlike delight at the inspiring sight of Dmitri's tart. After laying eyes on it, Jasper knew he'd never be able to refer to the like as "pie" ever again.

As Dmitri enthusiastically began to run through the steps he had taken to create this gorgeous delicacy, Jasper couldn't help smiling at his excitement. Other than Sadie and the occasional acquaintance of hers whom he had met, he had never seen anyone who gushed over food like Dmitri did. He suddenly found it very sad that Sadie hadn't learned to like Dmitri. They had a deep appreciation of food in common at heart.

As if summoning her with this thought, Sadie suddenly appeared at his side, bobbing up with unnatural ease.

"So," she announced by way of greeting.

Jasper recognized the sparks shooting from her eyes and realized, once again too late, that by hanging out with Dmitri he had committed the blackest of sins.

"Sadie, it's nice to see you." Dmitri smiled with warmth—although it wasn't enough to melt the ice wall Sadie forced between them.

"Mmm," she weakly responded. A very long, very awkward pause stretched between the three until she belatedly added, "You too."

Jasper stifled a groan. Sadie began to rock back and forth slightly on her feet. It reminded Jasper of an action Kylie took when she was about to work him over for something she wanted.

"Is that your entry?" Sadie gestured with her chin to the decadent delight resting on the table before them.

Dmitri nodded. "Chocolate ganache and ginger tart topped with poached pears."

Jasper could have sworn Sadie's coloring flushed to almost purple.

"Mmm-huh. I see."

Ever the gentlemen, Dmitri offered, "I noticed your own entry. It looks lovely. A chocolate mousse with berry compote?"

Jasper noticed Sadie's teeth grinding together from the corner of his eyes.

Her jaw was clenched so tight she lisped her reply. "Yeth, thath's right."

By now, it was obvious that nothing Dmitri could say would thaw the awkwardness between them. With a regretful smile, her competitor said, "Well, best of luck to you. Excuse me while I go have a word with Miss Lowell."

Sadie's plastic smile remained in place until Dmitri's back was turned. She then transformed from forced politeness to narrowed eyes, straight lips, and sagging shoulders.

"Chocolate ganache and ginger tart topped with poached pears? Now why didn't I think of that?"

Jasper remained silent, hoping to be momentarily forgotten...but he had no such luck. Sadie turned on him with an accusing glare.

"How *could* you?"

"We were only talking," Jasper responded with his hands held up in defense.

"Put your hands down," she commanded. He obeyed.

"This is *Dmitri Velichko* we're talking about! You *know* how I feel about him!" she chastised.

Jasper sighed. "Yes, I know *how* you feel about him. I'm just not quite sure I understand *why*."

She sputtered. "What—you—why? *That man*—" She pointed a finger, but Jasper slapped it down, afraid she would make a scene. "He's my *competition*, Jasper! They say he's opening up a restaurant *right across the street* from mine!"

"Have you asked him about it?"

For whatever reason, surprise or fury, this question dropped her into silence.

"Well, have you?" Jasper pressed. When she remained silent, he continued. "Maybe you should talk it over with him before you sentence him to the gallows."

Sadie appeared to be working up a decent retort when Kylie appeared, chattering happily about ponies and rainbows and all things decent and light in the world. She was speaking at such a high rate of speed that Jasper could barely understand a word of it, other than when she attached herself to his legs and demanded, "Lift Kylie! Lift!"

He picked her up and she carried on with her story, lips green from a lollipop's remains and fingers sticky with candy.

"…and then maybe Mommy can too!"

"Maybe Mommy can what?" Sadie distractedly questioned her daughter, finally pulling her gaze from the tantalizing perfection of Dmitri's dessert.

"Ride the ponies," Mac filled in as he sauntered up. "We found the pony rides as they were setting up for the day. They gave this little horsewoman"—he gestured to Kylie, who beamed at this appellation—"the first ride of the day for free."

"And a lollipop," Kylie added, rather unnecessarily. "After the people eat Mommy's dessert, maybe Mommy can have a ride too!"

Sadie had shifted her attention to the room at large and was scanning it desperately, most likely for the arrival of the judges. "Mommy's got a very busy day ahead of her," she murmured.

"But, Mommy," Kylie protested, "they'll give you a lollipop too!"

Sadie now focused on her daughter, who was sticking out her lower lip in a very precious, very sulky display of disapproval.

"There's plenty of time before the judging starts," Jasper pointed out. "Why don't you go now?"

"Yes, Mommy, yes!" Kylie inserted her own feelings on the subject.

Sadie hesitated. "But when the judges arrive…," she trailed off meekly.

"When the judges arrive, you can't do anything but stand there and wring your hands anyway, so you might as well be happily occupied," he suggested. Shifting Kylie to his other side, he leaned over to whisper in Sadie's ear, "Besides, Kylie's been really patient during the past few weeks, and you haven't spent much time with her lately."

Before she could ask, Jasper offered, "I'll keep an eye on your entry until you get back."

With no more excuses to prevent her, Sadie held out her arms and Jasper deposited a happy Kylie into them. Then he and Mac stood together and watched her carry Kylie out of the building, presumably off to the pony rides. Their heads were next to the other's in animated discussion. It was the first time Jasper had seen Sadie really smile in weeks. He hoped it wouldn't be the last for weeks to come.

Mac cleared his throat once Sadie was gone.

"Whose entry is that?" he asked, clearly impressed by the tempting display before them.

"Dmitri Velichko's," Jasper answered. "Chocolate ganache and ginger tart topped with poached pears."

"Uh-oh," Mac said.

"Yeah," Jasper replied. "I know."

Mac turned his back on the mouthwatering tart. "I don't suppose you've had a chance to tell Sadie your news, have you?"

Jasper scuffed his boots along the floor. "Nope."

"Oh," Mac responded.

Jasper thought he might as well have said "Uh-oh," like he had in reference to Dmitri's tart.

"The right time hasn't come up," Jasper defended himself. "Between this stupid dessert contest and watching Kylie and making sure everything's running smoothly at the restaurant…"

Mac didn't say anything.

"I will," Jasper reassured the older man, for his own sake more than Mac's. "Soon. I will soon. Who knows? Maybe she'll win the competition and she'll be in such a good mood when I tell her, she'll actually be happy…."

Mac's expression indicated what he thought of the likelihood of this scenario. Jasper frowned.

"Yeah. That's what I thought you'd say."

* * * * *

As the morning wore on, a large crowd gathered in the church and on the grounds. People overflowed the kitchen and gymnasium, where the Cocoa Cook-Off and talent competition were slated to take place, and dozens more made their way through the outdoor venues, taking in pony rides, balloon making, carnival games, ministry expositions, funnel cakes, and french fries. By the time Sadie and Kylie had indulged in two pony rides, an army of balloon animals, a round at "Throw the Ball in the Bucket," and a funnel cake, the chocolate competition was rapidly approaching.

Sadie found herself growing queasy, and it became harder and harder to concentrate on Kylie's steady stream of chatter. They greeted dozens of friends and acquaintances, but more than anything, Sadie wished Jasper would show up and reassure her frazzled nerves.

Grudgingly promising Kylie a cone of cotton candy for later in the afternoon, she at last herded her daughter back toward the church gymnasium, where it seemed as though most of the town had turned out to watch the Cocoa Cook-Off.

Mac stood by her display and waved her over with a smile when he saw her nearby. She nearly sobbed with relief at his encouraging grin, and for the first time in years, she felt like throwing herself into her father's embrace and crying on his shoulder. She had forgotten how much the strain and pressure of competition weighed on a person.

Kylie let go of her hand, raced through the crowd, and vaulted herself into her grandfather's outstretched arms. Sadie swallowed back a lump of emotion. She remembered doing that a very long time ago when Mac would ride back into town for a visit. She'd hear his old Harley in the drive, fly out of the house, and be in his arms almost before he could turn off the ignition.

She had been happy in those moments, and she hadn't needed anything else to make her feel worthwhile.

Why did she need something else now, years later, when contentment should have been secure at last? A lot of different things would pass through her life. When would any of them become enough? What was "enough" exactly?

This thought was cut off as Sadie pushed through the mingling crowds and arrived at her table just as Jasper reached it as well.

Her heart thudded with relief. "There you are." With her current emotional state, it sounded far more accusatory than she wished.

"Sorry. I got tied up by Dwayne," he explained. Dwayne Roop was the principal of Agape Christian Academy—and therefore Jasper's boss. "But I also ran into Lucinda. She just finished registering the last contestant."

He relayed the final instructions from Lucinda, rubbed Sadie's back in reassurance, and planted a kiss on her temple...and then there was no more time for encouragement, as the Cocoa Cook-Off competition got underway.

The judges moved from table to table, sniffing, tasting, writing on their clipboards, sniffing and tasting some more. Sadie thought the select group of church board members were really taking the dramatics to extremes and couldn't help but wonder how many late-night competitions on the Food Network they'd watched to lead up to this day.

When the judges reached Smith and Jones's table, Sadie cringed. The two elderly women had joined forces to create a Reese's peanut butter cup pie, which looked much fancier than it sounded. She had to give it to them; their replacement of mascarpone cheese in place of the plain old cream cheese called for in the recipe, along with their spiced nut graham cracker crust, was a brilliant strategy. The panel's satisfied expression as they tasted the results indicated that it had been the right move. Who knew that Smith and Jones could be such formidable competitors? Sadie ground her teeth together in distress.

There were two tables between Sadie's and Smith and Jones's, and as the judges moved on, Sadie flitted around to make sure everything was just right. Her dessert certainly *looked* impressive with its crumbly shell, creamy bottom layer, and the glossy reddish-purple berry compote dribbled over the top. The generous dollop of whipped cream along with the strawberry fan slices on top certainly made things *appear* convincing. She could only hope it tasted that way.

Nightmarish visions of every failed dessert (and heaven knew there were plenty) in her lifetime came washing over her in waves of nerve-racking assault. She closed her eyes and took a deep breath, felt Jasper's hand in hers, and determined that it would be fine. Everything would be fine this time. She had put far too much effort and thought into this dessert for it not to turn out right. She had spent hours in the kitchen, neglecting her family and her business…. What more could she do? Her sacrifice had been worth it. This was the moment where she proved them all wrong. This was it….

At Jasper's squeeze, she opened her eyes to find the panel of judges standing before her. She cleared her throat and quickly presented them with their individual plates and forks. They went through well-practiced motions: marking off numbers on their clipboards for presentation—no worries there. Then sniffing carefully like bloodhounds on a scent. This part left Sadie a trifle nervous. Truthfully, there wasn't much *smell* to her dessert, although she couldn't be sure why. Of course, it wasn't as if she had loaded her entry with savory scent factors such as *chocolate ganache* or *Reese's peanut butter cups*. She forced herself not to glare at her competitors nearby.

A wash of indignation touched her momentarily as the judges each exchanged nervous glances before raising their forks. What was that about? How far had word spread of her dessert disasters, anyhow? Not that she really had to ask. Thanks to Smith and Jones, pretty much everyone in her acquaintance, and even a few outside of it, knew that desserts had never been her strong suit.

And then came the moment of truth.

The spoons dipped into the compote.... Was it her imagination, or had the berries started to congeal? Bite-sized portions were scooped onto the utensils.... Was it just her, or did the judges choose *very* small bites? The spoons raised and slowly, ever so slowly, entered each judge's mouth. Sadie found herself actually widening her own mouth and pantomiming the bite.

Their jaws closed shut and the tasting began, the judges' tongues seeming to roll thickly inside their mouths. Someone cleared their throat. More tasting...and then...was that a gulp? Did they really just *gulp* down that itty-bitty bite of mousse? And had Mrs. Strausbaugh, the judge on the far end, actually held a handkerchief to her mouth to dispose of her tiny mouthful?

Sadie's eyes darted to each face, measuring their reactions. To their credit, they kept their expressions rather impassive. But Sadie had been feeding people for a very long time. No one needed to tell her, and not a single judge need show their score sheet, to prove what she could read in their thin lips and quivering jaws.

Failure. Absolute and utter *failure.*

She bit her lip and forced back tears as she exchanged the expected pleasantries and watched in disappointment and frustration as they moved on, now only one table away from Dmitri's entry.

"Sadie?" Jasper's voice sounded softly beside her.

"Give me a spoon," she demanded, still staring after the panel's retreating backs.

There was a silent pause before Jasper once more spoke. "Sadie, sweetheart, don't worry about it. Let's get out of here, go home…"

"Give. Me. A. Spoon."

He handed one over without protest. She reached for her dessert on display, dug the plastic spoon into it with angry force, and cut through the layers of whipped cream, berries, and mousse in one decisive motion. She didn't hesitate as she raised the bite to her mouth and stuffed it in. Beginning to chew, she immediately noted several errors in texture. The whipped cream was grainy, the berries tasted rubbery and chewy, and the mousse felt thicker than it should have been. And then came the taste factor. The almond extract was far too strong. The berries were bitter and the syrup acidic. The whipped topping had a sharp flavor. Her delicately spiced graham cracker base had no taste at all. Was that her fault? Or had she once again been the victim of a cosmic conspiracy?

She threw the spoon down on the table without a word and turned to watch, with the rest of the spectators, as the panel approached Dmitri's table.

The difference in reaction was unmistakable. Where Sadie's dessert had caused hesitation, Dmitri's invited eagerness. Where hers had provoked pinched expressions, Dmitri's garnered smiles. Where hers triggered puckered lips, Dmitri's drew circles of awe.

Chocolate ganache and ginger tart topped with poached pears. Why had she thought she could compete with that?

The judges sniffed in appreciation and marked wildly on their clipboards. Before, with the other entries, they had restrained themselves to only a few bites (and in Sadie's case, only one), but now they gorged themselves shamelessly, taking up to six and seven bites apiece before reluctantly lowering their plates back to the table. Mrs. Strausbaugh actually carried hers away, and Sadie had suspicions that the older woman planned to lick the plate later.

As the judges shuffled off with obvious unwillingness, casting several longing glances behind them at the second ginger tart still on display, Sadie watched several people rush forward to congratulate Dmitri, even though the results wouldn't be officially announced for another thirty minutes or so.

Jasper laid a hand on her shoulder, but she found the action irritated her. Without being too obvious, she shifted and turned so he was forced to draw it away. With her back turned to him, she missed the frown that creased his forehead.

She filled the next half hour with cleaning up her display table and the surrounding area, ignoring Jasper's worry-filled eyes and Mac's decision to take Kylie for a walk. When it finally came time to announce the winners, every inch of Sadie's area shone neatly, the remains of her dessert entry bagged somberly in the trash.

Her mind wandered during the opening preliminaries—who needed to hear how happy they were at the turnout and the impressive level of skill at their little old Cocoa Cook-Off, anyway? Her thoughts simply slipped away to her culinary training, her mother's deft touch at making truffles, and Ned's constant delight in the meals they had shared at the table. Jasper didn't touch her again, and she found herself both disappointed and relieved.

Why did this have to be so hard?

She ran a finger against the freshly scrubbed tabletop and tuned in briefly to the announcer. He was still rambling on about all the different kinds of chocolate desserts and how this expressed the unique individuality of every person who had competed, blah, blah, blah. She turned inward once more, her shoulders hunched protectively against the outside world.

When had desserts become such an issue for her? She actually remembered laughing over them with Ned, back when they were dating. He had presented her engagement ring in a white cake filled with raspberry torte, and she had joked how she almost preferred the torte to the ring since it was far more edible than her desserts had ever been. Ned had laughed, giddy with her answer to his proposal, and they had finished the torte together and spent the rest of the night gazing at the stars.

These days if someone had brought her a ring tucked in torte, she'd probably shove the entire offering—ring, torte, person, and all—off the top of the Hersheypark Kissing Tower. What was wrong with her?

"And without further delay, it is my great honor to announce the winners in our first-ever annual Cocoa Cook-Off competition."

Her head snapped up. Despite her bitterness, she found herself drawn to the announcement. She didn't expect to win anything, but somehow it made all the difference in the world just who *did* win.

Dmitri was practically assured first place, but since it had become clear to her that he was her archrival in the restaurant business, she could only pray such a thing didn't happen.

Fourth and third place went to people Sadie knew relatively well. One was a darling gentleman widower from her church's smaller group class, so she really couldn't begrudge him the prize. She even managed to applaud rather nicely. But when second place was announced, her stomach twisted with sourness.

"…for their Reese's peanut butter cup pie—Mrs. Eugenia Smith and Mrs. Dorothy Jones. Congratulations!"

As Smith and Jones ambled up to accept their shared ribbon, Sadie folded her arms against her chest—and even Jasper's subtle nudge couldn't prompt her to applaud them.

And then it came, the blue ribbon…first place.

She held her breath.

"I think it goes without saying which dessert, if you can even call such a delicacy by so humble a name, deserves to be presented with this little honor of distinction we have here." The announcer waved the blue ribbon back and forth, its golden trim glittering in the flash of camera bulbs exploding here and there throughout the gymnasium.

"He may be a newer member of our town, but it's clear he's earned a place here with us."

Sadie snorted. "Because he baked a pie?"

Jasper's soft "*Shhh*" left her feeling ashamed. The next words, however, erased all feelings of guilt.

"In fact, rumor has it, our winner plans to open his very own eatery here in town. Renovations are already underway."

They were? How had she missed that? *Oh.* She blushed. It wasn't as if she'd been spending a lot of time at the restaurant in the past few weeks. Otherwise she might have noticed.

"But enough introduction. It is my honor and privilege to announce as first place in our first annual Cocoa Cook-Off competition…"

The announcer paused with a deep breath while Sadie mumbled ferociously, "Out with it."

"Chocolate ganache and ginger tart topped with poached pears by Dmitri Velichko!"

Applause thundered the gymnasium as Dmitri made his way to the front, his perfect white teeth glowing brightly in his face. The local newspaper photographer snapped away as Dmitri shook hands with the head of the judges' panel.

Sadie's conflicting emotions left her feeling drained. Jealousy raged furiously within her, but at the same time—against everything within her screaming that she had to remain ruthless—a part of her felt happy for Dmitri. He was a nice enough guy, and it wasn't as if he'd been smug about the competition.

On the other hand, it was probably all part of his plan—to be all sweet and charming while he took her out at the knees, inching out her restaurant for his. She huffed in annoyance and blew a stray strand of hair out of her eyes.

Smith and Jones ambled by, grinning like two Siamese cats with a bucket of cream, while they flashed their ribbon none-too-demurely.

"We're so sorry you didn't win, Sadie," Smith practically purred.

"There's always next year," Jones offered with a smirk.

For the first time ever, Sadie turned her back without acknowledging them. If they wanted to be snooty with her, then she could be snooty with them. They were just two old ladies, after all. What did their good opinion matter?

She reached for a rag and moved to wipe down her table, only to remember that she'd wiped it down three times already. But Smith and Jones had shuffled on, whispering furiously and throwing sharp looks behind them.

Well, if they wanted to gossip about her, let them. She didn't care. It was only dessert, after all. She twisted the dirty dishrag in her hands and searched for something else to occupy herself.

"It's just a competition," she muttered with an attempt at nonchalance. "It's not that important...." But as her words faded softly, she felt tears filling her eyes. It had been more than that to her. It had been her last chance to prove to herself, and to everyone else, that she could do the impossible.

The stress and tension of the last few weeks suddenly fell fully upon her, and she sagged beneath the strain of her own making. Tears filled her eyes, and she was suddenly so very, very tired.

And then Jasper was there, his arm holding her up, as she laid her head against his chest. He smoothed her hair and murmured words she really didn't understand, but it didn't matter, because he was there. He was always there. He'd *always* been there, and he always would be.

"I wanna go home, Jas," she murmured. "I just want to go home."

He nodded his understanding. "Why don't I find Mac and ask if he can bring Kylie back to the house when she's had enough?"

Sadie nodded gratefully and allowed him to wipe her face with his T-shirt, hoping with all her might that everyone was still so distracted by Dmitri they hadn't seen her emotions on display.

"Wait here. I'll be back in a minute."

As he waded into the crowd in search of Mac and Kylie, Sadie hoped they hadn't gone far. She didn't relish spending another minute more than necessary at the Cocoa Cook-Off. Let Dmitri have his moment; all she wanted was the safety of her own home and Jasper's comforting arms around her.

As she gathered her things and stood waiting, the enthusiastic throng pressing around Dmitri broke a little and several people moved on toward the talent competition. Much to her vexation, Principal Dwayne Roop appeared out of the crowd and approached her table.

"Sadie, good show! It's a shame you didn't place at all!"

Sadie gritted her teeth, smiled graciously, and made some inane remark about not winning them all. She had never really liked Kylie's principal. He seemed to think himself superior to women just because he was the head of a school where Jasper was the only other male employee. His occasional comments about guiding his "flock of hens" had never impressed her...not to mention that his teeth were big and his breath horrendous.

"...anyhow what with Jasper's new job."

The endless drone of Principal Roop's voice suddenly struck her with earth-shattering significance.

Sadie swallowed. "I'm sorry, I didn't catch that. What were you saying?"

"I was only saying it's just as well you didn't win since you likely won't be here next year to compete again anyhow, what with Jasper's new job. I assume you and Kylie will be moving with him?"

In that moment, the final thread holding together Sadie's fragile world snapped, and the bottom fell out from everything keeping her sane for the last five years. Something, however, some last shred of rationality, held her poise and expression momentarily intact though she had shattered into tiny pieces inside.

Roop remained clueless as she demurely questioned, "Now, Principal Roop, how did you find that out?"

Roop guffawed, his fetid breath fanning Sadie's face. She stifled a gag. "Why, my dear girl, as Jasper's boss and the man who recommended him for the job, how could I not know?" He laughed and slapped his thigh as though this were a tremendous joke, and it was just as well that the remains of Sadie's mousse lay at the bottom of a nearby garbage bag. She might have upended it into Roop's red face otherwise.

"Fact is, Ms. Spencer, I'd wager I knew about it before you did!" He laughed again.

Only her deepest reserves of self-control kept Sadie from slapping him silly. "And do you plan to come visit us in…oh, where is it we're going again?" she queried.

"Colorado," he easily supplied, none the wiser for her baiting him. "I rather doubt it, my dear, what with all my responsibilities here. I'll miss that daughter of yours, though, that's for certain."

He positively beamed at her, as though she should kiss his balding head with benevolence for singling out her child in this manner. She couldn't help recalling last year's interview with Principal Roop, when he'd informed her of Kylie's attempts to wallpaper the school bathroom with construction paper. "Unacceptable shenanigans" had been the words he used.

"I assume you and Jasper are planning to tie the knot before the school year begins?"

Sadie gripped the edge of the table with abnormal force. "Oh, I don't know. I suppose we'll have to take it slow and see."

Roop nodded sagely. "Quite right. That's just what Jasper said when I mentioned it to him."

Sadie unclenched her jaws long enough to ask, "And tell me again, Principal Roop, what sort of job is it that Jasper's been offered?"

Now at this point, even the dim-witted Roop seemed to be finding Sadie's tightly clenched fingers and expressions somewhat suspect. Her last question left him a bit flustered.

"Well, now, my dear…of course you already know.…"

"Oh, but Principal Roop," she cooed falsely, "I'd like *you* to tell me."

Roop's naturally crimson shade had lessened by several degrees, and he bordered on what could even be considered "pale" for a man of his perpetually florid complexion.

"Why…it's, er… The offer to teach…at Westing's Private Academy for Boys in Colorado. Where you and Jasper will be headed this fall."

He delivered the words in a prompting tone, as if he could recall them to Sadie's mind just by speaking them. When this answer was met with silence, he began looking around none too casually for an avenue of escape.

"Ahh, you recall the job offer? It came through weeks ago. Surely you and Jasper have discussed it?"

Sadie watched the perspiration bead along the principal's brow as his eyes made frequent darts toward the exit doors. She suspected that he had never been overly fond of her and was only speaking to her now out of a sense of duty to Jasper.

Sadie narrowed her eyes. "You've never liked me much, have you, Mr. Roop?"

"Oh, now…well, m–my dear…I don't think…" He continued to stumble until she cut him off.

"Did you happen to try any of my dessert entry?"

His jaw sagged. He may not have tried it, but he'd likely heard plenty about it. "I—I do wish you all the best, Ms. Spencer," he offered and began backing away. "And do…keep us up-to-date on…on…"

She took one step in his direction, and he uttered a strangled "*Eep!*" before rushing off, merging into the mingling crowd, and blending seamlessly into the landscape.

Sadie glared at his departing figure, and for a moment she knew how cavewomen must have felt—this overwhelming urge to club something…or some*one*.

And then for a brief moment, the anger dissolved…and all that was left in its place was an aching, hollow space thrumming with emptiness as she realized what Roop's words truly meant.

Leave her. Jasper meant to *leave* her? How was that possible? Not Jasper, the one constant—the steady anchor. Not him. But what else was there to think? It sounded as though things were finalized. An honorable position at a prestigious academy—why *wouldn't* he choose that over her?

But then her spirit rose up in protest. *No!* She was his best friend—and now so much more! There was Kylie and Aunt Matilda, his students at the school, his church friends…he wouldn't just think of leaving all that, would he?

Would he?

For the first time ever, she doubted Jasper.

Maybe it was her. Maybe he thought it was a mistake to have taken their level of friendship to true love. Maybe he wanted out and this was the easiest way to do it. A clean break. No awkwardly running into each other or explaining to Kylie why he couldn't come around anymore. After all, the last few weeks had probably been hard on him. He'd seen more than he cared to see of her life. He didn't enjoy the prospect of full-time care of Kylie, even though he'd been pretty much her full-time caretaker for years now.

In the end, her excuses didn't matter. It all came down to this—people left her. That was what they did. She could never be what she needed to be in order to keep them. She hadn't been good enough to earn her father's constant presence, she couldn't make a decent dessert without failure, and now she couldn't even compete with Westing's boys' academy. She should have known better. She should have listened to that tiny voice of doubt, whispering in between her reason and her newfound love for Jasper.

She should never have let Jasper this close. Their friendship had been safe—it had worked for years. Love was not so simple.

So much for it conquering all.

It was as she reached this devastating conclusion that Jasper finally broke through the crowds and approached.

* * * * *

Having been successful in his mission to locate Mac and place Kylie into the older man's care for the remainder of the day, Jasper approached Sadie with a mixture of relief and sympathy. She had tried so hard with this competition, and his heart ached, having witnessed her disappointment. As he closed the distance between them, he saw her expression in profile, face partially hidden as she stared at the floor. The deep concentration on her brow made him hope she wasn't still dwelling on her dessert failure.

Despite the slump to her shoulders, Jasper was hopeful she would rebound quickly from the dessert affair. And once she did, he could share his news and ask her what she thought. He had no doubt moving to Colorado was the furthest thing from her mind, and he was willing to turn down the job rather than leave her. But he wanted her thoughts on it first...if he could present it in such a way that she didn't automatically assume he was pulling up stakes on her and heading out.

But there was time for that later. Right now she needed his love and reassurance, and he was determined to provide it for her. As he approached her at the table, he reached out a hand and laid it against her shoulder, planning to pull her into an embrace. But as soon as he touched her, she shot forward, stepping away from him and whirling around as though she'd been tightly wound, just waiting for his touch to set her off.

Then she exploded.

"COLORADO?!?"

He froze, completely unprepared for this assault. His delayed reaction caused Sadie's lip to quiver.

"What were you going to do, Jasper—leave a note? Call me from the airport? *Send an e-mail?*"

She let out a shriek of dismay, fingers clenching into fists at her side. Jasper winced at her reaction.

Unfortunately, most of the rather substantial crowd in the nearby area heard her outburst as well, and within seconds, Sadie and Jasper had an absorbed audience.

Thankfully, at this point, Jasper was catching up. He held up a hand.

"Now, Sadie, listen to me."

"No."

He clenched his jaw. "I can explain."

"I don't care," she volleyed back. "It was *your* idea to begin dating! If you didn't want a relationship, you should have just said so!"

"Sadie, I *do* want a relationship! That's why I was going to ask if you wanted to come to Colorado *with* me. You're totally blowing this out of proportion."

She seemed to have lost all sense of reason as she shouted, "That's not true! If you really wanted a relationship with me, you'd never ask me to leave here in the first place. This is my life, Jasper—*my life*. I have a career and a daughter to think about. I have the restaurant and my mother's home—the home I grew up in. I have friendships and memories.... You *know* I'd never leave all that behind."

Jasper felt a slight tingling of guilt—she made a valid point—but at the same time, he was indignant. He *had* been thinking of her all along—if he hadn't been, he would have accepted the position straight away rather than putting off the board for weeks while he tried to find the right time to ask her opinion. But beyond all this was the piercing knowledge of what he felt Sadie was trying to tell him—she had a life. A life filled with things far more important than he could ever be. A life that would go on...with or without him. How could he have ever thought otherwise?

"Of course you have a life!" Jasper rarely raised his voice, but when he did, it became unforgettably raspy with emotion. "How could we forget?" He waved his hand to encompass their large audience. Sadie's gaze followed his gesture briefly, and she blinked at the sight of so many onlookers.

"'Cause you see, Sadie, it's always about *your* life. It's about the restaurant or Ned's death or your mother's cancer or your father's leaving, and when all else fails, it's just about *desserts*." He had worked himself into a state of high passion now, feeling every bit as tortured as she did.

Her face flamed, either with anger or shame, he wasn't sure which. "Don't minimize my problems! I've had a hard time the last few years," she savagely defended. "Anyone here would admit that!" She copied his gesture to gather the crowd to her side. "And I thought if anyone would understand the pressure I've been under the last few years, *you* would. You're supposed to be my *best friend*."

"Why?" he demanded angrily. "Why am I your best friend, Sadie? Is it because you care about me, because you love me for who I am?" His voice dropped several levels, and the crowd gathered in tighter to catch what he said as he stepped toward Sadie. "Or is it because I made a convenient doormat—free babysitting for Kylie, free shuttle service when you needed a ride, a shoulder to cry on, someone to sympathize with all your problems—was it that, Sadie? Did you really convince yourself you cared about *me*? Or did you just care about needing *someone*?"

The crowd expelled a soft "Ooh" at this point.

"So that's how you solve it when people you *supposedly* love become an inconvenience?" she asked with more than a touch of sarcasm. "You decide to disappear to Colorado, move yourself up in the world and, oh—see ya, sorry if you need me, but I'm *gone*. Is *that* how it works, Jasper?"

All eyes shifted toward Jasper to see his response.

"When have I ever...*ever*...not been there for you?" he countered.

She ground her teeth together, eyes sliding to the side as she shifted from foot to foot. She was clearly at a loss to recall a single episode to throw back in his face. After a moment, she chose instead to retort, "Maybe you never felt like you had a choice if it's *always been about me.*"

"Maybe I didn't," he shot back. "But I have a choice now, don't I?"

The crowd gasped at the implications of this statement. Even Sadie took a step back at these words.

"Wh–what are you saying?"

"Maybe I should choose Colorado," he answered darkly. "After all, the winters there can't be half as cold as the summer I've spent *here.*"

And with that parting shot, he turned on his heel and strode for the door.

Chapter Thirteen

....

Sadie watched as the crowd melted around Jasper, shifting like the parting of the Red Sea to let him through. She felt hot tears well up in her eyes with frustration, sadness, and triumph—though what she'd accomplished she did not know.

Wounded to her very core, she acted on the first impulse that overtook her, walking quickly to Jones and Smith's nearby table. The two old biddies had watched the entire scene with a malicious sort of glee on their hawklike faces. But at Sadie's expression, they drew back, not daring to interfere, as she scooped up the remains of their award-winning Reese's peanut butter cup pie filled with mascarpone cheese…and lobbed a large handful at Jasper's retreating head.

Though she had never possessed much skill at softball, no one could have thrown a more perfect pitch. The pie smacked Jasper square on the back of his scruffy blond head, and the crowd let out another gasp.

He paused and stood there for a long moment. Inwardly, in the deepest part of her soul, Sadie begged for him to turn around. *Laugh,* she silently begged. *Look at me and laugh.*

But the moment passed, and Jasper kept walking. He never turned around to face her.

Sadie felt the tears begin to rise.

Great.

Humiliated by the presence of so many onlookers, Sadie mustered every ounce of will she possessed to staunch the flood of tears threatening to overwhelm her. What a horrible, rotten day. It was enough to make her crawl into bed and lock the door for the next three weeks. But she didn't let any of this frustration show as she turned, head held high, to gather her things and go in search of Mac and Kylie.

The crowd stared at each of her actions with mute fascination, seeming to wonder just what she would do next.

Now she knew how the prairie dogs at Hershey's ZooAmerica felt: the object of a crowd's absorption.

She wiped her fingers on a paper towel, cringing at the stickiness but deciding to wash them later. Right now she didn't care to do anything except make her escape from this horrible scene.

The crowd parted much more hesitantly for her than they had for Jasper. It was as if they were reluctant to let this last part of their entertainment escape. She forced her way around several people, her tears building to an anguished fury inside her, when suddenly someone stepped in front and began nudging people out of the way. Through the blur of tears she refused to let slip, she could make out the tall, dark figure of Dmitri Velichko, forcing people aside to help her cut a path to the door.

She didn't think, after throwing the pie at Jasper, that her humiliation could run any deeper. But the sight of the man she had sworn as her archenemy, the one who had defeated her in her own town at her own game, stepping in with such chivalry made her feel as though she had touched an all-new type of low. Her mouth filled with a sour sort of taste, but she could not focus on anything beyond getting away from the stares of the crowd.

Dmitri reached the door one step ahead of her and held it open. She slipped through without so much as a glance at his face, too disgraced to even offer him a thank-you.

The chatter outside was a welcome relief to the silence she had caused inside. Laughter and shouts served to veil her embarrassment and blanket her in a blessed cloak of anonymity.

But the feeling didn't last long.

Apparently, word had spread even faster than she had thought possible, and several of the festival's outdoor participants had clearly heard about the incident that had taken place just minutes earlier. As she walked through the venues, searching for Mac and Kylie, more than one couple turned aside to whisper, giving Sadie furtive glances. She clenched her jaw and forced her chin into the air. They couldn't begin to understand what she'd been through today.

Despite her proud demeanor, she nearly sank to the ground in relief when she spotted Mac and Kylie by the cotton candy stand. Kylie's face was smeared with a sticky palette of pink and blue, and for once, Sadie didn't much care how much dye and sugar her daughter had consumed.

The look on Mac's face as she strolled up told her he'd already heard—from whom she couldn't guess—about her very public confrontation with Jasper. He went to her without a word and awkwardly patted her shoulder. His stilted movements only exasperated her further—not that she had expected him to offer a fatherly embrace or anything.

Come to think of it, she'd probably have pushed him away even if he had.

"Time to go, Kylie," she announced, mortified at the way her words trembled.

Kylie protested, "But, Mommy, Kylie hasn't gone to the petting zoo yet!"

Sadie was in no mood to placate her daughter. "*Now*, Kylie."

Kylie looked from Sadie to Mac. He shook his head at her and, with a weary sigh, Kylie left the cotton candy stand and led the way to the parking lot.

"What about Jasper?" she asked as they exited the festival and stepped onto asphalt.

Sadie opened her mouth to answer her and discovered she had no words. She didn't know about Jasper, so she didn't know what to tell Kylie.

"Jasper had to go home early," Mac filled in for her.

Kylie frowned, but whatever five-year-old logic she was mustering, she kept it to herself.

On the ride home, she chattered on to Sadie about everything she had done that day—the friends she had met up with, the animals she had seen, the way her Sunday school teacher had fallen off the pony at the pony rides... But nothing lifted Sadie's mood, and Kylie's childlike intuition seemed to sense that something was very wrong. She finally fell silent, and by the time Mac's pickup pulled into the driveway of their home, the three of them had spent an agonizing eight minutes in complete silence.

As Mac turned the key in the ignition, he turned to look at Sadie.

"You shouldn't be too hard on him," Mac softly said, eyeing his daughter with a sad expression in his brown eyes.

Sadie's jaw clenched, but she didn't say anything. Mac paused before saying, "He tried to tell you about it several times. But you were so caught up in the dessert competition, you never heard what he was saying."

"I would have listened to something like that," Sadie stated, her tone brittle.

Mac frowned. "No, Sadie girl…you wouldn't have. He'd been scared for weeks to tell you."

Sadie shook her head. "No, see, that's the problem. If he was *scared*, it was most likely because he'd gotten cold feet and didn't know how to break that to me."

Mac shook his head sadly. "He was scared of *this*. This is what he was afraid of—that you'd see it all in the wrong light and then decide to punish him for it."

Sadie suddenly realized her daughter was listening. "Kylie, go wait for me on the front porch."

Kylie hesitated. "Kylie can wait here," she responded softly.

"*Go*, Kylie. *Now*."

Sadie helped her out of the truck and Kylie retreated to the front porch.

Once Kylie was out of earshot, Sadie turned to Mac angrily. "I don't appreciate your arguing with me in front of my daughter, and I certainly don't like you bringing up punishment in front of her. I'm her mother, therefore it's necessary for me to discipline her at times, and I certainly don't need that authority undermined."

Before she could forge ahead, Mac surprised her by saying, "You're right about that. I'm sorry."

She paused, her thoughts broken, and muttered a brief "Thank you" before starting again. "Secondly, Jasper's and my relationship isn't any of your business, and *if* Jasper had a problem with me—*IF* he did," she emphasized a second time, "then he should have brought it to *my* attention, not yours."

Mac threw her a second time by nodding. "I agree with you."

She heaved a breath. Okay, it should have felt like she was winning this argument…so why did she feel like such a loser?

It suddenly seemed as though everyone was trying to make her feel bad—Jasper, Dmitri Velichko and now her so-called father on top of it. Were they manipulating her guilt; was that it? She grew indignant at the thought and stiffened her spine as she spoke once more.

"Everyone seems to want to blame *me* for Jasper's mistakes. But the fact of the matter is, I didn't do anything wrong. If Jasper wanted to go to Colorado, he should have told me sooner so I didn't have to hear it from his soon-to-be-former-employer."

"He tried," Mac defended again, "but you never allowed him the opportunity. You have to admit, Sadie girl, you've been rather… preoccupied…these last few weeks."

"If you think you can live my life, you're welcome to it," she snapped, the weeks of pressure and strain releasing in a rush of words. "I buried my husband and my mother in less than three years' time, I lost a career in television and publishing, I started another career by building a restaurant from the ground up, and all the while, I've been single-handedly raising my daughter. And oh, let's see, how much love and support have I had from my father over the past twenty-nine years? Well, I think we know the answer to that," she responded to her own question with more than a touch of bitterness.

"The thing is, Mac…"—she fought to control tears, determined that he would *not* see her cry at this low point—"you weren't *there* before when I needed you…so what makes you think I even want you here now? And if Jasper doesn't want to be here either, far be it from me to keep him in my self-indulged little world."

She gripped the door handle and tugged at it with a sharp motion, sliding out of the pickup and grabbing her bag as she went.

"Sadie?" Mac called before she could slam the door. She wanted to slam it anyway, blocking out whatever else he had to say. But her curiosity—and a perverse sense of hope—wouldn't let her. She paused.

"You haven't been raising Kylie alone," Mac pointed out. "Jasper's been raising her too."

This completely rational observation shattered her final wish for understanding. "She's *my* daughter, Mac. *Mine*. And I think it would be better if you—and Jasper and whoever else wants to interfere in our lives—just left us alone from now on."

And with that, she slammed the door with such force that the truck body swayed. She turned and stalked up to the porch, and her fingers trembled as she tried to fit the key in the lock. Kylie's round, worried eyes on her didn't help matters.

"Mommy?"

Sadie ignored her and fumbled desperately to get inside, away from the eyes of the world. The tears she'd been fighting for the last hour rose and blurred her vision, slowly seeping from her rapidly blinking eyes and falling onto her hands as she continued to struggle with the lock.

"Mommy?" Kylie's voice held her own desperation as her tiny fingers clutched at Sadie's blouse. "Mommy, are you okay?"

The heartfelt concern in that tiny question, spoken with such worry from her five-year-old's heart, served to do what weeks of worry, stress, and strain hadn't accomplished. Sadie sank to her knees as she heard Mac's truck leave the driveway, wrapped Kylie's little form in her arms, and held her for several minutes while she wept, as the key patiently waited in the lock.

* * * * *

The week that followed convinced Sadie that everything she'd been through thus far was only a test for the greater battle to come. Dmitri's winning first prize at the Cocoa Cook-Off was local headline news for several days after the competition ended. Sadie tossed the papers into the recycle bin without reading them and even toyed with canceling her subscription. Kylie, bereft without Jasper to watch her, behaved abominably for their neighbor, Mrs. Snelling, who had offered babysitting services out of the goodness of her heart. But after four days of Kylie's worse-than-usual antics, even Mrs. Snelling's charity had reached the limits of its endurance. Sadie attempted to take Kylie with her to the restaurant one day, but after several Kylie-inspired mishaps in the kitchen, that proved to be a bad idea.

She could have called the local day care, but for a child who had never known anything except personal one-on-one attention, Sadie feared the day care might not be the ideal solution, and she loathed the thought of Kylie being permanently banned from there.

Without any other options, she once again begged Glynda to take on extra duties while she sorted out her personal life—a conversation filled with such humiliation and begging that Sadie feared she'd never reestablish her self-respect.

She didn't have much time to worry over it, however, because Kylie-at-home was a full-time career in itself. Sadie found herself racing upstairs and downstairs, from one end of the house to the other, to keep Kylie entertained and out of trouble. Kylie seemed determined to wreak even more havoc than usual, probably out of her frustration in being denied to visit Jasper, although Sadie didn't want to admit as much—to herself or anyone else.

So she tightened her emotional resolve, hid her face from the world, and worked to keep up the facade that although things were a bit rough, everything was business as usual. All the while, she was dying inside…wondering how she had ever thought she could manage without Jasper's help and why she had ever told Mac to stay away. While her heart ached at these thoughts, her indignation rose to remind her that *Jasper* had chosen to abandon *her*, not the other way around. And besides, Mac had never been around much in the first place, so it wasn't like there was a lot to miss on that score anyway.

But it was at night, when she finally had Kylie tucked beneath the covers and sleeping the satisfied sleep of the young, that the worst of it came. It was when she lay in bed, exhausted but unable to sleep, that she curled into a ball and nursed the pain inside her. Although she was surviving without Jasper's assistance, she was longing for his presence—the touch of his hand on her back or her hair…the way he raised his eyebrows at some of the crazy things she said…the warmth of his lips on hers. This was a void nothing else could fill. At night, trapped in the silence of her own making, she missed him. Missed him more than she had ever thought possible. And the hurt and anger grew to drown out the sorrow that threatened to overwhelm her.

It wasn't the same as missing Ned. Death had a finality to it that cut harder and deeper but grew to forced acceptance because life went on, even without the person in it. The loss of Jasper was harder to accept. He still moved in the world, was still a part of life…just no longer a part of hers.

She found herself talking to Ned at night as she cradled the anguish inside her, asking him what she should do and when life had become so impossibly hard. She never found an answer, but there were times when she was sure he wrapped his arms around her and held her fast. It was only then she was able to drift off to sleep at last.

By the beginning of the third week following her breakup with Jasper, Sadie felt as though she were reaching the end of her rope. She worried about the restaurant in her absence, she wearied of Kylie's incessant demands for attention, and she weakened at the thought of Jasper preparing for the move to Colorado. It was in the midst of one such moment, when she felt sure that within another second she was going to lose her mind completely, that the doorbell rang, rattling her from her musings and sending her flying to the front door. She would never admit she hoped it was Jasper who stood there, but in the deepest well of her soul, that was precisely the hope she cherished.

It wasn't Jasper, however, who greeted her on the doorstep with a wide smile and outstretched arms.

"Hello, sugar darlin'! And how *are* you?"

It was Mama Belva.

Before she could respond, she found herself engulfed in the ample breadth of Belva's arms and her chest squeezed so hard she thought she might burst. By the time her mother-in-law released her, she was gasping for breath, whether from shock or the force of Belva's greeting, she wasn't quite sure.

"Why, you're lookin' as peaked as whipped toppin' on a Ju–ly morning, Sadie dear."

Sadie used to giggle endlessly at the way Belva pronounced *July*. *Joo–lie*—always emphasized, always two syllables. She would giggle so hard she'd soon have Ned chuckling with her, although with his Southern roots, he didn't say it much differently himself. But this time, Sadie wasn't laughing.

She stared at her mother-in-law, taking in the familiar memory of her stylish, silvery white hair and twinkling blue eyes. Plump but undeniably graceful, Belva was one of those women who would be as equally beautiful and charming at eighty as she had been at eighteen. Sadie recalled how awkward she had felt during her first meeting with Ned's mother, shortly after they'd gotten engaged. Belva's genuine Southern hospitality had soon set Sadie at ease, though she often recalled that feeling of awkwardness each time she set eyes on Belva after a long while apart.

"Mama Belva." Hearing herself, Sadie wanted to wince. It had come out flatter than she'd intended. She attempted to perk up a bit. After all, this was *Belva*. "What are you doing here?" She wasn't very successful. This one came out with just a touch of accusation and not nearly enough hospitality. She almost feared Belva might reprimand her and ask if her mother hadn't raised her any better than that, but Belva didn't seem to notice her lack of excitement.

"Now, sugar…" She swept into the front hall, closing the door behind her. "When you didn't return my phone calls for several weeks,

I began to get worried." She moved from the hall into the kitchen, familiarly opened a cupboard, and pulled out a glass.

"Whew, I tell you, I am just *parched*. I drove all the way up here—I swear, y'all don't have a clue about good iced tea up here in the North."

Sadie was feeling a bit fuzzy-headed. She wondered if she had fallen asleep in the middle of the day and this was part of a twisted dream she was having. It wouldn't have surprised her. She'd been so tired lately....

"Why are you lookin' at me like that, sugar? You look almost disappointed to see me." Belva affected what Sadie supposed could be called a pout, but considering her age, Belva really did pull it off quite well.

Sadie shook herself to attention, remembering her manners. She wouldn't mind a tall glass of iced tea herself—something with lots of caffeine and lemon to take the edge off this haze.

"No, Mama Belva, not at all. I'm thrilled to see you." It still sounded unconvincing, so she cleared her throat and tried again. "Really, I *am*."

Belva cocked an eyebrow and didn't look the least bit inclined to believe her. Sadie didn't blame her. She tried shifting the topic.

"You drove up from Alabama? That's quite a trip."

Belva shrugged. "I needed some distraction…and some time to myself," she offered cryptically. "Besides, Clay's been busy building some fancy shed out in the backyard. So long as Ginny"—Ginny was their neighbor—"keeps puttin' supper on the table each night, I don't think he'll miss me for another two weeks or so." Her eyes twinkled mischievously. "Two and a half, if I'm lucky."

Sadie found herself smiling without trying. That hadn't happened in quite awhile, and it felt good. Belva appeared to be pleased with this progress but didn't draw attention to it.

"Now, where's that rascally granddaughter of mine?" she drawled.

Sadie's smile grew, and she suddenly felt an unexpected relief. She could still smile. It was a good sign.

"She's upstairs," Sadie offered. "Playing Barbies."

Sadie didn't add that leaving Kylie unsupervised with her Barbie collection wasn't always a smart move. After all, that's how Malibu Ken had lost his leg.

"Oh, that reminds me!" Belva exclaimed. "I've got a present for her in the car. Some new toy—a pet for Barbie. You should see it, sugar; it's the most darlin' little dog. And he comes with these ador- able little biscuits that you feed him, and then he…well…" Belva paused for a moment. "It comes with a magnetic pooper-scooper and everything, sugar, so it shouldn't be a problem."

Now Sadie found herself completely unable to control her grin, and she began to fear she'd start giggling helplessly. If Malibu Ken's leg had ended up in the toilet, she couldn't begin to imagine what Kylie would do with this new toy.

She suddenly found herself throwing her arms around Belva's thick neck and holding on tightly.

"I really am glad to see you, Mama Belva," she murmured, unable to control the tremble of emotion in her voice.

Belva patted Sadie's back in her typical gentle way. "There, there, sugar. I never doubted it for a minute."

* * * * *

Belva's arrival changed everything. From the moment she appeared on the doorstep, things began to look up. Belva took charge with a matriarch's deft hand, wrangling Kylie and freeing Sadie to return to the restaurant. Belva did this gladly, grateful for the days spent with her granddaughter and the nights in her daughter-in-law's company.

She never asked Sadie about not returning her phone calls, and Sadie never offered to explain. But somehow Belva seemed to know, and it was the one thing that left Sadie slightly uncomfortable through their long chats, as they caught up on the last few months since they'd really talked.

Even though she'd never considered herself close with Belva, Sadie loved to talk with her. Her amused drawl sounded, at times, almost lyrical enough to lull you to sweet, restful sleep even when she was telling the silliest of stories. Belva felt like home, and Sadie hadn't had that since her own mother died. She drank in the older woman's presence, drawing closer to her memories of times long past. It was easier, after all, to dwell in days gone by than to consider the ones ahead… without Jasper, maybe even without Mac.

Belva asked about Jasper only once after her arrival. Their first night at dinner she had questioned his absence, having known him to be a permanent fixture at Sadie's house on previous visits.

But when she mentioned his name in the same breath as, "Pass the biscuits please, sugar…and where *is* that Jasper boy who's always hanging around? I'd have thought you'd nailed him down by now, Sadie," it was obvious within seconds that she'd made a mistake.

Kylie, who had been humming and swinging her feet for the first time in a week, fell deathly silent and still. She stopped eating and looked at Sadie, who had dropped her fork to the floor with a clatter.

Sadie slowly leaned over, picked up the fork, and sat straight in the chair. With very deliberate movements, she laid the fork aside and covered it with her napkin.

"Jasper's leaving," she calmly announced. "At the end of the summer. For Colorado. He got a prestigious teaching position at a private academy."

Kylie's lower lip trembled, and without asking permission, she laid her own fork aside and twisted her way off the chair and onto the floor. She left the room silently, and her tiny footfalls could be heard thumping up the stairs to her room.

"I see."

Later, Belva took Kylie some ice cream for dessert in her room, and within a half hour's time, she was rolling with laughter as Kylie happily described the adventures of the bathroom volcano. Sadie heard them and smiled with bittersweet relief.

Belva didn't mention Jasper again for some time.

Chapter Fourteen

....

Mac hesitated for a long moment on the front porch of Sadie's house. He stared at the polished wood door, feeling a pang of both gratitude and regret—gratitude to Jasper, who had helped to keep the house in excellent condition over the years…and regret for himself, for not being there to help with the little bits of upkeep. For all its memories, he no longer felt any personal claim to this home. It had been Amelia's, and now it was Sadie's. Just as it should be.

Swallowing his emotions, he forced himself to raise a hand and ring the bell. Once this act was completed, his shoulders sagged in defeat. He was both eager and uncertain about seeing his daughter's face. She'd made it more than clear he was not welcome.

Moments later, as the door opened, he steeled himself for a frigid greeting. He was startled by the warm voice he encountered.

"Hello there, is there something I can help you with?"

Mac's head whipped upward at this unfamiliar Southern drawl. He blinked in bafflement at the charming woman who greeted him, her cheeks pink and her white hair swept up off her shoulders.

"I, um…"

He looked around, wondering if he'd somehow managed to knock on the wrong door. He noticed a weathered Cadillac in the driveway and determined that he must be getting older than he thought, to have completely missed his daughter's house.

"I'm sorry, I must have—"

"Oh, are you lookin' for Sadie?" the woman questioned and then squinted. "You do look familiar, sugar."

Mac, in turn, stared a little harder at the lady before him, his mouth parting slightly. "I'm Mac, Sadie's father—"

"Oh! Darlin'! My apologies!" She moved her plump frame out of the doorway and pulled him into the foyer before he could protest. "I'm Belva, Ned's mother. I haven't seen you in…well. Since my son's funeral, I daresay."

Mac felt a stain of remorse upon his cheeks. "Um…yes, ma'am, I believe that's right." He stood awkwardly in the foyer, shifting from foot to foot and entirely too aware that Sadie would not be pleased with his presence here.

"Is Sadie about?" he nervously asked. "I only came by because she had said there were some things—"

"Oh, come in, darlin'. No, I'm afraid she's at the restaurant." Belva began leading the way into the house, and to his chagrin, Mac had little choice but to follow.

"Apparently things have been busier than a set of jumper cables at a family reunion the last couple of weeks since Sadie has no one to watch Kylie through the day."

Mac frowned. He hadn't realized Sadie was struggling so much. But of course, she would be, now that Jasper… He cleared his throat. "I wasn't aware of her difficulties. If I had been…"

What? He'd have been more than happy to help out? Certainly he would have. But that was something his daughter would likely never allow him to do.

Though he didn't voice these thoughts, Belva must have heard the distress in his tone. She looked him over with what he feared was a critical air.

"Have a seat, sugar." She gestured to the sofa. "I'd tell Kylie you're here, but she fell asleep while we were watchin' that *Lion King* film. I never did understand that little cat and pig." She shook her head.

"Meerkat," he corrected her as he took a seat.

"What's that?"

"It's a meerkat. I heard Jasper explaining it to Kylie one night."

"Hmm. So I was right."

"Right about what?" he asked.

She clicked her tongue in dismay but didn't answer him. "Would you like some tea, darlin'?"

Mac shook his head. "No thank you, ma'am."

"Hmm. Well, I would. Won't take but a minute." She left the room, and Mac sat tensely waiting for her return and fearing Sadie might appear at any moment. As much as he wanted to see his daughter, he feared her reaction if she found him, as unwelcome as he was, inside her house.

Though Belva promised it would only be a minute, Mac could have sworn it was ten before she reappeared, carrying a tea tray loaded with steaming mugs and a plate of cookies.

"There you are, sugar." She placed the tray on the coffee table and then sank into the recliner with a sigh, cradling her cup in her hands.

"Now. Tell me everything."

Mac looked at her askance. "I don't believe I understand."

Belva blew on the surface of her tea and said, "About Jasper. And Sadie. And whatever turned that granddaughter of ours into a rebellious little munchkin."

Mac frowned with sadness. "Kylie's been misbehaving?"

Belva huffed. Mac chewed his lip for a moment before asking, "What do you know already...about Sadie and Jasper?"

She took a tentative sip of her tea and swallowed before answering, "I've never possessed any illusions about that Jasper Reeves. He's always had a hankering for Sadie, and there was no denying it. If he was too blind to see it while she was married to Ned, so much the better. But now..." She trailed off thoughtfully and then softly finished, "Now I'm just grateful, sugar, that Sadie has him in her and Kylie's life."

"Had," Mac forlornly corrected. "Had him in her life."

Belva arched an eyebrow at these words. "Out with it," she insisted.

And Mac did, to the best of his ability, bring her up to speed on the last few months. When he finished, Belva let out a long, low whistle. "These Yankee girls. Never knowin' what to do with a man." She paused for a thoughtful moment and then asked, "What about you, sugar? What do you think of all this?"

Mac found his mouth dry, with the telling of Sadie and Jasper's story, so he first reached for the mug of tea cooling on the coffee table. He took a large swallow, thoughtful for a moment. Then he said, "I love my daughter. But Jasper didn't deserve the judgment she gave him. That boy placed plenty of faith in me when I hadn't earned it, so I tried to speak up on his behalf. It didn't feel right to let him down, after all the times in my life when I've backed down on someone."

The truth was, he'd always been fond of Jasper. The kid was honest, but more than that, he was loyal. Those were qualities Mac admired, especially since he had such a hard time refining them in himself.

But now, Mac shook his head in remorse. "I don't think I was much help to him. Sadie probably placed another mark against him just because he'd found favor in my eyes."

He could hear the sympathy in Belva's tone as she murmured, "Oh, sugar."

His eyes met hers with an apologetic smile. "No need to feel sorry for me, ma'am. I burned my own bridges." He bit his lip for a moment. "That's what I appreciate about Jasper. He gave me hope that I could rebuild 'em."

Looking down, he stared into the translucent depths of his tea. "No one really knows," he explained, "except those who have already walked it, how rocky the road to redemption really is. There are no smooth paths, and not many people offer recognition for one's efforts along the way." He tore his eyes from his mug and glanced back at Belva. "But Jasper did, for me." Mac struggled for a minute or two, tamping his gratitude into a smaller container. "I wish Sadie knew what she had in that boy."

Belva worried her lip, her expression sober. "If she didn't know before, sugar, I'd say she's beginning to learn."

* * * * *

With Belva's arrival and her offer to watch Kylie through the day, Sadie was once again free to work at the restaurant full-time. To her surprise, her many absences hadn't created the number of crises she'd feared—Glynda had managed things with impressive skill during the gaps. Upon Sadie's return, she found everything almost in better condition than she had left it, and for a brief moment, she wondered if even her own restaurant fared better in other hands. But then Jimmy blushed when he saw her and mumbled how glad he was that she'd be coming in more regularly, and Karl pulled her aside to tell her that she really needed to have a talk with Jimmy—he'd nearly caused two grease fires last week. And Willow was asking for a raise because her tips weren't stretching to adequately cover all the hours she'd been working the past few weeks, and after all was said and done, Sadie was quite satisfied that her own position was secure.

She lingered in the kitchen longer than usual, however, helping Karl as he put the final touches on several breakfast dishes. Jimmy was stretching her patience thin with dozens of simple questions. How could he be sure the eggs were cooked? How long before he turned the French toast? Should he put more honey in the raspberry yogurt sauce?

She sighed. No wonder Karl was nearly driven to madness. With Jimmy momentarily distracted by the dish in front of him, she knew now was the moment to escape. But she found herself reluctantly staring at the neatly lined rows of pans and utensils and longed to jump in between Karl and Jimmy and create something fabulous. Something *other* than desserts.

But as Jimmy raised his head and seemed to zero in on her for another question, she abandoned the thought and escaped out into the main dining room. Things had slowed since the initial breakfast rush, although there were still several tables filled with latecomers. She headed for the hostess station and stopped.

Jasper stood there, in his typical faded jeans and T-shirt, his hair choppy and his face scruffy. His shoulders were slightly hunched, and he was looking at the ground, not seeming to notice anyone else.

For a moment, Sadie's stomach felt as though it was in her chest. He looked *lost*, standing there like that. He looked exactly how she felt. She was tempted to run straight into his arms and ask him if they just couldn't go back to the way things were.

But then reality interceded. They couldn't go back because Jasper wouldn't *be* here. He was leaving for Colorado soon. Leaving her for a whole new life out West. Just like some old-time pioneer, abandoning the old life without a backward glance and forging onto something new and different.

Something that didn't include her. He was leaving her, just like Ned had. But Ned hadn't had a choice in his fate. Jasper had a choice, and he'd decided to go.

Steeling herself, she straightened her spine and approached him with a desperate attempt at appearing nonchalant. Pleasant but distant. Calm but cool.

"Hello, Jasper."

His head shot up in surprise, and she felt a moment's hesitation in her resolve. His eyes were bleary and red, and there were sleepless lines cutting into his temples. He looked miserable.

"Hey," he answered her greeting. He didn't attempt to smile, and neither did she.

"I wondered if you had a minute," he said. "I was hoping we could…talk."

She considered this request, stealing a sideways glance around the restaurant. Other than several patrons' obvious interest in their conversation (they'd probably been among the crowd at the Cocoa Cook-Off), everything seemed to be quiet for the moment. Still, she balked.

"Why couldn't you come by the house?" she quietly demanded, letting irritation rise at him for showing up where there was the possibility of causing another scene.

"I didn't want to upset Kylie," he explained. "I know you told her she couldn't see me for a while."

Sadie's jaw clenched. "How do you know that?"

Jasper licked his lips, obviously reluctant to tell her. She crossed her arms and waited.

"She called me last week," he finally admitted. "She's really getting good at using the telephone."

Sadie felt a clenching in her chest. That was just the sort of thing he always used to know—the sort of thing he'd made a point to tell her. How was she ever going to manage without him in her life? Belva couldn't stay forever.

She shook her head slightly. But what did it matter? She could never have asked for Jasper's help ever again. Not now that she knew how he really felt—how he thought *she* felt…just using him for babysitting and free rides.

She sighed. "I don't have a lot of free time right now."

He ignored the tone in her voice. "I can come back later, if that's more convenient."

She didn't want him to come back later. She wanted him to leave her alone, to let her be miserable and attempt to rebuild things without him. The last thing she wanted was for him to keep looking at her with those mournful blue eyes, conjuring up dozens of delightful memories from the past few years and especially the past few weeks.

"No, it's fine," she finally acquiesced. "Follow me."

She led the way out of the dining room and down the hall to the office. It was empty. She purposely took the seat behind the desk and gestured for Jasper to grab a chair from along the wall. The desk placed a solid barrier between them, and she preferred being in the position of power on the opposite side.

She could tell by Jasper's momentary hesitation that he noticed the distinction. But he took a chair and drew it up to the desk without commenting.

Sadie folded her hands and leaned back, making every effort to appear relaxed when her muscles were coiled as tightly as springs.

"If this is about the items you left at my house, I've boxed them up and can have them delivered to you. I know you'll be wanting them for the move."

The voice speaking these words had the crispness of a business exchange. Sadie hated the sound of them but didn't know what other tone to take.

Jasper shook his head. "No, it's not that." He raked a hand through his flyaway hair, causing it to stick up in several more places. She couldn't help thinking how it looked endearing on him. It always had.

"No, listen, Sadie…I wanted to talk to you about…about what happened."

"About your decision to move to Colorado? I don't believe there's much to discuss." Again, that cold, calculating voice.

These words seemed to stop him dead in his tracks. He sighed, covered his face with one hand, and leaned back in his chair. After several seconds of silence, Sadie began to worry for him. At last, he dropped his hand and stared at her out of those melting blue eyes.

"I wanted to tell you about it. I tried, several times, but there was always something getting in the way."

"The dessert competition, isn't that what you mean?"

"For the most part, yes."

She flinched at his honesty.

"Maybe you should have tried harder," she suggested, her voice fluctuating from cool to scorching.

He shrugged. "I don't know. Maybe I should have."

"You're awfully nonchalant about it," she remarked with irritation.

He leaned forward quickly and suddenly, and she almost drew back as his hands gripped the desk, resting less than a foot from hers.

"But that's the problem, Sadie—I'm not feeling nonchalant about it at all. I miss you," he admitted. Her heart wrenched. "I'm sorry we fought, and I'm sorry I didn't tell you about the job sooner. I never meant for you to feel like I didn't care about you—that's precisely what I was trying to avoid."

His words struck deep within her, and she had to keep her gaze lowered for several minutes as she worked to regain her emotional footing. With her eyes still focused on her lap, she said, "Whether that's true or not, Jasper, I think it's quite obvious there are things about our relationship you've always wanted to change."

"Sadie—"

She rushed ahead, not allowing him to stop her. "I guess you've come to think of me as selfish and demanding rather than the selfless and giving friend I hope I once was to you. And while we've shared some wonderful memories over the years, it's understandable at this point why you'd want to move on without me. I mean, it's become obvious to me that Kylie and I are holding you back from realizing your true potential." She was very glad she'd kept her gaze down. She had managed to control her voice, keeping it smooth and matter-of-fact, but she could not hide the tears threatening to spill over. "And the truth is, perhaps you've been holding us back too."

This statement was met with such a long silence that eventually Sadie had no choice but to look up. Jasper's mouth was closed and he was looking off to the side, not even at her. She wondered if he'd just tuned out or if he'd really heard what she said.

"Well," he finally spoke, slowly bringing his eyes around to hers, "if that's the way you feel."

She had contained her emotions reasonably well, but Jasper didn't have the same luck. His eyes held a sheen of tears, and she could tell by the bitter twist of his mouth that what she had said had cut him deeper than she could have imagined. She had meant to let him go in such a way that he would feel no further obligation to them. She wondered if maybe she should have chosen a different method to say it.

No, she decided. It would be better for them all this way. He could start over in Colorado without worrying about them. He might hurt a little over this, but he could heal now, knowing that she would move on without him—just as she expected him to do without her.

She only hoped this mind-numbing ache in her stomach would ease with time. *Please, God, let it pass.* Because she didn't see how she could function if she had to carry this with her all the time.

"We wish you all the best," she filled the silence, hating how it sounded as though she were laying him off. The desk between them only served to enhance the feeling.

"Yeah." He said it with only the faintest trace of bitterness; she had to give him that. He rose to his feet and stared at her for a minute, and she found herself unable to look away.

What if this was the last time she saw him? What if this was really their last good-bye? She had known him all her life—she'd never had another best friend. Could a person replace a best friend? Or did only one ever come around in a lifetime?

He turned to go, and a part of her inwardly fractured, feeling a momentary panic that it was over—all over—between them. But she couldn't think of any good reason to stop him, never taking into consideration, in that moment, her life's happiness or his or even Kylie's.

He was reaching for the office door when it flew open and Kylie tumbled into the room. There had been an exclamation on her lips that dissolved at the sight of Jasper, replaced with a simple and absolutely satisfactory *"Oh!"* Her eyes darted from Sadie's face to Jasper's, back again and back once more.

And somehow she could tell, as children often can, that nothing had been mended and had perhaps been rent forever.

Disregarding Sadie's admonitions not to speak to Jasper, Kylie cried out his name and threw herself at his legs, clinging there tenaciously. With tears still wetting his eyes, he grinned and worked to disentangle himself.

"Lift Kylie, lift!" she demanded, and he did. She wrapped her arms around his neck and buried her face against his cheek.

Belva stepped inside, huffing slightly as she announced, "I declare, sugar, that child is the hardest thing to keep up with—oh." She noticed Jasper still smothered in Kylie's embrace.

"Hello there, darlin'."

"Hey, Belva," he greeted.

Belva did her own glancing back and forth until she seemed fairly satisfied as to what had gone on moments before. Sadie couldn't help but blush at the interested look Belva gave her.

Kylie pulled back to look at Jasper's face. "Mommy said you were leaving for the collie rodeo, but I told her that was silly. It's *horses* in the rodeo."

He laughed softly and planted a kiss on her cheek. Sadie's heart ached for them. This was exactly what she'd been afraid of when Jasper had pushed for more than friendship. Now look at the heartbreak it had caused her daughter. Jasper was leaving, and Kylie would be left behind.

Kylie grew serious then, placing one little hand on each of Jasper's cheeks. "Tell Mommy she's silly. Tell her Jasper's not going."

Jasper looked into her eyes for a moment. "I am going, Kylie," he quietly answered.

Kylie looked back at him. "Is Jasper teasing?"

Sadie didn't think she could take much more. Jasper looked like he couldn't either. He slowly shook his head. Kylie's lower lip began to tremble.

"But…but…*why*? Why's Jasper leave?"

Jasper shifted a glance toward Sadie and quietly asked, "Would it be all right if I took Kylie for a walk?"

Sadie hesitated, wondering if enough damage had been done. But before she could answer, Belva stepped in, saying, "You go on, sugar. I need a break anyhow."

Jasper nodded to Belva, but his eyes still sought Sadie's. She let out a little breath. "Go ahead," she finally allowed.

Jasper and Kylie left the room. Sadie busied herself with papers on the desk, mentally preparing for a salvo of questioning from Belva. But the older woman said nothing, eyed the paperwork with a sigh, and then sank into the seat Jasper had vacated.

Sadie was just about to exhale with relief when Belva launched into her second-least-favorite topic these days.

"Sugar, I've been hearin' folks talking around here. The rumor is that your father's moved back into town and you won't have anything to do with him."

Sadie slid a few documents into a file and slammed the drawer.

"That's not exactly true. Yes, he's back in town, and I've had him over for dinner a few times. He even came to Kylie's birthday party awhile back."

"And have you had him around lately?"

Sadie sighed and wished there was somewhere for her to escape. "No," she admitted, "not in the last few weeks."

"Not since you quit seein' Jasper, is that what you mean?"

Sadie clenched a fist out of tension. Why did her life have to be the topic of public debate? "How much do you know about me and Jasper?"

Belva waved a hand airily. "I know all I need to know, darlin'. Now be a dear and answer my question."

Sadie suppressed the urge to make a face. "That's right, I haven't seen him since Jasper and I…stopped…seeing each other." She found it a very awkward phrase to speak. "But I wouldn't worry about Mac. He's been in and out of town many times during my lifetime—I'm sure he'll be in and out several more."

"Hmm," was all the acknowledgment to this statement Belva would give. Sadie had the sinking suspicion she was working up to something.

Sadie always found it better to get right to it where Belva was concerned. "What do you mean by that?"

Belva glanced up from a critical study of her well-kept nails. She appeared completely oblivious—an act Sadie had witnessed many times before.

"What's that, sugar? What were you sayin'?"

This time, Sadie didn't restrain. She gave Belva a face that made things clear. "Out with it, Mama Belva. What do you want to tell me?"

Belva clucked her tongue and shook her head. "Sadie, sugar, you should *never* go makin' faces like that. It's hardly becoming."

Sadie made a face to rival her first one, and Belva couldn't help smiling.

"I always did admire your spunk, darlin'."

Sadie drummed her fingers on the arm of the chair and waited.

"Friends of yours about town are saying that your father is moving into Jasper's house to take care of things while he's away."

This announcement rattled Sadie considerably. It represented a degree of permanence for the two most influential men in her life, which startled her. Mac's decision to move into a house meant a presence of stability she had never known him to have. If he lived in a house, he couldn't just pull up stakes and move on when the idea took hold of him. It meant he really was serious about staying near her this time.

But more disconcerting than that was what it meant for Jasper. If Mac was moving in, then Jasper was moving out. He really would move to Colorado. He really was going far beyond her reach.

Sadie suddenly felt the most desperate urge to cry.

"You know, sugar, I'd love to see your father again."

Sadie swallowed, unable to think past the hollow ache accompanying her knowledge of the permanence of Jasper's good-bye.

"I—I don't know," she stammered out, vaguely realizing it summed things up pretty well. She didn't have a clue about anything right now.

Belva opened her mouth to comment further, but before she could say anything, a knock sounded on the office door.

It was Willow.

"Ms. Spencer, we've got a problem."

Sadie thrilled momentarily at the possibility of a distraction.

"What is it, Willow?"

She chewed her lower lip and paused, seemingly searching for the exact words. Finally she just threw out the only ones that summed up the situation: "Jimmy chopped off the tip of his pinkie finger."

"He *what*?"

"An ambulance is on the way."

Sadie's head began to throb. This really wasn't the distraction she'd been looking for....

"I'll be right there," she promised Willow. "In the meantime, make sure Jimmy stays in the back and see if the ambulance can come around *without* the sirens on."

"Karl already saw to that, Ms. Spencer. He's got a friend at the EMS."

What would she do without Karl?

"All right. Is the...appendage...on ice?" She had the insane urge to giggle as she asked this question, but she kept her expression neutral.

Willow nodded. "Karl took care of that too. And he's got Jimmy applying pressure to the wound."

"How much food was contaminated? And what about utensils and such?"

"Nothing. He wasn't even in the kitchen when he did it."

Sadie frowned. "Well, how did it happen, then?" She had automatically assumed it had happened while he was chopping vegetables or something.

"He was on break, showing off with his pocketknife, when the blade snapped shut."

Sadie winced. Way too much information there. She shook her head.

"Okay, thanks, Willow. Get back to the dining room, and I'll go wait with Jimmy until the ambulance arrives."

Willow nodded and disappeared down the hallway.

"Excuse me, Mama Belva—"

She waved another hand, completely nonplussed by such excitement. "You go ahead, sugar. I'll just wait around in the dining room until Jasper brings Kylie back."

Sadie exited the office, and Belva followed. She left her mother-in-law in the main dining area and headed to the kitchen. Karl gestured her toward the back exit, where she found Jimmy leaning on the doorjamb, his face as pale as vanilla ice cream. A rag was tightly wrapped around the smallest digit of his right hand, not even so much as a drop of blood showing through.

Recognizing Karl's deft forethought brought a relieved smile to Sadie's face. Her own relief must have reassured Jimmy, because he regained a shade or two of color at the sight.

"Sorry, boss," he mumbled, clearly feeling guilty over the incident.

Part of her wanted to smack him alongside the head and begin a ten-minute presentation on just how risky this sort of thing was for a restaurant—or for anybody, for that matter. But he obviously felt badly enough, and his hangdog expression wouldn't allow her to reproach him further.

"You should be more careful next time," she gently suggested, to which he nodded fervently.

"Absolutely. Yes, ma'am."

She folded her arms across her torso as a breeze blew in through the open door. Summer was slowly winding down, and Sadie found herself looking ahead to fall, a season she had always loved. Some people thought spring was the time of renewal, but Sadie had always equated that feeling with autumn. It felt like a shedding of mistakes—falling leaves, crisp breezes. As if you could cast off an old skin to work on a new one. She always looked forward to fall: piles of leaves she and Jasper used to jump into as children, dressing up together for Halloween pageants, riding the roller coasters at Hersheypark in the Dark, corn mazes, hayrides, sharing candy apples, carving pumpkins to see who could make a scarier face… And then with Kylie, they had shared those traditions together with her. One happy family.

Sadie shivered.

"Are you cold, boss?"

She shook her head. "No, I'm all right."

Jimmy stared at his finger, trying to see through the layers of bandaging to assess the damage. Sadie felt sorry for him.

"Look at it this way," she offered, "it's a great excuse for your girl-friend to give you some serious nursing. What's a lost fingertip when you're up for some TLC?"

Her teasing tone provoked a bashful smile from him. He seemed to be pleased at the thought. "Yeah, I guess so."

The ambulance pulled up then, and Karl appeared to greet his EMS friend and hand over a container filled with ice and Jimmy's pinkie tip. Sadie answered a few questions, reassured Jimmy and told him to call his girlfriend from the hospital, and then waved as they drove off.

Karl shook his head once they were out of sight. "That kid ain't got the sense God gave a duck."

Sadie wrapped an arm around his shoulders. "Yeah, but he's *our* little gosling."

Karl snorted and hurried back inside to catch up on the incoming lunch orders. When Sadie at last made her way back to the dining room, she found Belva seated at the counter, her brow furrowed in concern.

She felt a pricking of irritation.

"Jasper hasn't brought Kylie back yet?" she asked with an attempt at nonchalance.

Belva distractedly shook her head, but her vision remained fixed on a table in the corner. Sadie followed her gaze and noted two gentlemen seated in a booth with a pot of coffee resting between them.

"Mama Belva?" she questioned, disturbed by the other woman's intensity.

She forced her eyes away from the two men and onto Sadie's face.

"Sugar, who are those two?"

Sadie's glance flickered back to the booth and was momentarily disconcerted to find the men in question staring at *her*. She swallowed.

"I don't know; I've never seen them before. Why?"

Belva's eyebrows remained knitted together as she looked back in their direction. They had returned to their coffee, each taking occasional sips from their mugs. They didn't appear to be talking at all.

"Mama Belva? What's wrong?"

Except for at Ned's funeral, she had never seen Belva so disturbed. Her normally carefree face was lined with worry.

"Have you ever noticed them around before?"

Sadie shifted from one foot to the other, embarrassed to admit how little she'd been paying attention to her surroundings these days. And she hadn't even devoted any decent amount of attention to the restaurant in weeks. If not for her skilled and dedicated staff, who knew where she might be at this moment, after all her carelessness?

"No," she confessed, "but that's not really saying much. I don't always notice things like I should, in case you hadn't realized."

Belva didn't comment on this remark but continued to assess the two men.

"Okay, you're starting to freak me out, Belva. What's going on?"

Finally, the other woman turned and focused her attention on Sadie. "You don't remember seeing them before, sugar?" she questioned carefully. "Because I can promise you that as long as I've been here, they've been around."

Sadie straightened a few mugs behind the counter, feeling rather uncomfortable. "What do you mean—around?"

Belva watched her carefully. "Around your house, Sadie. Here at the restaurant. They followed us to church this past Sunday, although I didn't see them inside," she admitted. "I've even seen them around your neighborhood."

Sadie shrugged, relieved. For a moment she had feared they were restaurant critics and had gotten wind of Jimmy's mishap. "They're probably just tourists. Or maybe they just moved here. We've had all sorts of newcomers in the past few years," she remarked, thinking of Dmitri. "I wouldn't worry about it—I've seen all sorts of types come through this town."

Belva shook her head. "No, Sadie, that's not what I mean. I've seen them parked on your street. Watching your house."

Sadie felt a ripple of unease. Her house? Where she and Kylie lived?

"Maybe they're in real estate."

Belva's stare drilled into her. "They were at that table when I sat down here, Sadie, and they haven't touched a menu yet. Willow said they've been coming in quite a bit recently."

Sadie shrugged again. It was no different than Dmitri Velichko. "They're probably just trying to see how a restaurant is run."

Belva clearly didn't think so. "By coming to your house? By following you to work?"

She could not deal with this now. On top of everything else, she was being stalked by—she took a glance at the two men in the booth— two burly guys wearing dark sunglasses and Italian suits?

She bit her lip. Okay, so maybe that *was* a little odd…. Or maybe Belva's imagination was running away with her.

"You're not going senile on me here, are you, Mama Belva?"

Belva's expression could have withered a magnolia. "I can assure you, sugar, my mental faculties are as alert as ever."

Sadie couldn't resist the opportunity to tease. It was such a rare thing to actually ruffle Belva's feathers. "Of course they are," she soothed with an impish smile.

Belva's lips thinned to a straight line. She did not appear amused. Before she could muster a perfectly scornful Southern retort, Sadie noted Jasper's return from the corner of her eyes.

Unable to bear the thought of facing him once more, especially after knowing that he was letting Mac move into his house while he flew off to Colorado, she muttered something utterly nonsensical to her mother-in-law and disappeared into the back, momentarily forgetting the two men who watched sharply from their corner booth.

Chapter Fifteen

. . . .

That night, Sadie dreamed of Ned. He was with her in the herb garden behind Suncatchers, a place he had never lived to see in real life. She was leading him by the hand, pulling up clumps of herbs as she went, for him to sniff and taste.

Parsley. Basil. Mint. Thyme.

The textures and aroma were startlingly real for a dream. They walked in the moonlight, its watery glow washing the plants with a silver cast. Ned followed behind her, his fingers warm in the palm of her hand. She felt rushed—as though the minutes were slipping through the cracks and she must show Ned everything before he had to leave again.

"This is my life," she gestured around her. She remembered a verse from the Bible, from the Psalms: *"These things I remember as I pour out my soul."*

Ned was shaking his head at her, his eyes sad. They seemed to echo her deepest thoughts—*This is* not *your life.*

She looked at him for a moment, still feeling an urgency as she sought to capture approval in his loving green eyes.

"I keep pushing," she whispered to him. "I keep pushing to have it all until I can't hold anything."

Ned nodded in encouragement.

Family. *Her* family. Jasper. Kylie. Mac. They were her life. The thought was both warm and chilling at the same time. Such fragile threads that wove the tapestry of time. So fragile…

Her hand gripped Ned's until she felt the blood drain from her fingers. She could not let him go. Not again.

She suddenly felt overcome with the weight of loss. Her mother. Her husband. What would Ned think of her now? What would he think of the mess she had made of her life?

"I think you're too hard on yourself."

She was startled by his words. She hadn't expected him to speak. Deep in her conscious, she knew she was dreaming. But his voice sounded so startling real—so much like the voice she remembered— that her flesh tingled in response.

"There's not enough time," she desperately explained. "There's never enough."

"All life is fleeting," he answered. "Isn't that what the Bible says? Meaningless—a chasing after the wind."

Her eyes pierced deeply into his as she asked, "Then what's the point?"

"You know the point, Sadie," he answered. "You've always known. And if you don't…then it's not something I can tell you."

Sadie let go of his hand to rub her palms across her arms. She could not stop shivering. The garden was cold.

"Why grasp what you can't hold onto?" she asked.

"Because what you hold in your heart is far greater than the things you hold in your hand."

She could only look at him sadly, unable to understand what his sad eyes were trying to tell her. "That's easy for you to say," she accused.

He didn't answer her this time. She turned away from him for a second, and from the corner of her eyes, she watched him begin to walk away. She turned back.

"Wait. Ned, *wait*. I want to understand!"

He kept walking, but she felt like she was the one pulling away. A cloud covered the moon, bathing the garden in shadows. She could no longer see Ned.

"Please," she whispered to the darkness, "please help me to understand."

"Stop holding on to what doesn't last." She couldn't see Ned, but she could hear him.

"I don't know what you mean," she faintly protested, but in her heart she did know. She grasped tightly to the very things she *knew* would fade with time—the restaurant, her career, her abilities... Why not love? Why not Jasper? Why not Mac?

"It's too risky. I can't love and lose again. I'm so tired of loving and losing." She sighed with weariness and then called out to the blackened sky, "It's *not* better to have loved and lost! It's *not!*"

Suddenly the clouds shifted and Ned stood right in front of her. His presence was so unexpected that she gasped. He was just as she remembered him—his dark hair, his green eyes...and yet he wasn't real. This moment wasn't real.

"What are you afraid of, Sadie?" he asked her.

She could answer him now. "I'm afraid of what I can't hold onto."

She feared the time when her happiness passed. And pass it would. It always did—a lesson learned from her own loss.

Sadie swallowed.

"Why grasp what you can't hold onto?" she asked again.

Ned shook his head, unable to give her answers she had yet to learn herself. She awoke with a struggle for breath, shivering without her covers, and the remnant of dried tears itching her face.

* * * * *

That was only the first of Sadie's dreams. They continued night after night, in different scenarios and settings, but always with the same sense of urgency and the dissatisfaction of unanswered questions. The major difference was that other than that first night, Ned didn't appear in her dreams again. He was replaced by Jasper, who spoke far less than Ned had and only looked at her out of somber blue eyes.

She began to miss Jasper dreadfully, even worse than she had before their conversation at Suncatchers. Since that time, she'd had no word from him. She supposed he was going through last-minute preparations for the move, but her pride forbade her from asking about him, picking up the phone, or swinging by his house. She didn't trust what she might do if she saw him. And despite what her dreams might be telling her, she could not bring herself to consider asking him to stay. He clearly felt as though she had demanded enough of him. She would not ask this on top of everything else.

Belva's visit continued, and Sadie was relieved—not only for the babysitting services, but because she couldn't bear the thought of her and Kylie alone in the house without Jasper. He had become such an indelible fixture of their daily routine that living without him felt like leaving out an important part of the day—like forgetting to brush her teeth or eat dinner. Belva's presence helped to mask these feelings, but on the one day she had been absent—gone to visit a friend two hours away—Sadie had been near to insanity with trying to fill all the gaps Jasper's absence left.

She could only pray that once school started, new routines would be established and leave them to bury the past and move on with their lives. Kylie would be starting first grade, and Sadie was working out an arrangement to end her daily shifts sooner so she could be home by the time Kylie ended school.

As for Kylie, the possibility of first grade didn't thrill her as it once had. She was a different child these days—still endearing, still loving, still Sadie's little girl. But the spark had gone. Whatever Jasper had told her during their talk had calmed her rebellion, but it had ended her playfulness.

Sadie tried to make up for it, tried to devote more free time to Kylie's interests, but it didn't seem to make a difference. And Sadie soon realized that she wasn't Kylie's playmate. Jasper had been that, and she had lost him. Without intending to, Sadie had done the very thing to Kylie she had always accused Mac of doing to her—taking away the one man who should have been a constant in her life.

The thought ate away at her. And when Kylie returned to regular speech, no longer speaking of herself in the third person, Sadie thought nothing would ever be the same again. She had tried for such a long time to convince Kylie to refer to herself as "I" and "me," but when she finally did, Sadie felt as though something absolutely precious had been lost forever.

She began to wish that she could rewind time, forget the Cocoa Cook-Off, and forestall Principal Roop's conversation with her that day. But she knew it wouldn't have changed anything.

People left. Happiness ended. She wasn't sure she believed in anything else. Not anymore.

But she found herself wishing she could.

＊ ＊ ＊ ＊ ＊

One night after Belva had been with them about two weeks, she and Sadie put Kylie to bed and retreated to the back porch, where they bundled up with throws from the living room against the unseasonably cool evening air. The night was brilliant, clear and midnight blue with glittering stars pebbling the flawless backdrop. It was a sight to make one feel rich, no matter how few jewels one actually possessed.

Sadie wrapped her throw tightly around her, mentally reviewing her dream of the night before and unintentionally wondering if Jasper was watching the sky tonight. She pictured him with her, picking out constellations and wrapping stories around them that had nothing to do with Greek myths. The memory made her smile sadly.

"Penny for your thoughts, sugar?" Belva spoke up.

Sadie sighed, not inclined to admit where her mind had drifted. "It's just such a beautiful night," she offered instead.

"That it is, sugar. That it is." Belva paused. "But are you sure that's all you're thinking of, darlin'?"

Sadie loved Belva, but she didn't appreciate it when she pried. She wasn't about to admit how much she missed Jasper. Such a thing would have indicated a level of weakness that Sadie wasn't about to own up to possessing.

"On nights like this, it's better to *not* think about anything else." She felt as though this were a sage piece of wisdom. She'd spent many nights this past year thinking on things she had no control over—Dmitri Velichko and his upcoming restaurant…her ineptitude with desserts…Mac's reappearance…Jasper…. She stifled a sigh and indulged in a moment of feeling very old and wise.

Well, very old at least. She was almost thirty. That was old enough for all life had thrown at her, wasn't it?

She came to herself after a moment and realized Belva was staring at her. She looked back at her for a moment and then blinked.

"What?"

Belva shook her head, her silvery white hair flashing elegantly in the starlight.

"You really don't know why I'm here, do you, Sadie? All these weeks, and you still haven't figured it out." She looked away, back up at the sky. "Or maybe you haven't even thought about it."

Sadie frowned. "You just said you wanted to visit. You haven't seen us in a while."

Belva didn't say anything. Sadie waited but finally realized Belva had no intention of filling her in.

"I don't understand," Sadie spoke honestly.

Belva tore her eyes from the magnificence of the night sky and looked at her. "No, sugar, I really don't think you do."

Sadie found herself shrinking before Belva's stare. What had she done now? She didn't have a clue.

"Have I done something to…to offend you, Belva?" she asked.

Belva gave a most unladylike snort. "Not necessarily, darlin'." She and Sadie locked eyes for several moments.

Sadie was desperately trying to discern why Belva was looking at her with that odd glitter in her eyes. After a while, the coldness of it softened until Belva's stare was filled with nothing more than pity and sadness.

"What day is it today, Sadie?"

"Wednesday," Sadie immediately offered.

Belva shook her head. "No. What *day* is it?"

"August 5."

For a minute, Sadie thought Belva was going to shake her. Instead, the older woman simply stared as though Sadie had announced that she'd forgotten which way was up.

And then she remembered.

"August 5," she repeated.

Belva nodded.

"It's been five years today since Ned died."

Something in her chest sank with this realization, and she immediately began thinking about all the things she'd done today. She awoke from another dream about Jasper, fixed Kylie breakfast, ran off to work but spent at least thirty minutes glaring at the remodeling of Dmitri's restaurant across the street, went through a perfectly normal workday, returned home for dinner and a movie with Kylie and Belva, read Kylie a story, put her to bed, and escaped to the porch to relax.

Had she thought about Ned today? Had she missed him? What was wrong with her? What kind of horrible person was she? Could she sink much lower than this?

Belva's expression was filled with such pure, undiluted sympathy that Sadie found tears pricking her eyes.

"It's not that you forgot, sugar. It's *why* you forgot."

"I'm a bad person," Sadie immediately offered.

Belva took her hand. "You're *not* a bad person, darlin'. But you're certainly a misguided one, that's for sure."

To her horror, Sadie began to cry. She hadn't meant to break down in front of Belva—she hadn't done that since the night she'd had to call and give her the news of Ned's death. But now she found herself wracked by sobs she couldn't control.

Everything had fallen apart. Everything. And for the first time in her life, she was willing to admit that most of it had been due to her own selfish stubbornness.

She began mumbling explanations, dragging her sins through the mud behind her as she tried to work her way out of the mire. Dmitri Velichko and her wicked judgment of him. Trying to compete with Dmitri and others out of vanity and nothing else. Her near-murder of Aunt Matilda, not to mention sending Dmitri to the hospital at Kylie's birthday party. Her inability to forgive her father. Her neglect of her daughter. And the icing on the cake she could never make— her rejection of Jasper even after his attempts at reconciliation.

Belva let her sputter and stumble for a while before she disappeared inside and returned some minutes later with a steaming mug of tea.

"No wonder you're so worked up, sugar," she lightly chastised. "I couldn't find a drop of chamomile in the entire house. What would your mother say to that?"

The mention of her mother sent Sadie off into self-recriminations and blubbering once more. Belva soothed and encouraged her to take a sip of tea—Lemon Ginger—to calm herself.

After blowing repeatedly on the top to cool the beverage, she was able to gulp down a swallow. Belva was right. The warmth settled her stomach and caused her to take a few sniffling breaths.

"There," Belva declared triumphantly. "That's better. Now why don't you start from the beginning, sugar—first with this Dmitri character."

So with a deep breath and another fortifying sip of tea, Sadie did.

By the time she'd finished, Belva had covered them both with another throw against the night wind, and the moon looked down on them from high in its lofty perch. As Sadie wrapped things up with her final description of her and Jasper's last conversation, Belva drew her near and wrapped an ample, loving arm around her.

"Well, sugar, I'll certainly say, that explains quite a lot."

Sadie wiped her nose with a well-shredded tissue. "I'm hopeless, Mama Belva. There's nothing that can be done for me."

Belva clucked her tongue in disapproval. "I hardly think you're beyond redemption, Sadie. After all, look at what humanity has given the good Lord to work with over the years. I don't think you're the first lump of clay He's had to start over and work into something worthwhile. Besides, I think He's got a pretty good head start on you."

Sadie scoffed and leaned into Belva's warmth. It felt good to be wrapped in someone's arms. It made her feel anchored, safe, loved. It gave her hope, and she began to realize she'd been lacking that important attribute for quite some time.

"I've been very proud," she whispered, to herself as much as to Belva.

The older woman didn't disagree. "Yes, you have, sugar. But pride can be broken. You just take one step of humility, and you'll see what I mean."

"I've been selfish too."

"Start giving to other people. Start small and work your way up to the people you like the least. Like those two old harpies you mentioned—what were their names?"

"Smith and Jones."

"Not very original. But see if you can get yourself to give something, really *give* something, to those two. It may take some time, but I think you can get there."

Sadie was silent for a while, thinking things through. "What about Mac? How do I learn to forgive him?"

"Start by letting yourself love him. I know it's in there, sugar, even though it may be buried a little deep. Let yourself remember the things you've always liked about him, and then give him a chance to prove that he's changed. And maybe try loving yourself a little too. That might just help it all along."

Sadie absorbed this before Belva continued.

"You can't have everything, sugar, and sometimes just when you've got your hands on what you've always wanted, life takes it away and won't give it back."

Sadie thought of Ned and how much pain Belva must have been in today. Ned was her youngest, her baby. His death had taken something Belva could never get back. And yet she hadn't lost faith. She was thankful for her son's salvation and looked forward to the day she could see him again. She hadn't resented that Sadie had forgotten the anniversary of his death.

Sadie wondered if she could ever cultivate such grace in herself. Grace like Belva's. Grace like her mother had possessed. Grace like Mac had learned. Grace like Jasper had tried to teach her.

"I guess you could say," Sadie reflected ruefully, thinking on what she had lost the past few weeks, "that I've gotten my just desserts."

Belva chuckled, and the vibration of it shook Sadie's cheek as it rested against her mother-in-law's shoulder.

"Not hardly, sugar—more like a slice of humble pie. If we always got what we deserved, we wouldn't have much. That's where grace comes in."

"True," Sadie admitted.

They studied the night sky once more, and Sadie felt the first real peace she'd known in quite some time sneak up on her and fill her with light.

"I'm glad God is so forgiving. And I'm glad He's got patience, too. I think I'd have given up on me some time ago."

Belva reached a hand around to pat Sadie's cheek affectionately. "It's a good thing," she agreed, "or He might have gotten so weary of you, He'd have thrown you down Kylie's volcano."

Sadie laughed.

"How *did* that Ken lose his leg?" Belva questioned.

Sadie was still laughing softly. "I don't know, but I'm beginning to suspect that it wasn't an accident."

Knowing her granddaughter so well, Belva was inclined to agree. The two women sat in contented silence for some time until Sadie felt her eyelids growing heavy. Soon she'd have to head up to bed. But she wasn't dreading it as she had been all week. She didn't think she'd have any confusing dreams tonight.

As fatigue weighed on her eyelids, she sighed with relief. "I'm glad God sent you, Mama Belva."

Belva kept her eyes on the sky, the green in her gaze glittering with unshed tears. She held Sadie's hand tightly in hers, warm beneath the weight of the blankets.

"So am I, sugar. So am I."

Chapter Sixteen

. . . .

Sadie faced the next morning with mixed emotions. A part of her felt cleansed, renewed. Just as she had always viewed autumn, she felt as though she had shed something old and was preparing for the new.

But being armed with this knowledge didn't make the steps she had to take any easier. She had to swallow her pride, like Belva had said. And that meant she had to stop trying to best Dmitri Velichko. She had to accept him as inevitable competition and let the chips fall where they may. But more than that, she had to apologize to him.

It would be easier if he had acted poorly toward her, she reflected. She had to admit, Dmitri Velichko had been nothing but a gentleman, no matter what she'd done. He had performed with perfect grace. In many ways, she envied that in him. But that was her goal—to start acting with grace. Heaven knew enough had been doled out on her. Now she had to learn how to return the favor.

She went through the motions at the restaurant, barely aware of what she was doing; she was too focused on her plans for after work. She turned things over to Glynda with relief, glad she was finally free to get this over with.

She exited Suncatchers through the front, which was uncharacteristic of her—but she wanted to look at it again.

Dmitri's restaurant. Right there on the corner, across from hers. Remodeling was wrapping up, and she had to admit, the place looked classy. Chocolate brown awnings jutted out over large windows

303

flanking the gold-trimmed entrance door. Bronze light fixtures were spaced evenly along the exterior with antique scrollwork decorating the mounts. Everything was polished to an impressive gleam, but there was still no sign in place. She sighed.

It was hard to think what this could do to her business. But that was free enterprise, and railing against it wasn't going to change things. She would do what she'd always done—her very best. And this time around, she wouldn't flagellate herself for what she couldn't do. If Dmitri's restaurant beat out hers, so be it. It was out of her hands.

The thought felt wildly liberating, and with an intoxicating mixture of freedom and trepidation weighing on her shoulders, she started to walk toward her neighborhood. But instead of taking the road to the left, leading toward home, she veered to the right and headed for Dmitri's house.

She had thought to catch him at his restaurant, but the work had obviously closed up for the day. She couldn't think where else to look for him but at his home, and she could only pray he was there. She didn't much feel like waiting any longer to do this.

As she walked along, she drew her collar up higher against the sudden breeze. It seemed the seasons would turn quickly this year, with the promise of a long winter. She sighed, wondering how she'd make the walk to the restaurant each morning through ice and snow.

Before, when the winters had turned nasty, she'd relied on Jasper to see her to the restaurant. She forced the thought from her mind.

"One thing at a time, Sadie girl," she encouraged herself.

As she marched along the maple-lined drive toward Dmitri's, she became aware of a creeping feeling. It started in her shoulder blades and wiggled its way up her neck. She couldn't shake the sensation of being watched or followed. Finally, unable to ignore it, she paused and pretended to study the sole of her shoe for some obstruction while she slid a glance behind her.

What she saw made her give up all pretense. The two men from the restaurant—dark glasses and Italian suits still in place—stood watching her from several yards away.

Oh, this was just what she needed. Stalkers times two. Double the pleasure, double the fun. After all she'd been through—in the past five years and even the past few months—she wasn't about to put up with one thing more.

Gathering her courage and being grateful for the well-lit street, she turned and marched right up to them. She couldn't quite judge their reactions behind those sunglasses, but she sensed that they were surprised.

"I've noticed you gentlemen watching me for the past couple of weeks. Since you don't seem to know how to approach me on your own, I thought I'd make it easy for you. Is there something I can help you with?"

The two men exchanged glances, and before she knew it, Sadie was flanked on both sides as they lifted her up between them and dragged her behind a nearby shed. Once she realized what they were doing, she began to pull away, attempting to kick them in the shins and run.

She tried to shout, but the one on her right clapped a large, beefy hand over her mouth. She whimpered.

Not good, Sadie, not good.

What had she been *thinking*?

They pressed her up against the shed's walls. The one who hadn't covered her mouth now pressed a hand against her throat, severely diminishing the supply of air to her lungs. She choked and wheezed, but he did not release the pressure. When he spoke, his voice was thick with a Russian accent.

"You will not scream or make noise, do I make myself clear?"

She attempted to nod but had little success with the hand at her throat. Instead, she bobbed her eyes up and down, hoping that was sufficient.

It was. He released his hand from her throat, and the other man took his hand from her mouth.

The one who had already spoken removed his glasses, revealing one brown eye. The other was a film of white, and the skin around it showed where a knife had long ago marked the eyelid. Sadie suppressed a shudder of revulsion, but her stomach churned madly.

"We know you are in competition with Dmitri Velichko," the white-eyed one said, his words precise enough that she could understand him through his accent. "You must stop."

She was incredulous, despite her fear. "Stop? What do you mean—*stop*?"

The second one spoke. With his glasses still in place, he was almost more intimidating than the first man. "You will allow Dmitri's restaurant to outdo yours. Are we clear on this point?"

Her anger got the better of her fright. She drew herself up so she was eye-level with them. "Excuse me? *Excuse me!* Do you have *any* idea what I've been through in the last few months? My restaurant was there *first*—before your buddy Dmitri came along! I worked *hard* to get that place up and running, and I refuse to be told—"

She didn't refuse very well when a large hand clamped over her throat once more.

"You have daughter, yes?" the white-eyed one said.

She swallowed with a whole new kind of fear now. She forced a nod until he got the idea.

"She is, how you say...cute kid. Kylie. Likes to play with Barbie dolls."

Sadie's eyes were wide and fully alert. How had they learned so much about her daughter? When had all this happened? Sadie knew she had been rather oblivious of late, but this was beyond ridiculous.

The second one spoke now, drawing her eyes to him. "Would be shame if something happened to precious little girl. Accident."

"Hit and run."

"Or accidental drowning."

"Maybe even kidnapped."

Sadie felt bile rising up in her throat, burning its way to the surface. Not Kylie. Anything but that. She couldn't bear it if something happened to her daughter.

They watched her for a long time, watched the fear worming in her eyes and the way she had to fight the vomit down. She choked and sputtered against their grip on her until tears of desperation rose in her eyes. When she tried to talk, it came out in rasps, but she kept trying, wanting them to know that she would do whatever they asked so long as they stayed away from her child.

After an indefinite amount of time, they released her. The pressure disappearing was so unexpected after so many long moments of agony that Sadie slid to the ground in a heap, sobbing.

The one with the glasses glanced around, making certain no one had seen them.

"What do you say, Sadie?" White-Eye asked. "Will you leave Dmitri Velichko alone?"

She nodded emphatically, gasping and struggling to regain her breath and keep herself from being sick.

"Yes, yes, yes—whatever you want. But please leave my daughter alone. I swear, Dmitri can do whatever he wants—I don't care. Just please, please..." She grabbed at their coats, begging shamelessly. "Please don't do anything to her."

Her sincerity convinced them. After what had to have been hours, at least in Sadie's mind, they nodded.

"Very well. We will hold you to it."

They left her in a heap on the ground, weeping uncontrollably. She wasn't sure how long she lay trembling in the dirt, but the light slowly dimmed and eventually dusk fell. She was relieved that Kylie was with Belva and felt mildly reassured by the fact. But as the minutes dragged by and the terror of the ordeal lessened, she became aware of one overwhelming need.

She wanted Jasper. More than anything, she wanted him to be here now, holding her, telling her she was all right—that Kylie would be all right.

What had she gotten herself into? What had she done?

But Jasper wasn't here. She was on her own. She shook herself. No, not on her own. She had God. Wasn't it high time she started relying on Him? After all, when somebody had a terrific support system, they used it. They didn't let it languish in the background when they needed it.

She drew herself up to a sitting position, brushing away the dirt and mud layered in her hair.

Lord, she prayed, *I don't know what's going on, and I don't know what's going to happen. But I'm asking You to keep Kylie safe for me. I admit it's kind of hard for me to believe, but the Bible says that no matter how much I think I love her, You love her even more than that. If that's the case, let me be reassured. And please send Your angels to guard my little girl.*

She paused, feeling a bit better. She thought of something else and felt a little foolish but couldn't help adding it anyway.

And please be with Jasper, God. I totally botched that one—not surprisingly. I treated him like one of my desserts, trying to make him into something he's not. He's a better man than I thought he was. If I had just thought it through and taken off my blinders, I would have seen that he'd never just leave me. He loved me. He really did. If you can make something right out of the mess I made, I'd sure appreciate it.

She swallowed.

Thanks. Really.

Something about sitting there on the muddy ground, admitting her mistakes and asking for help, made her feel better. She felt some strength returning.

Finally she dragged herself to her feet. A bit of reasoning came to her. She didn't know who those men were, but she knew without a doubt that Dmitri wasn't aware of their presence. She may not always have been the best judge of character, but she knew enough of Dmitri to know that he'd never send people after her like that.

She'd had enough of playing games. She wanted to clear the air and find out exactly what was going on.

Straightening her clothes and hair as best she could, she headed for the street and picked up her pace once more.

She was going to Dmitri's, and this time, they were going to set a few things straight.

* * * * *

There was no better description for Dmitri's reaction than *stunned* when he opened the door and found Sadie on his porch. But his confusion went even further when he surveyed her appearance. Her legs were smeared with mud, and a mix of leaves, grass, and dirt was tangled in her hair.

"Sadie," he murmured in surprise, "what happened?"

She looked over her shoulder rather nervously.

"Can I come in?"

Embarrassed at his lack of manners, he instantly stepped aside. "Of course, of course."

She entered the doorway and headed straight for the kitchen, absently patting Mikhail's cage in greeting as she passed. The ferret only blinked at her in wonder, much as Dmitri was doing. Running water in the kitchen sink, she grabbed a handful of paper towels and spent a few minutes attempting to make herself presentable.

Finally, she turned to face him with a certain determination off-setting the weariness in her eyes.

"First things first," she announced.

Dmitri had a feeling he should be sitting down for this. He pulled a chair away from the kitchen table and slid into it, his eyes wide. He had never known anyone like Sadie Spencer. And he had certainly never had someone like her appear on his doorstep out of the blue, make her way into his home and his kitchen and then start speaking to him as though they were about to lay out a battle plan.

Truth be told, he was a little in awe of her.

"I owe you an apology," she continued, oblivious to his trepidation. "Several, in fact."

He licked his lips but said nothing, at a total loss as to what might come next.

"I don't know if you realize this, but ever since you moved here—or at least ever since I heard the rumor you were opening up your own restaurant—"

He opened his mouth to say something, but she swung her hand down in a chopping motion to halt him.

"You have no idea how hard this is for me, so please let me get it all out at once."

He closed his mouth.

"Thank you. The truth is, Dmitri, for a long time I've seen you as competition. And I've despised you in accordance with that view. For whatever reason—maybe because I could never quite figure out why my television show failed or because I couldn't hold my dad's interest long enough to keep him around permanently when I was a kid…for a very long time, I've had this obsession with being the best at everything. And when I meet people who threaten my abilities, I get very…uncharitable.

"I'm a control freak," she admitted. "And I don't like not being able to control who challenges me or what they're good at. The fact that you definitely take the cake—pardon the pun—when it comes to desserts…well, maybe it wasn't even so much that you were better than me. It was just the one thing I couldn't win at. I guess I've got a problem with pride on top of everything else."

She sighed. "But don't worry. I've learned my lesson. There are some things in this life I'll never have, and one of them is an award for the best dessert." She held up her hand even though Dmitri hadn't moved. "It's okay. I'm over it now. I've come to realize that while I was chasing rainbows, I was running *away* from the pot of gold behind me. And I have to live with the consequences of that.

"So, all that to say...I'm really, really sorry. And I wish you the best of luck with your restaurant. If only one of us manages to stay in business in a year's time...well...may the best restaurant win."

She stopped there, seeming to deflate following this speech. She rubbed a palm over the back of her neck but dropped her hand when Dmitri spoke.

"I don't suppose it will be too much of a problem," he remarked, the traces of his accent lilting against the words.

Sadie looked up. "What? What do you mean?"

"I'm not opening up a *restaurant*," Dmitri corrected her. "If anything, it's more of a...how would you call it? A dessert parlor? That was how the newspaper referred to it."

Sadie's eyebrows drew together. "Wait a minute, wait a minute. Back up. What did you just say?"

Dmitri stood to his feet. "Haven't you been reading the papers since the Cocoa Cook-Off, Sadie?"

She scoffed. "Yeah, right. Like I want *that* humiliation rubbed in my face."

He stared at her sympathetically, and her eyes narrowed.

"What are you saying, Dmitri?"

He sighed. "If you had read the papers, you'd understand. I never planned to open a restaurant. My passion lies in *desserts*. So I'm opening up a café selling only desserts, pastries, and the like. I chose that location because it is near the art gallery and bookstore. I thought it an ideal location to lure in customers. It was just a fluke that it happened to be across from Suncatchers. Although," he admitted, "I must say I so admired everything you did with your own restaurant, I sort of took you as the ultimate example and incorporated a few of your better business ideas."

Sadie had paled so considerably that Dmitri reached out a hand to steady her.

"Sadie?"

She stumbled toward the chair he had just vacated and sank into it. He went to the cupboard and took out a glass, filling it with water and carrying it to her.

She took a long gulp, draining half the glass.

"You mean…all that worry? All my obsessing? For nothing." She shook her head in disbelief. "And what about a name?" she asked. "What are you going to call it?"

He blushed a little. "Just Desserts," he answered. "I know it's not very original, but it's a play on words—"

"Say no more." She smiled at him. "I get it. I think it's perfect."

He beamed with pleasure.

She laughed, the sound echoing an evident relief. "Dmitri Velichko, I wish you had told me sooner."

He was smiling too, but it faded as she glanced out the window, her brow creasing.

"Well, that's one load off my mind, I can tell you. But, Dmitri, there's something else. Something far more serious."

He pulled out another chair and sat down. The soberness in her eyes told him he'd better.

"I don't know when it started. I've been a little preoccupied, which goes without saying, but my mother-in-law has come for a visit, and she was the first one to notice these two guys hanging around my house and the restaurant. And tonight, on my way here, they were following me." She shuddered as she reached for the glass of water.

"When I confronted them, they threatened me. They said if I didn't back off in my competition with you they'd—they'd—" She swallowed. "They made horrible threats against Kylie," she whispered. "And...they were Russian."

He stared at her, eyes widening. When he saw her watching him, he turned away, covering his face with his hands. "Oh, Sadie...I am so sorry."

"Do you know who they are?" she asked. "We could call the police...."

"No! We can't. It doesn't work like that." He pulled his hands away from his face. "But don't worry. I can get them to go away, to leave you alone."

"What? How?" she asked suspiciously.

He became reluctant, pulling back in shame.

"Dmitri, come on. I just poured out my heart and soul in an apology to you. Give me something to go with here. I'd enlighten you on my mistakes, but since you were there to witness most of them, I don't think I need to catch you up on the highlights. So, I told you mine; now you tell me yours."

He sighed and ran a hand over his face. "Do you remember the night we went to the movies and I asked you if you believed people deserved second chances?"

She nodded.

"Well, this is mine. Or…more than a second chance, it's a fresh start." He drew in a breath and came out with a story Sadie couldn't ever have dreamed up about him.

"I am the youngest son in a Russian crime family syndicate. We were good at one thing in Russia, and when we came to America, we put our skills to even better use here. Everything was arranged that I would follow in the family business after I finished school.

"It is true I went to college for business—although a completely different kind of business than my professors had in mind. But while I was there, several things happened. My roommate was a Christian, and he led me to the Lord. And while I had always had a certain love of food and desserts, it came full circle when I joined a culinary group at our church. From there my life took on a different direction and purpose than I had had before.

"I tried to reconcile my old life with my new one—after all, my old life included my family, no matter what they might do for a living. And they made several attempts at understanding, although it was difficult for them. Our family had owned a restaurant for several years—it was a legitimate business but also a front for our many other activities. I asked for a job there, and I started washing dishes. But I watched, and I learned. And in my spare time, I took classes at a local culinary institute. Eventually I became their best pastry chef. And as time passed, I gained more and more notoriety for my skills. But I also came to realize I could not stay with my family without eventually being pulled back into the life I'd grown to despise."

He drew another breath. "So I made plans and explained to them as well as I could. And I left them and came here, to start another life doing what I love."

"Making desserts," she supplied.

He nodded. "But my family has had a hard time accepting what they call my 'defection.' They truly want the best for me, but they do not trust my being beyond their reach and control. I thought they had let me go to try to make a life for myself on my own. But if they have sent Yuri and Petrov, then they are still trying to watch out for me."

He reached out a hand and gripped hers. She looked startled for a moment but then squeezed his fingers back.

"I will speak with my family," he reassured her. "Nothing will happen to Kylie, I promise you. They will give orders for Yuri and Petrov to leave, although they will probably still send them to check on me occasionally. But they will do what I ask of them, and your family—your restaurant—will be safe. I swear it on my life." He shook his head. "I am so sorry, Sadie. If I had known…"

She smiled at him. "But you didn't. And I believe you. I just *knew* you were hiding something all along. But here I was thinking it was some sinister plan to overthrow all my hard work." She laughed. "I never would have guessed it. You're part of the *mob*."

He corrected her. "*My family* is part of the mob. I had never joined in the family business, by the grace of God. And now I never will." He paused. "But I pray for them. Every day, I pray for their lives and their souls."

"No wonder you've been such an enigma," she commented. "That is one heck of a secret to live with." She paused. "But you're a good man, Dmitri Velichko. I'm sorry I couldn't admit that sooner."

Dmitri dismissed her apology and continued, "I must plead with you, Sadie, not to share this with anyone. It would mean the end of my business before it has begun. And I would have to leave."

"Oh, Dmitri. I should have put a little more faith in you. Your secret is safe with me," she promised. "Besides, knowing all this, I'd be afraid of what you'd do to me if I blabbed."

For a minute, he was startled. And then he saw the teasing glint in her eyes and smiled.

"You say you did not like me when I first came," he softly remarked. "But you were the first person here to show an interest in me beyond what you initially saw."

She shrugged. "God can still use us, even in our worst moments, I guess." She rolled her eyes. "I hope so, anyway. Heaven knows I've had some bad ones."

She chewed at her lip for a moment. "So...what do you think of the dessert menu at Suncatchers?" she asked Dmitri.

He hesitated.

"Seriously," she prompted. "Tell me the truth."

He winced a little when he answered. "It's a bit...unoriginal."

"Exactly!" she agreed without malice. "Maybe I should just eliminate desserts completely and incorporate a new line of appetizers. Besides, with your place only a few steps away, they could head out of Suncatchers and right over to Just Desserts if they're craving something sweet. Maybe we could offer discounts or something for people who eat at *both* our establishments."

Dmitri grinned. "I would like that."

Sadie affected her best Humphrey Bogart imitation as she said, "You know, Dmitri...I think this is the beginning of a beautiful friendship."

Chapter Seventeen

....

Sadie left Dmitri's house feeling quite pleased with her fellow man and life in general. Her heart swelled as she realized that Dmitri had been a little lonely. Not that she'd ever tell a soul about his past, but now that she knew, she'd really have to find a way to help him start meeting more people. Maybe even get him dating—she knew plenty of girls who'd be up for a chance at that.

Sadie had a feeling of triumph inside her. It was even better than the time she'd pulled her first successful soufflé from the oven and realized it hadn't fallen. She had never equated this feeling with anything other than personal success.

But now she realized there was a whole other type of personal success she'd never known about. She felt more airy and light than she had in weeks. It made her think of angel food cake—spongy and slightly sticky and faintly sweet.

She felt so buoyant and indestructible that she thought now was the time to swing by Jasper's and have the long-overdue talk with him she knew she'd been avoiding.

The truth was, she didn't know what to expect from Jasper. He'd been right on so many counts that she was more than a little ashamed to admit just how *wrong* she'd been. But the points that hurt the most were the ones he'd made about her selfishness. She *had* been abominably selfish, continually taking from their friendship without putting anything back into it. It was only inevitable that this tendency would grow worse once they moved from friends into a relationship. But she had recognized the error of her ways as well as realized that there was little she could do to make up for the imbalance she had created over the years. The best she could do was apologize and hope Jasper understood if he wanted to be friends again that she would try to live up to a different standard from here on out.

She had learned her lesson, but she didn't know if Jasper would even care. After all, he had a whole other life to tempt him now. But even if he chose that life over this one, she had to let him know he'd been wrong about one thing.

She *did* care about him. Their friendship and relationship *wasn't* just about her needing something from him. She loved Jasper. She'd loved him for a very long time. If she hadn't met Ned, who knew how things would have gone?

She didn't regret that, and she wouldn't change a thing about her courtship and marriage to Ned. He'd given her Kylie—he'd given her himself, totally and unconditionally. And she had loved him for it. But Ned had been a high, an exhilarating, breathtaking fireworks display of beauty and light.

Jasper was something different. Steadier. The anchor that had always kept her grounded and sane. Ned made her happy; Jasper made her feel safe *and* happy.

She loved him enough to not want to hold him back. But she was still just selfish enough to tell him how much she needed him, wanted him, back in her life.

She held a thousand of these thoughts close to her heart as she walked the distance from Dmitri's house to Jasper's. She had a million things to tell him, and she couldn't think how she was going to begin.

But just the thought of seeing him again sent darting thrills through her. She'd missed him like a drowning man craves air.

She would tell him that, she decided. She would tell him he was like air and water to her—she couldn't live without him. She never could.

With this thought, she found herself under the faint glow of his porch light. Drawing a deep breath and mumbling an incoherent prayer, she rang the doorbell and waited.

Air and water, air and water, she kept reminding herself.

"Jasper," she tentatively tested the sound of her voice in the stillness, "I love you." She cleared her throat and tried again. "I love you, Jasper. Please don't move to Colorado."

She swallowed. It sounded good.

And then there was the sound of shuffling feet and the doorknob rattling as it turned. She braced herself and ran a brief hand over the mess that was her hair, wishing she'd asked Dmitri for a comb.

The door slid open, and she hoped she looked properly humbled. But the effect was rather wasted, as Mac stood before her in the light of the porch lamp.

"Oh," tumbled out of her before she could catch it.

Mac was on her "talk-to" list as well, but she had momentarily forgotten about his moving into Jasper's house. She had planned to catch up with him tomorrow, maybe even invite him over for dinner so he could see Mama Belva again, as well.

"Hi, Dad."

Mac seemed stunned as much by this greeting as by her disheveled appearance. To be honest, she was rather surprised herself. She hadn't really planned to call him that. It had just sort of popped out.

"Hey there, Sadie girl," he greeted once he recovered.

She cleared her throat again. "I was planning to call you tomorrow to see if you wanted to have dinner with us—Kylie, Belva, and me."

Mac smiled at this. "I'd sure like that, Sadie girl."

Belva was right. This was getting easier by the minute.

"I know there's a lot we need to talk about, Dad"—there it slipped out again, though she didn't actually mind this time—"but I came to see Jasper. Is he around?"

As she waited for an invitation to come inside or hold on while Jasper was told he had a visitor, she watched Mac's smile dissolve by centimeters. He finally ended up sadly shaking his head, and Sadie felt her heart drop to her feet and land with a sickening flop.

"Oh, Sadie girl." He shook his head, and Sadie fought a wave of panic. "Why don't you come inside?"

She decided if she pretended everything was fine, then it would be. "That's all right; I'll just wait here for him," she perkily declared.

Mac eyed her sadly. She felt queasy in her stomach.

"Come inside, Sadie," he urged before reaching to draw her in.

She let him, feeling rather helpless as well as hopeless. He got her settled at Jasper's kitchen table and rummaged around for something to drink. Neither he nor Jasper was very adept at grocery shopping. The best he came up with was a glass of water.

Sadie only stared at it, remembering the words she had prepared.

"Air and water," she mumbled to herself, but Mac didn't comment on the phrase. Instead he announced what she already knew.

"He left for Colorado already. Moved his flight up by a week."

"When?" Sadie listlessly asked. "When did he do that?"

Mac sighed. "After he went to talk to you at the restaurant that day."

She nodded in complete understanding.

"I'm too late," she muttered. "Too, too late."

"I have his new address," Mac offered. "Or you could call his cell phone," he suggested hopefully.

She shook her head. "No. It was one thing to ask him not to go. It's another thing entirely to ask him to come the whole way back. Especially after…everything."

"He would do it, Sadie," Mac determined. "He would come back for you."

Her eyes drilled into the tabletop, searching for the words to explain. "I know he would. But it's *why* he would do it that would bother me. Would he feel guilty? What would he expect from me? What would I expect from him? It's too much pressure. He'd have to find another job or beg for his old one back. He'd have to leave the boys' academy in a tough position, which I know he'd hate to do." She sighed. "It's too much to ask of him. Maybe I'll send him a letter eventually, once he's settled. Maybe he could…"

Her face suddenly scrunched up in anguish as she left the thought unfinished.

"I'm really sorry, Dad," she choked out. "All these years I've been judging how you lived your life, and look what a great mess I've made of mine."

She laid her head on her arms, leaned into the kitchen table, and wept. Mac came around and knelt beside her, patting her back gently and holding her while she cried. These actions, as loving as they were, caused her to cry harder. For years, this was what she had longed to experience. She had wanted Mac to be there and hold her while she cried. It was a moment of bittersweet proportions.

"I'm so sorry," she began repeating. "I'm so sorry."

He let her cry it out for a good long while before he finally pulled her up and drew her face toward him.

"I love you, Sadie girl," he told her. "And if I could make your pain go away, I would. But I can't. So all I can tell you is—Jasper Reeves wouldn't give up on you, so don't you give up on him. You fight for that boy, Sadie. I guarantee you, you'll win."

She didn't know if she believed him or not, but she'd never heard a better speech from anyone in her entire life. Sadie threw her arms around her father's neck and hugged him so tightly she thought she might choke the life out of him. But he never uttered a word of protest.

"You're not going away, are you, Dad?" She pulled back to see his face. "You're going to stay...for Kylie? We'd really love it if you stayed, you know."

He smoothed the hair back from her forehead. "I know you need to ask that, after all the times I walked out on you in the past. But I promise you, I'm staying right here, Sadie girl, for as long as you're here. And if you pack up and move to Colorado or Asia or Timbuktu... that's where I'm going."

There was a part of her that Jasper's departure had left broken. But there was another part that felt whole and pure. She hugged him again.

"I love you, Dad," she whispered. "I always have."

He held her tightly. "I know, Sadie girl. I always felt it...because I loved you too."

And as she talked with her father long into the night, Sadie wondered at the miracle of a heart—how it could be broken and restored all at the same time.

* * * * *

The day after Sadie's reconciliation with Mac, Kylie sat quietly playing in her bedroom. She didn't bother looking up from her toys as her mother came into the room but continued to arrange the Barbie she held into different positions, bending the doll's legs as far back as they would go. Sadie entered the room and watched for a moment, wincing. Kylie remained silent as her mother settled herself on the floor beside her and picked up a doll gown at random. Sadie toyed with the shiny fabric for a long time, running the scarlet material through her fingers.

"Kylie?"

"Yes, Mommy?"

Kylie continued to contort Barbie's limbs until Sadie very gently reached out and took the toy from her fingers.

"Mommy has something very important to say to you."

Kylie folded her hands and politely gave Sadie her full attention. She watched as her mother met her eyes and then looked away again.

"You've been a very good girl lately. Ever since Jasper...ever since Jasper took you for a walk, that day at the restaurant."

Kylie didn't comment on this. Her last day with Jasper was not a memory she felt like sharing right now. After a moment of silence, Sadie began speaking again but kept her face lowered, just like Kylie herself did when she had done something wrong and didn't know how to admit it.

"Mommy's been—" Sadie cleared her throat and started again. "*I've* been very bad recently. I haven't"—she drew a breath—"I haven't listened to you the way I should have. I've had a hard time…getting things in order."

"Priorities," Kylie supplied.

Sadie's eyes darted to her daughter's face and stared at her for a long moment. "Who taught you about priorities?" she asked with curiosity.

Kylie blinked, feeling a rush of sadness. She dropped her eyes and sighed.

"Oh, right," Sadie whispered. "Jasper." She cleared her throat. "Kylie, the truth is…" Sadie laid aside the doll and the dress she'd been holding. "The truth is, I sent Grandpa away. And it's my fault that Jasper moved to Colorado."

Kylie looked back up at this confession but said nothing. Sadie's voice began to tremble as she continued.

"I haven't been very smart lately, but I'm going to get better. I'm going to pay more attention, but sometimes…sometimes when you mess up your priorities like Mommy did…sometimes you can't change some things."

Sadie drew a shaky breath. "You c–can't…get…everything back." She sniffed. "Now the *good* news is that Grandpa's coming back. He wants to see you again, and I want him to too. In fact, he's going to be watching you after school some days in case I have to work late at the restaurant."

Kylie felt a rush of joy at this. She liked having another grampa. She had Papa Clay, of course, but he lived the whole way down in Alabama with Nana Belva. Just like her daddy who lived way up in heaven with Jesus. It was hard, saying good-bye to Jasper, but it helped to know that now she had Grampa Mac too.

She smiled in relief at her mother's words.

Sadie continued, "The *bad* news is that…Jasper's gone to Colorado, and I…well, I…" She began wiping at her eyes as the tears started to fall. "I—I don't know when we'll ever get to see him again." A sob broke loose, and Kylie frowned with concern.

"So, I—I need to ask…" Sadie was full-out crying now, seemingly unable to stop. "I need to ask your forgiveness." She drew a deep, shaky breath. "I need to tell you I'm sorry. But I've prayed about it, and I'm going to try harder from now on. I'm going to hold onto the things that count, Kylie. Just like your daddy told me."

Kylie felt a lump in her own throat as her mother continued to cry, softly murmuring, "I'm sorry, baby…. I'm so sorry…."

Distressed to see her mother in such a state, Kylie scooted across the floor and climbed into Sadie's lap. She began to stroke her hair as she'd seen Jasper do a thousand times before and whispered, "There, there, Mommy. Is all right. Don't cry. Shh."

Sadie cried harder, wrapping her arms tightly around Kylie and holding her close.

"I forgive you, Mommy. I was never mad, not really." She drew a tiny breath and offered, "Sometimes I think you're mad, but you're really not. Sometimes you're just scared. And hurt. Like you were with Grampa."

Sadie sniffled and brushed a hand along the top of her daughter's head. "How did you get to be so smart?" she asked her.

Kylie sighed as if this were common knowledge. "Jasper. He 'splained it all."

Kylie felt a few more tears fall from her mother's eyes and into her hair. They sat together for a long time until Sadie calmed and

Kylie felt no more tears falling. And then Sadie rocked her back and forth, and Kylie curled tight into her mother's stomach, warm and comfortable.

"Mommy?" Kylie finally whispered.

Sadie rubbed her back. "Yeah, baby?"

"Kylie loves Mommy."

"And Mommy loves Kylie," Sadie whispered, and Kylie thought she heard a smile in her mother's tone as she began speaking of herself in third-person once more.

"And Jasper loves Mommy too," she added. "You'll see."

Sadie pressed a kiss, hard and long, to her daughter's forehead.

"As long as I still have you, Kylie girl…that's enough."

* * * * *

As Sadie had wished, life returned to a normal routine—or as normal as it had ever been in Sadie's world—after all that had happened. It was a sweet time, but Jasper's absence left a bitterness there as well. Still, the world didn't stop for a broken heart, and Sadie found herself swept up into so many things that at times there were whole hours where she didn't devote more than a passing thought to Jasper being gone.

Following their family dinner and a few more days of visiting, Belva returned home to Alabama. The anniversary of Ned's death had passed, and with it came a sort of benediction. Whatever Belva had come looking to find, Sadie believed she had found it. It showed in the peace radiating from the center of her eyes, engulfing them in a well of love and understanding.

Kylie was sad to see her grandma go, but the installation of her grandpa as her new playmate invited all sorts of new and exciting possibilities. She bounced back from the farewells with all the enthusiasm a five-year-old first grader could muster.

It helped that Mac had started visiting nearly every night, in addition to the afternoons he served as babysitter. Plus, Dmitri was coming around more too, always with some sort of sweet in hand for her and Sadie to taste. The only thing missing was Jasper. But his absence no longer seemed to weigh on Kylie as it once had. This became clear to Sadie one night as Kylie was in the kitchen, sampling the petit fours Dmitri had brought while explaining the hierarchy of elementary school.

"Kindergarten is for babies, Uncle 'mitri," she loftily informed him.

Sadie inwardly smirked at this. After all, it was only due to an advanced placement test that Kylie had begun school a year ahead of other children her age.

Dmitri's lips twitched. "I see. But first grade is different?"

She nodded. "First grade is for big kids."

"Like you?"

She shifted on her stool and daintily nibbled her dessert. "Like Kylie," she confirmed.

Sadie grinned as she left the room, carrying a mug of coffee and a petit four to Mac, who was upstairs disassembling pipes in an attempt to retrieve the latest sacrifice to the volcano—Kylie's toothbrush.

When she returned to the first floor, Kylie had evidently changed topics. Sadie approached the kitchen just in time to overhear her daughter announcing, "But Mommy shouldn't worry. It's okay. Jasper will be back."

Sadie had stilled, just beyond the kitchen's threshold, her hand clutched to her chest at her daughter's confident assertion.

Sadie possessed no such illusions. She hadn't heard one word from Jasper since his departure, although she was certain he and Mac kept in touch. If Mac had told Jasper how she felt, it certainly hadn't been enough to provoke a response from him. It confirmed some deep dread she'd harbored—that, secretly, Jasper was glad to be rid of her. She was glad she hadn't asked him to come back.

She kept herself busy by investing a whole new interest in Kylie's life and by taking care of Mac and Dmitri, drawing them out into the community around them. They went with her to church, and Sunday lunches at Suncatchers became an even larger event with Dmitri, Mac, Pastor Samuel, and a myriad of others joining her and Kylie each week.

The grand opening of Just Desserts was a smashing success, and to both Sadie's pleasure and chagrin, she found her profit margins rising each week following the dessert café's opening. *No wonder hindsight is so much better than foresight,* she thought.

She and Dmitri kept close tabs on their restaurants and each other as they exchanged business scenarios and assorted recipes. They shared many laughs and several prayer requests as they learned what it meant to be friends rather than rivals. The females on staff at Suncatchers were thrilled with the arrangement, as they got to see more and more of the handsome, dark-haired Russian. Sadie even made a few matchmaking attempts, which harried Dmitri considerably until he told her to stop.

She had seen Yuri and Petrov only once more after the night they threatened her. The pair was standing in front of Just Desserts when she exited Suncatchers through the front entrance one evening. She froze, feeling very much like a deer in the crosshairs of a hunter, fearful to move or breathe and confirm her own presence to them. But they had certainly recognized her, and she relaxed as they bowed, each offering her a salute of respect. She breathed again and moved on with a curt nod of greeting. She told Dmitri about it later, and they had a good laugh.

She was thankful for Dmitri's friendship. It was good to have someone to talk to, to confide in, even if he was no replacement for Jasper.

But Sadie did all right, and the weeks slid by with deceptive speed. She made it through Thanksgiving—the first spent without Jasper since Ned's death—and laughed at Belva's e-mail containing a recipe for pumpkin pie, declaring that neither Russians nor Yankees could possibly create a pumpkin pie better than a distinguished Southern belle.

Sadie took advantage of the holidays by rewarding Glynda with a day at the Hershey Hotel's Chocolate Spa, complete with Cocoa Massage and Chocolate Fondue Wrap. She also made a few changes at the restaurant, promoting Glynda from evening and weekend manager to general manager. The promotion included a substantial pay raise, but Sadie recognized that Glynda was worth every penny. For her part, she began to spend more time in the kitchen, working and exchanging barbs alongside Karl as they began to create a new level of cuisine. Following Jimmy's return to work after the "pinkie" incident, Sadie and Glynda decided to demote him to busboy and dishwasher. Jimmy actually didn't mind. But he had saved all his extra wages from his time as a line cook and bought a ring from the corner jewelry shop. He planned to ask Annie to marry him, come Christmas.

With one big exception, Sadie's life had never been sweeter. And as the holidays drew near and snow coated the ground, she began to think she could go on like this forever and learn to live with the permanent ache shadowing her heart and happiness.

She did indulge in one weakness, however.

She wrote Jasper letters. Reams of them. She sat down every night, after putting Kylie to sleep, and poured her heart out on paper. She told him about her everyday life and filled him in on Kylie's antics and stories about first grade. She explained how she and Dmitri had come to an understanding and how their friendship had grown out of their diverse backgrounds but with the common love of food and business. She informed him of the gems of wisdom Belva constantly gave her through letters, e-mails, and phone calls…and how she had never known what a treasure her mother-in-law was until recently. She thanked him for believing in Mac until she could believe in him too, and she told him how solid their relationship was now—how good things had become between them. She mentioned local gossip and how she had called to check on Aunt Matilda a few times and related each of the insults Matilda had flung at her during their chats. And when the time came that she ran out of things to tell him, she told him the one thing she wanted to say most of all: *I love you. I miss you. Please come back to me. My life is full, but it's hollow without you in it.*

And she always signed it: *Love, your best friend, Sadie*

She never sent a single one of these letters to Jasper, although Mac had given her his address several times. But she piled them in a box and kept them tucked away back in her closet, saving them for reasons she couldn't fathom.

And then came the holidays, when the rush of the season didn't allow her enough energy to write the letters anymore. While a part of her was relieved at this, a part of her mourned it as well. Writing to Jasper had been her only connection to him. Now she fell exhausted into bed each night, falling asleep as her head hit the pillow and sleeping a dreamless sleep where she did not see Jasper's face nor hear his voice.

She felt him slipping further and further away, and while she ached inside, there was no help for it.

Then came a day shortly before Christmas when she was sneaking a box full of presents for Kylie into her bedroom closet that she noticed the letter box was missing. She searched for it like a woman possessed but couldn't locate it anywhere.

In the end, she determined it had gone to Goodwill with the other items she had sent—her donation for the holidays. She only hoped the pages had been incinerated rather than read. Most of her lesser moments had been the stuff of public observation—she hardly wanted her letters to Jasper to be more of the same.

But even her prayers that the letters be burned filled her with agony. They had been her link, her lifeline. To lose them was as devastating a loss as giving up on Jasper entirely.

She heard nothing, however, as to their fate...and in the days leading up to the holiday, she put them out of her mind as best she could. Instead, she began to wonder how Jasper was spending his first Colorado Christmas and wondered if the winter weather was worse there than it was here.

On Christmas Eve, both Just Desserts and Suncatchers closed—a move Dmitri and Sadie had decided on together. Dmitri had flown home for the holidays, but not before bringing her and Kylie a week's supply of sugar cookies, Russian teacakes, and eggnog-flavored cream puffs. Mac came for dinner, and they gorged themselves silly on sweets as Kylie serenaded them with several rounds of "Jingle Bells."

They exchanged presents—a sweater Kylie had chosen for Mac all by herself, a new set of measuring cups and hot pads in the shape of ladybugs for Sadie, and a tea set and a book about volcanoes for Kylie from her mother.

Sadie drew a proud smile from Mac as she related Smith and Jones's stunned reception of her Christmas gift to them—lunch on the house for the entire month. A lingering case of cynicism left her reflecting that Smith and Jones would take full advantage of her offer by upping their weekly visits to daily ones, but the expression of surprise on their faces had been worth every penny of such an eventuality. The old adage of the holidays held true—it really was better to give than to receive.

As their evening with Mac drew to a close, both Sadie and Kylie kissed him under the mistletoe before sending him off into the night, and then Sadie announced bathtime for Kylie.

Kylie balked. "In the morning," she declared, but Sadie shook her head.

"You'll be too interested in those other presents under the tree in the morning. Better to have bathtime *now*."

With a defeated sigh, Kylie climbed the stairs and entered the bathroom. She soon regained her holiday spirit, and by the time Sadie had cleaned things up downstairs and made it into the bathroom, Kylie was happily splashing away, muttering dire predictions for the "canninabals" and offering Barbie's new shoes as a sacrifice to the volcano.

Sadie shook her head. "What kind of daughter did I raise? Not only are you a little pagan, but you should know better than to *ever* sacrifice shoes."

She rolled up her sleeves and knelt by the tub to begin shampooing Kylie's hair. Kylie began a lusty chorus of "We Wish You a Merry Christmas," and Sadie joined in with a fair share of joy. But a part of her felt removed from the Christmas spirit as she wondered where Jasper was tonight and who he was with. Colleagues? New friends? Was he alone?

She shuddered a little at each thought until a particularly boisterous turn in the tub splashed a substantial amount of bubbles onto her face.

Kylie giggled with delight. "Mommy looks like Santa Claus!"

Sadie wiped the bubble beard from her cheeks. "Mommy is *not* amused," she declared. But Kylie's laughter soon had her smiling.

She had just placed the final rinse on Kylie's hair when the doorbell rang. She sighed with a glance at her watch.

"Ten thirty. That's awfully late for carolers. Maybe Grandpa forgot something, huh?" She helped Kylie out of the tub and placed her on the mat. She wrapped her in a towel.

"Okay, you stay here," she instructed. "I'll be right back."

"Don't worry, Mommy," Kylie called as she left the room. "The volcano will keep me company!"

Sadie shook her head as she headed downstairs, muttering in a singsong voice, "That's exactly what I'm afraid of."

The doorbell rang a second time as she stopped to check her reflection in the hall mirror to make sure all the bubbles were wiped from her face. Her cheeks were flushed from the effort of Kylie's bath, and several strands of wet hair clung to her neck. Oh well, it was Christmas Eve, and she was the mother of a five-year-old. What did people expect?

She opened the door to a gust of wintry air, but the frigid blast didn't serve to startle her half as much as the occupant of her doorstep did. There, in living, breathing color—his nose tipped with red and snowflakes melting on his eyelashes—stood Jasper, shivering against the cold despite his boots, jeans, and heavy winter coat.

Common decency dictated that she invite him in, but the sight of months of longing and confusion staring at her with enough heat to melt several inches of snow only served to strike her immobile. She couldn't move, she couldn't speak—she wasn't even sure she was breathing.

It was only when she expelled enough air to talk that she realized she was still drawing breath.

"You came back," she murmured softly.

And with these words, she found herself swept backward into her own hallway as Jasper drew her into his arms and planted the warmest, tingliest kiss ever flat against her lips. Her reflexes were really in poor shape, she reflected, because it took her a full fifteen seconds to begin kissing him back.

Warmth flooded her face, replacing the coolness of the winter air, and by the time they pulled apart, she felt heated to the core. Jasper kept his arms around her as he drew back, holding his face within several inches of hers.

"I got your letters," he murmured breathlessly. "All three hundred and eighteen pages. I read them twice—and then read them again on the plane here."

She laughed softly, more than a little breathless herself. "It was that many pages? I knew that box was filling up fast...but, Jasper, they just went missing on their own at some point. I didn't send them."

Jasper shrugged. "I didn't really think you did. But you wrote them, didn't you? That's what counts."

She couldn't help herself. She planted a kiss square on his mouth and lingered there for some time, trying to convey without the help of words just how much she'd missed him. When she pulled back again, she thought she must have done a pretty good job, if the light in Jasper's eyes was any indication.

"I was such an idiot," she whispered. "You were right about so many things—about everything—except about me not caring for you. You were absolutely wrong on that. I love everything about who you are."

"As long as you remember that," he breathed, "about me being right nine times out of ten, then I think we'll do just fine."

She laughed, a sound of pure, undiluted joy. It was complete now. Her heart felt whole. But then, after they'd spent several more moments under the mistletoe, she began to consider a few things.

"But what about the academy—and your job? You can't be thinking of moving back, can you?"

"Of course I'm moving back," he declared. "Staying away this long has been torture enough—don't make me go through any more. Do you realize not a single one of the boys at that academy knew what the sub-definition for a volcano was? I need to come back to civilized society, where people are more practical." He kissed the tip of her nose. "*My* people."

She wasn't going to argue with him. She may have had her moments, but she wasn't *that* stupid. There was a familiar thunder of footsteps on the stairs behind her.

"Speaking of your people…," she murmured with one last brush against his lips.

"*JASPER!*"

Kylie rocketed from the stairs and into Jasper's outstretched arms, her bath towel wrapped in a regal toga around her form. Sadie leaned on the doorjamb and let them have their moment, whispering secrets she'd never share in. But she didn't mind. That was the way it should be with a father and daughter.

She thought of Mac and smiled, wondering if he had known all along that Jasper was flying back from Colorado tonight. And what about her letters? Had it been Mac who sent them to Jasper? Somehow she didn't think so. It didn't strike her as something Mac would do. And Kylie was too young to have taken care of it on her own… unless Dmitri had helped her….

Sadie finally shrugged. She didn't need to know—she didn't even want to. It would be her own Christmas miracle, a gift from God she hardly deserved. But she looked upward anyway and silently thanked Him.

Thank You…for not giving me some of the things I justly deserve… and blessing me with others that I don't.

Jasper sent Kylie back upstairs to put on some pajamas while he returned to Sadie's side. He rested a palm against her cheek, and they just stood there drinking in the sweet taste of their own happiness.

"I've got presents," he finally whispered to her.

She immediately frowned. "Oh, Jasper…I didn't know. I don't have anything for you…."

He winked at her. "Well, you might," he cryptically said, before disappearing outside to retrieve the presents from his car.

By the time he returned, Sadie and Kylie were snuggling together on the couch, tickling each other and giggling, completely content and perfectly happy and not needing a single thing more to make this Christmas any better.

But when Jasper entered the room, Kylie tore away from Sadie's embrace and gasped with delight at the gift Jasper carried into the room.

It was the most perfect, adorable puppy with coal black ears and round, dark eyes. Sadie wanted to protest but knew it was hopeless. It had been love at first sight, and the damage was already done.

Kylie had the round little ball in her arms, rubbing her cheek against its silky fur. "Is *perfect*, Jasper! Now Kylie is a mommy too!"

Sadie held her breath, just imagining all the adventures Kylie would have with this. *Oh, Lord.* But her happiness extended to include the newest addition to their family, and she moved to kneel beside Kylie. She smiled as she touched a hand to the puppy's nose and it sneezed.

"Kylie will call him *Lava*," the five-year-old announced with determination.

Sadie frowned. "Lava? What kind of a name is Lava?"

Kylie stared at her. "Because of the volcano, Mommy. And because we *love* him. Don't we, Jasper?" She looked up at him.

Jasper winked at her. "We sure do."

Sadie knew for certain she was defeated, but it had never been so sweet.

While Kylie became acquainted with her new friend, Jasper helped Sadie to her feet and pulled her aside.

"Now it's your turn."

Sadie still felt ripples of guilt. "No, seriously, Jasper. You didn't need to get me anything. Just you being here…" She felt tears of emotion prick her eyes. "It's more than enough," she whispered.

He appeared to be ignoring her as he reached into his pocket and drew out a ribbon of beautiful red silk. He handed it to her, and she raised an eyebrow. The string lay between them, but whatever was on its end remained tucked in Jasper's pocket. She bit her lip, already having a good feeling where this was going.

Her hesitation made Jasper pause, and she sensed his nervousness rise. She ran her fingers down the silky thread and tugged lightly when it became taut. Nothing happened.

She reached down and, with Jasper's help, pulled the rest of the string from his pocket. She held it up to her face, the diamond ring glittering brightly between them in the illumination of the Christmas lights.

He cleared his throat. "So…this is where your gift for me comes in." His voice cracked with worry.

"Say you'll marry me, Sadie…and I'll never need another present for as long as I live."

The ring was swinging back and forth like a pendulum, and she felt hypnotized by it. She followed it for a moment, seeing a whole world of possibilities flashing before her eyes. Finally she lowered her hand to look in Jasper's eyes.

They were blue and clear and ringed with hope. This was what she had been waiting for, all those months without him. She just hadn't known it until now.

"You do realize I'm not catering the wedding. The stress would just break me."

It was good enough for him. He let out such a loud whoop that Lava emitted a squeaky bark, and Sadie laughed as he lifted her in his arms and swung her around.

He planted her down under the mistletoe and took full advantage of tradition as he kissed her thoroughly. He only let up once Kylie tugged at his jeans, demanding to see the ring and saying, "Lift Kylie, lift!"

So it happened that Jasper spent Christmas Eve with his two favorite girls in the whole world and received the best Christmas gift of all, sheltered in the love of those who held him close.

Sadie thought it was only his just desserts.

Epilogue

....

Sadie stood in front of the full-length mirror that had been set up in one of the Sunday school rooms at the church and surveyed herself critically from head to toe. Her wedding dress was simple, but she thought it had class, and Belva's last-minute arrangements to her hair looked stunning.

She turned to the side and held her bouquet in front of her.

"I don't look half bad, do I?" she asked Lucinda, her maid of honor, whose hair Belva was *still* attempting to tame after three previous tries.

"You look g–gorgeous!" Lucinda enthused. Sadie knew she stuttered out of sheer nervousness. Dmitri was serving as the best man, and the sight of him in a tux would be enough to set even the most levelheaded woman to stuttering.

Except Sadie, of course. All her babbling was reserved for Jasper.

As the bride watched Belva attempt to flatten another strand of Lucinda's flyaway hair, Kylie bounced into the room with Lava tripping on her heels. In the seven weeks since Lava's adoption into their family, he had made himself a permanent part of their lives, especially Kylie's. Where Kylie went, therefore went Lava. When Jasper drove Kylie to school in the morning, Lava rode along. And before she came home in the afternoon, Lava sat on the doorstep waiting for her, his little tail thumping a furious staccato of happiness.

Sadie understood how he felt. Her own heart had been thumping the exact same beat for nearly two months solid.

And now, here she was, on her wedding day. It was only appropriate that it fell on Valentine's Day, as well. She spread her veil around her bare shoulders and smiled at herself.

"Grampa says they're almost ready," Kylie announced, twirling beside Sadie and watching her own dress of pink-and-white chiffon flare out around her.

Belva immediately gave up on Lucinda's hair and stuck a flower above her ear instead.

"There," she declared. "That oughta hold things in place through most of the service, sugar."

Kylie tugged on Lucinda's hand. "Guess what! After the wedding, Mommy and Jasper—I mean *Daddy*," she corrected herself, "are going to see *real* volcanoes in Hawaii!"

Kylie had been announcing this to nearly everyone she'd encountered in the last month.

Lucinda smiled patiently at the little girl as she tried to remove the hem of her gown from Lava's mouth.

"And Jasper—Daddy," she revised again, "even promised to bring Kylie back a piece of a volcano!"

Belva leaned down to help free Lucinda from Lava's chewing. "Just so long as you don't flush it down the commode, darlin'. Especially not while I'm stayin' with you the next two weeks."

Sadie interrupted this exchange in momentary panic. "Kylie!" Her voice stretched to a crescendo. "Where's Lava's ring pillow?"

Kylie continued to dance around, performing a series of pirouettes. "Grampa has the rings and pillow," Kylie informed her as she executed another twirl.

"All right then, sugar, we'd better get going," Belva announced.

And with her help, Lucinda and Sadie herded Kylie and Lava out of the room and toward the church foyer. Mac was waiting, pillow and rings in hand.

He took hold of Lava with an expert touch, attached the pillow, and made sure everything was in order before entrusting him to Kylie's care.

Dmitri wished Sadie luck and offered her an encouraging wink before extending his arm to Lucinda. He graced her with a warm smile, and Sadie couldn't help thinking that if Lucinda hadn't already fallen for their tall, dark-haired Russian, she surely would soon. Sadie cocked her head with interest. Sure, Dmitri had put the kibosh on her other matchmaking attempts, but Lucinda was different....

She shook herself out of this reverie. There would be plenty of time to consider her friends' love lives later. Right now, it was time to focus on her own.

With Dmitri and Lucinda on their way to the front, Belva took charge of the rest.

Under her direction, Kylie and Lava headed up the aisle, side by side. Kylie scattered rose petals, and Lava trotted happily alongside her. Sadie couldn't watch. She was filled with too many imaginings on what could go wrong.

Then things moved in a bit of a blur—Belva kissed her cheek, tears in her eyes, and shared a glance with Sadie that only the two of them could understand. She drew her in close and whispered, "Ned would be happy, sugar."

Sadie told her to cut that out or she'd be applying her mascara all over again. She blinked back the tears as Belva slipped inside the sanctuary.

Mac threaded her arm through his. He stood up straight, still a little shorter than her, and said, "I wish I'd been here the last time, Sadie girl."

She squeezed his arm. "It doesn't matter. You're here now."

And then came the music that propelled them forward, and she reached the front without stumbling—miraculously, since she had stumbled no less than three times during the rehearsal. Mac handed her to Jasper, and for a moment, nothing existed but the two of them. Him in his tux, his blue eyes such a rich cobalt blue she felt she could swim in them forever. His hair was combed, but it still had the choppy edges that were so familiar to her. She wanted to reach out and touch it, but she didn't think that would be appropriate just yet.

The service commenced and things went smoothly. Even her fears about Lava were laid to rest—he behaved like a true gentleman, and the rings were easily removed and placed on their fingers without a single hitch in the plan.

She was beginning to relax and content herself with the knowledge that this was the last time she had to go through with this, and she could soon rest easily and happily as she assumed the honored role of being not only Jasper's best friend but his wife, as well.

But just as Pastor Samuel was bidding Jasper to kiss her, it happened.

Aunt Matilda, seated in the front, had broken free from her nurse's grasp and stood to her feet. She pointed a shaky finger and trembled with indignation as she cried out for all their friends and family to hear, "This hussy...has stolen my bifocals!"

Everything fell silent. The preacher stood speechless. The pianist froze. Every row along each aisle sat frozen with surprise.

Jasper looked at Sadie, and she stared back at him, their happy smiles fixated in place. Kylie groaned and shook her head while Lava simply sat back on his haunches and stared, his tail thumping with amusement against the carpeting.

"If she brings up an eye for an eye, I am *so* out of here," Sadie hissed at him.

Jasper couldn't help it. His happiness overflowed, and he ended up laughing so long and so loud that eventually the entire congregation joined in. Indignant over this reaction, Aunt Matilda huffed her way into the aisle and began the long walk to the back of the sanctuary. Kylie ran after her with Lava yipping at her heels.

Sadie pulled Jasper's attention back to her and went ahead with the kissing part—and as everyone laughed uproariously around them, Sadie couldn't help thinking...

Great.

POST CARD
CARTE POSTALE

Love Finds You

Want a peek into local American life—past and present?
The *Love Finds You*™ series published by Summerside Press
features real towns and combines travel, romance,
and faith in one irresistible package!

The novels in the series—uniquely titled after American towns with unusual but
intriguing names—inspire romance and fun. Each fictional story draws on the
compelling history or the unique character of a real place. Stories center on romances
kindled in small towns, old loves lost and found again on the high plains, and new
loves discovered at exciting vacation getaways. Summerside Press plans to publish at
least one novel set in each of the 50 states. Be sure to catch them all!

Now Available in Stores

Love Finds You in Miracle, Kentucky by Andrea Boeshaar
ISBN: 978-1-934770-37-5

Love Finds You in Snowball, Arkansas by Sandra D. Bricker
ISBN: 978-1-934770-45-0

Love Finds You in Romeo, Colorado by Gwen Ford Faulkenberry
ISBN: 978-1-934770-46-7

Love Finds You in Valentine, Nebraska by Irene Brand
ISBN: 978-1-934770-38-2

Love Finds You in Humble, Texas by Anita Higman
ISBN: 978-1-934770-61-0

Love Finds You in Last Chance, California by Miralee Ferrell
ISBN: 978-1-934770-39-9

Love Finds You in Maiden, North Carolina by Tamela Hancock Murray
ISBN: 978-1-934770-65-8

Love Finds You in Paradise, Pennsylvania by Loree Lough
ISBN: 978-1-934770-66-5

Love Finds You in Treasure Island, Florida by Debby Mayne
ISBN: 978-1-934770-80-1

Love Finds You in Liberty, Indiana, by Melanie Dobson
ISBN: 978-1-934770-74-0

Love Finds You in Revenge, Ohio by Lisa Harris
ISBN: 978-1-934770-81-8

Love Finds You in Poetry, Texas by Janice Hanna
ISBN: 978-1-935416-16-6

Love Finds You in Sisters, Oregon by Melody Carlson
ISBN: 978-1-935416-18-0

Love Finds You in Charm, Ohio by Annalisa Daughety
ISBN: 978-1-935416-17-3

Love Finds You in Bethlehem, New Hampshire by Lauralee Bliss
ISBN: 978-1-935416-20-3

Love Finds You in North Pole, Alaska by Loree Lough
ISBN: 978-1-935416-19-7

Love Finds You in Holiday, Florida by Sandra D. Bricker
ISBN: 978-1-935416-25-8

Love Finds You in Lonesome Prairie, Montana
by Tricia Goyer and Ocieanna Fleiss
ISBN: 978-1-935416-29-6

Love Finds You in Bridal Veil, Oregon by Miralee Ferrell
ISBN: 978-1-935416-63-0

Coming Soon

Love Finds You in Homestead, Iowa by Melanie Dobson
ISBN: 978-1-935416-66-1

Love Finds You in Pendleton, Oregon by Melody Carlson
ISBN: 978-1-935416-84-5

summerside
PRESS

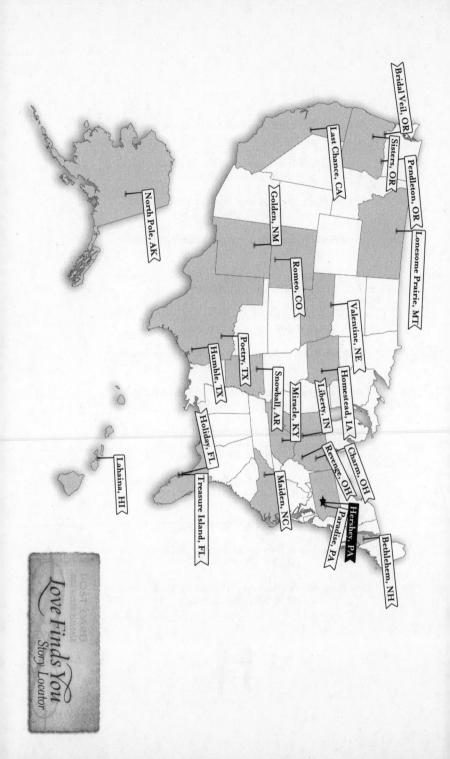